MW01633328

SHOOTING STARS

Shooting Stars

SKYE BOTHMA

This is a work of fiction. Names, characters, places and incidents are either a product of the author's imagination or are used fictitiously. Any resemblance to actual persons, living or dead, events or locales is entirely coincidental.

Copyright © Skye Bothma, 2023
www.skyebothma.com

The moral right of the author has been asserted.

All rights reserved. No part of this book may be reproduced or used in any manner without written permission of the copyright owner except for use of quotations in a book review.

Cover design by BetiBup33

ISBN 978-0-473-67421-2 (e-book)
ISBN 978-0-473-67419-9 (general paperback)
ISBN 978-0-473-67422-9 (on-demand paperback)

Road Less Travelled
www.roadlesstravelled.nz

First printing, 2023

For Deighton

Until we meet again,
I know God holds you
in the palm of His hand.

Note: Sunrise Cove is completely fictional.

"*W*here the hell is she!" barked Alistair Steele, mediocre business executive, but first-rate asshole. He slammed his hand down on the reception desk for added effect.

I sank deeper into my seat, looking away; instinct telling me not to look the predator in the eyes. *Don't move. Don't make a sound.*

"I asked you a question," he leaned over the desk coming in for the kill, "how much longer do I have to wait?"

I glanced up from behind the flimsy protection of my computer screen, "I'm sure Alex won't be much longer," I said, regretting the squeak in my voice, "perhaps one of our other attorneys can help you in the meantime?"

"I don't want to see someone else. I'm here to see her," he spat, saliva foaming in the corner of his mouth. "Get her here now!"

"Yes, of course. I'll try her mobile again." Shaking, I dialed her number for the fifth time. *Typical! Today, of all days.* I just knew when I saw this piece of work was booked to see Alex after lunch that she would pick *today* to go on one of her AWOL jaunts.

Come on, answer your phone, you selfish cow. I strained a meek pleased-to-serve-you smile while I listened to the phone go to voicemail. I was about to leave another message when the elevator doors opened. Breathing a sigh of relief, I hung up the phone. *Finally!*

The relieved sigh was premature. Amira, the office intern stepped into the office, clutching some files to her chest, having returned from an errand. She looked at Mr. Steele and then mouthed to me, "Is she still not back?"

I shook my head.

"Mr. Steele," Amira said, extending her hand, "would you like to come through to the boardroom? I can get the paperwork started."

He ignored her outstretched hand, grabbing his briefcase, "Thank you!" He barked, "Finally, *someone* with initiative," he glared at me before storming off ahead of her.

Amira turned to me, and using the pretense of adjusting her hijab to block his view, rolled her eyes and hissed, "He's such a jerk".

"Good luck," I whispered and leaned back in my chair feeling drained.

The reception phone started ringing again and I sighed heavily, my finger hovering over the answer button, before making contact, "Good afternoon, Andrews and Andrews, Cathy speaking. How may I help you?" I repeated the scripted greeting for the zillionth time into the headset.

"Hi, Cath. It's me."

I rolled my eyes. "David. Now's not a good time." Not that there was ever a good time to speak with him these days.

"That's okay, I won't keep you."

Yeah, well, that was probably true. Staying around wasn't his strong suit. "Fine. What is it?"

"I have a favor to ask."

"Seriously, if you don't collect your things soon, I swear I'm going to throw them out."

"Yes, yes, I know. It's not that. I need the plane tickets to Hawaii."

"Excuse me?" I grunted. "You're making it sound like you contributed towards them. They're *my* tickets. I paid for them." I felt the bitterness bubbling up again.

"It's not like you wanted them."

"No. You're the one who made me spend the prize money *I won* in the writing competition *I entered* on a holiday you never intended for us to take, instead of on the screenwriting course I wanted to do."

"Oh, come on. You know you'd never have used it."

"You don't know that!" I yelled, feedback squawking in the headset. "You never supported me in—"

"Cath, I don't have time for this. Just let me have the damn tickets."

"What do you want them for anyway?"

"I'm taking Tiffany to Sunrise Cove to—"

"And you expect me to pay for the airfare? You've got some cheek!" Had this been his plan all along? First distract me from wondering about all those 'late nights at the office' with plans of a romantic holiday over Valentine's Day, hinting that he was finally going to propose. And then, knowing I wouldn't have a use for or want to use two tickets to Hawaii, bamboozle me into giving them to him. For someone who liked the expensive things in life, he was exceptionally skilled at getting others to foot the bill. "If you can afford to take her to Sunrise Cove you can bloody well get your own flights."

"Oh come on, Cath, you're not going to use them. You hate the beach."

I gritted my teeth. "My name is Catherine." I hated the way he called me Cath. It sounded like it was short for catheter. "The answer is no."

"For goodness sake, I'll pay you back."

I rolled my eyes. I'd heard that before.

"I'm just really stretched at the moment. I can't let Tiff down. The hotel cost a fortune and the ring damn near bankrupted me, so I really need th—"

"Ring?" I went cold, a sudden flash filling the sky.

"Yes, we're engaged. That's why we're going to Sunrise Cove. To celebrate."

"Engaged!" I spluttered, as the revelation hit, a loud thundering crack that shook my body.

The projectile ripped a hole in me, like in an aircraft, explosively sucking the air from my lungs. I lurched forward, unable to breathe, clutching my chest with one hand and ripping off the headset with the other. The room spinning, hurtling towards disaster, I staggered into the hallway and headed for the ladies washroom. Falling against the door, it swung open and deposited me onto the old tile floor as tears engulfed the sinking wreckage. I pulled myself into a stall, pushing the door closed behind me before lunging for the toilet bowl and throwing up my lunch.

Engaged. After only eight months. We'd been together for five years. So, all the whining about not being ready, about needing more time were just excuses. He was more than ready to get married, just not with me. I grabbed another fistful of toilet paper and mopped up my blubbering before dropping it onto the growing mound on my lap. After all I had sacrificed for him so that he could start his own business, and then the minute he no longer needed me, he dumped me for *her*. His office receptionist. Receptionist – the very job he mocked me for having even though it paid the bills when his business had yet to make an income. The blond bimbo with perky breasts, only a year out of high school and half his age, who was nothing, yet everything I wasn't. If it wasn't so insulting, the cliché of it would be laughable.

I blew my nose again, adding another scrunched-up soggy mass to the damp pile, steeling myself to go back.

My absence would not go unnoticed for long. I bundled up all the wadded-up toilet paper and pent-up emotions and stuffed them into the toilet. I was reaching for the flusher handle when the washroom door opened ushering in the unmistakable voices of the firm's accountant and Alex's BFF, Jess.

I stood and waited for one of them to take the free stall before I made my exit. To my relief, I heard Jess' tell-tale heels clattering on the floor next to me as she entered the stall and closed the door. I could handle facing Kim right now, but not Jess. I flushed the toilet, straightened up, and headed to the wash basins.

Kim was reapplying her makeup and showed no sign of noticing me. I washed my hands watching her in the mirror out of the corner of my eye. She smacked her lips, popped her lipstick into her designer cosmetics bag, and went on to patting her perfectly quaffed silver hair into place though it required no adjustment. She had decided to go grey gracefully, the only way she could. I sighed inwardly. She was the kind of woman who excelled at everything. In high school, she was top of her class, prom queen, president of the debating team, and all-around sports star and cheerleader. In adulthood, she slipped easily into a career that fitted her like a figure-hugging evening gown, married the equally-perfect Dr. Right, and produced two perfectly unblemished children, now in their teens at private school and following in their perfect parents' perfectly-formed footsteps.

She gave her hair one final pat and headed into the stall I had just vacated, just as the other toilet flushed. I grabbed a paper towel and hurried to dry off my hands. The stall door swung open and Jess strutted out. She pushed past me and started washing her hands while turning her head from side to side and pouting her lips as she admired herself in the mirror. I snorted under my breath and she whipped round and glared at me.

"Um, did Alex tell you where she was going for lunch?" I sputtered.

"No. Isn't she back yet?" she hissed.

"No, and Alistair Steele has been waiting for her for almost an hour."

"No idea," she said turning back to the mirror, "why don't you try her on her mobile?"

"Thanks anyway," I mumbled, rolling my eyes, as I left her to her primping and preening.

I found Amira sitting in my seat, minding the fort. At just twenty-one and ten years my junior, she was my only friend here, probably because we found solidarity in being at the bottom of the corporate food chain together. "Has Alex arrived?" I asked.

"Not yet. I left Mr. Steele in the boardroom with the contract and a cup of coffee."

"Thanks for that." I said as I retook my seat, "I bumped into the other Barbie Twin in the washroom. I asked her if she knew where Alex was and she told me to 'try her mobile'," I gestured in air quotes.

"Seriously?"

"I know, right? Like, why didn't I think of that?"

We both roared with laughter. I felt my eyes moisten again and I looked away.

"Are you okay?" she asked noticing my eyes.

I sniffed, blinking back the tears waiting in the wings, and told her about David's phone-call.

"You're better off without him."

"I know. I just didn't need this today."

"No. You didn't," she put her arms around me and squeezed me, enveloping me with the sweet smell of incense that always clung to her clothing. She pulled back at the sound of the elevator arriving and we both watched as Alex waltzed into the office carrying two large Swishique shopping bags. She was wearing a new short-sleeved white blouse and her skin was more bronzed than ever, "Oh-em-gee, doesn't my new spray tan look simply divine? This top shows it off so well," she purred, doing a small turn holding out her arms for full effect.

"Is that where you've been? I've been trying to get hold of you since two," I snapped.

"Well, I can't answer my mobile while I'm in the tanning booth, can I? And then I saw Swishes was having a sale, so I simply had to have a look. What's so important anyway?" she idly took out her mobile to check it.

"Mr. Steele has been waiting for you for an hour!"

"Oh God, was that today? Shit!" Alex quickly scanned the empty waiting room in a sudden panic, "Did he leave?"

"No, he's in the boardroom. I gave him a coffee and the contract to look over," said Amira

"Good thinking. Here look after these will you," she said, handing Amira her shopping bags and dashing over to the boardroom.

"Alistair," she gushed as she opened the door and went in, "so good to see you. Sorry for the wait, I was unavoidably detained."

He stood up, reaching to shake her hand, "No problem at all, I completely understand".

The door closed and Amira and I shook our heads rolling our eyes at each other. *Typical.*

Amira rested the bags on the desk and nonchalantly peeked inside. A silk scarf was hanging over the top and Amira pulled it out, looking at the label, "Versace. Of course. Four hundred and ten dollars, marked down from four hundred and ninety-five! Even on sale, it's more than I can afford for an entire outfit. Nice for some, eh?"

I nodded, "Though, I'm sure you'll be able to afford it one day. Me? Probably never."

She shoved it back in the bag. "I'm not sure I'd want to. She's well..." she pulled out a copy of *In Touch*, "trashy magazine says it all, right?" showing me the cover. A headline of 'Hawaii Hots Up' was splashed across the front above a photo of Hollywood super-star, Jake Donovan. He was dressed in a business shirt, several buttons undone showing his smooth ripped chest, with a stetho-scope slung round his neck. He was looking side-on into the camera with his signature steamy smirk, piercing blue eyes, stubbly chin and tousled dark hair; sporting a more mature version of the bad boy look that had shot him to fame for his role in a teen-angst vampire drama. A show, which like his current hit, I had never watched. His shows, like him, were a bit too vacuous for my taste.

I snorted, "I'm guessing she bought it for the pictures."

Amira, flipped to the relevant page, "Yup, plenty for her scrap-book," she giggled showing me the double spread of stills of him sitting in a leather armchair, tie undone, sipping a glass of bourbon; walking barefoot on a golden sand beach in a tuxedo, bow-tie undone with the jacket slung over his shoulder; driving a Porsche with one hand on the wheel, wearing too-hot-to-handle sunglasses. "Says here, he's in Hawaii for the next two months filming the third season of *Hawaii Heartbeat*."

"Oh, how exciting," I said, unimpressed.

"So, what *are* you going to do with those air tickets of yours?"

"Well, I'm not going to give them to Alex, if that's what you're suggesting."

"Ugh no, I was just wondering what you'd decided. I thought that's why you requested time off next month."

"No, I have to take the leave otherwise I'll lose it, but I'll probably just stay at home. I tried getting a refund for the tickets but because I got them on a special deal, I couldn't. They wouldn't even let me change the destination." I sighed. "Hawaii was what David wanted; if I went I'd be reminded of him and his blond tramp. I think I'm just going to let them expire and go to waste. Just to spite him."

"Oh, that's a shame. I was just thinking Alex would be so jealous of you walking the same streets as Jake Donovan."

I smiled, "She would, wouldn't she?"

"Wouldn't it just kill her if you actually met him?"

"Wouldn't it just!" I laughed. "It's almost enough to make me go. Does it say where they're shooting?"

Amira scanned the article then quickly closed the magazine and shoved it back in the bag at the sound of footsteps coming towards us.

Jess glared at both of us, then spotting the shopping bags hissed, "Have you only just come back from lunch now?"

"No, these are Alex's, I was just—" Amira started.

"Never mind. He's ready for you now," she said to me, then turning to Amira, "Don't you have work to do?"

"Yes, of course," I said curtly, "that's why she's here. To relieve me while I see Mr. Andrews."

"That's right," said Amira, taking my seat as I got up.

Jess snorted. "Fine, get on with it then." She turned and sashayed back down the hall in her impossibly-high heels.

I blew out my cheeks, "Well, here I go." I stood up and brushed my hands through my hair, tucking it back behind my shoulders and straightening my shirt and skirt, then slipped on my jacket. "How do I look?"

"Good. You'll be fine."

"Liar, but thanks anyway."

"Good luck," she smiled sympathetically, having been through the same fate earlier in the morning.

"I'll take these through to Alex's office," I said, picking up the bags.

Amira smiled and showed two thumbs up before turning to answer the phone, leaving me to walk the green mile.

I went into Alex's office and popped the shopping bags on the floor by her coat stand and noticed a poster of Jake Donovan hidden behind her door. He was shirtless of course, leaning against a concrete pillar, thumbs hooked through the belt of his jeans, the buckle hanging loose, button undone, and zipper of the jeans slightly open and poised precariously, just enough to allow the bulge in his underpants to peek out. *Eww. Just eww.*

Although... I had to admit it... *Damn!* He was drop-dead gorgeous. But, he obviously saw himself as God's gift to women. Beautiful women. Beautiful artificial self-centered women. The superstars and the supermodels. Women who got ahead in life thanks to their looks. Women like Alex, Jess... Tiffany. Women like me... well... we didn't get gifts from God. So, yeah, *eww*. God's taste in women left much to be desired. I swallowed back the bitterness beginning to form, wiped my watery eyes, and closed the door.

Chapter 2

$\mathscr{I}$ turned into the hall feeling new waves of nausea build as I headed to my dreaded annual performance. My every step seemed to echo in rhythm to an executioner's drum roll along the executive equivalent of the green mile. Did I have any final words before facing my fate? *Please make it quick.*

How the hell did my life come to this? I had dreams once, didn't I? How did I come to be headed towards yet another passing of judgment for work that numbed my soul in a job I hated? I hadn't consciously chosen to be a receptionist. It just sort of happened. It was supposed to be a stepping stone, a stop gap while I focused on 'what I really wanted to do' – as my parents put it – since writing was of course 'a silly dream' and not a viable option. Then David came along with his empty promises, 'we need your income now. When the business is off the ground, I'll support you to do whatever you want'.

The psychologists called it inattentional blindness – the way we could miss seeing the person in the gorilla suit while focusing on whatever task at hand. I had been distracted by all the expectations and promises over the years that I hadn't noticed my dreams dying, and was left completely blindsided by David's betrayal. Not only had I not seen the gorilla, but now I was the one left behind wearing the monkey suit, invisible to everyone around me while they pursued their own dreams.

The donut-shaped frosted decals on the glass walls, strategically placed to provide privacy, seemed to watch me, studying me like a specimen in a glass tank. I looked down at the floor, the white marble reminded me of the white pebbles that decorated the bottom of the fish bowl I had as a child. My goldfish had committed suicide; flipped itself right out of the bowl. I had wailed for days; didn't Nemo like me? But, I got it now. It wasn't suicide – it was a desperate leap for freedom; a bid to be released from the mind-numbing monotony of swimming round and round and round, and sheltering in the same fake cave day after day after miserable day. Every hour seeing, through the glass wall, a world full of wonder and longing for the life just beyond its reach.

My goldfish hadn't chosen to live in that fish bowl, but I had surrendered my will to live in this one. I had damned myself to captivity while watching others live the life I longed for. But, like my goldfish, I had no idea how to escape. Unless someone took pity and released it into a pond, its fate was pretty much sealed. I stopped at the hallway window next to the boss' office and placed my hands against the glass as I stared down at the street below. At this level, the windows didn't open, which was probably a good thing. I sighed heavily. The day was coming when I would have to jump, to make a break for freedom, but would I land in a pond, another cheerless tank or would I hit the sidewalk to lie gasping and twitching as the life left my broken body while staring at the existence I longed for, fade?

I wiped my eyes, straightened my clothes, and turned towards the senior partner's door. I paused for a moment and looked over at the alcove beside it. It contained a single Victorian cabinet that displayed an assortment of law-themed antiques – some old law books, brass scales, a dusty barrister wig from the UK, a gavel, and an oil painting of a dour-faced eighteenth-century gentleman. I snorted to myself. This supposed homage to the firm's roots was a fraud. The antiques were real but hadn't been passed down from one Andrews' ancestor to the next; they had been collected by Mr. Andrews and his wife on many road trips to antique stores and estate sales. In truth, none of the Andrews' ancestors had been attorneys and Trevor Andrews had been the first to break out from the family's blue-collar origins. The law firm itself was only ten years old, established by Mr. Andrews with his son, shortly after Maxwell passed the bar. However, six months after the firm launched, Max decided he was better suited to being a barista rather than a barrister and left to start his own business, a coffee truck named the Gavel and Bean that he parked outside the San Francisco courthouse just to piss off his father. Maxwell's name was never mentioned and the second Andrews in Andrews and Andrews was only ever referred to as the 'silent partner'. The fact that I knew any of this was because Amira had gone out on a date with Max once and he had spilled the beans with her and of course, she had told me everything.

The sound of coughing from inside the office brought me back to the present and I knocked on the door taking a final deep breath before turning the handle and plunging to my fate.

"Ah, Cathy," Mr. Andrews gushed, smiling broadly. I saw right through it. Not getting up, he motioned to me to sit in the straight-backed chair opposite him. "We'll just get straight into it, shall we?" he started writing in the large notebook on his glass-top desk.

"Of course," I said forcing a smile. *Yes, let's. Let's get this pointless box-ticking exercise over and done with.*

"Right," he looked at me over the top of round-framed reading glasses, looking something like a Charles Dickens character with his curly grey hair and sideburns, completely out of place in the ultra-modern white and chrome décor, "Firstly, I'll outline the objectives of this review..."

He repeated the same old routine, spewing the same ridiculous corporate buzzwords, lauding the benefits of this annual shaming as a constructive exercise towards building a better future for me at Andrews and Andrews... blah blah blah.

Yeah, whatever. I heard the words but didn't listen. I threw in a few 'uh huhs' at appropriate pauses for good measure and stared past him at the world map on the wall behind him. It was a useful technique I learned in an assertiveness training course I once attended – if looking at someone eye-to-eye feels intimidating: then look at, or just past their ear. The person won't be able to tell the difference. I'm not sure I learned much assertiveness; however, it did give me confidence I never had before to be rebellious on occasion. But then maybe rebelliousness is the height of assertiveness.

A small spider was in the process of trekking south, about to invade Mongolia. I imagined terrified Mongolians on horseback racing towards the safety of their yurts while this horrifying giant eight-legged creature shook the ground with every thundering step.

Mr. Andrews cleared his throat and I returned my gaze to him to check if he had noticed that my mind had left the room. He hadn't.

"Your work over the last year has been faultless and you get along with the staff... blah blah blah," he continued his monologue.

I stifled another sigh – it was becoming a habit – and returned my attention to the spider. Dead Mongolians cocooned in silk littered the landscape as riderless panicked horses bolted for freedom.

"But..."

There it was. The word punctuated the white noise like the sound of the trapdoor falling open below the feet of a condemned person, right before the rope snaps taut. *But*. The one word that summed up the story of my life. As a child, all my report cards read 'Cathy does well in class, *but* could try harder'. Ever since I started working, my performance reviews were the same: 'performance good, *but* could be improved'. In dating it was always, 'I like you, *but* I just want to be friends. And then there were David's words to me in February, 'I do love you, Cath, *but* I'm in love with Tiffany'. Just another but in a long line of buts and other assorted kicks in the butt.

I became aware that Mr. Andrews was staring at me. My cheeks flushed hotly as I realized I'd sighed out loud this time.

"Do you understand what I'm saying?" he hissed. "I need everyone on the team to be out there on the field giving it a hundred and ten percent."

I hated sports and hated sports analogies even more. "I see myself as the member of the team who observes the game, provides feedback, support and encouragement, and hands out the towels." I replied flatly. I was only the receptionist for goodness sake, no one ever expects the ball boy to be out there scoring the touchdowns.

"That's not good enough," he snorted, "everyone else here works late into the evening, but I've never seen you work late once."

Seriously? That didn't even make sense. My main duty was to answer the phone and greet visitors. After five o'clock the doors closed and the automated answer service kicked in. What exactly was I supposed to do after hours?

But this wasn't about work, it was about appearances. Andrews and Andrews was a small firm. It didn't deal in million-dollar lawsuits. There really was no reason for anyone to work late, yet the mindset persisted even here that normal working hours were the minimum and you weren't pulling your weight unless you regularly worked overtime. Merely being seen in the office after hours gave the illusion of an acceptable level of dedication. The truth that most were likely making personal phone calls, watching videos on YouTube, or reading trashy magazines to avoid going home to an empty apartment or tiresome spouse failed to be acknowledged. And it didn't matter that I was the human glue that kept the firm together, from being the office trouble-shooter, whipping boy, and therapist who solved every crisis from a jammed photocopier to a clogged toilet, to taking the blame for others' mistakes, to listening to everyone's problems and offering a shoulder to cry on. None of that could be quantified in any measure of profitability and was therefore meaningless and irrelevant.

"That's because I don't need to work overtime. I work efficiently, always meet deadlines and take a short lunch break, if I take one at all." *Unlike some people who have to work late because they go for two-hour lunch breaks and keep clients waiting.*

"Well, I suppose that's true," he grunted.

Thank you! I nodded triumphantly and sat back in my chair.

He raised an eyebrow, studying me, "Where do you see yourself in five years?" he asked, changing tack.

Oh god, not that one. He knew full well I had no desire to be here. He was baiting me to commit perjury, to deny what he already knew to be true. *I won't lie for you.* If that makes me a heretic, then so be it. I'd rather burn at the stake than spend my life as a slave. *Give me liberty, or give me death!* I narrowed my brow, puffed out my chest and declared, "I plan to be following a career in writing perhaps as a novelist or a screenwriter."

Mr. Andrews scowled, mumbling under his breath and I immediately regretted my answer. Why didn't I just lie? This wasn't the Spanish Inquisition. Why did I have to be so melodramatic? It's not as if I really believed my own words. It always seemed like such an impossible dream and given where I was sitting at that moment, it just made me sound like a five-year-old saying I wanted to grow up to be an astronaut.

Mr. Andrews rolled his eyes and looked at me with the same disapproving look my father would give me when I spoke about my writing. It's just a hobby – you'll never make any money from it. You're just dreaming, he would say, rolling his eyes crushing my spirit, snuffing out my soul.

"You've proved my point." Mr. Andrews growled, exasperated.

I stifled another sigh and sank back into the chair.

Mr. Andrews leaned forward, "I need people who are committed to the work we're doing here. You need to get your priorities straight. I don't want people whose loyalties lie elsewhere."

Excuse me? Having dreams didn't make someone a traitor, did it? Or maybe it did. I had ignored the signs, wanted to believe it was harmless flirting when David started paying attention to Tiffany. Maybe he believed it himself at first, but eventually he left me for her.

"I'm loyal. I'm here every day, I do everything..." I trailed off. If I was flirting with my dreams then maybe I was already leaving here in spirit. In reality I'd never been here to begin with. It was pointless saying otherwise. "You said I met all my performance requirements this year, so will I be getting the raise you promised last year?" May as well get straight to the point.

"No. As I said, everybody in this firm goes the extra mile and I need you to do the same."

"But, you said my work has been faultless. You said... I need..." Mr. Andrews' expression was unchanged. I gave up, sinking against the hard back of the chair feeling like that five-year-old again.

"Look, I know you've been through a rough patch with you and David going your separate ways."

That's a nice way to put it.

"We're all sorry you broke up, but you need to get over it. It's time for you to step up and do your part."

I looked back at the map on the wall. The spider had disappeared.

"To that end, I've enrolled you in some professional development training next month."

Oh yippee. "Professional development?"

"Team building skills, lateral thinking, problem solving. That kind of thing. It'll help you become more proactive. I need you to start showing initiative—"

"Initiative!" I blurted, "How do you know I don't show initiative? I deal with half a dozen things every day that you never see because I solved the problem before it ever makes it to your desk." I was on a roll now. "If you want me to step up around here, why don't you give me something that'll make use of *my* strengths? Like giving me the firm's newsletter to write. Alex does such a shocking job of it, I wonder how she ever made it through high school English, let alone law school. But because it's *Alex*, you..." I stopped myself just in time.

Mr. Andrews sat back in surprise, "Now this is what I've been wanting to see from you, though with perhaps a little less venom."

I bit my lip, scowling; I wasn't looking for his approval.

"Taking over the newsletter is an excellent idea. As you say, Alex is simply far too busy to give it her full attention. We'll look at it when you get back from the training."

Of course, he'd defend her. "So, when exactly is this training happening?"

"The last week of next month, which I realize happens to be at the same time you have requested leave, so you'll have to shift your leave to September."

"I can't."

"What do you mean you can't?" he fumed, "You're just going to sit around at home."

"That's when I'm going to Hawaii." I grinned.

"I thought that was canceled."

"Postponed. I'm going on my own." I proclaimed triumphantly. "I've already booked everything and the tickets expire at the end of August so I can't change it. You'll just have to cancel the training."

Mr. Andrews' face turned red, at a sudden loss for words he looked down at his notepad and scribbled away grumbling under his breath, "Oh all right. Fine," he spat, not looking at me, "your vacation stands. You can go."

Did he mean Hawaii or now? I felt so giddy, I was afraid to stand up so I stayed seated presuming he meant the former.

"We're done here. You can leave," he grunted, not looking up.

"Of course," I stammered and stood up cautiously, trying not to wobble, adrenalin and euphoria from my victory flooding my system.

"Cathy," Mr. Andrews said as I got to the door.

I turned and he looked at me, his expression softening as he took his glasses from his nose, "I am sorry that things didn't work out for you and David."

"Thank you." I smiled weakly.

"A holiday away will be good for you."

I nodded. Maybe he had a heart after all?

"It'll give you time to sort yourself out, eh? Help reform your attitude."

Nope. I closed the door behind me, shaking my head. The only thing I would be reforming was my resolve to get away from here. But, I couldn't very well do it at home now. I didn't put it past him to check on whether I had indeed gone away. Looks like I was going to Hawaii after all.

Chapter 3

Ethan jogged on the path along the beach leaving another crazy shift behind him. His soaked T-shirt clung to his chest and every powerful footfall sent droplets of sweat into the air from the ends of his drenched hair. He didn't need his Fitbit to tell him his heart was pounding.

A young boy chasing a ball ran out in front of him and Ethan swerved hard, jumping off the path onto the grass to avoid colliding with him. He stopped abruptly and leaned against a palm tree catching his breath while he watched the boy run over to re-join his family building sandcastles on the beach. It was another perfect afternoon at Waikiki. Surfers rode the turquoise waves while other people swam and played games on the white sand. Behind him, in the distance, several large trailer vans were parked with a large cordon set up around them and blocking off access to the beach. Beyond the cordon, a crowd of curious onlookers was gathering, but Ethan paid no attention to them.

He took off his aviator sunglasses with one hand and lifted the edge of his T-shirt with the other and wiped his forehead, showing off his perfectly-sculpted abs. He checked his Fitbit then slipped his sunglasses back on and turned back to the path when a sudden cry drew his attention to the water.

A surfer was dragging a body from the water. "Someone, get a lifeguard!" he screamed.

Ethan reacted instantly and sped across the grass verge and

onto the beach, kicking up plumes of sand as he ran toward the men. Several people were gathering round and Ethan pushed them aside, "Let me through, I'm a doctor," he shouted as he fell to his knees beside the lifeless man.

He ignored the bleeding minor gash on the man's shoulder as he felt for a pulse and signs of breathing. Nothing. He tilted the man's head back, squeezed his nose shut and gave two breaths. "Does anybody know what happened?" He asked as he interlaced his fingers over the man's chest and began compressions.

The crowd murmured, but no one answered.

Ethan moved back to give the man some more breaths when he noticed blood pooling at the base of the man's head. "He's got a head injury!" he exclaimed, whipping off his shirt and bunching it up. "You," he motioned to the young woman in a bright pink bikini who was staring at his naked chest, "hold this here," he grabbed her by the arm and directed her to press his shirt against the side of the man's head as he gave two more breaths and continued compressions.

The surfer paced back and forth and picked up his board which was still tethered to his ankle, noticing blood on the fin. "Oh man, I killed him!" he cried, "I must have hit him with my board. I never even saw him until he was floating there."

"It was an accident," said the girl in the bikini, turning to him.

"Keep pressure on the wound!" Ethan hissed.

She returned her attention to the man's injury, "It wasn't your fault," she called to him.

The crowd parted to let through two lifeguards. "We can take it from here," said one as he began taking tubes and gear from his kit bag, and the other set down a backboard and took over the compressions.

"Has someone called for an ambulance?" asked Ethan.

"Already on its way," said the lifeguard as he inserted a breathing tube into the man's airway and attached an ambu-bag.

Ethan reached over and grabbed the lifeguard's kit bag, "I take it you've got an AED in here."

"Yes sir, but please let us do our job—"

"I'm a trauma surgeon at Honolulu General." Ethan pulled out a plastic box and unraveled a set of leads, plugging them in.

"Oh, okay, I didn't—"

"Yeah, yeah. Out of my way," he ripped off the backing of the electrode pads and placed them on the man's chest, and switched on the defibrillator, charging the device. "Everyone move back!"

The lifeguards stopped what they were doing and backed away from the lifeless body.

"Shocking!" Ethan yelled as he pressed the shock button. A jolt of electricity surged through the man's body jerking his torso off the ground. Ethan stared fixedly at the unit's display screen. "Restart compressions!"

The lifeguards jumped back to action.

"He's going to make it, right?" pleaded the surfer, "He can't die. You've got to save him!"

"We're doing everything we can. Please stand back." Ethan barked, watching the defibrillator's screen as the device recharged, "Clear!"

The lifeguards backed off and Ethan pressed the shock button again, "Shocking!" Again, the man's body jerked violently but did not respond. "Damn it!" Ethan shook his head, "Restart compressions!"

The lifeguards took up their positions again and continued CPR.

"Come on, come on," Ethan mumbled under his breath as he waited for the defibrillator to charge up again, "Clear!"

The lifeguards jumped back as Ethan sent another jolt of electricity coursing through the man's body. They watched the gruesome jerking repeat, keenly aware that the man's chance of making it was fading with every round. The lifeguards moved back to continue their efforts when a beeping sound broke the hushed tension.

"Hold compressions!" Ethan cried out, "I've got a rhythm."

Cheers and applause rang out from the crowd and the surfer dropped to his knees, staring up at the sky as he wept, "Oh, thank God!"

"Okay, let's pack him up." Ethan directed the lifeguards to move the man onto the backboard, while he dealt with the head wound and stabilized his neck.

Someone called out, "Ambulance's here" and the crowd parted to let through two paramedics.

"Ethan!" The female paramedic with a blond ponytail cried out in shock. She stood back leaving her male partner to join the lifeguards in preparing the man for transport.

"Britney." Ethan looked up from securing the cervical collar around the man's neck. He sighed heavily and stood up.

"You haven't returned any of my calls."

"Now's not the time, Britney."

"He's in good hands," she gestured to the man on the backboard being carried over to the waiting ambulance. "We need to talk."

"There's nothing to talk about."

Britney snorted, "We need to talk about us."

"There is no us."

"That's not what it seemed like when you had me pressed up against the wall in the on-call room."

"That was a mistake."

"A mistake?" she hissed.

"It should never have happened. I love my wife. I know that now."

"And you needed to screw me to figure that out?" she slapped him across the face.

Ethan pressed a hand to his stinging cheek, "I don't owe you anything."

"We'll see about that."

"You just have to forget the whole thing ever happened."

"That's going to be hard—" A shout from the waiting ambulance interrupted her and she turned to see her partner motioning for her to hurry up. She turned back to Ethan, pausing for a beat, "I'm pregnant." She let the words drop, then turned and jogged for the ambulance.

Ethan dropped his hand and stood motionless processing the gravity of her revelation. He watched her leave, his eyes wide, not seeing the man with the camera mounted on a body-hugging metal framework walking towards him with slow deliberate steps, or the furry mass hovering above his head while he waited for the sign.

"Cut!" the director's voice squawked over a distant megaphone.

Jake blew out his checks, relaxing his stance, but maintained his position. He clenched his fists, resisting the urge to run his hands through his hair. The last thing they needed was him delaying what had already been a long day by making them wait while he had his hair reset for another take.

The boom operator stifled a yawn, but kept his grip on the boom, keeping the microphone levitating above Jake's head, and the Steadicam operator stayed where he was holding the camera on Jake. All eyes turned to the assistant director. She had her hand pressed over her ear as she listened for further instructions through her ear piece.

"Yup, gotcha," Emily muttered holding the microphone of the headset close to her chin. She turned to the group, giving them a double thumbs-up, "It's a wrap everyone."

A round of weary whoops and relieved sighs rang out from the group. The Steadicam operator backed off and the hovering dead cat descended as the boom operator set it down, with a yawn and stretched his arms while a couple of grips moved in to help dismantle and pack up the gear.

"Great job," Emily said to Jake as they headed towards the grass embankment, "you really nailed Ethan's shocked expression. I'm looking forward to seeing the dailies."

"Thanks." Jake snorted, "It's easy to look exasperated when Kristie is on set."

"I know what you mean," she laughed. "Are you coming to the party tomorrow night?"

"Nah, giving this one a miss. Making an early start on the vay-cay."

"Ah well, you have a good break."

"Will do. Have fun tomorrow."

She nodded and they stepped up onto the grass. Emily headed over to the video village that was set up in the shade of some palm trees to confer with the director and producers who were gathered around the monitors. Jake waved as he passed and then cut across the empty beach car park towards base camp, the corral of trailers that formed the hub of the day's operations.

He passed the production trailer and rounding the corner came face to face with Kristie who was standing in front of the door to his own trailer. She had changed out of the paramedic uniform into a white bikini and had let her hair down.

"I've been waiting for you," she said coyly, twirling a few strands between her fingers.

"Going for a swim?" He asked as he tried to get to his door.

She laughed, and blocked his way, "Oh Jake, this is Luis Vuitton. You don't get it wet."

"Ah, so it's only for show." He tried sidestepping her but she pivoted round, effectively pinning him against the side of the trailer.

"What time are you picking me up tomorrow night?" she ran her tongue over her top lip and dragged a finger down his chest.

"You'll have to make your own way there. I'm not going," he tried reaching for the trailer door, but she blocked him again, pressing her hands against the trailer on either side of him.

"What? But we have to go. We're like the prom king and queen, we have to be there." She said pouting.

"We are not a thing."

"How can you say that? You can't deny we have chemistry." She pressed herself against him and kissed him hard, full on the lips, wrapping her arms around his neck.

Jake pulled away, pushing her off him, "Damn it, Kristie! Enough!" He lunged for the door and yanked it open.

"We belong together! You'll see." Kristie crowed as he jumped inside, slamming the door in her face and locking it behind him.

He leaned against the door and exhaled heavily. God, he wished the writers would kill her off. He had made the mistake of going with her to the last wrap party and ever since then she had deluded herself that they had shared a spark when all they had shared was a cab. Things only got worse when the writers decided to give her a larger role as Ethan's femme fatale. No matter how much he denied it, she was convinced he had pressured them to write it for her and that he just needed time before he would finally declare his feelings for her. Until then she hounded him and set traps trying to trick him into surrendering and leaked tips to the gossip columns that their 'onscreen chemistry' was real off camera, which the fans were desperate for and added fuel to the fire.

'Such raw animal attraction'. 'Savage passion simmering below the surface'. Viewers loved the tension between Ethan and Britney, but it wasn't desire Jake drew on, but contempt. He deserved an Emmy for pulling off their love scene – if a sordid hook-up in an ER on-call room could be called a love scene. He hated every minute of it and that had translated into a fevered and primal carnal act that the production team loved, fueled Kristie's delusion further, and left Jake filled with anger. Anger at the industry he loved for asking too much of him. Anger at himself for submitting. *Smile, Jake. Lose the shirt, Jake. Show like you're loving it while you fake climaxing with a woman you despise.* Sometimes he felt like he was merely a trained monkey expected to perform on command, locked in contracts and made to dance for the highest bidder.

Take the abuse, the criticism, the insults; never step out of line, never fight back, because if you do, those who adore and worship you will crucify you. The industry was no stranger to sex scandals, idols who abused their power and influence and were toppled by sexual harassment charges. Always men. Jake was powerless against Kristie. If he said or did anything to put her in a bad light, he would be seen as the aggressor. She was skating on thin ice, but he was the one who would be plunged into the freezing water if it cracked.

Changed and refreshed, Jake zipped up his duffel bag and slung it over his shoulder. He slowly opened the door and looked around to make sure Kristie wasn't waiting to ambush him then left the trailer and made his way to the production trailer. He popped in to say a quick goodbye then made a brief stop at crafty to grab a snack for the road. He ripped open the bag of nuts and shoved a handful in his mouth before turning for the parking lot. A man in his twenties stood watching him and nodded at him apprehensively as he approached.

It took Jake a moment to recognize him without the prosthetic latex lacerations and fake blood. "Oh hey," he mumbled with his mouth full while wiping the salt from his hand on his cargo pants. "Great job out there," he cheered, extending his hand.

"Thanks man! It was an honor working with you," he shook Jake's hand eagerly.

"Anytime." Jake nodded and tossed another handful of nuts in his mouth and munched away without a second thought, leaving the young man to bask in the glow of having shook hands with Hollywood royalty on the day of his first real onscreen role, which would get him listed in the credits as 'Bleeding Man' or 'Injured Swimmer'.

Chapter 4

$\mathcal{J}$ake drove along the coastline watching the sun sink into the ocean while activity on Waikiki's beaches migrated to the night life of restaurants and thumping nightclubs. He cut through the downtown and exited onto the Lunalilo freeway heading away from the high-rises, past the Diamond Head crater, and on towards the less-populated coastline on the southeast of the island.

The further he got from the noise and chaos the more the tension drained from his body and he relaxed his grip on the steering wheel. He breathed deeply, filling his lungs with the salty air thick with the scent of damp vegetation, and rested one arm on the open window feeling the humid air blow over his skin.

He needed this. Whenever filming wrapped for a season he would take some alone time to recharge. It was his way of shedding the character; of shedding all the stress and bullshit that went with it.

He could get so wrapped up in the many personas he had to play that he lost track of who he really was. Sometimes he even ended up carrying baggage that wasn't even his own. He needed the physical break, the disconnect, to re-establish his hold on reality.

It was like working on a jigsaw puzzle. He had to tip out all the pieces and spread them out, and then sort the pieces into different piles: those that made up Vincent Dubois, those that made up Ethan Temple, those that made up Jake the Celebrity, and those that made up Jake the Man. He suspected Jake the Man was missing a few pieces. He never seemed to be able to finish that part of the puzzle. He'd lost the box years ago and had no idea what he was supposed to look like. Jake the Man was the one character he still struggled to get right.

He was on the Kalaniana'ole Highway now, heading towards Makapu'u Point, the lighthouse visible on the right, bathed in gold waiting for the light to go before sending out its beacon into the darkness. Although the sun was setting on the other side of the island and had disappeared behind the mountains the view of the twilight sky reflecting on the calm ocean was breathtaking. He made a mental note of finding out if it was possible to visit the lighthouse. It would make for some great sunrise photographs.

Makapu'u Point behind him, he was now heading towards Sunrise Cove, a little-known private resort nestled in the small bay before Waimanalo Beach, a few miles south of the location that had been used as the site of Robin's Nest in the original *Magnum PI*. He took the turn-off following the road in the direction of the beach, but had yet to see any sign of the resort. The road curved round into a stretch of dense bush plunging the car into darkness and flooding it with the smell of wet earth and dripping vegetation. Jake took a deep breath relishing the fragrance. It was like the smell that comes after the rain, full of life and renewal. The road curved again and led him into the parking area in front of a modest five-story hotel, flanked on either side by a series of small cabins.

Jake parked the Jeep and made his way along the path, lined with frangipani trees covered in perfumed blossoms and strung with twinkling fairy lights, to the courtyard. A large fountain stood in the center, spilling water into a fish pond, encircled by stone benches and orchid-filled tubs. In the distance, the sound of the tide coming in, added to the buzz of night insects.

The glass doors of the hotel slid open ushering Jake into the lobby. Cool jazz trickled through from a piano being played in the lounge while guests sat and chatted and glasses filled with ice cubes and early nightcaps clinked against each other.

A large Hawaiian man dressed smartly in the hotel uniform looked up from the front desk.

"*Aloha*, Sir." He smiled broadly, "Welcome back to the Sunrise Resort."

"Thanks, Keoni. It's good to see you again."

"To the airport, right?" asked the Uber driver after I settled in the passenger seat. He was an attractive guy in his mid-thirties, with sandy blond hair, neatly dressed in jeans and a button-up shirt.

"Yes," I was really in the mood to make some sarcastic comment about stating the obvious when that's what was listed on the booking, but he was just being polite, "that's right." I smiled, "thank you."

I made an instinctive cursory glance at his left hand as he maneuvered the car out onto the road. *Married.* The nice ones always were.

"Righty-O." he chirped cheerfully.

I sighed as I detected an English accent. *Married and British.* I turned away and watched the apartment recede from the side window. It was overcast and dreary, but not yet raining. Ordinarily, I'd be excited to be going to the airport. But I hated everything about this trip. I hated the reminder that David had left me. I hated that I had let him bully me into purchasing those damned airline tickets. I hated that my boss had set me an objective, to 'sort myself out'. And I hated the goddamn beach.

"Are you going somewhere exciting?"

"My aunt died. I'm going to the funeral."

"Oh, I'm so sorry for your loss." He stammered.

I cringed at simultaneously inventing and killing off a fictional relative and shutting down his enthusiastic attempt at making conversation, but I just didn't have the energy. "Thank you. It was unexpected..." I trailed off as the clouds opened up and I watched the rain beat against the window. He took the hint and didn't press me further and we continued the rest of the journey in silence.

The rain eased by the time the driver delivered me to the departures terminal. I stood for a moment outside the entrance listening to the roar of an aircraft taking off and inhaled deeply. There was something about airports; the sound of the engines, and the smell of aircraft fuel in the air that always lifted my spirit. Perhaps it was the idea that air travel promised new experiences and opportunities just beyond the horizon. I extended the handle of the suitcase, gliding it along behind me, and walked through the sliding doors into the terminal. Maybe this trip was going to be good after all.

David could never understand why I liked to get to the airport early. Ever impatient, he didn't like to wait, and whenever we went anywhere together getting to the airport, checking in and boarding was a frenzied dash that left him invigorated and me, a nervous wreck. On my own, I liked the waiting time, I found the wind-down and build-up therapeutic. I checked my suitcase at the self-check-in and paid extra attention this time to the usual pre-flight questions so that I didn't repeat the mistake of my last trip by answering 'yes' to the one that asked if I was carrying any explosives. A rerun of that fiasco successfully avoided, I began my airport departure ritual. First I took a casual walk about the terminal, watching people and tuning into their different energies. All strangers, all anonymous faces; people I would never see again or if I did, I would pass by in the street without recognizing, but each one of them told me their story without saying a single word. There were the businessmen and women in their suits, Bluetooth phone attachments perched on their ears, wheeling and dealing while walking across the tiled floor with proactive strides, pulling their designer mini suitcases behind them; the foreign tourists sitting in groups next to small mountains of combined hand luggage; the haggard parents clutching fussing children by the hand, on the endless quest to find a washroom; the global backpackers on another overseas adventure sitting at tables drinking coffee in paper cups while flicking through well-worn *Lonely Planet* guides; the workaholic frequent flyer tapping away at a laptop on his knees; and the newbie airport worker sporting her brand new lanyard and ID badge, wide-eyed and full of optimism on her first day, while her grizzled grey-haired colleague shuffled along beside her counting the days to his retirement.

I moved on from people-watching and popped in at the news agent and browsed the newspaper stands, shelves set with candy, travel gadgets, gifts, and the usual assortment of T-shirts, Golden Gate Bridge postcards, and authentic San Francisco souvenirs made in China. I made my way to the books and perused the current top-sellers and latest casualties to land in the bargain bin. Lastly, I stopped at the magazines and flipped through a few cookery and home decorating titles. I put them back and glanced over at the tabloids with their garish assault of bright colors, bold lettering and gossipy headlines. Predictably, Jake Donovan was splashed over the covers of most of them. I snorted at the latest exposé: Jake Donovan was dating co-star Kristie Jephson. *People* had a picture on the cover of him (shirtless, of course) standing with his back against the side of a movie trailer while she wore a skimpy white bikini and stood gazing into his eyes and caressed his cheek. The headline read 'Kristie says it's official'. Next to it, *In Touch* had a different picture of the same moment, this time he had his tongue down her throat with 'The Kiss!' spread across in giant fuchsia pink letters.

So, Jake Donovan was no longer on the market. *Aww, what a great loss to beautiful women everywhere.* I couldn't help grinning; Alex would be devastated.

Chapter 5

I left the shop without buying anything and wandered on to the food court. Though it was lunch time, I wasn't really hungry, but felt I should eat something, since the inflight meal was likely to be insubstantial. Besides, this was all part of my pre-flight ritual. I reviewed the various options, but couldn't decide. I wasn't even sure if I wanted something sweet or savory. I found myself standing in front of a cabinet of food at a coffee shop, staring at the assortment of sandwiches, muffins and pastries. What did I want? What *did* I want? Considering the whole point of this 'holiday' was to sort out my life, how was I going to make any decisions about my future if I couldn't even make up my mind over a sandwich versus a muffin?

"I'll have the Mississippi mud cake and a large latte," I announced when I got to the head of the queue and then immediately began to doubt my decision as I swiped my card to pay. I probably should have bought something sensible. Still, I was on vacation, so I may as well eat like it.

I settled at a table towards the back, near the windows overlooking the tarmac. I sat for a while watching the workers below buzz from one plane to the next collecting and delivering luggage in carts, refueling, restocking and rechecking. Repeating the same routines over and over. Even here, in the enviable world of airline travel, repetition had the power to turn the exciting into the mundane.

I sighed and turned my attention to my cake, a glorious mound covered in smooth chocolate frosting. Just the pick-me-up I needed. I dug my fork into the ganache, looking forward to layers of cake, marshmallow cream and fudge sauce, but sank back in disappointment. The cake was a fraud. It was solid all the way through; no creamy indulgent interior and when I put the first forkful in my mouth I discovered that the frosting wasn't a ganache at all, but a thick butter icing, and the cake was a dry cake-from-a-box sponge.

This new thick gluggy betrayal stuck to the roof of my mouth and was hard to swallow. So full of promise... a lot like this holiday, I grunted as I felt the stodgy mass slide down my throat. If David had been with me, he would have told me to take it back. But, technically there wasn't anything wrong with it and I wasn't the kind of person to take food back just because I didn't like it. I committed to my choices. I didn't discard people when they no longer served me. I stayed loyal even when things got hard or the excitement dulled. I wouldn't give up on this cake just because the person who baked it lacked inspiration and the café had a tight budget. And so, I kept plowing on, feeling virtuous in my noble effort to keep this piece of cake from the sting of rejection.

But then, perhaps that was my problem. I paused, holding my fork upright in the remaining nub of cake. Did I stay with people, places and jobs out of some kind of misguided loyalty? Forgiving broken promises, ignoring mistreatment, giving endless second chances to those who let me down? Was loyalty only a strength when it was selfish, but a weakness when it was selfless?

A waitress delivered my latte and snapped me out of my downward spiral. I sniffed back my failures and took a big swig of the coffee, grateful to be able to wash down the cake.

"Damn it!" I cried out as the scalding liquid hit my tongue. I slammed the cup on the table and noticed people were staring at me. I looked away and glared at the cup. The contents-may-be-hot warning glared back at me. *Yeah, hilarious.* I took another mouthful of cake to sooth my mouth. It stung with more regrets than simply poor café choices. Any remaining obligation I felt towards the cake had vanished and I pushed the rest aside uneaten. I got up, slinging my bag over my shoulder, and taking an extra napkin to wrap around the coffee cup, walked towards my departure gate.

There were no more seats available so I stood by the window staring out at the waiting plane cautiously sipping the cooling coffee. I idly read the message on the side of the cup: 'Kafé Kulchur supports sustainable living, please recycle'. So much for sustainable living, what about sustainable loving?

I guess that was it, people were like cups. Some were high-maintenance porcelain tea cups with gilded edges and delicate patterns that had to be handled with care and were kept on display or only brought out to impress. Others were the mass-produced ceramic mugs, sturdy and practical that endured for a lifetime. They had memorable witty sayings or commemorative decorations printed on them and were collected, loved and valued for decades even if the designs were faded, the glazes cracked or the handles broken off. While other people were single-use, disposable, easily crumpled in the palm of a hand, replaceable. At best they were recycled, reused, repurposed; at worse they became unsightly rubbish lining the road lying helpless to be flattened by passing cars. The drivers, oblivious of your existence, drove over you, not feeling even the slightest bump as they pushed you into the dirt on their way to the drive-through to pick up a new fresh cup.

The sound of the attendant announcing that passengers should begin boarding brought my mind back to the present and I drained the last of my coffee. I gave the cup a parting glance; now empty, its function served, no longer 'coffee cup', just 'cup'. It had once been filled with purpose, once had belonging and value to someone, and within a matter of minutes it had become obsolete, contaminated, and as I dropped its empty shell in a nearby rubbish bin... abandoned.

I settled into my seat and buckled the seat belt. At least I had scored a window seat, though as usual I was seated next to the wing which obscured most of my view. I leaned over to watch the workers below load the last of the luggage and then drive away, their carts now empty, off to collect the next load like ants scurrying around collecting crumbs from a picnic blanket.

I reached for the inflight magazine and idly flicked through the pages of fashion trends and exotic travel destinations. The last page fell open at a full-page picture of Jake Donovan, his eyebrows furrowed, resting his chin on his fist, staring off into the distance all broodily as if in deep thought, while showing off an ostentatious Tag Heuer watch on his wrist. I grunted, slapping the magazine shut and stuffed it back in the seat pocket, and turned my attention to the flight attendant going through the safety procedures. I always felt it was the polite thing to do, even if you had seen it a hundred times before. With a gentle lurch the plane started moving backwards and turned to taxi towards to the runway.

The plane lined up and then paused while the engines built up power and I peered out the window feeling my excitement grow. Even if I had been traveling for a real funeral, even if I was dumped by the man I thought I would marry, even if I had to 'sort myself out', none of that could spoil what was to come, that best part of flying... the takeoff.

As if pawing at the ground impatiently, the cabin shook with trembling anticipation. And then released, the giant beast bolted forward, thundering down the runway. I watched the tarmac speed past while I was pushed back in my seat, the cabin tilted upwards and I felt that euphoric rush as the ground fell away, taking my troubles with it, and I was free.

For a while anyway. The cabin leveled out and was filled with the sound of seat belts being unbuckled and people moving about again and getting stuck into their inflight entertainment as if being inactive for the next five hours would cause them actual physical harm. I, on the other hand, appreciated the excuse to do absolutely nothing, free from the guilt of thinking I ought to be doing something productive. As long as you were in the air, between here and there, between today and tomorrow and your life was in someone else's hands, you got the freedom to put life on hold, to leave all your burdens on the ground and simply *be*.

I left my own seat belt buckled and shifted over onto my side so I could look out the window while resting my head against the seat back and aircraft wall. I loved to watch the clouds drifting over the changing landscape below. It was a remnant of my childhood when I would lie on the grass in our backyard and stare up into the sky, letting my imagination run loose. I would strain to see higher and higher, beyond the clouds, beyond the blue veil, up into where the blackness began and the stars appeared, imagining what I might see on alien worlds and in the space between. It had been many years since I had lain on the ground staring up into the sky, but staring out an aircraft window brought me right back. I never tired of it.

Before I knew it, the evening meal was being served. People complained about airplane food, but I loved the novelty of it. I delighted in the little fit-together dishes, all hermetically sealed and perfectly arranged in the small tray. It was probably another reminder of my childhood playing with a beloved toy kitchen set. I removed the lid of the vegetarian lasagna and dug in. I winced, feeling the sting of hot food against the raw patch in my mouth. But, determined not to be discouraged, I peeled off the lid of the tiny plastic cup of red grape juice and lifted it up to make a toast. *To me, to new beginnings.* A sudden shudder of turbulence knocked the cup from my hand spilling its contents down my white blouse. *Maybe not.* I dabbed at my blouse up with the small serviette, thankful that the cup contained no more than approximately three mouthfuls. This, in hindsight, was probably the reasoning behind the tiny quantities and not necessarily economic cost-cutting.

A flight attendant noticed my distress and brought a damp cloth to my aid, which only made the stain spread. *Great. Just great.* She offered me another drink, but I declined. One stain was enough, though my blouse was now effectively ruined anyway. I ate the rest of the lasagna and dessert of fruit salad with custard cautiously and shied away from the coffee service though, like the first part of the flight, the remainder was equally free of turbulence. *Naturally.*

By the time the trays and rubbish were collected we had started our descent and the sky had turned pink. We followed the sun, sinking towards the ground and leaving the sparkling ocean behind us as the world we approached was bathed in gold. A picture-perfect scene, yet as the wheels struck the ground I felt the gravity of reconnecting with reality hit me with the same double g-force as the plane experienced touching down.

I sat back heavily, readjusting to the weight, and watched the other passengers compete in the mad race to disembark, whipping off their seatbelts, scrabbling for their bags and jostling for the door. Outside the worker ants swarmed over to the open belly of the plane to start offloading the luggage. Once the mass of passengers had moved to the front of the plane I left my seat and followed them out, pausing to thank the flight attendants and gaze out onto the tarmac from the windows in the air-bridge. I was in no hurry. No one was waiting for me.

By the time I had got to the baggage claim carousel my suitcase was the only piece of luggage left and it stood waiting patiently for me, on the floor next to the now-motionless conveyor. I extended the handle and pulling it behind me, made for the exit. But, instead of rolling, my suitcase bounced and shuddered. I stopped and looked down to find one of the wheels had broken off in transit. I dropped my head, letting out a defeated sigh and stood for a moment staring at the floor while I collected myself. Despite the audible drone of air-conditioning, the terminal was warm and stuffy inside and my head felt equally hazy.

I scanned the hall for an empty luggage cart and the nearest was on the opposite end to the exit. I decided not to bother with the extra walk when I was literally a few feet from the exit. For goodness sake, it wasn't as if I couldn't carry the thing. I shoved the expandable handle back down and turned the suitcase on its side, and with my carry bag slung over my shoulder, I lifted it by the carry handle and marched off towards the exit.

Within a few paces, my modestly-packed suitcase began to

weigh a ton and I had to carry it with both hands. It banged against my legs and I cursed as the hard edges dug into my flesh and threatened to snag on my linen pants. I swear I had only packed the essentials, but now I was beginning to question the necessity of those essentials. How the hell could a few clothes, toiletries and a change of shoes weigh so damn much?

With a final heave I lurched over the threshold and the automatic doors spat me out onto the arrivals' forecourt, sliding closed behind me. The hot humid outside air hit me with an unexpected blow, sucking the air out of me and I gasped, setting the suitcase down. Almost instantly my hair clung to my head in a moist matted mess and rivulets of sweat began to steam down my back. The thick air smelled musty of wet vegetation, damp concrete and jet-fuel. *So, this was paradise.*

Aged fluorescent lights began to flicker on, their glow barely bright enough to soften the growing shadows left behind by the withdrawing sun. Despite my temporary deafness from the descent, the high-pitch buzzing cut through my head until I became aware of another buzzing. Mosquitos. I was a sitting duck. I grabbed my suitcase and made a mad dash to find a taxi.

"The Waimanilo Hotel, please," I said, craning over to speak to the cab driver through the open window.

A bulky Hawaiian man in a floral shirt frowned at me, "Never heard of it."

"It's in Diamond Bay."

"You mean, Diamond Head?"

"Yes, yes, just past Waikiki."

He nodded, popping the trunk and leaned out the window, as I started towards the rear of the car, "What street?"

I paused, setting down my suitcase again and dug out the print-out of the booking from my shoulder bag. I handed it straight to him without looking at it.

"Lady, this is for the Diamond Day Hotel in Waimanalo Beach."

I took the paper back and skimmed over it. He was right. How had I got it so muddled? "Okay, well there then. Is it far?"

"About half an hour but it'll cost you over a hundred dollars."

Shit. I'd budgeted on half that. "Is there any other way of getting there?"

"The bus, but it doesn't go directly there or a shuttle."

"A shuttle, where do I get that?"

He grunted and pointed to some minivans I had just passed on my way to the taxi stand. One was pulling out and heading towards the exit, and the other appeared to be about to do the same. I grabbed my bags and made for the vans waving my arm madly to get their attention and left the taxi driver cursing as he got out the car to shove closed the trunk.

"Where to?" asked the shuttle driver who had seen me waving and stood beside the van, his arms crossed.

"Wai...man...lo...bay. ...Beach." I panted. I handed him the printout and leaned against my suitcase to catch my breath. "Can you take me?"

"Yeah, you'll be the last stop."

I nodded, "That's fine. How much?"

"Sixty bucks."

"Okay." I nodded again with gritted teeth.

He pulled open the van's side. "Get in," he motioned and then took my suitcase from me to store it in the back.

I climbed in to find the van full of people. If I was the last stop then it was going to be a long ride. I groaned and made my way to the only vacant seat in the back, squeezing past the passengers in the front who glared at me for delaying their departure.

I settled into my slot in the sardine can, squashing myself up against the side of the van as much as I could. The door slammed shut, trapping us in and we were off. There was no inside light and the dark interior smelled of damp upholstery, body odor, car grease and air freshener. All strangers, no one talked and the only sounds came from the engine, traffic and the radio tuned to a local Hawaiian station. Though I was next to a window, I couldn't see much in the darkness, so I rested my head against it and stared up at the roof watching lights and shadows dance across with every turn and passing vehicle.

I must have drifted off when the sound of someone shouting stirred me awake. I opened my eyes to find the van empty and the driver standing by the open door calling to me. "Hey lady, we're here."

"Already?" I mumbled and looked at my phone. The journey had taken close to two hours. I blew out my cheeks; at least I had slept through most of it. I slipped my phone back into my bag, pulled out some cash then clambered out of the van. The driver deposited my suitcase at my feet and I handed him the fare. "Thank you," I said with a sagging smile.

"*Mahalo*," he said, yawning, "have a great stay." He took the cash from me and stuffed it into his pocket before slamming the side door and hopping back into the driver's seat.

The van drove off leaving me on the side of the road in the dim glow of a street light. I scanned the street ahead; I could make out a row of suburban houses and realized I had no idea where I was or if I had even been delivered to the right place. I walked on, half-carrying half-dragging my sodding suitcase, starting to feel a mild panic. I felt like a kidnap victim, in an abduction gone wrong, who gets dumped in some sketchy neighborhood so that the kidnappers can make a hasty getaway. I had to be going in the wrong direction. I turned round to look behind me and saw it, a large double-story Queen Anne-style Victorian villa with a signboard out front hanging from a post. I had been standing right in front of it, with my back turned, the whole time. I let out a string of expletives under my breath and retraced my stumbling steps.

In its day it wouldn't have been a hotel so much as a boarding house. Lost in the dark and painted with the jaundiced glow from the street lights it looked twisted and gnarled, like an old person slumped over in a wheelchair with contorted fingers. I stepped up onto the creaking wood porch and turned the front door knob with trepidation.

Inside, the atmosphere was a lot more cheerful. The front living room, now the common room was buzzing with young people on laptops and phones, playing cards at a corner table, curled up in armchairs reading books or seated together on the couch discussing their days' adventures. It was a nostalgic scene from my own overseas travels in my early twenties, but now being on the wrong side of thirty, I felt somewhat out of place. I made my way to the office, a small reception desk, built into what had probably been a large closet or utility room.

Though I had been reduced to staying at a youth hostel I had drawn the line at staying in a dormitory and had booked one of the three available private rooms.

A young man with acne handed me a key and a pillow and a bundle of sheets and thin blanket, "It's room number three, on the third floor," he muttered in between chewing loudly on gum. "If you want to use the Internet, the Wi-Fi password is on the keychain. Bathrooms are on the second floor and the kitchen is just behind the common room. Laundry is outside, coin-operated machines."

I thanked him and left him to return his divided attention back to his phone. Slipping the key chain on my finger and grasping the bedclothes under my arm while gripping my suitcase with both hands and my carry bag swinging about from my shoulder, I headed for the hall to look for the elevator.

There wasn't one. *Of course, not. What was I expecting?* I stared up at the single staircase. It was steep and narrow, barely wide enough for one person, let alone one person lugging a modestly-oversized suitcase. *Perfect. Just perfect.* I waited till I was sure no one was on the stairs and began my perilous ascent, stepping onto each new step with both feet then heaving my suitcase up onto the step below, one step at a time.

I ground my teeth and cursed under my breath with every step as I inched my way up to the top. The further up I got, the more I feared I'd lose grip and my suitcase would go bounding down to the bottom, bowling over some poor international student. A small Scandinavian family would be mourning the loss of their only son.

Dearest, beloved, Bjorn – he was just eighteen and taken so trag-ically! We told him it wasn't safe, his mother would be wailing, *all those drugs and mass shootings!* Only for poor Bjorn to be crushed to death by my fucking suitcase.

With a final grunt and outburst of swearwords, I hauled the damned devil's trunk onto the third-floor landing. Little more than a large attic, the top floor was divided into three small rooms and the landing was not much wider than the stairway.

Too tired to lift my suitcase over the last few feet, I dragged it across the floor into my room, picturing the people on the floor below hearing and wondering if I trying to dispose of a body. *Yeah, welcome to the Bates Motel,* I smiled to myself.

I closed the door and switched on the small bedside lamp, which added little illumination to the weak glow of a single over-head incandescent bulb. I spread out the bedding over the narrow metal frame bed, being careful not to bump my head against the sloping wall then lay down, cringing as the bed let out a loud squeak in protest. I sighed wearily, feeling the bed springs dig into my back through the thin foam mattress. Daring not to move, in case the bed complained again, I lay staring up at the ceiling as the outside sounds seeped in through the small window and under the door. These were not the sounds the brochures promised – no seabird calls, no sound of the ocean, no music from a distant luau, no shell ornaments tinkling in the breeze. Not even a low rhythmic swish swish swish of a ceiling fan that might have lulled one to sleep. Instead, there was the tinny buzzing of air-conditioning units, loud conversations and laughter from the other guests, passing cars and the thumping bass from a nearby backyard party and one lone mosquito.

My body felt heavy and the mattress seemed to engulf me like I was sinking into a slab of wet cement. I was too tired to resist. Yet as drained as I felt, I knew I wouldn't be getting much sleep. My mind started to wander, pulling me to watch as it started to replay my past regrets, tormenting me. It was trying to provoke me to break down, but I was too exhausted to engage, too worn out to cry.

My tears had left me, gone on strike, left the premises. I zoned out, and paid no attention as the sound of the film running out on my mind's projector and slapping away against the reel of *My Greatest Disappointments* added to the white noise filling my head and I stared at a blank screen until I eventually closed my eyes.

Chapter 6

$\mathcal{A}$ brisk sea breeze had picked up by the time Jake got back to the Makapuʻu Point car park. The morning had been perfect for the walk down to the lighthouse and he had captured some amazing shots of the squat building with its red spinning-top roof set against the majestic backdrop of the sun rising above the ocean. He had certainly not been disappointed at the display of reds, purples, pinks and golds that splashed across the sky as it moved through all the shades of blue.

He unlocked the Jeep and climbed in, placing his camera bag on the passenger seat and inserted the key, giving it a half turn, switching on the electrics. He typed in the next destination for the day into the GPS and while it calculated the route he reached for the key again to start the ignition, and this time he noticed the fuel gauge was pointing to low. He'd have to make a detour. He looked up the closest gas station, and with the new course laid in, started the car and headed back onto the Kalanianaʻole Highway towards Waimanalo Beach.

The noise had died down around two in the morning, but what little sleep I did get was restless. I awoke to the sound of glass crashing on glass when someone emptied a crate of glass bottles into a metal bin. It was just gone half past five. *So much for sleeping in.*

I got up and slipped on my gown, pulled my towel and toiletries from my suitcase, and made my way down to the communal bathrooms, figuring I might as well take a shower before there was a queue. Once refreshed and back in my room I dressed in a red floral blouse and white linen shorts and slipped on my gold-painted sandals. I stuffed some cash in my pocket, packed up my suitcase and pushed it under the bed, locked the room and headed downstairs.

The common room and office desk were deserted. There were some sounds coming from the kitchen and I popped my head in. The pimply-faced teenager was at the stove frying an egg.

"Morning," I said, "I hoped I'd find you."

"Oh?" He turned in surprise.

"Yes, I was wondering if you could recommend any places for breakfast."

He looked at me as if I'd asked for directions to the Ritz, "There's really not much around here, other than a Seven-Eleven and a McDonalds."

"Okay, and where is that?"

"Take a right and head for the freeway. It's about a fifteen-minute walk."

McDonalds was bad enough, but having to walk fifteen minutes to get it... I sighed. It would have to do. "Thanks," I nodded and left him to his breakfast. I would have to find a convenience store to pick up some supplies to do the same. I refused to endure eating McBreakfast for eight days in a row.

In the growing daylight, the villa looked a little less ghoulish. It sat alone, the sole survivor of a bygone era among rows of modest suburban houses. It seemed to watch me forlornly as I walked away as if to beg for some attention like a dog in a corner longing for someone to tickle its belly or throw it a ball. Please, it whimpered, just one coat of paint, fix just one window...

I shook my head and continued down the street, passing gardens with lush tropical plants and palm trees. It was a tired, aged neighborhood: porches with old couches and sleeping dogs, vintage cars propped up on blocks in unused driveways with weeds growing over, flower beds littered with faded forgotten toys. Life moved slower here.

Even though it was early and the sun had only just appeared over the horizon, the air was heavy and humid. There was the smell of vegetation, not a sweet moist forest smell, but the smell of dank decay. There was another smell too, an unpleasant whiff, sulfurous, like rotten egg. I pressed on and passed a sign that explained the odor. It pointed the way to the Waimanalo waste water treatment center. *Delightful.*

Jake paid for the gas and a coffee, thankful for the cashier's lack of recognition or interest. "Thanks buddy," he said, stuffing his wallet in his back pocket, and picked up the paper cup. The man nodded and returned his attention to the game playing on the TV. Jake made his way to the door and paused noticing the magazine rack, pictures of him supposedly kissing Kristie against the side of his trailer splashed across the covers. "Christ!" he cursed under his breath.

A group of young men passed him on their way to the door, carrying six-packs of beers and bags of chips, talking so that everyone could hear whether they wanted to or not.

"Hey, lookie here!" the larger of the group exclaimed, "It's that doctor from that show."

Jake made for the door but they blocked his way, jeering.

"Ooh, big-shot *haole* come here to save the natives, eh?" the taller sneered, pushing Jake on the shoulder, "like we need help from pretty shark bait."

"It's just a TV show," Jake sighed as he edged towards the door. *Different town, some bunch of wise-ass jerks.*

"Yeah, I know that," the tall one snapped, "you think I'm stupid or something?"

Jake shook his head, "Look, I don't want any trouble."

The boy looked at his friend, "I'm not being any trouble. Yo think I'm mak'n trouble?"

His friend shook his head.

Jake stifled a sigh, "Come on guys, please, I need to get going," trying to get to the door.

The third of the group noticed the magazines, picked one off the shelf, flicking through the pictures, "Oh man, I get it, if I had pussy like that waiting for me, I'd wanna get outta here fast as too," he made suggestive hand movements above his crotch. Then bowed and stood aside, holding the door open for Jake, "Respect, man!"

Jake quickly stepped through exhaling with relief, but the youths followed him to his car.

"Oh man, what happened to your ride?"

"Where's the Ferrari?"

"No man, you dick," laughed the tall one, "that's Magnum. Donovan drives a Porsche."

"Actually, I prefer Mercedes," Jake muttered under his breath as he unlocked the car door, while they continued to amuse themselves.

"Ain't gonna get no tail driving that!"

Jake climbed in, set down the coffee cup, closed the door and locked it as the three continued to circle, jeering and laughing and kicking the tires. He noticed a lone shovel leaning against the parking railing and entertained a brief thought of grabbing it and smacking the stupid grins off their faces; smiled at the image of driving off leaving them cradling their bloodied noses and picking their teeth from the dirt.

He started the car and backed out of the parking space with a little less care than usual. Accidentally running one of the wankers down would have been a guilty pleasure. He headed back towards the freeway, but feeling his fingernails dig into the steering wheel, he instead turned off onto a side road towards the beach. He focused on his breathing, in through the nose, out through the mouth. *Let it go. Let it go.* So much of his work revolved around emotion. Show the pain. Show the grief. Show the love. Bring the viewer to tears of joy, tears of sadness. Take the words from a page and mold them into something palpable. Create something from nothing, express feelings and emotions that were not his own. And yet his *own* feelings – anger, longing, fear, loss – those had to be suppressed. Never let those show. Never let them see you break.

When the beach came into view, I realized I had gone the wrong way. I would have to go back. I released a few choice expletives while I stood at the end of the road staring out at sand and waves. The sun was hovering above the horizon, slowly making its ascent, sending golden trails across the water. Palm trees lined the beach and swayed in a gentle breeze. Everything was quiet except for the sound of the ocean and the call of seagulls.

I was in no rush. Since I was here, why not dip my toes in the water? I crossed the road and walked down to the beach, my feet sinking into the sand with each step, filling my sandals with grit. I stopped and took off my sandals, looping them over my finger and then headed for the water's edge. Breathing in the fresh sea air, I curled my toes in the wet sand and waited. A wave rolled in and washed over my feet, surprising me with its warmth. This wasn't the cold West Coast ocean I was used to and I splashed about in the water, letting the waves curl around my ankles and suck the sand from between my toes.

My inner child satiated, I turned back towards the road to renew my mission to satiate my stomach. But, the bland neighborhood stretching ahead did little to motivate me and I didn't move from the water's edge. As I returned my gaze to the ocean I spotted some cliffs and a lighthouse in the distance. Makapu'u Point... which put Sunrise Cove somewhere ahead of me. It was that close.

Without thinking, I started walking in that direction; wading further into the waves, water swirling around my calves with every step. I pulled the tie from my hair letting it fall loose and blow in the breeze as I focused on the lighthouse, feeling inexplicably drawn towards the cliffs.

Before long, I had forgotten about breakfast – I had forgotten about pretty much everything – and had been walking for some time. The water was now past my knees, but I couldn't turn back. Not yet. *Just a bit further*. I had to keep going. I *had* to see it. Sun-bloody-rise Cove.

Jake followed the road down to the beach and then, reaching a cul-de-sac, pulled over to park in the shade of some palm trees. He took his coffee from the holder and sat back looking out to the ocean and watched the waves roll in. Unlike the popular tourist beaches of Honolulu, this beach with its golden sands and turquoise water appeared to be deserted. He noticed a woman wading in the water. She was wearing a red floral blouse, cap sleeves flapping in the breeze. The sea water was over the hem of her white shorts, sticking the fabric against her thighs. She didn't seem to mind and was lost in her own world, looking down into the water, one hand trailing through the surface, while she held the other arm outstretched, a pair of golden sandals hanging from her fingers above the water. Jake put down the coffee and pulled out his camera. Though she was too far away to hear, he quietly opened the door of the Jeep, and using it as a shield, zoomed in firing off a few shots. She was turned away, her long brown hair cascading down, obscuring part of her face. The sun reflected off the water sending a shower of shooting stars that made her shimmer like a mirage, and the golden sandals sparkled in her outstretched hand. She seemed, not just out of place, but also out of time, as if she had stepped through a portal in space and time, a Greek goddess to be immortalized by a Renaissance artist. But instead of capturing her with horse-hair brushes and egg-emulsion pigments on a canvas, he was capturing her in his camera, trapping her image like a genie in a bottle.

She looked up and turned her gaze towards the road and he quickly shrank back into the car.

The waves were lapping the edge of my shorts and I held my sandals up with one hand while I looked down and trailed my other hand through the water. The sunlight reflected off the water, surrounding me with hundreds of shimmering shooting stars and I paused, standing transfixed by the dazzling sparkles and bright flashes. They started to move about me like circling fireflies. Faster and faster, they spun around me blurring the tiny starbursts into thin lines of light. The axis tilted, became unstable and I clamped my eyes shut till the swaying subsided.

A throbbing headache suddenly gripped my head as I slowly opened my eyes again. I squinted against the brightness and turned towards the beach; it was much farther away than I had realized. I felt a pit in my stomach at the realization of how far out I had waded and that I hadn't had so much as a glass of water since the evening before. I started to head back, but each step toward the beach seemed to go nowhere; I seemed to be stuck in place. I must have been walking for over an hour, so it would take me at least that long to walk back and that wasn't including the energy it was going to take me to break the water's hold on me. The pit was growing into a full-blown tangled knot of anxiety.

I could hear my mother telling me off for not carrying my mobile phone when I went out walking alone. I never took it with me – the whole point of going for a walk was to get away from people. But, she was right. Today was the day I really needed to have it with me. I wouldn't be able to phone for a taxi or even an emergency delivery by Uber Eats. The beach was still deserted, not even a life guard station this far down and no one around I could ask to borrow a phone. There was a lone white SUV parked under a palm tree, but I couldn't see if anyone was in it, and knowing my luck they'd have driven off by the time I got there. There was nothing for it, but to keep pressing on and look forward to spending the rest of the day, stretched out on that squeaky bed, sleeping off a dehydration migraine, when I got back to the hostel.

Though I was moving towards the beach, the water was now up to my waist. I pushed forward again, swinging my arms for extra momentum, and my sandals flew out of my hand and splashed in the water. I turned back and lunged to grab them and as I put my foot down there was no ground beneath it. I fell into a void and the water swallowed me up, rushing over my head. When I bobbed up to the surface and gasped for air, I couldn't see the beach and in a sudden panic, I flailed about trying to swim and kicking wildly reaching for the ground. Then in horror, I realized I was heading in the wrong direction, and with every attempt I made to get back to shallower water I was in fact being dragged further out.

The more I struggled, the more the water pulled me in. Each wave washed over my head, pushing me down; the salt water stung my eyes and forced its way into my ears and nose, and rushed into my mouth. I swallowed it down and gasped for air only to suck in another mouthful of salty water, over and over till gasping and swallowing became the same thing. Water filled my stomach, flooded my lungs with a searing pain while my body shuddered, and jerked violently. Everything around me became quiet and I could hear my heartbeat, amplified, racing uncontrollably. And then in a growing stillness, my heartbeat began to slow and my body fell limp, twitching occasionally. Now weightless, suspended between worlds, time paused, calm and peaceful, I watched a piece of seaweed drift in a slow waltz beneath me as darkness crept in like a tunnel collapsing around me.

Chapter 7

Jake switched off the camera and put it back in the bag feeling a pang of guilt at taking photos of someone without their knowledge, without their consent. Right now he was no better than the paparazzi who stalked him, no better than every fan who begged for a selfie with him. But he wouldn't sell these photos. No one else would ever see them. Was that an excuse though? How many people out there had photos of him he would never know about? Even with the millions of photos that filled the internet, the thought that his privacy could be invaded so easily still got at him. He picked up the camera, switched it on, and waiting for it to boot up looked out to sea again.

The woman had disappeared. He looked up and down the beach, but there was no sign of her. He hadn't imagined her. He opened the car door again, and stood up, scanning the beach more closely. No sign of her, no one walking nearby, not even any footprints. She couldn't have just vanished. Jake looked back towards the ocean, when a flash of red floating on the water caught his eye, like a tiny flag fluttering weakly in the breeze. And then as the ocean undulated he saw the outstretched limbs.

"Shit!" Jake cried, pulling off his shirt and shoes, and tossing them in the Jeep. He slammed the door and bounded the beach barrier in one leap. He tore towards the surf, kicking up plumes of sand and spray as his feet hit the water. Then plowing through the waves till he was waist-deep he dove forward and swam towards her body, which was moving further from sight with every wave.

This time there was no body double or stunt man to take over, to carry the risk, to make it look easy. There would be no second takes, no time to reset and do it again. This would be the most important performance of his life and he had one shot to get it right.

Within a matter of seconds his muscles began to cramp and with every wave that washed over him, dunking him below the surface, his own life flashed before his eyes. The childhood memory of when his father pulled him out from under a wave flickered through his mind. He had been only four years old, but it had left him with a healthy respect for the ocean and he never swam this far out. Ever. Had he made a fatal mistake? Was this how it would end? Would they find his body and think it was suicide, or would his disappearance go unsolved, shrouded in rumor and mystery for decades? Scenes from every ocean thriller he had seen flashed across his mind: doomed submarines and deep dives gone wrong, abandoned swimmers and killer sharks, giant sea monsters and mountainous waves. He spat out another mouthful of sea water. This was not going to end well if he continued; his character would not be the hero, but the side character whose sole contribution to the story was to provide a gruesome on-screen death.

He stopped swimming and treaded water, bobbing in place while he looked out at the horizon. He had lost sight of her and now she was gone; he was too late. He closed his eyes for a moment and whispered, "I'm sorry," then turned back to the beach. The best he could do now was alert the authorities. He swung his arm over his head and it struck something solid. A leg. With a fresh surge of adrenalin, he grabbed the woman by the ankle and pulled her with him as he headed for the beach. He'd seen the videos, he knew this wasn't the right way to do a water rescue, but if he didn't get them to shallower water fast, they would both be swept out to sea. He headed for the beach swimming diagonally across the current.

The current did not want to release her and her weight was far more than he anticipated. It was a dead weight. A weight that threatened to drag him down with it, not the life-preserver buoyancy of a prop dummy, and a poignant reminder that this was very real and no one would be calling 'cut' at any time.

Finally, his feet made contact with the ground and as he lunged forward to get better purchase, he pulled the woman closer to him and rolled her onto her back to get her face out of the water. She didn't respond. Lying on his back, he clamped his arm around her chest, and swam backwards towards the beach, not looking at the open unseeing eyes and blue lips. His own energy waning, he put his all into slow powerful strokes, making each one count. At last the water was shallow enough for him to stand and wade the rest of the way. He then scooped her out of the water and she hung lifeless in his arms as he carried her out onto the beach.

Airways, breathing, circulation, he repeated as he lay her down on the sand. He leaned over and placed his cheek to her nose. He felt no air movement; her chest didn't rise and fall. He tilted her head back, pinched her nose and opened her mouth.

"I've done this before. It's just like on the dummy," he said, willing Ethan Temple to take over. Taking a deep breath he pressed his lips over hers and blew into her. He recoiled in shock at the feeling of her cold lips and porcelain-like teeth. So much more colder than silicone and plastic. So much more dead than lifeless or inanimate.

"Get a grip!" He inhaled deeply and shutting his eyes to block out her blank stare gave her another breath; then pressed two fingers to the side of her neck.

"Oh, thank God!" he cried with relief. But, her pulse was weak. He repeated a few more breaths. Water gurgled from her mouth and he rolled her on to her side till it drained then checked her breathing again. Still nothing. He repeated the breaths and felt again for a pulse. It was still there. Barely.

Jake scanned the beach. He needed to get help.

"Hey you!" he screamed to a young man walking on the path that ran parallel to the beach. He didn't appear to be wearing headphones, but was so engrossed in his phone that he didn't look up.

"Hey! Hey! Over here! Help!"

Finally, the man looked up and, first turning to look around behind him, pointed to himself.

"Yes, you!"

He walked down to the beach and when he saw the body, shouted as he jogged closer, "Do you want me to get the lifeguard?"

"They're too far," Jake panted after administering two more breaths to the woman, "just call an ambulance."

The man nodded, about to dial when it clicked. "Hey, no way!" he shrieked, "You're Jake Donovan!" He turned the phone to face himself as he leaned in next to Jake.

"For fuck's sake," yelled Jake, "forget the fucking selfie and call 911."

"Uh, yeah, sure," the man mumbled and started dialing.

"Tell them it's a drowning and go wait for them on the road. Can you do that?"

The man nodded, "Um, yeah. Totally."

"Okay, then go!"

The man jogged off and Jake continued his efforts to revive the woman. "Come on, come on!" he cried pinching her nose again to give her another breath, "You're so close. Please!" On the next breath her body twitched, and she spluttered and started coughing up water. "That's it! Keep going!" He sat behind her, holding her on her side so she wouldn't slump face-first into the sand. Slowly her shuddering and gasping eased and she began to breathe normally, but she remained unconscious. "It's okay, just take it slow," he repeated in a whisper. He sat supporting her head and rubbing her arm, feeling the warmth return to her skin. "You're going to be okay."

I was floating in the darkness of space, surrounded by stars in every direction. So quiet, so peaceful. Though I was suspended motionless, I was moving slowly forward, toward a light that grew brighter. Then suddenly, I was snatched away and flung into a fury of swirling water, flashes of light and dark, noise crashing in my ears and pain, blinding pain. I was dropped on the ground, no longer weightless; I felt the pull of gravity and myself collapsing under my own weight. I jerked awake to the sensation of hot air being forced down my throat. Gasping and shuddering, I opened my eyes and was blinded by the light, dizzied by the world spinning around me. I tasted salt, felt water up my nose and in my ears, the breeze cold and foreign against my skin. I was a fish out of water, gaping and flapping, desperate to return to the water.

Then in time the shuddering subsided, the pain eased and my body began to warm, and the spinning world came to rest. At last calm and quiet, I looked out onto a foreign landscape – desert sand and slanting trees – a world on its side. Somewhere in the distance there was a faint sound. A voice. Disembodied.

I rolled onto my back and stared upwards. Blue sky and thin wispy clouds filled my view. I was a child again, back home lying on the grass in our yard staring heavenward. I imagined I was a balloon floating up into the sky. I wanted to see beyond the clouds, drift higher and higher, beyond the veil of the atmosphere, up into the stars where I belonged.

A shadow moved overhead, eclipsing my view. The sunlight hit this dark mass creating a halo around it and as my eyes slowly adjusted, the dark object began to take on features of a man's face. Black hair, steel blue eyes, soft red lips set in stubbly growth. Breathtakingly handsome as I imagined an angel would be, yet somehow I expected angels would be clean-shaven.

The angel spoke, "Hey, there. Just take it slowly."

I stared up at him. I knew this man. Confused, I sat up, the world suddenly tilting again, pain gripped my head and I started to fall backwards again. He grabbed my arms and held me till the spinning subsided.

"Take your time," he said comfortingly.

I studied his face. I knew I knew him, but from where?

"David?" I asked.

I knew it was the wrong name, but it was the first one that came to me, like it was written on a slip of paper drawn randomly from a bowl at a charity raffle.

"What, no?" he frowned, "can you tell me your name?"

I dipped my mind back into the bowl, randomly pulling out slips of paper, reading the names, but none seemed right. I knew him, but where was the name? The bowl empty, slips of paper strewn on the floor, a breeze caught them, scattering them like flecks in a shaken snow-globe. Then it caught the cover of a magazine sitting on the table next to the bowl, flicking through the pages, stopping on a spread of photos of a man with dark hair, blue eyes, soft red lips, bare-chested standing against a movie trailer holding a blond bombshell. I threw the magazine to the floor. I was losing it, the answer made no sense.

"Who are you?" I asked.

He narrowed his brow and for a moment, I wondered if I had not spoken the words out loud.

"I'm Jake Donovan," he said concerned, as if I should know him.

"No," I held up a finger to pause this figment of my oxygen-deprived brain, "no, you're not."

"I'm pretty sure I am," he said cocking his head to one side, a wry smile breaking.

"You're Jake Donovan?"

He nodded.

I could feel the sand, the breeze, my wet clothing against my body, his hands holding my shoulders. I could smell the vegetation, the salty air. I breathed in, catching the smell of expensive intoxicating cologne. A fragrance outside of my knowledge, something my mind could not be fabricating, like a reality totem. I wasn't dreaming. I looked back into his eyes, looked down at the smooth toned chest, water droplets and sand still clinging to his skin.

"You're Jake Donovan!" I blurted and promptly lurched forward, and vomited over his arm onto the sand.

Chapter 8

*J*ake jumped out of the way and moved behind me, holding my shoulders and rubbing my back, "That's it, get it all out. You'll have swallowed a lot of water."

The retching subsided and I sat back inspecting him, trying to make sense of it all.

"Now that we've established who I am, can you tell me who you are?" he asked sitting down opposite me.

"I'm Cath—" I paused. "My name is Catherine. Catherine Marshall."

"Well, Catherine Marshall welcome back to the land of the living."

"Thanks." I groaned, pressing my hand against my head.

"Tell me what's happening," he said, furrowing his brow.

"My head is killing me."

"Did you hit your head?"

"I don't see how, there was only water and sand out there."

"I'm just going to check, okay?"

I nodded cautiously.

He leaned forward and gently ran his fingers over my head and neck. "There's no blood and I don't feel any bumps or see any wounds." He pointed his finger and held it in front of me, "Follow my finger without moving your head," he said as he moved his hand from side to side.

I complied, feeling too exhausted to question if he really knew what he was doing.

He sat back and took my arm, pressing his fingers against my wrist and sat for a moment with his eyes fixed on his watch, a large manly stainless steel timepiece, the kind you see advertised in... *inflight magazines.* I felt my cheeks flush.

He let go of my arm, "Your pulse is much stronger," he announced happily, turning back to me, "And your color is coming back too."

I coughed and looked away, sucking in my lip, and stared at the sand as a sudden awkward silence descended.

"How's your breathing?" he asked.

"It's okay."

"Any other pain?"

"I feel like I was kicked in the stomach."

"Probably from the vomiting, but tell me if it gets worse, okay?"

I nodded and pulled my knees up, wrapping my arms around them, and rested my chin on my arms.

"What happened here?" he pointed to the bruises on my legs.

"My suitcase."

He raised an eyebrow.

"The wheels broke and it kept banging into my legs while I carried it."

"You sure?"

I raised an eyebrow in return. "Of course, I'm sure."

"I just meant, someone isn't hurting you?"

I laughed, but stopped as pain gripped my head again, "No, just me". I grimaced.

Jake's face fell, "Today, out in the water, you weren't trying to... to hurt yourself?"

"Good lord, no!" I cried, "I think I fainted. That's all. I didn't eat, walked too far."

"Okay." He nodded, relieved.

I smiled, "You've been very sweet, but I should probably get going." I pushed myself up to stand, but the ground tilted and knocked me over.

"Hey, you're not going anywhere." Jake caught me and helped me to sit up again, "An ambulance is on the way."

"Oh, that's not necessary," I muttered, "but, if you could call me a taxi I'd really appreciate it."

"I'm not letting you out of my sight until you've been properly checked out."

"Really, I feel fine."

"And if the paramedics agree, then I'll give you a ride myself to wherever you want to go."

I cocked my head to one side to consider his offer and the world started spinning again.

Jake moved round behind me and pulled me to him, "Here, lean against me."

I hesitated, but the dizziness and fatigue were advancing fast. "Okay, I probably just need to rest for a little while." I rested my head against his shoulder and closed my eyes feeling his warmth envelop me to the growing sound of a distant siren.

I had a vague awareness of the trip to the hospital. I lapsed between foggy moments of consciousness and flashes of dream-like images that made no sense. One moment I was being loaded into an ambulance, the next Alex was standing over me pressing her hand down over my nose and mouth, while Jake Donovan stood beside her, laughing. Then I'd be asleep, trying to roll over without making the hostel bed squeak, and wake to find myself floating in the ocean with no land in sight.

The sound of doors banging and the sensation of being jostled about brought me round and I opened my eyes to see alternating ceiling tiles and flickering fluorescent lights pass above my head. I tried to sit up, and a hand pushed me back. I turned to see who was there and saw a tall blond-haired woman in a paramedic uniform carrying a clipboard walking alongside me. She had the same impatient air about her as Alex.

We came to a small hallway in front of a set of double doors.

"Wait here." She barked at the person behind me, pushing the gurney, "I'll go get someone."

"What do you mean *get someone*? They should be ready waiting for us."

She grunted, "This is the *real* world. *This* Honolulu General is broke, under-staffed and Miss Hollywood here is breathing and has all her blood so she'll just have to wait her turn like everyone else." She dropped the clipboard on the gurney by my feet and marched off through the doors. The clipboard slid off onto the floor and the man behind me stepped forward and retrieved it and put it back securely. He walked up to the doors and cupped his hands to the window panels.

"Where the hell is everyone?" he grumbled.

The voice was familiar. I tried to prop myself up to get a better look and in my moving about, got my arm tangled in wires coming from my blouse and set off an alarm.

He turned quickly and came over to my side, "Hey, easy." He gently pushed me to lie back down again and bent over to retrieve a plastic device that had come loose and was now hanging by a wire.

I pulled the mask from my face. "I'd like to sit up, please." I croaked, my voice hoarse.

He straightened and clamped the device to my finger tip and the beeping alarm stopped. "No problem." He smiled and leaned forward reaching behind me and pulled on a lever that raised the back of the gurney.

I coughed. It *was* him. "You came?"

"Of course, I came. No one should have to go to the hospital alone."

"I... you..."

He took the mask from my hand and slipped it back on my face. "You need to keep this on."

"It hurts." I moaned, pointing to my cheeks where the rubber straps were digging in.

"Hmm," he murmured and scanning the hallway, spotted an equipment shelf. He went over and scratched through several trays of hermetically-sealed packages. Then finding what he was looking for, took one and tore it open, and pulled out a length of plastic tubing. He walked back to me unraveling it and then unhooked the mask from my face and slipped the tubing behind my ears and tucked a small nozzle piece under my nose. "How's that?"

"Much better," I said adjusting the nose piece above my lips, while I watched him take the other end of the tubing and connect it to the oxygen canister lying at the foot of the gurney.

"You know your way around this stuff," I said.

"Oh yeah, I've picked up a few things."

"Like how to save someone from drowning."

"Like that." His face was wan, his hair matted. He had put on a shirt and shoes at some point and he looked smaller now... more ordinary. He gripped the railing of the gurney with both hands, locking his elbows and shifting his weight, leaned forwards. He hung his head and exhaled heavily, pouring out a great weariness.

I reached over and touched his elbow. He looked up, startled, as if surprised that I could see him.

"It's okay," I whispered, with a comforting smile. "Everything's okay now."

He shifted his weight again, moving away from me and I pulled my hand back and tucked it in my lap. The double doors swung open and a stout charge nurse with her hair in a tight bun walked up to the gurney.

She took the clipboard and checked the chart, "you're the drowning victim?" she asked. I nodded and she turned to Jake, "and you're the one who pulled her out?"

"Yes, I was first on the scene, and I—"

"Yes, yes, the medic briefed me." She checked the monitors and noted the readings on the chart.

"How is she doing?"

"Much better. Blood pressure's still a bit low, but, oxygen saturation is coming up nicely."

"That's good," Jake squeezed my arm reassuringly.

"There's no contact person listed here," she said turning to me, "Is there someone we can phone for you?"

"No. Not locally. I'm here on holiday alone."

"Ah, that explains the suitcase," Jake muttered.

I snorted sarcastically, "It's turning out great so far... I only arrived yesterday. Today was—"

"We have a bay available now, so we'll move you inside." She muttered, interrupting me, and marched down the hall.

I nodded and turned to Jake, "Sorry. I messed up your day. Thank you for—."

"Hey, no need for that. Besides, I'm on vacation too. I've got nowhere to be".

The nurse returned, grumbling, "Damn. Where's an orderly when you need one?"

"I can do it," Jake offered.

"Okay," she sighed, "follow me."

Jake moved behind me again and stepped on a lever at the base of the gurney, releasing the brake, and started pushing the gurney and followed the nurse through the double doors into the main emergency room. She pointed to a bay and Jake maneuvered the gurney in beside the bed. He helped me scoot over to it and was about to start transferring the tubes and wires from the portable monitors on the gurney to the ones in the bay when the nurse swatted his hand away.

"I'll do that," she hissed. "These aren't toys. You can wait outside."

Jake nodded obediently and ducked behind the curtain.

"I need to get your medical history," she said, plugging in leads and switching on monitors, and transferring the oxygen hose to the hospital supply.

"Of course."

She took out a pen and scribbled notes on the chart while she asked me the usual questions, whether I had any medical conditions or allergies and what medications I might be taking. I didn't pay much attention, I'd have to repeat myself to the doctor anyway. I kept my focus on the curtain – each movement reassuring me that he was still there.

"Are you pregnant?" she asked.

"No."

"Are you sure?"

"Yes, I'm sure." I snapped, "There's no chance of that. I haven't... for some time." I wondered if he was listening, a celebrity eavesdropping on my sorry life story. What a joke.

She clicked her pen and slipped it back into her scrubs pocket, "Okay, that's everything." She hooked the chart on the foot of the bed and handed me a gown, "You need to put this on. If you need any help, press the buzzer."

"Thank you. Um," I stammered as she collected the gurney and headed out, "would you please let Mr. Donovan know he can come back... if he wants to."

She nodded and drew the curtain closed behind her.

A few minutes later, Jake called from behind the curtain, "Are you decent?"

The heart monitor registered a jump in my heart rate at the sound of his voice. "Yes, come in," I called back, breaking into a smile.

He entered the cubicle carrying two water bottles and a chair. He set down the chair beside me and then uncapped one of the water bottles before handing it to me."

"Oh my goodness, thank you. I'm so thirsty."

"It'll be from the saltwater you swallowed. But drink it slowly, ok."

I nodded and deliberately sipped the water though I was desperate to chug it in one go.

Jake uncapped his own bottle and settled into the chair.

"Well, thank you for everything and for getting me here..." I started, "but, there's really no need for you to stay."

"I'll stay till you've seen the doctor."

"Okay. If you're sure..."

"Yeah. No problem."

From the hallway, we could hear squeals and excited chatter as the news of Jake's presence started to spread. Jake sighed and sank deeper into the chair.

"Sorry," I whispered.

He looked up and frowned, "For what?"

"For all that." I gestured to the noise.

"Occupational hazard," he feigned a smile.

"Still, it's my fault. Please, you can go. You've done more than enough. I can manage on my own."

"Hey, I'm not going anywhere until you've been checked out. Besides," he grinned, "you haven't told me your story yet."

"My story?"

"About how you ended up floating in the ocean this morning?" he drained the last of his water and replaced the bottle cap.

"Like I said, it was my own stupidity."

"I mean the backstory."

I sighed, "It's pretty clichéd, I wouldn't want to bore you."

"I doubt that," he persisted. "You said you're here on holiday."

I nodded

"Alone. In Hawaii?"

"I was supposed to be here with someone, but... well... it didn't work out."

Jake nodded. "I see. So where are you from?"

"San Francisco."

"And what do you do in San Francisco."

"I work at a law firm."

"Oh, a lawyer, hey?"

"Actually, I—"

The curtain was drawn aside and I left his assumption uncorrected as the doctor walked into the cubicle. No need to go into the sad details when I'd never see him again.

"Hello, I'm Dr. Evans," she said, taking the chart from the foot of the bed and skimming the notes, "you must be Catherine Marshall," she peered over wire-rimmed glasses.

"Yes, that's me." I nodded and shook her hand.

She folded her glasses and slipped them in the top pocket of her white coat and extended her hand to Jake, "And you'll be who's causing all the fuss out there."

He stood up, towering over her, and shook her hand, "Yeah, sorry about that." He smiled apologetically.

"Well, it's not every day we have a visit from someone famous. Though, it would be nice if our hospital looked as good as your TV show makes it out to be."

Jake shifted uncomfortably, "To be honest, all the interior is shot in our LA studio and the exterior is of a medical center in Burbank."

"Ah, that explains it." She turned back to me and referred to the chart, "so it says here you had a misadventure out on the water and Jake here pulled you out, is that correct?"

I nodded, "I was on my way to find somewhere for breakfast and got side-tracked. I ended up at the beach and decided to dip my toes in the water and before I knew it I had been walking for ages. I waded into deeper water and when I tried to head back, I... got dizzy and lost my footing or something. And the next moment I was in the water and then I must have passed out."

Jake continued, "I saw her floating in the water and went in after her and pulled her out. She wasn't breathing but did have a pulse, so I gave her mouth-to-mouth till she started breathing on her own."

"Hero in real life too, it seems. Do you know for how long she wasn't breathing?"

"It couldn't have been long. One minute she was walking in the water, the next—"

"You were watching me?" I blurted.

"Not as such. I had parked by the beach to drink a coffee and saw you walking; that's all," he confessed. "I looked away for a few minutes and when I looked up again she was floating facedown and that's when I acted."

"I see," Dr. Evans scribbled some notes in the chart.

"And how did she seem when she came round, any disorientation?"

"She did seem confused at first,"

"Well, to be fair I did wake up to see *Jake Donovan* sitting in front of me," I pointed out, "My first thought was that I had to be hallucinating."

Jake and Dr. Evans laughed, and Jake flashed me a bashful smile before continuing, "But, other than that, she seemed fully aware. She complained of headache and I checked for signs of head injury, but there were no bumps or bruises or nystagmus."

"My-stag-nous?" I repeated under my breath, frowning.

"She also mentioned a tender abdomen, but I think that was from vomiting. She brought up a lot of water at the scene."

"I'm impressed." Dr. Evans admitted, raising an eyebrow.

Jake cleared his throat, self-consciously, "Yeah, I did advanced paramedic training and shadowed trauma physicians and surgeons for my role."

I stared at him with new respect.

"Well, that training certainly paid off," said Dr. Evans "Ms. Marshall is very lucky Dr. Temple was at the scene."

The life suddenly drained from Jake's eyes, "I hope I never have to do that again, though."

"But, you've done water rescues before, right? On your show." I asked concerned.

"Yeah, but working with prop dummies and having a real rescue crew on standby if things go wrong doesn't prepare you for the reality of doing it for real."

"No, I suppose not." Dr. Evans agreed.

"We did a very similar scene a few days ago. It probably fooled me into a false sense of ability. But I wasn't prepared at all," he turned away and looked at the floor, "the dead weight, the cold skin... the blank staring eyes..." He went white and like a scene in a science-fiction movie, where the holographic projection flickers to reveal the real person standing behind it, Jake Donovan, the actor, flickered and for a moment I saw Jake Donovan, the ordinary man, who had done an extraordinary thing risking his own life to save that of a stranger.

I wanted to reach out and take his hand or squeeze his shoulder but he was too far.

He stood up abruptly, "I should go – let the doctor..." he gestured towards me and Dr. Evans.

"No, stay." I grabbed his hand as he brushed past me.

He turned to me and frowned.

"Please." I squeezed his hand, clasping it with both of mine.

He turned to the doctor, "If that's okay with you?"

"Certainly."

He sat down again, pushing the chair further back to give Dr. Evans more space.

I looked over and winked at Jake, "Nothing you haven't seen before, right?"

He smiled weakly and took out his phone as a discreet diversion.

Dr. Evans took out her pen light and shone it in my eyes, beginning her examination. "Have you had fainting spells before? Any family history of epilepsy or seizures?"

"No, never."

She continued, feeling my head for bumps and asking me the same questions the nurse asked earlier about whether I had any existing conditions and if I was on any medications. "Any chance you might be pregnant?"

Not that question again. "No." I sighed, "No. There's no chance." I stared down, twisting the blanket between my fingers.

"Okay, well I think we're just looking at dehydration and not eating for the headache, dizziness, and low blood pressure," she scribbled some notes in the chart, "we'll start you on some fluids to help with that. What I'm concerned about now is complications from the near drowning."

"Really?" I frowned, "I feel fine."

She took the stethoscope from her neck, inserted the ear buds and moved behind me, placing the chest piece on my back. "Deep breath in... and out," she said, listening intently, "and again," she repeated while moving the chest piece around my back and chest.

"Hmm," she slung the stethoscope back round her neck, "that's what I was concerned about."

"What?" I asked and let out several hearty coughs that I had suppressed while she had her ears to my chest.

"Mild bibasalar crackles," she murmured, writing some more notes on the chart.

"And, what does that mean?"

"It means you inhaled some water."

"Fluid in the lungs," said Jake, looking up from his phone, concerned.

Dr. Evans nodded.

"But that's not serious, is it?" I asked.

"Not right now, but it could be. There is a chance that it could develop into pulmonary edema or pneumonia.

"Really? I would never have thought of that."

"No, that's the big danger with near drownings. A tiny amount of inhaled liquid can turn deadly because the body responds with inflammation, producing liquid to eliminate the inhaled substance and a person can effectively experience secondary drowning when their lungs fill up with their own fluid."

"Wow, okay. So what happens now?"

"We'll send you for an X-ray and I'd like to admit you overnight for observation, in case we need to run further tests."

I frowned, "Seriously?"

"I want to make sure your collapse wasn't due to something more sinister and we also need to keep an eye on your organ function. Ingesting a lot of salt water can damage your kidneys so we'll do a full blood work-up to check that.

I nodded slowly, taking it all in.

Jake pulled his chair closer to the bed, "See?" he said, smiling sympathetically, "I was right to get you to the hospital."

"Yes, you certainly were," said Dr. Evans.

"I'm always right," Jake declared deadpan, watching me with that signature smirky Jake Donovan smile.

That was the Jake Donovan I expected. I sighed and turned away, and Dr. Evans rolled her eyes at me.

He sat back in the chair and said with a flippant shrug of his shoulders, "except when I'm wrong."

I turned back and he winked at me, the smirky smile replaced with a silly grin.

Dr. Evans and I burst out laughing and she turned to him and extended her hand, "You're not so bad, Donovan. It's been a pleasure to meet you, I may have underestimated you."

He stood up and shook her hand. "Hey. I'm glad I could help."

She returned the chart to the slot at the foot of the bed and grasped my hand with both of hers, "Well, my dear, I will see you later in the ward and for now I'll leave you in the hands of the nurses and Dr. Temple." She winked at Jake.

"Thank you." I squeezed her hand and she turned and left the cubicle.

Jake moved closer to the hospital bed, "Okay, well, I guess I should..." he trailed off as if unsure what to say.

"Yes, I guess this is it. Thank you for everything." I took his hand and squeezed it.

"Yeah, hey. Anytime. You take care now." He patted his hand on top of mine.

I nodded. "And you?"

"Me?"

"Will you be okay?"

He pulled his hands away and frowned, cocking his head in surprise.

"You look tired. You need to get some rest."

He stepped back and hopped up onto the side of the bed and let out a heavy sigh, "Yeah, I think it's all hitting me now."

"You've been through an ordeal yourself. It must have been harrowing."

"Yeah," he grunted, turning to look at me with a numb expression, "I've had a fear of the ocean, ever since I was a kid..."

I shivered with a sudden chill at the thought of him swimming after me surrounded by his childhood phobias.

"Instinct kicked in. I didn't think. I just reacted."

I stretched my leg and accidentally brushed against him under the blanket. He didn't move, didn't make any gesture that he even noticed, simply kept staring at me, past me, lost in thought. I gingerly moved my leg again, resting it against him. I could feel his warmth soaking through the blanket and wandered if he could feel mine.

"I was supposed to be here with my boyfriend." I sighed.

The light returned to his eyes and he focused on me again. "The backstory?"

I nodded, "It was meant to be a Valentine's weekend getaway. I was convinced he was going to propose. Well... he did. Just not to me." I explained the rest of the story of how David dumped me for his receptionist after making me book the tickets to Hawaii. "I didn't even want to go to Hawaii. I won the money in a competition I entered and I wanted to use it to do some courses online."

"I'm sorry."

"Oh, it's okay. I told you it was a sad story." I groaned, "And I'm not a lawyer. I'm the receptionist. Though obviously not the grade of receptionist that David wanted. I'm not a nineteen-year-old with perky boobs and blond hair. He said he 'outgrew' me," I surrounded the word with air quotes, "as if I were a sweater that was now too small. Though I guess that implies he'd gotten fat." I snorted at my sudden flash of brilliance, "I wish I'd thought to say that to him back then. Story of my life, I only ever think of the witty comebacks when it's far too late to use them."

I paused for a beat, catching my breath. I kept expecting Jake to cut me off, fire off a quick goodbye and make a hasty exit, but he sat and listened quietly, actually taking it all in. It was almost as if he was grateful for the excuse to stay.

"Then, he even had the nerve to ask me for the plane tickets, as if that had been the plan all along."

Jake shook his head with sympathetic indignation.

"I was going to let them go to waste, to spite him," I continued, "But, then my boss got on my case over my annual performance review and other corporate bullshit and I just had to get away."

"I can understand that." Jake commiserated.

"Right? It doesn't matter where you work; there are always the power-trip jerk managers and the stuck-up drama queens. In my case, two senior attorneys. My friend Amira and I say they remind us of Reese Witherspoon's character in *Legally Blond* – Lawyer Barbies. We call them the Barbie Twins," I laughed.

Jake grinned, "I know quite a few of those."

Of course, he would. "Sorry," I paused, "I shouldn't be offloading all this on you."

"Hey, you have nothing to be sorry for. You're the one being admitted to the hospital. I think you're allowed a little offloading."

"Oh God!" I groaned, recalling the events at the beach.

"What?"

"I just remembered I vomited over your arm at the beach and now I'm throwing up the details of my sad life all over you."

"That's okay. As long as it's helping you feel better."

"Actually it is," I smiled, "like when your stomach starts to settle after bringing up a bad meal."

"Better out than in." he grinned.

"Definitely. But, you've done more than enough. You don't need to stay and listen to my woes. You must have other things to do, people to see. Your girlfriend—"

"Nope. Like I said, I'm also on vacation."

"All the more reason for you to go and do something other than look after a disaster case like me."

He leaned forward and whispered cheekily, "You know there are women out there who would kill to spend time with me."

"I know," I giggled, "I work with one." I felt my cheeks flush and turned away abruptly, trying to plump the pillows behind me.

"Here, let me," Jake jumped off the bed and came up next to me. "Up or down?"

"Up a bit more."

He hunted around the head of the bed and found a control box attached to an electrical lead hanging down the side. "This must be it," he muttered, pressing what looked like an up arrow and the head of the bed slowly lowered. "Whoops, wrong way, other one," he chuckled and pressed the opposite arrow.

"I thought you knew your way around this stuff," I teased as the bed slowly inclined.

He reached behind me and while he plumped my pillows, I leaned forward, biting my lip and gripping the edge of the blanket, feeling his warmth against my bare skin through the gap of the hospital gown and his seductive cologne threatened to derail me.

"How's that?" he asked, stepping aside.

I leaned back, sinking into plumped perfection, "Perfect," I grinned and slipped my hands under the blanket tucking them under my thighs to avoid temptation.

"You're cold," he remarked, noticing the gooseflesh on my arms.

"No, no. I'm fine."

"Don't be silly. I'll get you another blanket," he muttered as he nipped out of the cubicle.

I let out a restless sigh. At least he believed I was cold and wasn't able to read what was really going through my mind – the irresistible urge to grab him by the shirt and pull him to me, to feel those lips against my own, this time while conscious.

He reappeared carrying a blanket. He unfolded it and laid it over me. "Better?"

"Much. Thank you."

"See? I have many talents." He smiled, the smirk breaking through.

"You do indeed. Though I don't think I should ask how you became an expert pillow plumper and blanket fluffer."

He laughed, "That's for me to know and for you to find out."

My cheeks flushed with heat. Was he flirting? With me? "You must—"

The grating sound of the curtain being pulled aside cut me short and we both turned to see a young nurse enter the cubicle, carrying a tray of medical supplies.

No! Not yet! I shot a look at Jake terrified her arrival would signal his departure. He moved away from the bed, but instead of leaving, he settled again in the chair next to me. I sank back against the pillows, relieved.

"Hi, I'm Rebecca," she said to me while watching Jake out the corner of her eye, "I'm here to take some blood and start your IV."

She put the tray down on the mobile bed table and then unable to contain herself any longer, spun round and rushed over to Jake, extending her hand, "Oh my God! I just love you!"

Jake nodded in acknowledgment. He stood up to shake her hand and she wrapped her arms around him and hugged him tightly. She let him go and he sat down again, forcing a smile.

"Imagine that, Dr. Temple, actually *here*! Though you'll always be Vincent to me," she pressed a hand to her chest, "Team Vincent forever!"

"Thanks, that's very kind." Jake cleared his throat and pointed at me, "Um, your patient?"

"Oh God! Yes! Sorry." She picked up the supplies again and moved over to the side of the bed. I glanced at Jake and he raised his eyebrows in amusement.

"Oh, you're soooo lucky," she gushed, leaning into me, "rescued by Jake Donovan! Sooo jealous!"

"Yes," I smiled, "though I wouldn't recommend the drowning part."

"No, probably not." She giggled, reaching for the tourniquet, "Okay, I'm just going to draw some blood first."

"Mm, yummy," Jake quipped with a sly smile, "always best from the vein."

Rebecca burst out laughing and had to pause what she was doing.

"Do you know?" I said, turning to Jake, "I've never watched a single episode of *The Blood Moon Prophecies*."

"What?" he clasped his hand to his chest in mock injury, "Ouch, that's harsh. I'm hurt."

"Okay, make a fist," Rebecca instructed, after regaining her composure and pulling the tourniquet tight around my arm. She reached for an alcohol wipe and syringe, "and... small prick."

I nodded and turned away, staring fixedly at Jake.

"Got a thing against needles?" he asked.

"Not really, I just don't like to watch." I grimaced as the needle pierced my flesh.

"I feel like I'm being evaluated by Dr. Temple," Rebecca remarked as she drew a second vial of blood.

"Well, he is a fully-trained TV doctor." I winked at Jake.

She disposed of the needle and applied a small wad of gauze to my arm with tape and set aside the vials. Then she set about setting up the drip. "This is just saline," she said hanging up the bag. She unraveled the tubing and took my hand. "There'll be another small prick, I'm afraid."

"Oh my God!" she cheered with a sudden realization, and shot Jake an excited glance while she rubbed the top of my hand with an alcohol swab and started the process of inserting the catheter, "The big news! Congratulations!"

"Sorry?" he stammered.

"You and Kristie. I just knew there had to be something going on with you two. The chemistry on screen is so real."

Jake shifted uncomfortably as she continued to prattle on. "I'm so happy for you but totes jealous of Kristie, I mean, who wouldn't be?" She nodded at me for confirmation, as she attached the tubing and applied a sticking dressing to keep everything in place, "Are you going to propose?"

Jake's eyes bulged at the question, but she didn't notice and kept musing as she gathered up the tray and leaned against the foot of the bed, "Would you have a beach wedding here in Hawaii? That would be amazing! Or maybe somewhere romantic like Paris... or a castle in Scotland. You could—"

"Um, would I be able to get some pain relief? My head's really killing me." I butted in, noticing Jake's growing exasperated expression.

"Of course," she refocused, "I'll get these to the lab," she gestured lifting the supply tray, "and be right back." She left the cubicle, pulling the curtain behind her, after stealing one more longing gaze at Jake.

I smiled sympathetically to Jake, "It must be difficult having your personal life open for public discussion like that."

"You have no idea." He let out a heavy sigh and leaning his head against the chair back, stared up at the ceiling.

It was as if a cloud had passed overhead, the air grew heavy and shadows crept across the floor. Rain was coming. Not happy rain, the rain of children skipping in puddles, but sad rain, the rain of parting lovers and coffins being lowered into the ground surrounded by mourners holding black umbrellas. This was the beginning of the end. The realization that this would be one of those few rare and precious encounters that punctuate our lives yet remain with us forever – a discussion with a local on a train in a foreign country, the kindness of a stranger on a bad day, a passing comment in a museum – random, fleeting, intangible. Never to be repeated. A blinding burst of light in the mundane, that burns up and is gone. Impossible to capture, easy to miss. The light of a shooting star.

"*M*e again," Rebecca emerged from behind the curtain carrying a glass of water and a tiny paper cup. "Tylenol for the headache."

"Thank you." I dumped the pills in my mouth and washed them down.

"X-ray's pretty busy at the moment, so it might be a while before someone comes for you," she said, attaching a band to my wrist, "but in the meantime, you're all admitted. They'll move you to the ward after the X-ray."

"I see. Thank you." I idly played with the wristband, trying to hold back the tears beginning to well, "That means you're free to go, Mr. Donovan." I croaked, staring down at my feet, unable to face him.

He stood up and leaned against the bed, his hands on the rail, a pained expression on his face. "Well, I—" he started.

"Don't mind me," Rebecca cut in while she made some notes on my chart.

"Again, thank you…" I mumbled, willing her to leave.

"Coffee!" Jake blurted, "I really need a coffee. What about you? Maybe an orange juice would be better?" He turned to Rebecca, "Is it okay if I get her something to eat?"

"No problem, it'll do her good. Meal service isn't for another hour yet." She replaced the chart in its slot and made her exit.

"Any preferences?"

"Um," I stared at him in disbelief, "I guess something light? Vegetarian. And I could die for a coffee."

Jake raised a questioning eyebrow.

"Oops, bad choice of words." I laughed, "I would *love* a coffee. Milk, one sugar."

"Right, but I'm getting you decaf." He wiggled his finger at me then turned on his heel and headed through the veiled portal to the outside world.

I lay back and shut my eyes. I couldn't believe it. Not the blackout. Not the near drowning. Not even the freak circumstance that Jake Donovan of all people saved my life. No, considering the absurdity of my life, the events of the last few hours were pretty believable. What I couldn't believe was that Jake was nothing like I imagined him.

My thoughts drifted to David. I had known him for years, convinced myself that our relationship was solid and that he truly cared about me even though he rarely showed it. 'That's just David's way', I would tell friends when they remarked about his coldness towards me. How had I ever allowed myself to believe that that was all I was worthy of? It was either the near-fatal dunk in the ocean or the unexpected kindness of a stranger, but I was beginning to see that I deserved a whole lot more.

I had prejudged Jake, believed him to be incapable of caring for anyone but himself, yet he was staying by my side though he had no need to do so. David on the other hand would have been 'too busy' or seen no reason why I couldn't manage on my own.

The memory of that day bubbled up to the surface again, repeating on me like bad chili. We were getting ready for the Christmas party; the inaugural one at David's new architecture firm. Even though I had contributed my own time and money to the business, David always referred to it as *his*, never *our* firm. He bought a hideous blue cocktail dress and heels for me and insisted I wear them despite my objections. It was no use arguing so I dressed and did my hair and make-up, and as usual, I ended up being ready long before him. I left him in the bedroom and went through to the kitchen, tugging at the hem of the dress as I walked, trying to extend the length even the tiniest bit.

With nothing else to do, I started emptying the dishwasher. My thoughts were far away when I took the mandoline slicer from the top rack. A pool of water had collected in it, which I tipped into the sink, and then I reached for a dishcloth and wiped it across the top, brushing my palm along the blade.

I let out an involuntary scream, more out of surprise than pain, and regretted immediately when David stormed into the kitchen and seeing the blood dripping from my hand yelled at me for being so stupid and making us late. I apologized over and over while I wrapped my hand in a towel and rested it on a bag of frozen peas. I told him I needed stitches and instead of helping me to the car, he told me to call a cab. He could've dropped me off before going to his precious party; the hospital was on the way. But, no, he 'didn't want me dripping blood on his leather seats'.

Still, there was no accounting for fate. Perhaps if I hadn't cut my hand, if I had gone to the party, David might not have hooked up with Tiffany and we might still be together. I doubted that though, it would have simply been a matter of time before he finally strayed. In the end, that damned mandoline saved me from perpetuating the biggest mistake of my life.

There's a flip side to the old adage 'that you don't know what you have until it's gone' – you also don't know what you're missing until someone comes along to show you. Just a few hours with Jake Donovan and I was starting to see that I had missed out on a whole lot.

"Knock knock," Jake peered round the curtain, "just checking you weren't sleeping."

I opened my eyes and gestured for him to come in. "I think I did nod off a bit, but not much."

He stepped into the cubicle and put a tray of goodies down on the over-bed table. "Right," he said, sitting down on the edge of the bed near my knees, "We have two coffees: one decaf with milk, one sugar," handing the coffee to me, "and one black, no sugar, very-caf." He took a long swig and then opened a pastry box, "And some half-decent muffins from the cafeteria. I got gluten-free just in case. He placed the box on the bed between us, offering me first choice."

I leaned forward and feigned stretching my legs at the same time so that I could shift my leg under the covers to rest it against his thigh. Again he didn't move away. I pretended not to notice, pretended not to be aware of the heat radiating from him being absorbed into my calf, like liquid being sucked up by a cloth, filling all the tiny gaps between the weave, warming me from a molecular level.

"Chocolate chip or blueberry?" he asked, pointing to the muffins, breaking me from my reverie.

I took the blueberry one and bit into it hungrily. "Oh, these are so goob," I mumbled with my mouth full, and took a sip of the coffee.

Jake laughed, "You really are hungry," and took a hearty mouthful of the chocolate chip muffin. "Mm, actually not bad."

We sat eating and sipping our coffees without saying much, but it wasn't awkward or strained. There was a sense of comfort, a familiarity, as if we had known each other for years. Psychics say when this happens it means the souls knew each other in a previous lifetime. I wondered if his recognized mine too. Or was I simply mistaking the lingering effects of my near drowning for the illusion of an indelible connection?

Jake finished his coffee and held onto the cup waiting for me to finish mine. "Finished?" he said as I drained the last mouthful and motioned to take my cup.

"Yes, thanks," realizing too late that I should have made it last, as I handed him the cup.

He squashed the cups into the pastry box, folding it up into a tight bundle, got up and dropped it into the rubbish bin.

"Well, I guess it's time..." *For you to leave.* I couldn't bring myself to finish the sentence. "Thank you, I really needed that."

Jake turned from the bin, his brightness fading, and looked about the room as if stalling, "Oh, I nearly forgot," he grinned, picking up two magazines from the tray on the table, "I bought some trashy magazines to keep ma'am entertained." He handed me one, and pulling the chair closer to the bed, sat down with the other.

"Thanks," I beamed, my mood lifting, "I only ever read these things in waiting rooms. I never buy them."

"You don't? I knew there was a reason I liked you." He said matter-of-factly while flicking through the pages.

Did I hear right? Or was it merely an irreverent turn of phrase? I opened the magazine, the same copy of *In Touch* I had seen at the airport kiosk with the picture of Jake and Kristie Jephson kissing on the cover, and paged through it, not really taking any of it in.

"I like to keep up to date with what's happening in my life," Jake said, "see, apparently I'm in love with Kristie." He lifted the magazine to show me a double spread of photos of their steamy kiss.

"And, that's not so?" I asked turning to the similar story in my magazine, "it's not 'official'?"

"God, no! I can't stand her."

I looked at him in surprise.

"What? You assumed, because I'm a Hollywood stud that I must be into women with plastic bodies and fake personalities?"

"I suppose I did expect the stereotype." I cocked my head as I studied him, considering his words, "You're not gay are you?" cringing immediately after I blurted it out, "I mean, not that I have a problem with that."

"No."

"Thank God." I let out a sigh of relief.

He raised an eyebrow, smiling at me with his signature smirky grin. He was enjoying this.

"Oh, God, I'm sorry, that all came out wrong, I mean it's just—"

"All the good ones are married or gay, right?"

I laughed, "Something like that."

I turned back to the magazine, "No offense, but you are kissing."

"She ambushed me. Of course, there're no photos of when I pulled away. She'll have engineered the whole thing."

"What makes you say that?"

"The only way the parasite could've gotten in a shot like that, from that angle, is if she had someone let him through the barricade and told him where to wait."

"But, why would she do that?"

"Publicity. Ratings. Fuel fan gossip. Advance her career at my expense. Take your pick."

"That's awful. I'm sorry."

"It is what it is."

"But it shouldn't be." I suddenly realized the risk he was taking being at the hospital with me. "I want you to know, I won't talk to the press about what you've done for me. I think it's disgusting the way the media feeds off and distorts the personal lives of public figures."

"Thanks. I appreciate it." He shrugged his shoulders, "The way I see it, the stuff the media writes, it's just another character I play – a fiction as much as Ethan Temple or Vincent Dubois. It's not me. People rarely see the real me."

"Oh, to be seen for whom we really are." I sighed, closing the magazine, and put it on the bedside cabinet.

"Sorry?"

"I mean, people always see what they want to see. They see us as who they want us to be, but rarely see the real person. For the most part, we appear to the others as projections of their own desires and expectations." I looked down at the blanket, staring into the weave, "Sorry, I get weird sometimes."

"I see you," he whispered.

I looked up and smiled, "I wouldn't be here if you hadn't."

I reached over and squeezed his shoulder. "Thank you. And I don't mean for rescuing me, I mean for being here now. You didn't have to... it means a lot."

"Just doing what anyone would have done."

"I doubt that. My ex would never have bothered."

"What do you mean?"

"The last time I had to go to the hospital, he made me get a cab."
I continued to relate the full story of that fateful day. "So, while I
sat getting stitches, dripping blood all over the awful dress he made
me wear, he was at his Christmas party screwing the receptionist
in his office."

"Sounds to me like you're better off without him."

"Yes, I think that wretched slicer did me a favor." I sighed,
Jake's shocked expression reaffirming that I had accepted David's
unacceptable behavior for far too long. "I guess it doesn't say much
for me that I'm willing to put up with a guy like that."

"Were."

"Sorry?"

"You *were* willing to put up with a guy like that. You've been
reborn, remember," he winked.

I smiled, letting his words sink in. He had a point.

"So, um, what made you stop in Waimanalo Beach this morning?" I asked, trying to lighten the mood.

"I just stopped for gas, actually. I was on my way to the north
shore."

"Ah." I nodded blankly, already at a loss as to what to ask next.

Jake smiled. "I had just come from the Makapuʻu lighthouse. I
got some great shots of the sunrise."

"You're making a movie?"

"No, no. Stills. Photography. It's a hobby."

I raised an enquiring eyebrow.

"Actors have hobbies," he chuckled. "You said you won the airfare in a competition. What sort of competition?"

"The San Francisco's Writer's Corner annual short story competition."

"So, you're a writer."

"It's a hobby," I laughed, "a distant dream," then let out a wistful sigh. "Not something that could pay the bills, unfortunately."

"Ah, so you're a *struggling* writer."

"I guess so."

"I don't think an artist can be great unless they've struggled at some point, experienced the darkness, battled inner demons.”

“You have inner demons?”

He frowned and looked away.

“Sorry, I shouldn’t—”

Jake jumped up and bolted from the cubicle.

“Jake?” I called after him, but he didn’t turn back and then he was gone. I dropped my head against the pillow and stared up at the ceiling. Surely, he wouldn’t leave like that, without saying good-bye. I could hear him talking to someone outside the cubicle, but couldn’t make out words.

Then the curtains parted and he reappeared, holding up a pen triumphantly. “For the crossword,” he declared and hopped up onto the side of the bed again, settling near my legs. “Okay, one across, six-letter-word for ‘wild cat’?”

“Tiger.”

“That’s only five letters.”

“Hmm,” I screwed up my nose in thought.

“I thought you were the writer.” He teased.

“Hey, my brain’s still pretty scrambled.” I kicked him playfully from under the blanket.

“Cougar,” he jotted down the answer and shifted his weight against my leg. “Three down, eight-letter-word for ‘part of a light bulb’?”

“Filament,” we both said simultaneously.

“Yes! Four across, five-letter word for ‘brings up the rear, but keeps going’?”

“Me.” I snorted under my breath.

Jake flashed me a sympathetic smile, “second letter will be an A, it intersects with three down, see,” he leaned over and showed me the puzzle page.

I shook my head, “No idea. Lag? But that’s only three letters.”

Jake turned to the back of the magazine, “Lasts,” he announced, scanning the answers.

“Cheat!” I laughed. “Oh, that’s sneaky. Brings up the rear – last, keeps going – lasts. Clever.”

“Seems like your brain’s doing okay after all.”

"I guess it's still in there," I tapped my head.

"Right, six down, seven-letter-word for—"

The curtain whipped aside and a tall skinny man with round glasses and hair that looked like it had been shot from a party popper entered the cubicle. "Oh, hi, sorry," he stammered, "I'm Chris. I've come to take you upstairs," he stared at Jake, "I mean, not you, her, the patient," he pointed to me, his eyes still on Jake, "I love your work man."

"Thanks," Jake hopped off the bed, "can you give us a minute?"

"Sure, cool. I'll be right outside." Chris retreated, pulling the curtain closed behind him, and stood outside fidgeting making the curtain move as if caught in a breeze.

"Looks like you'll have to finish it on your own." Jake handed me the magazine and pen.

I nodded, biting my lip, the growing lump in my throat threatening to drown me all over again. I grabbed his hand and squeezed it. "Thank you. For everything."

His smile wobbled, "I'm just glad I could help," he placed his other hand over mine and squeezed it in return.

"Um, can I..." I started, but how could someone like me ask someone like him for his phone number? "I... It's been really good meeting you."

"Yeah same, though not the you-nearly-drowning part. You take care now, okay?"

"Yes, you too." I sniffed, letting go of his hand.

He patted my shoulder then turned and headed for the curtain.

He dissolved in my tears as the world caved in around me. I curled up on my side and sobbed. I had cried when David left: bitter angry tears full of resentment and regret. But this was different: raw, pure, unblemished. I cried with uncontrollable shaking and retching wails. Hot salty tears drenched the pillow and plunged me into the inky depths of an ocean of anguish. This time, I could not be saved.

Chapter 11

I lay on my side with my back to the window. I was awake but kept my eyes closed, pretending to be asleep. Maybe if I ignored the cheerful sunlight tapping me on the shoulder long enough, it would go away and annoy someone else. As long as I didn't open my eyes, as long as I didn't let the light in, he would still be in my today. But the second I let the new day in, he would be consigned to my yesterday. And then, all too quickly, yesterday would become last week... last month... last year. As long as I kept my eyes closed, he was still a part of my reality. But the instant I opened my eyes he would be a memory, a ghost. No more real than a dream or a figment of my imagination.

A commotion in the hallway signaled the impending arrival of the breakfast service. I could hold off no longer... I opened my eyes and he was gone. Yesterday's ghost. I sat up and turned to the window. The sky was clear blue, growing brighter with the rising sun over a deep turquoise ocean. Butter-curl white-topped waves licked a golden sand beach, framed by tall palms swaying gently in the breeze along a road of happy pedestrians and orderly motorists. Perfect. Nauseatingly perfect. In the realm of my life it made sense that my holiday accommodation would overlook a dumpster-filled alleyway and it would take a hospital stay to get me the view the tourist brochures promised.

I sighed and turned back to look about the room. It was a small ward with six beds, three of which were empty. My companions were an elderly woman in the bed next to me – she flashed me a toothless grin as she fished her teeth from the glass beside her – and the woman across from me, cocooned in bedclothes, was still asleep. At least, I hoped she was still asleep. She didn't move at all and I couldn't hear even the slightest snore from her.

The sound of squeaking hospital trolleys, clanging of trays and cutlery, and muffled voices grew closer, a harbinger of the ordinary. I had been pulled from the brink of certain death by the most eligible man in America, only to be abandoned in the mundane. It was like rescuing a puppy from a well only to keep it on a chain for the rest of its life.

In the daylight, the idea that I had been rescued by Jake Donovan seemed absurd. Perhaps I *had* fabricated the whole thing. Someone had obviously pulled me from the water, but why had I imagined him to be Jake Donovan, of all people? Was there something my mind was intentionally trying to keep hidden? It was an accident, wasn't it? I hadn't tried to drown myself on purpose, had I? Surely not. Then I remembered the magazines I paged through at the airport. Somehow the memory of those pictures had been incorporated into my delusion. A silly daydream that my mind fixated on when it believed itself to be dying.

The barrage of noise reached our ward and a kitchen aide breached the threshold, wheeling in a shelved stainless trolley. She quickly handed out the morning meal, pulling a tray of food from each shelf and placing it on the appropriate patient's mobile bed table, before withdrawing and re-joining her ranks. I looked over at granny, drooling and dropping oatmeal down her front, then across to the woman emerging from her cocoon, still alive, but obviously injured, her face black and blue and an arm in a cast. I got up and pulled the curtain around my bed, blocking them out, hiding like a child in a fort under a table with a floor-length tablecloth.

I went through the motions of eating breakfast – spread the toast with margarine and jelly from little plastic tubs, peel and slice banana into a bowl of cornflakes, pour over cold milk. Chew while staring into space, swallow, repeat. Then ceremonially stacking the dishes and laying the banana skin over the top, I emptied a sachet of sugar and the remaining milk into the cup of coffee and chugged the cold sickly liquid down in one go. I pushed the table away and shrank back into the bed, staring up at the ceiling.

The curtains being yanked aside startled me. I noticed the breakfast tray was gone and realized I must have drifted off.

A young nurse, pushing a blood pressure unit walked over to the side of the bed, "Good morning, Catherine," she said, taking my arm and wrapping the cuff round it, "I'm Mia, I'm just going take a few vitals."

I nodded.

She made no mention of Jake. It seemed news of his visit hadn't been passed on to the morning staff. That is, if he was ever here. She pressed a button on the monitor console and the cuff inflated.

"I'm sure Dr. Evans will discharge you today." She said cheerily, noting the readings on the chart and the cuff deflated.

"Oh?"

"Yep, everything's normal." She removed the cuff, the loud ripping of Velcro intruding on my thoughts. "You must be looking forward to getting back to your holiday."

"What?" I mumbled.

She didn't hear and smiled at me warmly and taking the monitor, pulled the curtains back leaving me in the security of my draped fort.

Holiday? What holiday? I wanted to go home, yet at the same time, home was the last place I wanted to be. But, staying in that crumby hostel didn't fill me with joy either. Perhaps, I could feign some new symptoms and stay in the hospital for a few more days. The accommodation was better and it came with full room service. I didn't have the money or the energy to find another place to stay and what would be the point? My heart just wasn't in it; I wasn't in the mood for being on holiday. And, if I did stay, I'd end up wandering around like a lost soul looking for a phantom, vainly hoping to cross paths with him again. Better to go home and spend the rest of my vacation ignoring the world cocooned in my own bed.

"Good morning, Catherine" Dr. Evans threw open the curtain smiling brightly.

"Dr. Evans," I mumbled, propping myself up again.

"And, how are you today?" she asked, taking my chart from the slot at the foot of the bed.

"Very well, thank you," I replied automatically.

"That's good to hear. I'll examine you now, but," she scanned the notes, "as the X-ray and bloodwork came back clear, and you didn't have any issues overnight everything should be good for you to leave today."

I forced a smile as she pulled the stethoscope from her neck and popped the ear buds in her ears. She listened to my chest then slipped the scope back round her neck. "Excellent. Your lungs are clear, so I'm happy for you to be discharged," she remarked, making some notes on my chart, "I'll leave your discharge form at the nurses' desk and you can leave when you're ready."

"Oh. Okay." I blew out my cheeks.

"You don't sound very excited to go back to your holiday."

"No, I'm not. I don't think Hawaii really agrees with me. I think I'm just going to go back home."

"Well, I can understand. You do what's best for you."

I smiled and nodded, "Um, there is one thing…"

"Yes?"

"The man who found me… It really was Jake Donovan, right? I didn't imagine it."

She laughed, "Yes, it was him indeed."

"It just seemed too crazy to be real, but I was sure I hadn't been hallucinating."

"Nope, not at all. No need for a psyche evaluation," she winked, "though you might want to buy a lottery ticket considering your lucky streak."

"I think I'll just stick with a flight home. It is okay for me to travel?"

"Yes. You shouldn't have any problems, but if you feel unwell be sure to see your doctor back home."

"I will. Thank you. Everyone here was been so kind."

She took my hand and patted it, "You take care of yourself, sweetie. And I hope you have a better holiday soon." She left, pulling the curtain behind her and leaving me to my thoughts.

I didn't want to go home. I wanted to be with him. I snorted at the irony. *I wanted Jake Donovan.* I had become the same as Alex. Except we were nothing alike. She wanted the façade. I wanted the man I had glimpsed behind the façade. There had to be some way I could contact him. After all, I had a great excuse. I wasn't some hysterical fan; by virtue of the fact that I was the person he saved from drowning, we had a legitimate connection. If I could find out where he was staying I could drop by with a gift to say thank you. A bottle of wine? A gourmet food hamper? What exactly does one give someone as a thank-you gift for saving your life? Perhaps it would be better to write to him. A letter, something personal and private. But, how would I know he'd even get it? It would most likely end up being thrown in with all his fan mail and some assistant somewhere would probably read it, and what if they went to the press? He might think I leaked the story after all.

No, it was probably better to leave it alone. Better for me to sink into the depths of his memory quietly, with graceful dignity. I was already in his yesterday; to try and push my way into his today would be like trying to keep alive something that was already dead. Perhaps I may haunt a dream or my memory might flutter through his mind one day, but I was gone, no more real to him, than he was to me.

I folded back the sheets and gathered my clothes from the bedside cabinet and made my way to the bathroom. I washed quickly, the smell of bleach and hospital-grade soap didn't inspire much indulgence beyond a cursory rinse. I dried off, the coarse hospital towel prickling my skin and changed back into my clothes.

Feeling a bit more refreshed I padded back to the ward feeling the cold vinyl floor under my bare feet.

I folded up the gown and placed it on the foot of the bed then pulled opened the cabinet drawer looking for the hostel key. I froze, my hand gripping the drawer handle at the sight of two magazines. The key was next to them and I grabbed it and stuffed it in my pocket, and then carefully removed the magazines as if they were fragile parchments. My breath caught in my throat, paused waiting, while I leaned back against the bed and turned to the crossword in the copy of *People*, expecting to find it blank.

But, there in blue ballpoint, were the three words written by his hand in block capitals: *cougar, filament, lasts*. I ran my fingers over them, feeling the ridges and valleys of the meandering rivers of ink; rereading them as if there might be a hidden message in them. I felt my eyes moisten and sniffed, biting my quivering lips. It was real. He had been there.

I closed the magazine and rolled them up taking them with me. Many years from now, when I had passed away after a full life with someone else, my children would find them among my box of treasures. They'd wonder why I kept two trashy magazines when they'd never seen me buy a single tabloid, let alone read one. They'd never know what these meant to me.

Chapter 12

$\mathcal{T}$he nurses' station formed the hub of a half wheel, a crescent-shaded desk against a wall, with wards leading off from it like spokes. The nurse on duty was speaking on the phone and nodded to acknowledge me.

I smiled and stood staring at the abstract painting on the wall behind her, a random swirling of reds and blues exploding in a purple cascade down the middle.

"Thank you for waiting," she said, putting the phone down.

"No problem, I'm Catherine Marshall. Dr. Evans said I can leave; you have the discharge form?"

"Yes, that's right. I just need to check you out of the system and if you could just sign here and here," she handed me the form pointing to the relevant blocks, then sat down again and started tapping away at the computer. "I'm sure you must be keen to get back to your holiday. It's a gorgeous day out there."

"Actually, I'm going back... Yes, I've got so much planned." I applied a fake smile; she didn't need to know. "Would you be able to call a taxi for me?"

"Yes, that's already been arranged for you. You can wait here and an orderly will escort you out shortly."

"Oh? Okay, well that's very kind, thank you." I handed back the signed discharge form and sat down on the small couch opposite the desk. I returned my attention to the painting and tried to make out if there was an interpretation to be gained or if it was just a random spilling of paint.

"Ms. Marshall?"

I looked up to see the same orderly with party popper hair from the day before.

"I'm here to escort you outside," he gestured to the wheelchair.

"Right. I'm ready."

"Good to see you're looking better today."

"Yes, thank you. Yesterday was, well... yesterday." I sighed as I settled in the chair.

He didn't say anything more and didn't mention the J-word as he wheeled me down the corridor and through several sets of double doors to outside the main entrance.

"There's supposed to be a taxi here for me," I said as I stood up and scanned the forecourt.

"It must be on the way. Sorry, I can't wait with you, they need the chair inside."

"That's okay. Thanks for the ride." I watched him return inside and then walked over to the short wall bordering the paved area of the portico. It was still early, but already the ground was warm underfoot. I turned and hopped up onto the wall to let my feet cool off. I sat with one hand resting on the wall and the other clutching my precious magazines while I watched the cars come and go. I was so focused on looking out for a taxi that I didn't notice a white Jeep pulling into the drop-off zone until it had stopped at the curb in front of the entrance.

A man dressed in jeans and a white long-sleeve T-shirt with the sleeves pushed up to his elbows got out. He removed a pair of aviator sunglasses and slipped them through the collar of his shirt. I felt my heart skip a beat and plunge into my stomach disturbing a swarm of butterflies. He flashed a big smile at me and I instinctively looked behind me to see if he was smiling at someone else. I turned back, sucking on my lip, and gripped the wall unable to move as he jogged over to me.

"Hey, Catherine. You look much better today."

"Jake." I stammered in shock, still uncertain that this wasn't all an elaborate construct of my brain. Somehow the thought that I might wake up and find myself alone on the beach and that only a few minutes had passed during which I had hallucinated the drowning and Jake entirely was still more believable than the reality that he was actually here standing in front of me. "What are you doing here?"

"I'm your ride."

"Oh that's okay, the nurses called a taxi for me."

"I know. I asked them to call me when you were discharged."

My brain was still lagging. "Sorry?" *Jake Donovan was an Uber driver in his time off?*

Jake grinned and held out his hand and helped me down from the wall, "I promised you a ride. So here I am."

My knees buckled as I breathed in his heady cologne and he slipped his arm through mine to steady me,

"You didn't have to do that."

"No. I wanted to. But, I can call you a cab if you'd prefer."

I squeezed his arm and shifted closer to him, "Well, since you're here... if it's not too much bother."

"It would be a wasted trip otherwise." He said, guiding me to the Jeep.

"Oh? You're not staying in Honolulu?"

"No, I'm staying in Sunrise Cove, it's pretty much right next to Waimanalo beach." He opened the passenger side door.

"Sunrise Cove. Of course."

He raised a questioning eyebrow while he held open the door for me.

"I mean, that's why you were at the lighthouse so early," I muttered as I hobbled over the hot asphalt and climbed into the passenger seat.

"The hospital didn't give you a pair of slippers or something?"

I shook my head.

He let go of the doorframe and opened the back seat passenger door and reached in looking for something on the floor behind the driver's seat.

I tugged on the seat belt and jammed the latch plate into the buckle assembly but it refused to catch. I felt beads of sweat prickle my armpits as I struggled with it. *Oh, come on! Seriously?!* Surely I had embarrassed myself enough in front of him.

Jake swung the back door shut and handed me a pair of flip-flops, "You can borrow these till we get you back to your stuff."

I let go of the seatbelt and it recoiled away from me. "Thanks," I murmured as I took the shoes from him. They were well-worn, the fabric thongs faded and the soles smooth and dusty. I slipped them on my feet feeling the indentations made by his feet.

"Okay?"

"A bit big," I giggled, "but much better, thank you."

"Good. Then let's be on our way."

I nodded and reached for the seatbelt.

"Here, let me," he leaned over, taking the latch from me and shoving it in the buckle, and it caught right away, "the catch is temperamental. It responds to brute force." He winked at me and closed the door.

I inspected the interior while he made his way round to the driver's side. It was an older model Jeep and had obviously seen a lot of use. There was sand on the carpets, fraying stitching on the seats, and the trim was sun cracked. The dashboard was littered with creased maps, sea shells, and pages from the script for an episode of *Hawaii Heartbeat* folded back over the staple and marked with coffee mug stains and notes scribbled on the side. A water bottle, sunscreen and baseball cap were stuffed in the door cubby while an empty coffee cup, loose change and his mobile phone sat in the cubby hole next to the gear shift. There was a camera bag and beach towel on the backseat. The inside smelled of him and a high-tech GPS unit was mounted above the radio. This was obviously not a rental car.

His door opened and he climbed in. He noticed me watching him, "What?" he asked.

"This is your car?"

"Yup, I bought it the first season we came here."

"You bought a used car?"

"Sure, why not? I only use it when I'm here; it sits in a lockup the rest of the time."

"I just pictured you in a sports car."

"Oh..." he grinned, reaching for his seatbelt, "I have one of those too, back in LA."

Of course, he did. I felt my cheeks flush at the thought of him wearing his Hollywood sunglasses, driving with one hand on the steering wheel, along the palm-lined Santa Monica coast with the top down and the breeze in his hair.

"You said you were staying at the Diamond Day, do you know what road that's on?" He asked, interrupting my reverie, and switching on the GPS unit.

"Yes, that's right. It's on Wahine Street, Waimanalo."

He punched in the information and the map appeared on the small screen. He took his sunglasses from his collar, slipped them on, then started the ignition and turned the Jeep from the hospital drop-off zone, and headed for downtown Honolulu.

We passed through the downtown and once we were on the freeway Jake reached over and turned on the radio. It was mid-morning, predictably sunny and warm, and I had to confess, idyllic. I wasn't ordinarily a beach person, but the ocean view truly was spectacular. I was getting to see the scenery along the coast toward Waimanalo Beach that I had missed on the night-time drive up in the shuttle and it took my breath away. It, along with the heat and humidity. Even with the windows down, my blouse stuck to my back and I could feel beads of sweat on my forehead.

"It's a beautiful day," I said grappling for something to make conversation.

"Sorry?" Jake reached over and turned down the radio, "did you say something?"

"Oh, just, it's... it's a beautiful day, don't you think?" I cringed.

"Yes, yes. Beautiful." He turned the radio up again.

He seemed lost in thought. Or he'd lost interest. I sighed and turned back to the window.

"How did you sleep?"

"Sorry?" I blurted, startled.

He reached over and turned off the radio. "I mean, last night, were you comfortable? Did you get much rest?"

"I actually slept better than at the hostel."

"And the doc says you're all clear, right?"

"Pretty much."

"That's great. You're very lucky."

Yeah, great, real lucky. I knew I'd been given a gift, a second chance on life and I should've been grasping it with both hands, but it still felt more like a penalty – like being sent back: travel down the snake, back five squares, miss three turns and start the losing game all over. If I could have woken up as someone new, in someone else's life then maybe, but I didn't feel like I had gained anything, just ruined another outfit and lost my favorite pair of sandals. I couldn't see how nearly dying would magically make everything better.

"What do you have planned for the rest of your stay?" Jake asked breaking the long silence, as we headed into Waimanalo Beach

"Actually, I've decided to go back home, put this whole disaster behind me."

"Oh, I'm sorry to hear that, are you—" He was interrupted by the GPS announcing that we had reached our destination, "this is it?" he asked, shutting off the engine and peering through the window at the hostel, which looked even more dismal than it did the day before.

"Sadly, yes."

"I can see why you don't want to stay."

I let out a heavy sigh, this was it. The goodbye. The tears were starting to congregate at their designated egress points. I didn't have much time. "You've been very kind, I—"

"I'm going to have to tell our location scout to keep this place in mind if ever we need a site for a drug den."

I laughed, "Yes, it does have that skid row feel." I pressed the safety belt release button and it came free immediately. I reluctantly let it recoil back to its den.

"You can't stay here."

"I'm not intending to. I was going to look for somewhere else before I ended up being flotsam, but now I can't be bothered. I just want to fetch my stuff, get a taxi to the airport and go home."

"Have you changed your flight already?"

"No, I'll do it at the airport and hope for the best."

"What if you can't get a flight? I don't want you to be stranded at the airport."

"Oh, it's okay, I'll be fine, I'm sure I could find—"

"Come with me to Sunrise Cove!" he cut in, "You can make all your arrangements, relax, have something to eat, and you can get a cab later."

"You've done so much already, I couldn't—"

"It's nothing. I insist."

I hesitated, the offer was very tempting and it would mean having more time with Jake, but I had already imposed too much. *Oh sod Miss Goody Two Shoes.* "Okay. That would be nice. Thank you."

"Excellent!" he cried, pulling the keys from the ignition. He threw open his door, grabbed the baseball cap and jumped out of the car.

I watched stupefied as he rushed round to my door. Was I imagining it or was he actually excited?

He opened my door for me and offering me his hand, helped me out, then locked the Jeep and slipped on his cap.

"You're coming in?" I asked.

"You need a hand with your suitcase, right?"

"Yes, but..." I gestured towards a group of youths that were hanging out on the porch, "aren't you worried about being mobbed?"

He pulled the peak of his cap low over his forehead, "It'll be okay."

"Okay... if you're sure." I took his arm and we headed for the entrance. His flip-flops slapped against my feet, reminding me of when I was a child and used to stumble about the house in my mother's shoes.

Jake kept close behind me as we went inside, looking down, not making eye contact with anyone, and we made our way up the twisting stairs to the tiny room at the end of the top floor. I took the key from my pocket and unlocked the door. Everything was still as I left it. Jake walked over to the tiny window and peered out while I knelt down and pulled my suitcase out from under the bed. I opened it up and sat down heavily on the bed. It squeaked loudly and he spun round.

"I know. It's shocking isn't it?" I laughed and slipped on my other pair of sandals. "Thanks for the loaner." I handed the flip-flops back to him.

"Anytime, ma'am," he did a little bow.

I zipped up my suitcase and scanned the room to be sure.

"All set?"

"Yup, let's go."

He picked up my suitcase and grunted at its weight.

"I swear, there's nothing in there." I blushed, "I hardly packed anything."

Jake grimaced and heaved it over to the staircase.

We made our way back down the staircase again unnoticed. The people we did pass were more focused on keeping a healthy distance from my demon suitcase. I dropped off the key and followed Jake outside.

"I can't believe no one recognized you," I said as he lifted my suitcase into the back of the Jeep.

"It's like you said yesterday. People see what they expect to see. No one expects to see me in a place like this so they often don't recognize me even if I'm standing right in front of them."

"Like the guy in the gorilla suit."

"Sorry?"

"Oh, nothing. It was a psychology experiment – a guy walked around in a gorilla suit in a supermarket and people were asked later if they saw him and no one remembered seeing him even though he walked right past them. They saw only what they were focused on."

"Exactly," Jake smiled and shut the Jeep back, "Sometimes being invisible is a blessing."

"I guess so. Until they forget you exist." I sighed.

We got back in the Jeep and set off for the hotel. The Makapuʻu cliffs were up ahead and soon we turned into a winding side road that took us to Sunrise Cove. Considering the hype, the resort was surprisingly understated: a small hotel and a cluster of cabins hidden amongst palm trees nestled in front of a perfect golden sand beach with a turquoise sea.

"So, this is Sunrise Cove." I said, "I somehow thought there'd be more to it." I couldn't help but giggle inwardly thinking of the fuss David made about it being *the* most exclusive place in Hawaii.

"What? No limos and Lamborghinis parked outside?" mocked Jake.

"Well, yes." I laughed, "It doesn't even look like it's five stars."

"The people who come here come for the privacy, not the luxury."

David was definitely in for disappointment then. He wanted everyone to see him and the trophy hanging on his arm. I watched Jake put the Jeep into park. He kept surprising me, but the more I was getting to know him, the more it made sense that he'd choose to stay in a place like this. He noticed me looking at him again and I quickly turned away and dealt with my seatbelt. We got out and he fetched my suitcase from the back. Water splashed in a fountain in the center of the courtyard and the air was perfumed with the fragrance of frangipani flowers. Sliding doors ushered us into a cool lobby and in the distance someone was playing a piano.

"Ah, Mr. Donovan, are you enjoying your day?" A large Hawaiian man in a hotel uniform boomed as we approached the front reception desk.

"Hey Keoni, yes *mahalo*. I need your help."

"Certainly Sir, what can I do?"

"My friend here needs a room."

"A room?" I exclaimed, "no, no, just a place to change and freshen up."

Jake ignored me, "A room. One with a view of the ocean, please."

"No, problem." Keoni tapped away at the computer.

"But I'll only be staying a few hours."

Jake turned to me and implored, "Then use it for a few hours."

Fatigue was creeping up on me and I didn't have the strength to argue. "Okay." I relented, "I could do with a nap."

"Good!" He turned back to Keoni, "book it for a week, on my account, plus anything else Ms. Marshall needs."

"But, that's too much!" I gasped, "really you've done so much already. I couldn't accept."

Keoni looked over at Jake for instruction.

Jake nodded to him to go ahead and turned to me, "Yes, you can."

"But, I can't repay you."

"I don't want you to. Please, it's a gift. I have the means to help, so let me."

I shook my head, "I don't know what to say."

"You don't have to say anything. The room is here for as long as you want it. Leave whenever you're ready, okay? But, get some rest first – a few hours, a few days – as much as you need. "

I nodded. "Okay."

Keoni handed me a key card and Jake took my suitcase and we headed to the elevator.

"See? It has an elevator!" Jake said gleefully.

I shook my head. This was clearly nuts.

Chapter 13

I swiped the key card and opened the door. "Wow!" I gasped as I stepped inside. Large picture windows with a panoramic ocean view provided the backdrop to a room decorated in muted neutral colors. Two luxurious armchairs sat in opposite corners, framing the windows, while a king-sized bed piled with plump pillows took center stage. The white of the linen, smooth and folded to perfection, gleamed invitingly along with a fluffy bathrobe and complimentary slippers laid out across the foot of the bed. Opposite, a giant flat-screen TV took up most of the wall above a bar fridge and credenza topped with a coffee machine, a basket filled with a selection of teas and coffee capsules, and a glass bowl full of fruit. I poked my head into the bathroom and was dazzled by shiny marble and sparkling glass and brass fittings. A generously-sized shower cubicle with a ginormous shower head stood next to a large spa bath. Half a dozen white towels made for pampering, rolled into neat bundles were stacked into a triangle on a glass shelf and a basket full of soaps and lotions sat on the marble countertop next to the hand basin.

Jake heaved my suitcase onto the chrome luggage rack beside the dresser and I turned back to him, chewing on my fingertip, "Maybe I could stay for one night."

He grinned, "That's what I want to hear."

"It's very generous. I really do appreciate—"

"No more of that, okay? You're on holiday now."

"Okay." I nodded.

"Good. And, if you need anything, just ask the front desk and charge it to the room."

"I will." I lied, "And you, if I...? Are you—"

"I'm in one of the cabins."

"Ah, I see... Well, I hope you enjoy your holiday. I'm sure you must—"

"I'll let you get settled." Jake cut me off, walking towards the door.

"Yes, of course."

He paused, turning back to me, his hand on the door handle, head cocked to one side, "Would you like to join me for dinner this evening?"

"I'd love to." I smiled, sucking on my lips to prevent them from betraying my eagerness.

"Great. Seven o'clock?"

I nodded.

"Right. See you then." He gave me a cheerful two-finger salute and closed the door behind him.

I shook my head in disbelief and walked over to the window, and stood watching the sea. To the right were the Makapuʻu cliffs and lighthouse and to the left was Waimanalo beach in the distance. Just beyond the curve of the bay and the infamous sandbar that had stranded me was the spot where I had nearly died. Or maybe I did die. Perhaps this was heaven.

I turned away and went over to the credenza and peeked inside. The usual contents: glasses, cups and saucers, a clothes iron, telephone directory, and a leather folio containing hotel stationery. The same with the bar fridge: an assortment of sodas and mini bottles of alcohol, snacks and coffee creamer. I closed the door and picking up the room service menu idly flipped through the pages before putting it back on the credenza. I helped myself to some grapes; that would do for lunch. I wouldn't be ordering room service or taking anything from the mini bar. It didn't feel right.

Taking the bathrobe I headed to the bathroom and plugged the bath and turned on the taps. I added a capful of the complimentary bubble bath, taking a moment to breathe in the herbal fragrance rising with the steam. Then hung the bathrobe on the door hook and undressed. I stepped into the scented water and slowly sank into the bubbles. I lay for some time soaking in the warmth, not really thinking about much, grateful that for a while my mind had fogged up, hiding the doubts and angst that usually flashed across the mirror of my soul.

I took a deep breath and dipped my head below the surface. The water washed over my face and I sat up abruptly, coughing and choking as the memory rushed back. I could taste the salt and feel the sting of water in my eyes and nose, and the burning of my throat. I gripped the rim of the bath till my pounding heart slowed. The surreal suddenly felt very real. Reality hit me hard. I had been too distracted by Jake's incomprehensible presence in my drama that I hadn't been paying attention. I really had nearly died. I gulped down the cold truth and reached for the soap.

I carefully climbed out of the bath and gingerly reached for a towel – all I needed now was to slip on the polished floor and crack my head open on the Italian marble. I dried off and slipped on the bathrobe pulling its fluffy comfort tight around me and headed back to the room. The bed beckoned to me and I flopped onto it sinking into the white pillow clouds. Not a single squeak, groan or spring in the wrong place.

When I woke the sun was starting to drop. I checked the time: quarter past six. I'd slept for hours! I jumped up and bolted for my suitcase wrenching it open. While I wasn't the kind of woman that needed hours to get ready, I was the kind of person that needed plenty of time to prepare mentally, and I had only forty-five minutes to pull myself together.

I pulled out the entire contents of my suitcase, hoping that by some miracle, I might have unwittingly packed an appropriately stylish and sophisticated outfit. But, no such luck, just the expected assortment of shorts, jeans, skirts and tops... and one summer dress. It would have to do. I didn't even bring a fancy pair of shoes. My golden sandals might have worked; instead I slipped on their ugly cousins, my plain brown pair. I grimaced at the sight of myself in the mirror – all I needed was a wad of sticky cotton candy on a stick and I'd look right at place at a country fair. I added the final touches, a modest necklace and earrings and a light dusting of make-up. I bunched up my hair into a ponytail trying to decide whether to have it up or down, when there was a knock at the door. *Down.* Grabbing my hairbrush, I quickly brushed my hair again on the way to the door, and then threw the brush onto the bed, before opening the door.

I let out an involuntary gasp and felt the heat rush to my cheeks at the vision of male perfection standing in front of me. He had changed and was wearing black pants and a crisp black long-sleeve cotton shirt with the top two buttons open. He had shaved off the growing shadow and doused himself in fresh cologne and combed back his hair neatly, though an errant curl was falling across his forehead. He stood with one arm behind him.

"Hi," I squeaked breathlessly.

"Sorry, I'm a bit early," he smiled, "but I realize I forgot to say where to meet, so I came to you."

"Not at all."

He withdrew his arm from behind his back, revealing a large frangipani flower in his hand, "for you," he said and tucked the flower behind my ear.

I touched my ear shyly.

"You look amazing."

I laughed, "You mean, not drowned."

"No, you look great, but that too."

I gestured to my dress, "Is this okay? It's all I had with me."

"It's perfect. Shall we?" he offered me his arm.

I nodded and slipped my arm through his, pulling the door closed behind me and we headed for the elevator. The warmth of his arm radiating through the cotton of his shirt against my bare arm helped quell my nerves and I wondered if he could feel my shaking ease. Jake pressed the button and we stood waiting, staring ahead, not saying anything. My mind was all over the place, trying to come up with something to say, but everything it suggested was either too inane or too complex for my mouth to execute.

The elevator arrived and as we traveled down to the lobby, I couldn't help sneaking a look at the two of us reflected in the polished steel wall.

When we reached the restaurant Jake dropped his arm and gestured for me to go ahead of him. I noticed him shake his hand as if trying to get the feeling back and cringed with horror, realizing I had held onto him that tightly.

"Good evening, Mr. Donovan and ma'am." The maître d' glided over to us with a pair of leather-bound menus, "your table is ready, if you'll follow me," and ushered us towards the rear of the restaurant.

"Thank you," Jake nodded in acknowledgment and with his hand resting softly against the small of my back we headed to our table, leaving hushed whispers and stolen glances in our wake.

Before the maître d' had a chance, Jake stepped forward and pulled my chair out for me. He carefully nudged it below me as I sat down then took his seat opposite me. The maître d' handed us our menus and informed us of the specials before fading back into the background. I opened the large menu and peered over the top watching Jake. He held his menu open across the table, head downturned reading the options. Without looking up, he grinned and raised an eyebrow. Feeling my cheeks flush, I quickly returned my attention to the menu.

We were seated next to a clear glass wall that overlooked the beach. Once I made my selection I put down the menu and turned to admire the view. The sun was dipping below the horizon, the last rays of light bleeding into the ocean like a melting scoop of ice cream.

"Beautiful sunset tonight," I murmured.

"It is." Jake agreed, setting aside his menu.

"I can see how this place got its name. Well, I mean, it's Sunrise Cove and it's sunset, but—" I took a sip of water to shut myself up and stared down at the heavy silverware in front of me, sparkling with tiny stars of light reflecting from the flame of the single elegant candle standing tall in the center of the table like a wax lighthouse.

A waiter arrived and took our order while collecting our menus and Jake chose a wine. I looked up and noticed Jake watching me.

"What?" I asked confused, "Did I do something?"

"No. You just look so radiant."

"Radiant? What, me?" I frowned.

"Natural."

"Natural?"

"Natural."

"Ah. Like the girl next door." I sighed, forcing a smile.

"Maybe... To the boy next door."

I cocked my head, trying to work out what he meant. Surely he didn't mean... "The room is lovely," I said changing the subject. "Than—"

Jake furrowed his brow.

"Right. No more of that." I grinned. "I had a really good rest."

"Glad to hear it. You deserve a holiday. Talk to Keoni at the front desk. He can arrange anything you'd like to do tours, spa treatments, swimming, scuba diving—"

I raised an eyebrow.

"No. Scratch the water activities."

I laughed, "I think I'll be better off staying well away from the water. Besides, I'd be happier just sitting under a palm tree reading."

"So, you'll stay then?"

"I don't know. I'll see how I feel tomorrow. This holiday vibe thing is beginning to grow on me." I blew out my cheeks. "Honestly, I'm not in any hurry to go back to my real life."

"Then stay."

At that moment, the waiter returned with our food and I sighed inwardly with relief that I could let Jake's comment dissolve in the distraction. "What about you? How long are you here for?" I asked as the waiter left us once again.

"About a week. I've got a few day trips planned. A little R and R and then back to LA."

"To the show?"

"Well, my part's done for this season. It's in post-production now, but there're interviews, conventions, that kind of stuff to do."

I nodded. "Did you always want to be an actor?"

"I'm not sure I thought of it that way. It's more that performing has always been the thing I enjoyed doing most. Acting, role-playing..." he chuckled, "showing off... was always my way to step outside myself, to be someone I wasn't. I always loved make-believe games as a kid; I was in every school play. I did commercials and I had a supporting role in *Time Wrecked*."

"That was you? I loved that movie."

He smiled, "Yeah, I had a blast doing it and I was offered the sequel, but my father drew the line. Decided it was time for me to 'grow up'," he gestured the words in air quotes, "and concentrate on my schoolwork, otherwise, I would never make it into med school."

"Med school?" I raised an eyebrow.

"Yeah, I come from a family of doctors. Dad's the leading cardio-thoracic surgeon at John Hopkins. Mum's a pediatrician."

"I see. No pressure, then."

He grunted. "Yup. I tried. I did try. I made it into med school, but I dropped out after six months and left for LA."

"What do they think of you playing a doctor now?"

"*Playing* is the operative word."

"Even after all your real-life training?"

"That kind of makes it worse, like, why couldn't I put in the effort for the real thing?" Jake sighed, "Dad just can't get that I didn't quit because I found it too hard, but that I couldn't take the responsibility of having someone's life in my hands."

I felt a chill as he said that, imagining the thoughts that must have run through his mind when he pulled me from the ocean and gave me mouth-to-mouth.

He continued, "In acting you can do another take if you mess up, but with medicine there're no do-overs."

"Have you tried explaining that to him?"

"I have, but he just sees it as an excuse, says I'd get used to it, it's just part of the job."

"Hmm." I sighed, nodding in commiseration with him. I got it.

"My younger sister eventually took up the torch; she's a cardiologist, so at least I can be the family disappointment in peace."

"I'm sure it's not that bad."

"Oh, it gets worse, Dad really lost it when I changed my name. It was like I had disowned the family or something."

"You changed your name?"

He nodded, "I was just getting modeling work, parts in commercials and small supporting roles, and my manager said I needed a name with better star quality."

"Well, I guess that makes sense in your line of work. What was your real name?

"Jonathan Donaldson."

"Oh dear," I suppressed a giggle, "that's quite a mouthful."

"So, I've been told." He winked at me, flashing me his wicked smirky grin.

My cheeks flushed and I choked on my risotto. Swallowing hard, I took a sip of wine. Regaining my composure, I studied him thoughtfully.

"What?" He asked.

"I'm trying to work out which one suits you better."

"You don't think Jake Donovan suits me?"

"I'm not sure. I mean he's not what I expected."

"Oh? And what did you expect?"

"Honestly, I expected you to be shallow and self-centered. Fake."

"And you don't think I'm fake?"

I cocked my head, "No, I don't think you are. I think, perhaps Jonathan Donaldson is the fake, the one playing the role of dutiful son trying to please his parents who set impossible standards for him to achieve. While Jake Donovan is the real deal, the person you were meant to be, his name set you free. You worry about being artificial, you see Jake as a façade, but I think you left the façade behind with Jonathan. You are more real than you realize."

Jake put down his fork, his smile dropped and it seemed like a sudden hush had descended around us as he stared at me, his mouth agape.

"Sorry," I looked down at my plate and picked at my food, "I see things that others miss."

"The hallmark of a great writer."

"Oh, I don't know. Maybe one day." I sighed. "I wanted to spend my prize money on several online writing courses, but David told me not to waste my money, and well you know the rest. Writing competitions might be all I'm destined for."

"That's bullshit and you know it. You should be setting your sights much higher. I agree with your ex, don't waste your money on some budget online school. You're way better than that. You should be aiming for an institution like the Deighton Academy—"

I grunted, "I wish. It's my dream to go there, but even if I could get in, I can't afford it."

"They give out scholarships. You should apply, I'm certain you'd get in."

I laughed, "You're just being nice. You don't even know what my writing is like."

"I read your story."

"Really? You read *An Apple a Day*? How?"

"I know how to Google."

"You actually took the time to read it?" I repeated, shaking my head in disbelief.

"I can tell you why you didn't get first prize."

I sighed, "Sure, go ahead." Everyone else had offered their criticism.

"It was too short."

"Well, it was a short story. I couldn't make it longer. As it was I had to cut huge chunks out to make it fit."

"That's what I mean... it left me wanting more."

I cocked my head and eyed him curiously.

"It felt like a film treatment."

"A treatment?

"Yeah, it's the term we use for the synopsis of a movie, the proposal for a story before a script is commissioned."

"Ah." I nodded.

"It gave me a good sense of the basic plot and characters, but it's got potential for so much more. I wanted to know Martha's backstory, for a better understanding of her motivation to murder her husband, and to feel satisfaction when she gets away with it. But the idea that she injects an overdose of his own heart medication into the apple that she packs every day for his lunch, is brilliant.

I grinned, "Yes, I liked the idea that the police might suspect foul play but wouldn't have any real proof, and then there's all the symbolism of the apple. You know, the proverbial poison apple."

"Exactly... the sweet apple, which over years of resentment turns bitter and eventually becomes the thing that kills him. It's a great metaphor." He agreed, "It would make a great movie or miniseries. A network like Netflix or Amazon would snap it up."

I snorted, "Oh, I doubt—"

"No. I mean it. You have talent, so why aren't you using it?"

"Probably because no one's told me that before."

"Well, that can't be true."

"With the exception of some favorite English teachers who encouraged my writing, most people just say my writing is good, to humor me. You know what friends and family are like; they don't want to hurt your feelings. But, as far as it being a legitimate career... well, the general consensus has always been that that was never an option. First my parents, then David, all made it clear that writing wouldn't pay the bills and I shouldn't waste my time on silly dreams."

"Hmm, sounds familiar."

"True, but you at least had the courage to go after your dreams. I've always been too afraid of disappointing my parents. I'm an only child, so I don't have the luxury of having a sibling who can pick up the torch if I fail. I carry the sole burden of fulfilling their hopes and expectations.

"I guess that's true."

"I can't be the screw-up. I *have* to be the over-achiever." I let out a plaintive sigh. "And so far, I haven't achieved anything on their list."

"And, if you did, would that make *you* happy?"

I stared at him as his words slowly sank in.

"You'd only be feeding their flawed image of you. They still wouldn't see you for you. Like someone who buys drugs for an addict – you'd be an enabler, feeding their fantasy and not getting what you need in return because they can't see what you need, because they can't see you."

I sat back in my chair.

"Sorry, I went too far."

"No, you're absolutely right. I'd never thought about it that way. I always thought I was being the good daughter, the dutiful daughter; that it would be rebellious or selfish of me to stand up to them."

"That's the thing though, if you can't stand up to your parents, you'll never be able to stand up to anyone." His words hit me in the stomach. First it was my parents, then my teachers, then my bosses... then David. All the things I had done to make them happy, to get their approval and what did it get me in return? Did any of it ever make *me* happy? I turned and stared out the window at the dark undulating ocean, the sweeping beam of the lighthouse regularly coating the surface in a copper glaze, and barely noticed the waiter clearing away our dinner plates.

"The lady requires dessert, stat!" Jake declared.

"Very good, sir." The waiter bowed slightly and left to fetch menus.

"I shouldn't," I said.

"Of course, you should. You only live once. Well, actually in your case—" Jake cocked his head and held up a thoughtful finger then jumped from his seat and rushed over to our waiter who was on his way to our table with the menus. Jake whispered something to him and he passed the menus to Jake before heading back to the kitchen.

"What was that about?" I asked as Jake handed me a menu and sat down.

"Nothing." He smiled, breaking into that smirky grin.

I raised an eyebrow.

Jake tapped my menu, "Just pick a dessert, will you? They make a great crème brûlée."

"Oh, all right," I smiled.

We continued to peruse our menus and our waiter returned with an ice bucket, a bottle of champagne and two glasses. He set the bucket in a stand next to the table and proceeded to remove the seal from the bottle.

"Wait, this is for us?" I asked in surprise as he popped the cork, poured the glasses, then took our dessert orders before retreating.

Jake nodded, "It occurred to me, that it's not everyday one comes back from the dead and remains human. I mean, I only did it as a TV vampire. I think that's cause for celebration. "

I laughed and took my glass as Jake held up his.

"To second chances and new beginnings," he said.

"To starting over," I smiled and clinked my glass against his.

Our waiter came back with the desserts, setting down a crème brûlée for Jake, and for me, a chocolate mousse in a glass bowl with a lid nestled on a silver tray surrounded by chocolate shavings. I lifted the lid and a fragrant woody smoke swirled up from the bowl.

"Wow, that's awesome!" Jake cheered, leaning over the table to take a closer look.

"Regretting your choice?" I glanced at his ceramic ramekin of brûlée topped with a single shard of toffee.

"Want to swap?" he grinned.

"No way! But I'll let you have a taste." I offered a spoonful to Jake and watched as he put it in his mouth and drew it out between those gorgeous lips.

"Oh, that... is... good..." he moaned, handing the spoon back to me.

I took it back and not thinking, automatically put it in my

mouth instead of dipping it back into the mousse. I felt the warm metal against my tongue, sucked it, bit down on it, feeling a hot craving flood my body while I slowly withdrew it and watched him dip his spoon into his own dessert.

"Your turn," he offered his spoon to me.

"Hmm, that's good too, but I definitely think mine is better." I handed the licked spoon back to him, watching to see what he would do. He plunged it back into the brûlée, breaking the sugar crust and the spell.

Once the dessert plates were cleared away we continued talking over the rest of the champagne and after-dinner coffees. I forgot it was Jake Donovan sitting across from me, by now he was simply Jake and we chatted away about all the normal things normal people talk about when they're getting to know each other. Things that interested us, places we'd been to and wanted to go to, and sharing funny stories that made each other snort with laughter so much that champagne bubbled in our noses and people turned to stare.

At one in the morning, our waiter politely interrupted to tell us they needed to close up the restaurant. We hadn't noticed we were the only guests left and apologizing with embarrassment for keeping them so late, we made a hasty retreat, giggling like giddy teenagers. We walked back to the lobby, arm in arm, shoulders touching; our footsteps on the marble floor echoing in the deserted corridor.

"I had a wonderful evening," I said when we reached the elevator.

"Me too," Jake smiled softly – no mischievous cocked eyebrow, no wicked smirk and pressed the elevator button. The doors opened immediately and he reached across, holding them open, "Well, have a good night."

I nodded and as I stepped into the elevator, I leaned forward and kissed him on the cheek. He pulled back but kept his arm on the door. Feeling my face flood with hot regret, I shrank into the corner and staring fixedly at the floor buttons, I selected my number and hit the door close button. The doors lurched, but Jake's arm was still in the way. He leaned in, his head cocked, eyebrows furrowed, "Would you like to come sightseeing with me tomorrow?" he blurted.

"Sightseeing?" I eyed him curiously.

"Yeah. I thought I might head out to Honolulu, perhaps take in a museum. I just wondered if you'd like to join me?"

"I'd like that," I said, doing my best to rein in my smile.

"Great. I'll meet you in the lobby at 9.00?"

"Perfect. It's a date." I cringed, but let it go rather than make a bigger git of myself by trying to backpedal my way out of my choice of words.

"Great. I'll see you then." He grinned and stepped back letting the doors close.

The elevator began its ascent and I let out an excited scream then fell back against the wall laughing at the craziness of it all.

Chapter 14

My phone chimed and I reached over for it, holding a slice of toast in my mouth before taking a bite. It was a message from Amira wanting to know how my holiday was going. I tapped out a short message: *Eating breakfast, watching the ocean.* She'd imagine me sitting in front of a beachside bakery, a small box of pastries on my lap and a large coffee in a paper cup in my hand. How could I possibly describe to her in a single text that I was actually wrapped in a fluffy gown, sitting in an upscale armchair in front of a giant window overlooking one of the most exclusive views in Hawaii with a room service cart full of breakfast goodies at my side? I would explain everything when I got back. I had to explain it to myself first.

The hall seemed to be growing longer and rotating with every step. I twisted the fabric of my skirt between my fingers. This couldn't be real. *Me? Going out on a date with Jake Donovan?* I felt I was going to be sick. I stopped and took a deep breath. *Date?!* What was I thinking? This wasn't a date. This, the hotel, it didn't mean anything. Why did I always rush ahead? A guy just had to be nice to me and I'd jump to thinking he *liked* me. Jake didn't pull me from the ocean because he *liked* me.

I stood at the elevator and untangled my finger from my skirt and smoothed out the creases, trying not to think about my growing queasiness.

The elevator was empty and as soon as I pressed the button for ground, my fingers started playing with my skirt fabric again and a foot started tapping in time with my racing heart. What if he didn't show up? Maybe he'd only asked flippantly, a spur-of-the-moment suggestion he regretted in the morning. Maybe that's why he'd sent the breakfast.

The doors opened and I stepped out into the lobby. It was quiet except for the sound of water trickling from the water feature and soft piped music. I took a deep breath and scanned the room, hurriedly smoothing the creases in my skirt. Jake sat in an armchair near the grand piano and saw me at the same time I spotted him. He stood up and smiled broadly with that gorgeous crooked smile of his. I couldn't help it; I blushed like a silly school girl who caught the popular boy looking at her.

It felt like I was in a movie as we walked towards each other holding each other's gaze. He was dressed in jeans and a navy blue button shirt, the sleeves pushed up his arms to his elbows, top buttons at the neck undone, letting his smooth skin peek through. I swallowed hard and walked over to meet him, stepping slowly and deliberately trying not to show how much I was shaking.

He bounded over, calm and confident and the closer he got the more it felt like wrong, like when you wave to a friend in the street and then realize you were mistaken and you're waving at a stranger. I wasn't meant to be here.

"Morning," said Jake, "You look lovely."

"Thank you." He was being polite. I looked drab. I regretted my choice of the taupe maxi skirt and white blouse – the one without the stain – and brown sandals. "And thank you for the breakfast."

"No problem." He winked, "I wanted to make sure you didn't skip it."

I wondered if he meant nutritionally or if had he anticipated that I wouldn't order anything to avoid adding further charges to the room.

"Shall we?"

"What?"

Jake gestured towards the courtyard.

"Oh right, I..."

"Did you forget something?"

"No, no. All here." I mumbled tapping my bag, psyching myself up. This was really happening.

"Well then, let's go." He reached out his arm and ushered me towards the main doorway and as I turned he rested his hand protectively on the small of my back. His fingers came to rest on the bare skin of my back in the gap between my blouse and skirt sending tingles shooting through my body. He didn't move his hand and I didn't pull away.

Though still early, the air outside was already hot and humid and I started to panic at the thought of a rivulet of sweat running down my back and over his flawless fingers. I cringed at the thought of him removing his hand and having to wipe it on his designer jeans.

"This way," Jake said, taking away his hand and turning from the path to the cabins and over to his Jeep which was now parked in the courtyard.

I sighed with temporary relief. He had no idea what he had signed himself up for.

He unlocked the passenger side door and I hesitated, holding onto the door frame. "I just want to apologize for last night," I blurted.

Jake looked at me quizzically, "What for?"

"For kissing you."

"You are?" he asked raising an eyebrow.

"You must get women throwing themselves at you all the time. I don't—"

"I do. It's because I'm hot," he said flatly, breaking me off. "I'm insanely sexy and I'm a star. I get it. *All the time*!" He broke into a teasing grin and winked at me.

I laughed, "You don't take yourself too seriously, do you?"

"In my business, it's wise not to."

"It's just... I don't want you to think I'm like all those other women, hitting on you because you're Jake Donovan. I mean... I don't like you *because* you're Jake Donovan... I like you in spite of it."

His grin dropped and he cocked his head to one side, "You know, that might be the nicest thing anyone has ever said to me."

I climbed in and he closed the door after me. I watched him walk round to the driver's side, eyebrows furrowed, shaking his head in amazement, smiling shyly. Had I actually unnerved *him*?

"So, Mr. Tour Guide, what's on the agenda for today?" I asked while jiggling the seatbelt catch about in the temperamental lock, praying I wouldn't have to make an ass of myself by having to ask him for help. It clicked almost immediately. I was starting to get the hang of this.

He slipped on his sunglasses and started the engine. "How about we start with Honolulu... have an easy day, do some of the touristy stuff..."

"Sounds good. I'm glad you asked me to sightsee with you. I probably wouldn't have bothered with the sights otherwise."

"Me too. It's easier to go out in public if I'm with someone – people are less likely to approach me if I have company."

"Oh, so you're just using me then," I teased.

"Absolutely and without shame," he replied deadpan again.

I turned to him and he grinned at me as he rested his arm on the back of my seat and reversed the Jeep out of the parking space with one hand while looking out the rear window.

I blushed, catching a whiff of his cologne and seeing his neck so close to my mouth that I could reach out and sink my teeth into it. I sucked in my lips and stared ahead. "You can use me all you like," I said cheerily and immediately sank into the seat flushing in embarrassment at my choice of words.

The morning was stunning with a vibrant blue sky and clear views of the ocean which undulated calmly to a far distant horizon. I watched the gentle waves, mesmerized, breathing in the fresh air heavy with the fragrance of lush vegetation that wafted through the open windows. Jake drove with one hand on the steering wheel and his other arm resting on the window frame. He tapped his fingers in time to a song he was humming to himself.

"Up ahead is Makapuʻu Point," he said, pointing towards the cliffs.

"The lighthouse," I shifted in my seat to get a better view, "that's the one you visited before you stopped in Waimanalo Beach. Before..."

"That's it."

I watched it recede into the distance – the mighty lighthouse, savior of souls at sea – and reflected on the seemingly random sequence of events that had occurred for this lighthouse to have played an indirect role in saving my own life.

I turned back to the road ahead and became acutely aware of a growing palpable silence. I hated small talk and I started to sweat as I racked my brain for something to say. Everything I had that was worth sharing had already been told. My time was running out. He would soon discover that I was actually quite dull. *Think!* There had to be some anecdote in my past that he would find amusing.

"You can turn the radio on, if you like." Jake offered.

"What? No. That's okay. I'm fine. Unless, you want to... I'm sorry, I must be boring—"

"I rather like the quiet," he sighed softly, "you know... space to hear your own thoughts."

"Exactly!" I piped up, "Why do people have to talk all the time; be continually surrounded by noise?"

"It's exhausting, right?"

"So exhausting!" I turned to him amazed. Who would have pegged Jake Donovan as an introvert? My anxiety evaporated, I sat back and we enjoyed the rest of the drive in companionable silence.

We parked downtown and spent some time exploring the historic part of Honolulu on foot. Jake brought his camera and fired off photos of the various landmark statues and buildings while we strolled through the oasis of manicured grounds edged with colorful flower beds and tall palm trees.

I was awestruck by the Kawaiaha'o church. At first glance it seemed like a fairly ordinary grey brick building then Jake explained that the bricks were made of coral cut from the ocean floor some two hundred years ago and I stood marveling at it while he took photos from various angles.

From there we made our way through a small garden to the mausoleum of King Lunalilo, which itself looked like a tiny church with concrete pillars, steeple roof and gothic wooden doors. A group of students with Australian accents passed us talking and laughing loudly. One of them turned to take a second look then murmured excitedly to the group. They stopped and all turned to look our way.

We had paused to read a plaque next to a bubbling fountain and Jake was standing close to me, almost touching. He noticed the group turning back and bolted for the mausoleum shielding his face with his camera. I held up my hand at them in a weak wave and, not recognizing me as anyone worth recognizing, they assumed their friend was fooling around and continued on their way.

He doesn't want to be seen with you, said the voice in my head as I went to look for Jake. I know it wasn't the same, yet the encounter brought back a familiar feeling of unease. I had dated that guy before. The guy who always kept me at a distance. The guy who never held my hand in public and walked next to me maintaining an airy gap between us. The guy who broke off dates at the last minute or kept me waiting for hours before showing up. The guy who was always too busy to stay for long. The guy who never responded to voicemails or texts or did so with only monosyllabic or emoji responses. The guy who never introduced me to his friends or family, who never called me his girlfriend and didn't want me to tell anyone I was seeing him. Though we saw each other on and off for years, that guy was the boyfriend I never had. If I hadn't met David, he would probably still be orbiting me, keeping me conveniently trapped in his gravitational pull.

"Sorry, about rushing off like that," Jake said when I joined up with him round the back of the mausoleum.

"That's okay." I strained a smile, "I understand. It must drive you crazy, worrying that every person with a mobile phone is a potential paparazzi."

Jake sighed, "That and the endless stream of requests for a photo."

I craned my head round the corner and scanned the garden. "Well, they're gone now. It's safe to come out."

"Thanks." He whispered and tiptoed out of the shadows.

"Happy to help. I'm here today to be your decoy, remember?"

He laughed, "That's right. In that case, shall we continue?"

I nodded and we crossed the road to Iolani Palace – now a museum, it was once the home of the last monarchs of Hawaii. I vaguely remembered the history from school. The last ruler of Hawaii, Queen Liliuokalani, had been forcibly removed from the throne in the early 1890s and though she had led an uprising, it failed. She was captured and held prisoner in a room in her own palace. The toppling of the Hawaiian monarchy set in motion the annexation of the islands by the United States and ultimately the incorporation of Hawaii as an American state.

Jake took a series of photos of the exterior of the palace and surrounding barracks and pavilion buildings. I loved watching Jake with his camera – the way he got lost in the zone to get the perfect shot and cradled the large telephoto lens in one hand and focused with the other, the wide black Canon-emblazoned strap round his neck. It wasn't that he looked sexy doing it, which he did, it was that he was sharing his passion with me, letting me into his world. It made me feel special, but it was tinged with sadness because I knew I wasn't. He too, would be a boyfriend I never had. I longed to take a photo of him, to have some proof, but how could I? I didn't want to violate his trust by taking one without asking, and after the earlier incident, I didn't want to seem like everyone else, hustling him for a selfie.

Chapter 15

One of the places we both wanted to visit was the Honolulu Museum of Art and we spent a good two hours exploring the impressive collection, which consisted of art from a variety of periods, cultures and artists. The spacious building with its air-conditioning and tranquil garden courtyards was a welcome break from the city heat and noise.

Away from the public spaces and the possibility of being shot by a sniper photographer, Jake relaxed and seemed less conscious of our conspicuousness. Also, peak tourist season was still a few months away so the museum wasn't terribly busy and we could move about without much interruption. As long as Jake stared intently at an exhibit and kept his back toward the other visitors he was able to avoid being recognized. We only received a few second glances and hushed whispers from people near us. When this happened I would turn and frown at them and they would quickly look away and move on. Then I'd return my focus to whatever piece we were at and notice Jake sneak a sideways look at me while breaking into a big smile.

With the exception of a few notable paintings such as Van Gogh's *Wheat Field with Sheaves*, which I was surprised to see here of all places, the artworks started to look the same to me especially in the contemporary art section. It was difficult to pay much attention to a piece with him standing next to me. I couldn't tell if he was doing it deliberately; I wanted to think so. He would stand

129

so close that his arm hair would brush against my skin, making me catch my breath and bite my lip. Then he would make some bland comment about the composition or use of texture, as if either of us were particularly knowledgeable about art, before moving on to the next piece. When I had followed and was standing next to him again, he'd shift his weight ever so slightly till he brushed up against me once more, and repeat the routine. We continued this dance over and over, and on one turn, I leaned in against him, so that our arms touched. He didn't move away and I could feel the heat building as we both stared ahead feigning interest at some unintelligible mass of squiggles and splats. If it had been a movie, it would have been one of those scenes where you'd see the guy turn, grab the woman, press her up against the wall, and kiss her passionately while groping her all over, and then it would cut back to the same scene of them still standing there and you'd realize it was all in her head. I swallowed hard and turned to face him, ready to surrender. He turned his head to meet me and as I leaned forward, he smiled an oh-hey-I-forgot-you-were-there smile and walked over to the next painting. It was all in my head.

We decided to have lunch at the museum's café rather than venture out into the city chaos. After much insisting, I convinced him to let me pay. Just because he could afford to foot the bill, didn't mean I felt comfortable with it. I have principles and I wanted him to know it. He went to look for a table while I waited in the queue to settle up and I watched him cross the room leaving a wake of turned heads and excited whispers behind him. He found an empty table beside the large folding doors that opened out onto a grassy courtyard and pulled out his camera and sat reviewing his photos.

I picked up the tray and headed over to join him, walking slowly, terrified that I'd trip over my own feet and launch the tray into the air and shower him in salad and bread buns. He noticed me approaching and came over and relieved me of my potential ordnance.

"Good spot," I remarked as we settled down and I set out our sandwiches and sodas.

"Thanks for the lunch." Jake raised his sandwich to me before taking a bite.

"You're very welcome." I raised my soda bottle in a return toast and twisted the cap. My hands were clammy and the cap wouldn't budge. *Naturally.*

Jake reached over, took the bottle and popped the cap off with one quick twist, flashing a smooth and taut bicep below his sleeve.

"Thanks." I croaked and took a long swig of soda. "Did you get some good shots?" I gestured to his camera.

"Yeah, I think so. I'll transfer them to my laptop later and do a few edits."

"Mmm," I nodded. I was struggling to get through my sandwich. They had looked so appetizing in the cabinet, but had turned out to be a bit dry. Jake had already finished his and was beginning to look bored.

"No rush," he said, picking up his camera and pointing it at the courtyard, "take your time."

That made me feel so much better. Slowcoach Cathy taking up the rear again. "I'd love to see your photos sometime." I mumbled with my mouth full.

"Uh-huh." Jake was firing off some candid shots of a toddler on the grass walking to her mother's arms.

"I mean, if that's okay, if you want, you don't have to—" I took another large bite to shut up my blithering which sent a blob of relish and a slice of pickle down my blouse. "Shhi!" Hissing, I pulled my blouse collar forward and looked down searching for the fiend. Out of the corner of my eye, I could see Jake was still facing away and had his hand raised in acknowledgment with a nod and strained smile at someone across the courtyard who had recognized him and was waving madly. I didn't have the time to get visual confirmation; I sent my hand in blind.

Jake turned back and raised a questioning eyebrow at the sight of me with my hand stuck down my blouse.

"Oh God, I'm such a klutz." I yelped with embarrassment, scrabbling about my bra desperately chasing the errant pickle. If he doubted his decision to spend time with me, he surely would now. *Go on, run for the hills! Save yourself!*

"Need any help?" he smirked. He was enjoying this.

I burst out laughing and had to look away to stop myself from giggling uncontrollably. I had to focus, damn it! I caught my breath and resumed the chase. Finally, I caught hold of the offending piece of salad, pulled it out and held it up triumphantly, "Success!" I declared, before dumping the pickle on the tray.

"Well done," Jake clapped his hands softly, then cocked his head to the side frowning.

I looked down to see what he was looking at and saw a streak of red relish down my front. "Oh, crap!" I grabbed a serviette and desperately tried to rub it off, but only succeeded in spreading it further.

I was getting more flustered and Jake got up and came over to crouch beside me. He pulled his sunglasses from his shirt then slipped them through my own collar, positioning them so that the lenses hung over the bulk of the stain. The still-warm metal arm of the sunglasses came to rest against the skin of my breast sending a rush of heat through my body.

"That'll work for now." He stood up, then paused and reaching down, ran his finger slowly over my lip. "Missed a spot," he whispered and licked his finger, sucking it slowly and deliberately while keeping his eyes locked on mine.

I let out a strangled gasp. Oh God, he was doing it again.

He gathered up his camera gear and I wobbled to my feet. I leaned forward to clear away the lunch tray and the sunglasses swung precariously on the loose fabric of my blouse and I clutched my hand to my chest to stop them from falling.

"Hmm," he mumbled and taking my hand led me from the café to the gift shop. Once inside he dropped my hand, scanned the aisles and headed for the back on a mission.

I shrugged my shoulders and wandered around on my own browsing the shelves of the usual tourist souvenirs including leis, baskets and grass skirts while hoping that he hadn't done a runner and abandoned me in the store as a diversion. His sunglasses bumped my chest as I walked to a new aisle; I could always sell them on eBay for a nice profit. I sneered and held a coconut-shell bra against my chest.

"Suits you."

I looked round and saw Jake had reappeared beside me. He winked at me, grinning.

"Ha!" I snorted and shoved the thing back on the shelf.

"I thought this might be better." He held a gift bag and pulled out a light blue T-shirt with a large red heart and the words *I Love Hawaii* printed across the front. He held it against me checking the size, "The woman at the counter says you can swap it if it doesn't fit."

I raised my own eyebrow, "you're coming to my rescue again?"

"Not at all. Just providing a service. You've got to have the obligatory tourist T-shirt, right?"

I laughed, "well, in that case, we need to get you one too." I pushed past him and headed to the clothing aisle. I dug through the T-shirts till I found the same one in his size.

"Oh no," he raised his hands as I held it in front of him, "I'm not wearing—"

"You know what they say, when in Rome, wear the T-shirt," I laughed, but I had to admit, it didn't look right. I shoved the shirt back and he let out a sigh of relief. I couldn't tell if it was from the tacky design or the idea of us walking around in matching T-shirts, but I wasn't letting him off that easily. I pulled a floral explosion from the rack and held it in front of him, "Perfect!" I cried, "It'll do nicely. Very *Magnum PI!*" and marched off to pay for it before he could stop me.

"Here you go." I proclaimed, handing Jake the bag containing the shirt, when we were in the foyer outside the gift shop.

He took it with a mock scowl and handed me the bag with the shirt he bought for me, "All yours."

"Thanks. I'll be right back." I ducked into the ladies room leaving him staring into the bag and shaking his head.

I carefully placed Jake's sunglasses on the counter – the last thing I needed was to break them. I ripped the tag from the shirt and changed into it. It turned out to be a bit tight around my bust. Old me would have wanted to add a scarf to distract attention but new me decided to flaunt it. I repositioned my boobs for maximum effect, stuffed the old blouse in my bag – the second stained shirt of the trip – brushed my hair, freshened up and applied a fresh layer of lipstick. Then added the final touch: I slipped the sunglasses back in place on the collar of the T-shirt, positioning them strategically.

I left the ladies room and found him leaning against the foyer wall, checking his mobile. He had changed into the shirt I gave him. He saw me, slipped the phone into his pocket and swaggered over to me.

"I didn't think you'd actually wear it," I chuckled.

"Why wouldn't I? I totally rock it." He turned on his heel and jiggled his eyebrows at me, setting me off laughing again.

"Well?" I collected myself, "What do you think?" I held up my hands to show off the T-shirt, flaunting the rather obvious.

"Perfect! It brings out your... eyes."

I bit my lip and purposively slipped his sunglasses from my cleavage and handed them back, "Thanks for the loaner. Again." I breathed, doing my best to sound steamy.

"Any time." He slipped them through the collar of his new shirt and I felt a flash of heat rush through me at the thought of the metal arm, still warm from being against my chest, brushing against his skin. He reached out his arm and rested his hand again on the small of my back as we headed for the exit.

Jake parked the Jeep in the shade of some palm trees. He grabbed the baseball cap from the dash and locked up the car. Even with the Magnum shirt, sunglasses and cap pulled down low he was recognizable as Jake Donovan and I tried not to notice the stares of people we passed.

"So, this is the famous Waikiki Beach," I said, recognizing the backdrop to those infamous magazine pictures.

"The one and only." He turned and pointed to an area off in the distance behind us, "over there is where we filmed the last scene, the beach was blocked off and the trailers were parked up there on the concourse."

"Which is where Kristie's spy must have been staked out," I said understanding how it had to have been a set-up.

"That's it. He couldn't have got past those trees without someone letting him through."

I shook my head. No matter who you were or where you worked there was always someone to make your working life a misery. I had Alex, Jake had Kristie.

We walked down the path to the beach. When we reached the sand I stopped and took off my sandals. "Ffffudge!" I squealed as the hot sand immediately stung my feet and I sprinted over to the water's edge. Jake followed me grinning and slipped off his own shoes when he reached the wet sand.

I smiled sheepishly, feeling the water wash over my feet and the sand slip away. "I think this is as far in as I'll go today."

"Good thinking," he laughed. "I'll be happy if I never go that far out again myself."

"So..." I began as we started walking along the water side by side, "how do you manage all those surfing scenes if you have such a phobia of the water?"

"Oh, so you do watch the show then," he teased.

"I've seen a few episodes."

"A double does the surf scenes."

"Of course. D'uh."

"I tried learning, but I always wipe out and end head-first in the water. So, you'll see the close-ups are always of me going in or out of the water carrying the board but when you see me riding a wave, you never see my face, only the back. Well, the back of Chuck's head anyway."

"And, if you don't mind me asking, what happened to give you the phobia?"

"I nearly drowned as a kid. We were on a family vacation. I had wandered off into the water and got knocked over by a wave and caught in the wash. If Dad hadn't seen me and grabbed me... I've been afraid of getting too deep into the waves ever since."

"Wow." My mouth went dry. "I still can't believe you came in after me... You risked your own life..."

"I guess instinct kicked in. I didn't think. Though there was a moment when I thought neither of us was going to make it."

A chill came over me, "I'm so sorry. I'll never be able to repay you."

"Hey, no more of that okay?" He squeezed my arm. "You being here now, is all I could ever ask for."

I nodded, struggling to return his smile. I wasn't sure I would ever feel worthy of the sacrifice he came so close to making.

We walked along the shore in silence for a while, lost in our own thoughts, though it wasn't really the right kind of beach for reflecting on life. It was busy with beachgoers surfing, swimming, playing games and children making sandcastles. Bronzed bodies with bleached hair lounged on the sand tanning like lizards that had scuttled out from cracks to sit on rocks to soak up the heat. The breeze was heavy with the smell of salt and sunblock, and music from competing portable Bluetooth speakers clashed with the sound of sea gulls and waves breaking.

I felt uncomfortable in my long skirt and tight T-shirt, although even if I had been wearing a swimsuit I'd have still felt uncomfortable. I filled swimwear with bulges in all the wrong places and despite attempts at tanning remained pasty pale. And as for being graceful in the water, well at least I drowned with grace.

If Jake was aware of my conspicuousness, he was hiding it well. Jake, of course, oozed beach appeal.

"I'm feeling remarkably over-dressed," I sighed, noticing people staring at us.

"Don't worry. They're staring at me, not you."

"Gee thanks," I laughed.

"They're commenting on my questionable fashion choice," he

pinched his shirt cheekily, "and wondering who the lucky babe with Jake Donovan is."

"I'm hardly a babe. I—"

"Sure you are. You've just been around the wrong kind of men."

I stopped and turned to him, stunned.

"Men are asses. A pretty face and a short skirt and their Neanderthal brain kicks in. They have short attention spans and are easily distracted by empty play things and roller coaster rides. But when you're surrounded by all that every day, they start to lose their appeal. You start to develop a more refined taste... A woman who doesn't know how beautiful she is... a woman with standards... now that's sexy. A man can't seduce a woman who has no standards."

"So, you enjoy the conquest?" I asked confused.

"It's not the conquest, it's the feeling that you have discovered something rare and precious that others have missed, like a rock that is overlooked, but an enlightened person recognizes that if you tap it just right it'll break open to reveal glittering gems inside."

"And have you collected many gems?"

"Probably not as many as you think I have."

"You always seem to have a new flavor of the month."

Jake snorted, "most of the time it's just publicity. I can't be seen going to an event alone, so my manager arranges an escort."

I raised an eyebrow.

"Not that kind of escort. A date. Usually a model, or up-and-coming actress. Someone who needs to be seen to build their image."

"A stand-in," I said.

"Yeah, like a seat filler at the Oscars. It's all about appearances, good optics."

"But, why do you go along with it... all the needless rumors that must lead to? It's bad enough that your own co-star sets you up for fake stories."

"I figure, the more stories and rumors are out there, the more the media chase their own tails and keep occupied the better. It keeps them distracted from paying too much attention to what's actually going on in my life."

"I guess that makes sense."

"We play the press as much as they play us. We'll throw them red herrings to keep their heads spinning. A few years ago, I did a solid for Bryce—"

"Bryce?"

"Oh yeah, I forgot, you never watched the show. Bryce was my co-star on *The Blood Moon Prophecies*. He played my character's brother."

"Ah." I nodded.

"Anyway, we kissed, full-on mouth, tongue and everything, in front of a room full of press at a fundraiser. The press went wild for weeks digging for the big scoop that I was gay and in the meantime Bryce was left alone. The press already knew he was gay so no story there – and in that time he and his partner Anthony, were able to sneak off to the Bahamas and get married without anyone noticing."

"I remember that scandal, Alex was devastated."

"I'd do anything for that guy. Working that closely with someone for that long, you know... we're practically brothers in real life now."

"I bet that must build quite a bond."

"Yeah. And he's a great kisser." Jake winked.

We laughed and he leaned over and bumped his shoulder against mine then snatched my shoes from my hand. He dropped them on the dry sand along with his own then scooped me up into his arms and walked straight into the surf, carrying me above the waves spinning me around, threatening to drop me as waves lapped his legs.

I wrapped my arms round his neck tighter and playfully kicked my feet in the air, "Don't you dare!" I cried.

He pulled me up and dropped me to my feet so that I stood in the water in front of him, my skirt ballooning out around me as the air rushed in and then sank back down into the water.

He brushed the hair from my face, resting the palm of his hand against my cheek, "I wish you could see yourself right now," he whispered, studying me with his penetrating stare, "the sparkle in your eyes, the life in your smile." He brushed his thumb over my lips, "you don't know how beautiful you are." He wrapped his free arm round my waist and pulled me closer.

I could taste the salt in the air; smell his cologne, his sweat. I stood electrified, quivering, my breath shallow as we moved closer into an embrace. Our bodies pressed together, eyes locked, breathing each other in, our lips almost touching... I closed my eyes and surrendered.

His lips brushed mine; then he suddenly pulled back and swung me sideways. Bewildered, I saw a flash of neon pink as an errant Frisbee whizzed past my head and landed in the water next to us. Jake bent down and plucked it from the water, turned and flung it back to a group of kids on the beach. He gave them a friendly two-finger salute when they waved in acknowledgment. The waving turned to point excitedly when they recognized who had returned their Frisbee and was followed by more staring and questioning gestures as they looked at each other with who-is-*she* confusion.

I smiled at them feeling a wave of warmth wash over me. *Yes. It's him. And he's with me!*

"Come on," Jake said, breaking me from my reverie, "let's leave these posers." He slipped his hand in mine and we collected our shoes and walked back to the car.

I leaned against the Jeep, while Jake dug around in his pocket for the keys, and let out a huge yawn.

He raised an eyebrow and smirked at me as he unlocked the door. "Bored?"

"Oh God, I'm so sorry. It's the sea air." I gestured at the ocean.

"Sure." He laughed, holding the door open for me.

I hesitated. "Actually, I am starting to feel a bit tired. Would you mind if we called it a day?"

"Hey, not at all." He helped me in and fastened the temperamental seatbelt lock again, then sat back on his haunches, looking up at me concerned. "There's nothing else going on, right? We don't need to take you back to the hospital?"

"Just tired."

"You sure?"

I nodded. "I'm fine, I promise. It's just been a long day."

"Okay."

"You can drop me off at a bus stop, if you want to keep going. It is still early."

"No problem. We'll head back." He reached behind me and pulled a large beach towel from a duffel bag on the back seat. He folded it into a tight bundle and handed it to me, "for your head, in case you want to sleep."

I tucked it behind my head watching him walk round to the driver's side, and get in and start the engine. I closed my eyes when he reached for the gear shift and drifted off feeling his arm come up to rest behind me and the warmth of his breath on my shoulder as he turned round to back the Jeep out onto the road.

"Would you like the last spring roll?" Jake asked, offering me the box.

I held up my hand, "you go ahead. I'm stuffed."

We sat on the floor of Jake's private cabin, leaning against the couch, a selection of Chinese takeout boxes around us.

"Midnight snack, then." He folded the lid closed and set the box back down by his side.

"I'll take some more wine though," I said, holding out my glass.

He leaned over and taking the bottle from where it stood beside the couch leg, topped up my glass and his own, pouring out the last drop.

We clinked our glasses and let out a simultaneous mutual sigh of satisfaction as we sipped in unison.

"This was a good idea," Jake remarked.

"Definitely. I'm so glad you got us takeout. I just didn't have the energy for a restaurant."

"Yeah. I could tell. How are you feeling now?"

"Better. The nap helped. I guess it's going to be a while before I'm one hundred percent again."

"Yeah. You need to take it slow."

"Weren't you going to show me your photographs?" I teased, changing the subject. I didn't need reminding of my idiocy.

"That's right!" He remembered excitedly and jumped up, disappearing into his bedroom. He re-emerged carrying a laptop and sat down again next to me.

"Ooo, yes!" I emptied my glass and scooted closer to Jake while he opened the computer and logged in.

"So, these are all photos I've taken in the last few weeks while we've been in Hawaii. Hmm, let's see…" he scrolled through a series of shots that looked to be taken in the downtown area then opened a folder of boat-themed pictures. "I took these at the Ala Wai Boat Harbor. It's just north of Waikiki. We were shooting some scenes for episode eight. I took these early, while the crew were setting up." He clicked through a series of artistic images of rusty chains, the dawn light coating the water surface like a film of oil, barnacle-encrusted ropes, paint peeling off weather-beaten bollards.

"Ah, here we go," the photos changed to images of various crew members setting up various pieces of equipment – lights, scaffolding, rigs to hold cameras and microphones, and an assortment of tech gear that I couldn't identify. He stopped on a close-up of a guy with an AC/DC T-shirt and a baseball cap on the wrong way, mounting a tiny device to the wall above some dumpsters behind a utility building. "That's Travis setting a squib."

"Squib?" I asked.

"It's a small explosive charge like a firework which is used to create the illusion of a bullet striking an object. In this case, plaster flying off a wall."

"Ah. Though, a gun fight? I thought the show was set in a hospital."

"It is, in this scene though, Ethan is on his day off and gets caught up in the middle of a drug deal gone bad. And…" he clicked onto a selfie, a photo of himself with a bleeding shoulder wound and red, watering eye, "spoiler alert, Ethan gets shot."

I leaned in for a closer look, "What about your eye? That doesn't look fake."

"It isn't. A piece of the blood pack hit me in the eye when the squib fired."

"What?!" I turned to him shocked, "You mean those things are also triggered by little explosives?"

He nodded. "Yup, it's usually pretty safe. But, moron here

happened to have his head turned towards the thing at the wrong moment."

"Well, I'm glad you didn't lose an eye."

"So am I." He chuckled and clicked through some more photos of the shoot before opening a new folder.

"Oh, I recognize these. It's the lighthouse."

"That's it. I got some great shots out there the other morning. It was a fantastic sunrise." He scrolled through them slowly, each image becoming brighter and more colorful. "That was the same day we, as I, you. Sorry, I..." he tapped the forward button faster, animating the rising sun, "wow, I didn't realize I took so many."

"It's okay. It *was* a beautiful morning." I nudged my shoulder against his.

Jake clicked on, then stopped, "Hmm, where did I take that?" he mused as he stared at a photo of an unidentified beach with yellow sand and turquoise water framed by palm trees. He clicked on to the next photo which was of the same ocean, but had a woman wading in the water, walking towards the camera. She was looking down, sandals raised up in one hand and skimming the water with the other. She appeared to be showered in stars as the sunlight reflected off the water. She seemed strangely familiar. "Shit!" Jake screeched horrified, as he advanced through the photos, "I forgot these were on here."

"You were taking photos of me?"

"I'm so sorry. I'll delete them right now."

"No. Don't." I pulled his hand away as he headed for the delete button. "They're beautiful." I stared dumbfounded as I scrolled backwards through the images. "I've never seen myself like that before."

Jake smiled softly, "You reminded me of a Greek goddess in a renaissance painting pouring wine from a clay pitcher."

"No one's likened me to a goddess before," I whispered.

"Well, you deserve to be." He cocked his head to the side and smiled, holding me with his gaze. Static building, he shifted his weight towards me.

Feeling my hair stand on end and my breathing stall, I willed myself to lean in to meet him, eyes closed, lips pursed, but I froze.

His smile dropped and he turned away, sitting up, and snapped shut his laptop. "More wine!" He exclaimed, reaching over for the bottle.

"Didn't we finish it?" I mumbled, while mentally cursing myself for hesitating.

"Hmm. Yes, we did." He held the bottle upside down over his lap. He put it back and started gathering up the takeaway cartons. "Hang on. Fortune cookies." He handed me one. "Come on. Let's see what your future holds."

I broke it open and popped the cookie in my mouth as I read the slip of paper, and choked when I saw what was printed on it.

"Well?"

"Um, I... it..." I croaked.

"Come on, read it," he teased.

I cleared my throat and read it out loud, "'You will find the love of your life in front of you'. That's not awkward at all." I said, making a face.

"Let me see that," he frowned, taking the paper from me. "It couldn't have been scripted better." He laughed and put the paper on the table.

"Your turn."

He broke his cookie open and read the slip inside, "'Now is the time to make houses with soy sauce. Haste no more.' Huh?"

"Oh, that's much better," I laughed.

We smiled at each other, our eyes locking and the awkward silence descended again. I leaned in towards him, trying to recapture the moment, but he stood up and collected the empty cartons from the floor, and took them to the kitchen. I followed, bringing the empty wine bottle and glasses.

"Coffee?" He asked, stuffing the last carton into the rubbish bin.

"Sure." I nodded, I doubted I'd sleep anyway, and rinsed the wine glasses while he popped two capsules in the coffee machine.

I stood leaning my hip against the counter next to the sink as I continued to watch him... reaching for the mugs, adding the sugar, fetching the milk, and squeezing the corner of the carton to make a spout. All such pedestrian actions which should seem like the extraordinary in the hands of a superstar, yet with him they seemed so unexpectedly ordinary, so comfortingly familiar, so... normal.

"Here you go." He smiled and handed me my mug, turning it so that I could take it by the handle.

"Thanks." I took it with both hands, wrapping my fingers around the bowl and took a sip.

He leaned against the opposite counter and we sipped our coffee in silence watching each other. I wondered what he was thinking. Was he thinking or imagining? I was imagining dropping my mug in the sink and marching over to him, pushing him against the cabinets and slowly and deliberately undoing each and every one of the luscious buttons on his gaudy Hawaiian shirt, then kissing his chest and running my hands down his skin, to slip under his belt and pull his buckle... I caught a whiff of his intoxicating cologne and sucked in my lip, pressing my fingers tightly against the hot ceramic.

What was going through his head? Was he picturing striding over to me, taking the coffee mug from my hands and lifting me onto the counter; then pulling off my T-shirt and pushing up my skirt before ravishing me hungrily; his mouth against my skin, his hands on my bare back, unhooking my bra and pulling it free; feeling my thighs press up against his sides? I blushed and stared down into my mug. It was already empty, but I held it against my lips like a life buoy.

Jake held his mug above his waist, but hadn't taken a sip for some time either. Was his mug empty too? Tethering him to reality? Was he too, at risk of being swept away? Or was he simply wondering if he needed to get gas in the morning?

The light from a passing car flashed across the wall sending shadows racing towards the door, breaking the spell. Jake put down his mug and checked his watch.

The message was clear. I turned and quickly rinsed my mug and set it upside down on the draining board.

"I should go," I stammered. I looked around for a hand towel, avoiding Jake's gaze, and not seeing one, I wiped my hands on my skirt.

"You don't—" he started, but I didn't hear the rest as I darted for the living room. He followed me out and I continued, fetching my bag from the couch, "I've got to pack... got to leave for the airport early tomorrow."

"Are you sure?" he asked matter-of-factly, like a routine *are-you-sure-you-don't-want-fries-with-that* response.

"Yes, yes. It's time for me to go. I..." I stopped at the door, reaching for the handle and turned to him, side-on. "Thank you so much for everything. I've had a really wonderful time. I'll never forget what you—"

Jake reached past me and opened the door, "Can I walk with you? To the hotel?"

I nodded and turned away, unable to look at him, afraid my eyes would betray me.

He closed the door behind us and we headed up the track to the main hotel. The sun had set and the first stars were beginning to appear. Strings of twinkling fairy lights hung from the frangipani bushes lining the path and short pillar solar lights glowed, illuminating our way. Though there was a cool breeze my T-shirt still stuck to me within seconds of leaving the air conditioning of the cabin. The distant roar of the ocean and the buzzing of insects filled the quiet between us. We walked next to each other, facing ahead, our arms by our sides. I reached out with my fingers trying to find his. I hoped his fingers were doing the same, but I was too afraid to look down in case I'd see that they weren't.

"Well..." I croaked as we stopped in front of the main entrance. The automatic door slid open. "Thanks again for... You... it means so much..." I mumbled looking down at the ground. Jake said nothing and I felt unable to move. The door slid closed.

Jake smiled, frowned, and smiled again. The automatic door slid open again. "I'm just glad I could help. I..." he started as the door closed again. "I've really—" the door opened again.

I shifted my weight towards the door, but before I could commit to stepping over the threshold, Jake clutched my arm and pulled me away. He steered me towards a corner in the shadows and pushing me up against the wall pressed his lips on mine and kissed me. Hard. Urgently. His tongue sought out mine and once found pulled me into him.

With one hand pressed against the wall above my shoulder, his other hand sought out my leg and traveled along it, pulling my skirt up at the same time. My hands were on his back tugging at his shirt till at last they made contact with bare skin. Then slipping beneath the fabric my fingers dug in, pushing him closer to me so that I could feel his heat against my chest.

A roar of laughter startled us and we stopped dead, holding our breath and each other, as a loud group of men exited through the automatic door and headed down to the beach.

We parted slightly and holding my shoulders, Jake rested his head against my forehead. "Stay. Please stay," he whispered, "don't go back. Not yet."

"Okay." I breathed hoarsely. "Yes. I'll—"

He pressed his hands to my face and kissed me gently, lightly tugging at my lip as he slowly pulled away.

"I'll call you in the morning." He said beaming in the half-light, then turned and disappeared into the night.

I stood leaning against the wall for a moment, collecting myself. I'd wake up soon because this had to be a dream.

Chapter 17

$\mathcal{I}$ didn't sleep much. I kept replaying the events of the last few days, over and over, fast-forwarding through the awkward bits and pausing, rewinding, and playing in slow motion the good bits. The fantastic, amazing bits. He kissed me. *Jake Donovan kissed ME!* My brain finally shut down at around three in the morning. I then overslept and had to shower and dress in a hurried panic to meet Jake at eight.

After a light breakfast at the hotel restaurant, we set out in the Jeep for a new day of sightseeing. We left the coast at Pearl Harbor and then went north through the middle of the island along the Interstate, past the Wheeler Army Airfield and on into forests and tropical orchards. On our way, we visited the Dole Plantation where we learned about pineapple farming and left armed with a selection of dried pineapple snacks, pineapple candies, sauces and salsas, and more fresh pineapples than two people could ever need on such a short trip.

Around late morning, we reached the coast and stopped in the small town of Haleiwa for shaved ice to cool off. According to the guidebooks and travel bloggers, 'no visit to O'ahu is complete without a visit to the North Shore's famous Matsumoto's Shave Ice shop'. I had to agree. The small family business was established in 1951 and had been operating in the same corner store by the same family ever since. Its long history and reputation as the best shaved ice in Hawaii had made it a tourist attraction and the items that had stocked the shelves of this once-grocery store were now replaced with the usual assortment of souvenirs, postcards, candy, sodas, snack foods, and T-shirts and bags printed with the Matsumoto logo.

"Aw," said Jake while we casually browsed the aisles, "no coconut bras."

"Very funny." I laughed, elbowing him in the ribs as we headed for the shaved ice counter.

There was already a steady queue of people, despite it being a Monday, and although it meant waiting some time, it also meant that the other customers were more focused on making it to the head of the queue than on noticing that the man next to me in sunglasses and baseball cap looked familiar.

"What do you feel in the mood for?" asked Jake as we inched closer to the counter.

"I don't know. There are so many," I said mulling over the flavors listed on the board above our heads, "definitely not—"

"Pineapple," Jake said at the same time as me.

We laughed and moved another step forward. Behind the row of serving staff were several large machines that looked like drill presses. Each held a large block of ice at the base of a rotating arm. A blade pressed against the spinning ice shaved off flakes into a drum. These were then scooped up by hand and shaped into a ball on top of a cone or bowl and then drizzled with flavored syrup. Extras such as vanilla ice cream, condensed milk, sugared azuki beans and mochi balls added the Hawaiian and Japanese take on the familiar fairground snow cone.

Placing our order received several looks of recognition from the staff but they were simply too busy to follow through with the usual remarks of surprise and requests for selfies, much to Jake's relief. We took our syrupy concoctions outside and found a bench under a tree to enjoy them. We shared a side of coconut mochi balls and swapped spoonfuls of the sweet icy slush to taste each other's flavor combinations, talking and eating too fast, and smacking our foreheads in unison when the brain freeze hit, yelping and giggling like a couple of kids on summer vacation hyped up on sugar.

After we recovered from the brain freeze we decided to walk to work off the sugar rush and explore more of the historic town on foot before heading to lunch at a small pizzeria tucked between a laundromat and a pharmacy in a strip mall across from the beach.

"I've heard this is the best place for pizza on the North Shore," Jake said as he held the door open for me.

A young strapping Hawaiian man greeted us at the door, his eyes widening, "Hey, you're that actor," he said awestruck, pointing at Jake.

Jake nodded.

"Sweet. I'm Makoa." He extended his hand and met Jake's in a casual slap-fist-bump handshake.

"If we could have a table somewhere private…" Jake started.

"Sure, no worries." He escorted us to a booth tucked in the corner at the back of the restaurant and handed us two menus in laminated plastic, then left us to decide.

We settled in, sitting next to each other on the same bench seat on one side of the booth. Jake handed me his camera bag and I put it beside me along with my bag up against the wall. I brushed some crumbs from the red and white checker tablecloth and reached for a menu, and we sat for a while mulling over the assortment of pizzas and other dishes listed.

"How is it that there's no Hawaiian pizza in Hawaii?" I quipped.

Jake laughed, "That's the first thing we discovered when we started shooting here. It's not a Hawaiian thing." He replied just as our waiter returned to our table, "Isn't that so, Makoa?"

"Yeah, bruh. They say some dude in Canada invented it. We do make a pineapple and ham pizza if you want it. It's called 'The Mainlander'," he pointed to an item halfway down the menu.

"What would you recommend?" I asked.

"'The Luau'. Kālua pork – that's slow-cooked pork, luau-style – red peppers and Hawaiian barbecue sauce."

"Is there a vegetarian version?" asked Jake.

He sighed, "Roasted vegetables instead of pork?"

Jake turned to me and I nodded. "Perfect. We'll have that and a pitcher of iced tea."

Makoa took our menus and headed for the kitchen leaving us to an awkward silence. I could feel Jake's heat, we were sat so close we were almost touching. I wanted to stretch out my leg under the table and rest it against him like I had done in the hospital but I suddenly felt shy, like it might be too obvious of a move, especially in such a public setting. And Jake seemed preoccupied. He was staring towards the door people watching, lost in thought. Instead, I played with the edge of the tablecloth to keep my hands from wandering.

The food arrived quickly and I served out a few slices of the pizza onto our plates, while Jake poured the iced tea.

"Cheers," he said handing me a glass.

"Cheers." I clinked my glass against his, took a long sip and then dug into the pizza. "Wow, that's good pizza."

"Uh huh," Jake nodded, grinning, his mouth full.

I started on my second piece, maneuvering it carefully to avoid dislodging a chunk of roast pumpkin that was poised precariously on the tip.

"What?" I noticed Jake watching me.

"Nothing."

"Oh... You're waiting to see if I'll drop some down my front, aren't you?"

"Hey, just keeping an eye on you. You know... in case you need assistance." He winked, "Your blouse is quite billowy. I wouldn't want you to get your hand tangled in it."

"Ah, I see. How very noble of you."

He pressed his hand to his chest, "Upon my honor, I am your humble servant."

"Eat your pizza, will you," I laughed and nudged him with my shoulder.

He nudged me back, resting his shoulder against mine, and shifted in his seat so that our thighs were now touching. We ate and laughed, and wiped barbecue sauce from each other's lips and for a while the outside world faded away and we were two ordinary people sitting in an ordinary restaurant losing ourselves in the first flush of love.

"Oh my God, I love you!"

Our bubble burst and we looked up to see a girl in her late teens standing beside our table. She wore tight cut-off jean shorts with frayed hem and a loose off-the-shoulder crop top that revealed the top of a bright pink bra and exposed her midriff.

"Hi." Jake raised a hand in acknowledgment and strained a smile. "It's nice to meet you, but if you don't—"

She turned towards the main restaurant and yelled, "Ally! It's Jake fucking Donovan, get over here and bring my phone!"

Jake closed his eyes and sank back into the booth leaning his head against the wall, the life draining from him.

A younger girl, similarly dressed rushed over and handed a bedazzled phone to the older girl while pointing her own at Jake. "No fucking way!"

They stood in front of Jake's end of the bench seat effectively trapping us in. Jake looked away, holding his hand to his temple to shield his face.

"Girls," I said, "do you mind, we're trying to have a private lunch." I looked around for someone to help.

"What?" the younger leered at me and popped a gum bubble.

Jake turned to me, "it's okay," he sighed, his face ashen. His eyes were grey and sunken, like a cornered animal that's lost its fight. "You want pictures, right?" he addressed the girls and stood up.

"Fuck yeah!" they squealed and immediately planted themselves on either side of Jake once he stepped out of the booth. They fired off a series of primping and pouting selfies, posing with Jake as if he were little more than a gimmicky prop.

It made me sick.

Once they got bored and their attention shifted to reviewing their haul, Jake sat down again. We said nothing, waiting for them to move on. But, without looking up from their phones they slid into the seat opposite us.

I let out an audible groan and glared at them, but it went over their heads.

"So, who are you?" The older girl grunted at me.

"None of your business." I hissed back.

"Rude!" She made a face and helped herself to the last piece of our pizza.

"She's trying to steal him away from Kristie!" the younger girl mocked.

"As if," the older snorted, her mouth full.

Jake leaned over and whispered in my ear. I nodded and gathered our bags from beside me and followed him as he got up and left the booth.

"Ow!" the younger shrieked, "you stood on my foot!"

"That's my sister, bitch!" the older teen screamed, "Look where you're going!"

"I'm sorry, it was an accident." I cried, trying to apologize.

Jake took me by the arm, "Let's just go."

We turned towards the door when a heavyset bearded man wearing a stained singlet blocked our way.

"What's wrong baby?" he belched with breath that stank of alcohol and cigarettes.

"Dad! That bitch kicked Ally."

"I stumbled, that's all."

"It was an accident and we just want to be on our way now." Jake tried to pass him, but the man pushed in front of him.

"What, can't you spare any time for your fans?" he hissed, spittle raining down on his beard.

"They got their selfies!" I cried.

The man grunted, "He should be more grateful."

"Grateful?" I gasped. "For their rudeness? You could do with teaching your daughters some manners, please and thank you, would be a start. And why not clean up their language while you're at it."

"Lady, you need to show some respect!" he glared at me with intoxicated eyes.

"Respect?" I was on a roll now, "how about you lot respect his privacy."

A hush had descended over the restaurant and all eyes were on us.

"Look, we just wanted a quiet lunch," Jake edged in front of a large pillar blocking the audience's view of him.

"Yeah, so? My girls weren't doing any harm, you selfish prick!" The man shoved Jake on the shoulder with such force that Jake fell back and hit his head.

"Get your hands off him!" I screamed and rushed over to Jake. He rested against the pillar dazed, holding a hand to his head.

Makoa rushed over and grabbed the man by the shoulders, "That's enough, man!" he shouted as he pulled him aside and a tall smartly-dressed man in his fifties, carrying a cordless phone, joined the fray.

"I'm the manager. Is there a problem here?" he asked.

"Yes." I declared. "You can call the police. That man assaulted my... Mr. Donovan."

"The bitch is lying! I never laid a hand on him. He tripped. We're just having a friendly conversation."

"Yeah, sure," Jake mumbled, still rubbing his head.

The manager held up the phone, poised to dial, "I'll call if you want me to, Mr. Donovan?"

Jake shook his head, "That won't be necessary."

"But, he..." I started.

Jake turned to me and whispered, "It's not worth it."

"Okay. If you're sure?"

Jake nodded.

"Okay, well then. Show's over folks," he announced to the curious onlookers and then turned to the man and his daughters, "as for you three, you're no longer welcome in this establishment. Please leave."

The man continued to yell abuse, with his daughters cheering him on and whining about being unfairly treated while Makoa wrestled him towards the door.

"I'm really sorry about that, Mr. Donovan," apologized the manager.

"Hey, it's not your fault."

"Still, can we get you something else? On the house?"

I slipped my arm through Jake's, "That's kind of you, but I think we'll be on our way."

Jake nodded. "Perhaps, if we could leave through your back exit."

"Of course. Right this way." He led us through the kitchen and out into the alley way. "Again, I'm really sorry."

"Don't sweat it, man." Jake sighed and shook his hand.

We thanked him for his help and then made our way past the dumpsters and crates of empty bottles back to the front of the strip mall. After making sure the obnoxious trio wasn't waiting to ambush us, we darted across the street to an empty picnic table by the beach under some palm trees. I dumped the bags on the table and sat Jake down on the bench while I stood next to him and took a closer look at his head.

"I get so sick of this bullshit!" He slammed his fist against the table. "Sorry."

"That's all right. I can't believe people think they can treat you like that." I ran my hands over his head and smoothed his hair, "Looks okay. Just a bit of a warm spot. You'll probably have a small bump."

"Thanks." He touched his head. "It comes with the job. I'm public property."

"That doesn't make it right." I sat down next to him and rested my hand on his knee and squeezed it. "I'm sorry I shot my mouth off like that," I said, "I probably didn't help the situation."

"That's okay, you didn't say anything I wasn't thinking myself," he exhaled heavily. "I just can't engage, can't afford to lose it. It only makes things worse."

"I get it."

He turned to me, his eyes red, "But, it gets so hard, you know… to hold back."

I nodded and wrapped my arms around him drawing him into a tight hug. He rested his head on my shoulder and we held each other for what felt like several minutes while the world around us dissolved and all we could hear was our breath, the sound of distant waves and the call of sea gulls overhead.

He pulled away and wiped his eyes. "I don't think I can handle any more people today."

"Me neither."

"There's a Buddhist temple and garden on the way back, what do you think?"

"Sounds perfect."

We gathered up our things and headed back to the car.

Chapter 18

Jake pulled out his camera as we stepped onto the long footbridge that led from the parking area down into a beautifully landscaped garden over a grassy expanse. The sight of the Japanese pagoda-style building looming in the distance took my breath away and I stopped for a moment to take it in while Jake leaned against the railing and fired off a few shots. Set against the lush backdrop of tall pine trees and the Ko'olau Mountains the bright red beams, gold and white cornice detailing and grey slate tile roof of the Byodo-In Buddhist temple stood out with a brilliance that inspired reverence. A large reflecting pond stocked with hundreds of koi fish and black swans gliding across the surface surrounded the building, and perfectly-cut topiaries and stone statues decorated the edge.

"It's stunning," I murmured.

"I thought you'd like it," he shouldered the camera and slipped his hand in mine, "I've been here a few times now and it moves me every time."

"It's so tranquil, so soothing."

He squeezed my hand, "Yup. That's why I love it."

We spent an hour enjoying the quiet of the garden, the silence broken only by the buzzing of insects, waterfalls, peacock calls, our footsteps crunching on the gravel foot paths and the occasional low gong-like ringing of the meditation bell.

It was early afternoon, but the sun was already on the other side of the mountain casting long shadows over the garden. Jake was absorbed in his photography and I was absorbed in watching him. With each photo he took, the more freed of the burden of Jake Donovan, public personality, he became and the more restored to Jake Donovan, regular guy. I would find myself walking ahead of him and then turn to see where he'd got to and he'd be crouched down taking a photo of an overlooked flower or a hidden frog or pointing the camera at me waiting to catch me looking for him. At other times he'd get me to pose for him, leaning over the railing on a footbridge to toss a leaf into a stream, holding a flower to my nose, or standing with my back against a column of a garden pagoda, hands behind me, looking into the distance while a peacock paraded at my feet.

The tour of the garden brought us back to the temple and after taking a few more photos, Jake packed away his camera. We went up to the meditation bell and together drew back the large wooden log suspended on a rope and released it so that it swung and struck the huge bell sending out another low knell across the garden. We then took off our shoes and left them at the temple entrance. Jake's expensive leather ankle boots stood out amongst the assortment of well-traveled sandals, sneakers and flip-flops.

The interior was dimly lit and heavy with the smell of incense. A large statue of a Buddha seated on a lotus flower stood in the middle of the space. There was a small altar in front of it that held candles and large vases of purple orchids and red Hawaiian ginger flower spikes. The sacred statue and altar were closed off by a low wall topped with a red-painted wooden railing. There were people seated on benches praying and chanting meditations while other visitors talked in hushed voices and took discreet photos. Jake walked over to read an information placard on the wall and I went up to the Buddha to pay homage. In front of the gate to the closed-off area was a table with a box of short incense sticks, a red-framed glass lantern holding a candle and a large earthenware bowl filled with sand. I took a stick of incense from the box and held it between my fingers, pressing my hands together; I touched my thumbs to my nose and closed my eyes for a moment in silent prayer. Then carefully unlatching the glass door of the lantern, I held the stick to the candle flame to ignite it. I then closed the lantern door, blew out the incense flame and watched the smoke curl. "I miss you," I murmured as I pushed the stick into the sand and breathed in the jasmine fragrance.

"You okay?" whispered Jake.

"Oh hi, yes," I turned to him and he slipped his arm around my waist, "just remembering a close friend I lost a long time ago and thinking about how near I came to seeing her again."

He kissed my forehead and pulled me closer. I rested my head on his shoulder and we stood for some time watching the smoke drift heavenward while I thought of her, a best friend, my kindred spirit whom I had lost tragically in an accident when we were still in high school. *Until we meet again.*

"How about I cook us dinner?" asked Jake, as he turned the car and pulled into the parking lot of the Waimanalo Beach mini-mart.

"You cook?"

"Don't sound so surprised."

"I just imagined you'd live on take-out or have your own personal chef."

"Gees, I'm not that famous," he laughed, cutting the engine and releasing his seatbelt. "I'll just get a few things. Do you like pasta?"

"I do."

He slipped on his baseball cap and despite the heat pulled on a hoodie from the back seat.

"Would you like me to go for you?"

"That's okay, I'll be fine." He drew the hood over the cap and took his wallet from the glove compartment.

"Well, I'll come with you then." I grabbed my bag and climbed out of the Jeep before he could protest.

We were hit by a welcome blast of cool air after the automatic doors slid open and ushered us inside. Jake handed me a shopping basket and we headed to the produce aisle. He selected some fresh herbs and vegetables and popped them in the basket, before moving on to the cheese counter. I stood beside him holding the basket while he bent over the chiller and selected an appropriate ball of Mozzarella. I noticed a young woman with sun-bleached hair dressed in a beach dress staring at us. Jake hadn't seen her, but I could see that she was figuring it out.

"Hey, you're Jake Donovan!" she rushed over, pointing at him.

Jake stiffened and I jumped in front of him, blocking her view, "Him?" I snorted, laughing loudly, "no, that's my cousin, Pierre. He's visiting from Montreal, *n'est pas*?" I turned to Jake.

"*Oui, oui,*" he nodded.

She studied him clearly confused, "but... he looks just like Jake Donovan."

"I know, right?" I rolled my eyes, "He gets that *all* the time."

She frowned and tilted her head, about to say something more.

"He doesn't speak a lot of English."

"*Oui, oui.*"

"Oh, well, I hope your cousin enjoys his visit," she grumbled and marched off.

"Great improv," said Jake after she was out of earshot.

I smiled, "Thanks. You must be rubbing off on me."

"Not as much as I'd like." He grinned wickedly and tossed a packet of Mozzarella in the basket before turning for the frozen foods aisle.

I coughed, feeling the familiar flush of heat flood my cheeks as I stumbled and followed after him. We selected some ice cream for dessert and picked up a few other sundries before making our way to the checkout. We joined a queue, standing next to racks of those damned magazines with Jake and Kristie on the covers. It wasn't long before we received a few second glances and people started to stare and whisper. I stood close to Jake, my shoulder against his, leaning in towards him to shield him as best I could. He put his arm around my waist, drawing me closer and pressed his lips to my temple in the softest of kisses then rested his head against my shoulder, burying his face in the crook of my neck. Over the top of his head, I could see the woman with the sun-bleached hair in the next aisle over watching us. She was obviously not buying the cousin story anymore. I shrugged my shoulders at her apologetically as we moved up to the counter and set down our basket. Without looking up the sullen teenager on the checkout took the basket and, as slowly as humanly possible, passed each item over the scanner before placing it in a paper bag.

"Do you want a separate bag for the cold stuff?" He asked, letting out a bored sigh.

"No, no. One bag's fine. We're not going far." I blurted. *Just hurry up!* Jake's hand had moved downwards and was resting on my behind, his breath hot and wet against my neck, and I was pretty sure he had run his tongue along my skin. An involuntary moan escaped from my mouth and I bit my lip.

"That'll be sixty-five dollars and fifteen cents." The teen said at last.

Jake straightened and pulling his wallet from his back pocket handed the boy a hundred-dollar bill, "Keep the change."

"Whoa, thanks man!" The young man looked up, his moody air of resentment and teen angst instantly replaced with a look of awe and dawning recognition, "Hey, aren't you—"

Jake took the bag from the counter and slipping his hand in mine, we made a hasty exit.

Back at Jake's cabin, I offered to help, but he insisted I sit and relax, so we poured some wine and I perched on a bar stool at the kitchen counter and sipped it while I watched him work. I savored every moment, each mundane task – chopping the herbs, flicking the pan to toss the vegetables, adding the dry pasta to the boiling water – transformed into a sensual act by the contours of his chest and arms that his fitted T-shirt accentuated. The steam rising from the stovetop caused that errant curl of his to slip forward and hang above his eyebrow, and beads of sweat to form on his brow. He wiped his forehead and slung the kitchen towel over his shoulder, and caught me drooling from the corner of his eye. "Hungry?" He asked, draining the pasta.

"Very." I croaked, sucking in my lip.

He set the pasta aside and brought a spoonful of sauce over to me to taste, "what do you think?"

I licked the spoon while he held it to my lips, his eyes locked on mine. "Oh, yum!" I exclaimed, heat coursed through my body and it wasn't from the small amount of chili he had added to the sauce.

"Then, let's eat," he grinned and served up two plates.

We ate at the kitchen counter, sitting next to each other, our legs touching. We didn't say much, all that needed saying had been said and the small talk had dried up. Like my mouth. The pasta was tasty, but I was struggling to eat. I had a knot in my stomach and every nerve ending felt tense, primed. Jake reached for the salt, and as his arm brushed mine my hair stood on end charged with static. The weather was changing, a storm was coming.

Jake was done ahead of me and rinsed his plate while I finished up. "Hmm, we need to do something with all this pineapple," he remarked, taking one from the counter, "grilled pineapple for dessert?"

"Perfect," I said, scooping up my last mouthful of pasta, "and compliments to the chef. It was so good I had to eat it slowly."

"Any time." He smiled and cut a few slices, then coated them in brown sugar before dropping them onto a hot griddle pan.

I cleared away the plates, loading them into the dishwasher beside him, 'accidentally' bumping my shoulder against his and when I reached to fetch some bowls from the shelf I 'accidentally' brushed my hand across his back. He took the pan off the heat and came over to the counter, set it down on a trivet and reached past me for a serving spoon, 'accidentally' grazing his arm against the small of my back. The air was humid and the wind had picked up.

"Looks like it might rain," Jake mused, peering out the window on his way back from the refrigerator.

"Lovely. There's nothing like the sound and smell of rain, don't you think?" I took the ice cream tub from him and spooned a dollop into each bowl and handed the tub back to him.

"Absolutely." He popped the tub back into the freezer.

I handed him a bowl and spoon, and we took our dessert through to the living room and settled down on the couch. We both stretched out and put our feet up on the coffee table and ate in contented silence.

"That was delicious, but I don't think I want to see another pineapple for months." I laughed and reached over to put my empty bowl on the coffee table. I felt Jake watching me and turned to face him.

"Thank you." He whispered.

"What for? You cooked."

"You know..."

"Oh. I... you don't..." I mumbled and looked away.

He shifted closer to me and lifting my chin with his hand, turned my face towards him and kissed me. Softly, tenderly, like a gentle wave washing over my feet, and then as the wave receded, the sand falling away under my toes pulling me in, he moved closer again. He leaned over me, pushing me back against the couch and kissed me more urgently, slipping his arm under my waist. Then he moved back and I followed, wrapping my arms around his neck, and with his other arm cradling my legs he scooped me from the couch and carried me through to the bedroom.

He lay me down on the bed, the moonlight cast rippled shadows over a calm sea of sheets and he knelt over me, his eyes locked on mine. I grabbed hold of his shirt, clinging to it like a life buoy, as he continued to kiss me, the waves knocking me down, pushing me under. Then sitting up, I surfaced, gasped for air, the life buoy lost to the current, I ran my hands over his skin. Plunging below, my hands found his belt and I grappled with the buckle while he nibbled my neck. The rigging straining in the gale, I struggled with his zipper. At last, the anchor cut loose, released, he lurched forward and seizing hold of my blouse he whipped it off, flinging it aside, a flapping sail ripped free by the storm. Time running out, he wrestled with my shorts, hauling them from my body, and threw them overboard. But, it was futile, we were going down. In a last desperate attempt to stay afloat, underwear was torn off, the remaining weight jettisoned. Our fate sealed, succumbing, we sank into the sheets.

Submerged, beneath cotton waves, our naked bodies entwined, we held onto each other, thrashing and writhing, moaning and gasping in unison towards an inescapable end. And then a collapse, a release of held breath, a final twitching, and then stillness. The storm passed. The wind dropped. A distant dying rumble.

The sea calm once more, gentle waves lapped against two islands of skin, caressed the shore, washed over the curve of a back and down the valley of an outstretched leg. With salt on our lips, hair damped down and skin moist with droplets of sweat that sparkled in the moonlight, he traced a finger over my shoulder like a piece of driftwood being dragged across the sand.

Chapter 19

Thin shafts of sunlight filtering through the Venetian blind poked at my eyelids and I opened my eyes. The floor was strewn with clothes, debris from the storm; the crisp cotton sheet cool against my naked skin, like a soft sea breeze. I rolled over onto my side, tucking my hands under the pillow and watched Jake sleep. He was lying on his back, the sheet pulled up to his waist, a soft snore blowing from his lips.

I reached over and ran a finger over his chest, tracing every contour from his shoulder downwards.

He stirred and turned to look at me with those dreamy blue eyes. "Morning, you," he yawned with a cat-ate-a-bird-satisfied grin, "Sleep well?"

"Terribly. Someone kept me awake all night." I smiled, tracing idle circles around his navel.

"Ha!" He laughed, "And, what would you like to do today?"

"Apart from this?" I leaned over and kissed his chest. "There's a whole lot more exploring I'd like to do right here."

"I think that can be arranged," he purred and rolling over, climbed on top of me. He pulled the sheet over us and, attacking my belly, ravaged me all over again.

When I woke again, Jake was gone. I sat up, drawing the sheet around me and heard the shower turn on. Twisting the sheet between my fingers, I bit my lip, picturing him naked, surrounded by swirling steam, water rushing over his skin. I slipped out of bed, pulling the sheet with me, and tip-toed to the bathroom and carefully opened the door.

He was standing in the shower, his back to me, soaping his arms. I walked over, dropped the sheet, and stepped in behind him. I ran my hands over his shoulders and he turned to me, water rushing over his face and down his chest. He wiped the water from his face, smoothing his hair back and I bent forward and kissed his shoulders, then his chest, running my lips and tongue over every toned muscle, drinking him in. His stance weakened and he fell back against the shower wall.

I didn't think about all the women who had come before me or the ones who would follow. Right now, in this moment, he was mine; groaning and begging for *my* touch, powerless in *my* hands. I paused and he looked at me with an expression of surprise and aching need, as if it was rare for him to be made love to. He ran his hands down my neck, along my shoulders and pulled me to him then swung me round so I was pressed up against the shower wall, his lips sought out mine, and once connected we sank into each other, fingers digging into flesh pulling the other closer, threatening to break the skin, our heated breath and moans rising with the steam to a crescendo that threatened to topple us. And then subsided and we were left in a soft embrace, kissing tenderly under a warm rain.

Jake closed off the tap and we left the shower. I turned to reach for a towel and caught myself in the mirror. Usually, I'd look away, too self-conscious of all my bulges and blemishes, but this time I stopped and stared, as if I was seeing myself for the first time. Jake came up behind me and nestling his chin on my shoulder slipped one arm round me over my breasts and the other around my waist, sliding his hand downwards, making me quiver.

"You're so beautiful," he whispered, watching me in the mirror, and we held each other for a while, staring at our reflection. Then he kissed me softly on the temple and handed me a towel before reaching for one for himself. He wrapped it around his waist and padded through to the bedroom and then returned wearing a bathrobe and carrying a second one. He held it up for me to slip into.

"Hungry?" he asked as I knotted the tie.

"Ravenous."

"Oh, I know. I meant for food." He winked.

I swatted him on the backside and we shuffled through to the kitchen. Jake toasted some bread and I made two coffees and we took them outside to the private patio that adjoined the bedroom through a large sliding door. There was a small plunge pool in the middle and we set down the food on the paving between us and sat on the edge with our feet dangling in the water. We ate quietly, lost in our own thoughts. My mind was full of questions.

"How is it you're still single?" I asked, breaking the silence.

"Oh, you know..." Jake sighed, hesitating, "It's the world I'm in. It's not conducive to long-term relationships."

"I get that, but you have so much to give, any woman would be lucky to have you."

"You give me too much credit. I'm bad news."

I frowned. "I don't believe that."

"Well, you should." He looked down at the water, "there was someone once... we–" He let out a heavy sigh, "It's all over the Internet, I'll let you Google the sordid details."

There was a vulnerability to him, just below the surface, a thin layer of ice that would crack if mishandled or melt in the right hands.

"She hurt you..." I offered, reaching out for him to share his burden with me.

"It's just the way it is. The life."

"But you love it, don't you?"

"What do you mean?

"The work, the fans, the fame."

"I used to. These days, not so much. I still enjoy the work, but the studio politics get me down and well, you've seen what the public life is like. Sometimes I wish I could just go back to having a normal life."

"Can't you?"

"Not without breaking my contract and that's something you don't want to do in my business. Not if you want to get work in the future."

"Ugh, contracts, I know. I work for attorneys." I sighed sympathetically. "What would you do instead, if you could?"

"Shorter projects, movies. Roles with more complex characters; more depth. I'd like to start my own production company and make movies written by obscure unknown writers, like Catherine Marshall," he nudged his shoulder against mine, "and spend a lot more time at my ranch."

"You have a ranch?"

"Yeah, a big chunk of land outside of Santa Clarita, several horses, some I ride, others are rescues living out their retirement. The land is good for grapes. I thought I might plant some vines; make a boutique wine."

"That sounds wonderful."

"Yeah, well," he sighed, "it's just a dream." He stood up, drawing his bathrobe tighter, "I've got a few things I need to do – I'll meet you in the lobby at five-thirty for dinner?" He gathered the coffee mugs and plates and headed inside.

"Sure, okay." I scrambled to my feet and followed after him, grabbing a towel from the dresser to dry my feet. I dressed quickly and went through to the living room to fetch my bag. Jake sat on a bar stool at the kitchen counter, looking something up on his laptop.

"Well, I'll be going then," I announced, walking over to him.

Looking up, he quickly closed his laptop, then got up and walked me to the door. He pulled me into a tight embrace and kissed me hard before letting me out the door and I floated back to my room like a freed helium balloon.

The sun was beginning to sink toward the horizon by the time I went downstairs to meet Jake. He was already waiting for me in the lobby when I left the elevator. Again the sight of him made my heart jump. He was dressed in black jeans and the shirt I bought him, and he flashed me that steamy smile as he walked over to me. I ran a self-conscious hand over my drab summer dress, trying to smooth out imagined creases.

"You look amazing," he said, bending forward and kissing me on the cheek.

"Hello, Thomas." I teased, "You're wearing the Magnum shirt *again?*"

He grinned, "It's perfect for where we're going to dinner."

"Okay? And where is dinner?"

"You'll see." He slipped his hand in mine and we walked out to the courtyard.

"Are we walking?" I asked, not seeing the Jeep. "I might need to change my shoes—"

"Nope." He pulled me by the hand towards a bright red convertible parked near the fountain.

"A Ferrari?" I gasped, "I thought you didn't have—"

"I hired it for the night." He leaned over and opened the door for me.

"No way." I shook my head.

"Take care getting in, the seat's pretty low."

I gingerly put one foot in and pressed one hand on the seat and held onto Jake with the other as I slowly lowered myself in. The seat wasn't where I expected it to be and I kept going and partly fell, partly slid into the chair.

"Thanks for the warning," I laughed and pulled myself up the smooth leather seat. Even properly situated, I felt like I was only a few inches from the ground and the windows and windshield seemed higher than in other cars.

"Not bad for a newbie," he winked, closing the door, and walked round the driver's side. He climbed in with his usual grace and sex appeal.

"So, where are we going?" I asked as I reached for the seatbelt. The latch locked in place without any effort.

"Ka'ula Bay, it's just over an hour from here." Jake put on his seatbelt and then gripped the steering wheel with both hands, grinning like a boy with a new toy, "Though, in this baby we can be there in half the time."

"Umm, you're not going to—"

"Don't worry. I'll behave." Then, under his breath, he added, "sort of." He pressed a red button on the steering wheel and the engine roared to life. "Oooh man, listen to that sound!"

"Should I leave you two alone?" I teased.

Jake laughed, "Well, I was kinda hoping for a three-way – you, me and the car?"

I slapped him playfully on the shoulder, "so much for behaving!"

Jake backed the car out of the parking lot and with only the lightest touch of the gas pedal, we launched up the hill with a surge of power that made me cry out. He turned to me grinning, "You've never been in a sports car before have you?"

"No," I laughed, "it's like being on a rollercoaster." I lifted my arms above my head, waving my hands in the air and yelled, "Woohoo!" much to Jake's amusement.

Within minutes we were on the freeway heading towards Honolulu. Jake sank back in his seat, flipped on the cruise control, and casually held the steering wheel with one hand, reached over and rested his other hand on my thigh. I turned to him and he smiled. A comforting, familiar smile. I sat back in the seat, resting my head against the headrest and stared up at the sky turning pink with the setting sun and felt the warm air rushing over my head. Somehow, despite how crazy all this was, it felt like the most natural thing in the world – comfortable, safe. It was as if we had known each other for years and had gone on this drive, in this car a hundred times before.

Chapter 20

It had just turned dark when we pulled into the parking grounds of Ka'ula Bay Luau.

"A luau," I noted, reading the large welcome sign, "now I get the shirt choice."

"When in Hawaii..." Jake parked the car and turned off the engine. He then pressed another button and with a whirring of mechanics, a flap on the trunk opened exposing a panel that unfolded and slid into position over the roof, and then the trunk flap closed.

"Ah, so that's how it works."

"Pretty neat, huh?"

I nodded and reached for the door handle.

"Let me." Jake jumped out, jogged round and opened my door and offered me his arm.

"Thanks," I said, taking his arm and pulling myself up, "they need to add ejector seats for us unsophisticated types." I slung my bag over my shoulder and Jake rested his hand on my back and we walked towards the entrance.

I stopped and turned to him, "Don't you need to lock it or something?"

"It's all keyless," he pulled out a metal badge from his pocket, which had the Ferrari emblem on it, "there's a chip in this. That's all you need."

I shook my head in wonder and slipped my arm around his waist, and we continued toward the entrance.

Men and women dressed in traditional colorful floral dresses, grass skirts and garlands of glossy green leaves presented us with leis made of purple orchids and ushered us along a path lit with bamboo torches to a small open-air amphitheater. We found a place near the back and sat down. I leaned against Jake with my head on his shoulder and he rested his hand on my thigh. I placed my hand on his and we interlaced our fingers, and we listened to the sound of the ocean in the distance while more guests continued to arrive and took their seats around us. No one recognized Jake in the dim light and for a while we blended in again, an ordinary couple on an ordinary holiday outing.

Once the last guests were seated, the show started – an hour-long display of hula dancing, fire juggling, Hawaiian songs accompanied by ukulele players and a deafening log drum finale. After the show, we made our way to the dining area leaving the other guests to get their gift shop souvenirs and selfies with the performers. The noise faded behind us as walked along the torch-lit path, the air heavy with citronella, frangipani and orchid, smoke and food cooking. Being the first to arrive, meant we had first pick of a table and we headed to those on the periphery, away from the serving table.

"Jake!" someone called from behind us.

I flinched. *Not now, not here.* But, Jake broke into a huge grin and turned towards the voice.

"Bryce!" he roared, and taking the man's extended hand, clasped it firmly, pulling him into a slap-on-the-back man hug, "What are you doing here?"

"We're here on holiday." Bryce stood aside, letting a short man with blond hair and glasses step next to him.

"After all your raving about the place, I convinced Bryce that it was time we came to see for ourselves."

Jake turned to him and hugged him, "Anthony, great to see you again."

"Likewise, you're looking good, Jake."

"Why didn't you tell me you guys were coming?"

"We only arrived this afternoon. It was all very last minute..." Bryce continued.

I shrank back, disappearing into the shadow of a large potted palm, to give them space. I felt out of place, spare, surplus to requirements. I watched the three of them catching up on their unordinary lives and the latest Hollywood buzz. Jake looked like *that* Jake Donovan again, the Jake in the TV shows and magazines, the Jake that would never be seen with a woman like me, and in an instant the distance between us cracked apart like a fault line pushing two land masses away from each other. I crept away, looking for an escape route. I should leave and spare Jake the awkwardness of having to explain my presence. But, just as I made my move, I caught my foot in a broken paving tile and stumbled, knocking into the palm and making the fronds flap wildly.

"Catherine!" Jake grabbed me by the elbow helping me regain my balance and pulled me to him, "meet my best buddy ever, Bryce Deans."

I stepped forward cautiously, "Lovely to meet you," I croaked, extending my hand.

Bryce squeezed it, shooting Jake an enquiring glance, before introducing me to his husband.

"I apologize for those two," Anthony nodded toward Jake and Bryce, "when they get together, there's no getting a word in edgeways until they're all caught up."

"Err, yeah, sorry," Jake grinned at me sheepishly, "Bryce, Anthony... this is my friend Catherine Marshall. She's also here on holiday."

They both studied me as if trying to place me.

"You'll join us, won't you?" Jake, gestured towards a table.

"Of course," they chorused.

"So, how do you know Jake?" asked Anthony after we settled.

"Oh, we only met a few days ago."

"By accident," Jake added.

"Oh?"

"I had a small misadventure on the water and Jake came to my rescue."

"We need more than that. Details!" Bryce laughed.

"I was walking along the beach, wading in the water, and fainted. Next thing I knew I was waking up to see his face above me."

Bryce and Anthony turned to Jake questioningly.

"I was parked nearby, drinking a coffee, and saw her floating face down... Instinct kicked in. I went in after her and pulled her out."

"Oh, God!" Bryce clapped a hand to his chest, horrified, "How awful!"

Anthony reached over and squeezed my hand, "You must be traumatized."

"Actually, I don't remember much. I think it was worse for Jake."

"Did you have to do CPR?" Bryce asked, his face ashen.

"She had a pulse, but I had to help her to start breathing again."

"Thank goodness for all your medical training," said Anthony.

"Well, yeah. Though I think it's more a case of 'right place, right time'."

"And if saving my life wasn't enough, he's also saved my vacation." I nudged Jake playfully with my shoulder.

He laughed, "Yeah, after near-on drowning, I couldn't leave her to spend the rest of her vacation in that fleapit hostel she was staying at so I got her a room at my hotel."

Both Bryce and Anthony raised an eyebrow in unison.

"And, he's been taking me sightseeing."

"She's quite useful." Jake teased and went on to tell Bryce and Anthony about our run-ins with fans at the pizzeria and later at the mini-mart when I improvised the story about him being my cousin.

"Well done!" cheered Anthony. "I'm glad someone's looking after our Jake at last."

I blushed and turned to Jake beaming. He stiffened and forced a smile. I quickly looked away and stared down at my hands desperately hoping that the feeling beginning to take hold in my gut was wrong.

"So, you're not from Hawaii then?" Bryce asked.

"No. I'm from San Francisco."

"And, what do you do?" enquired Anthony.

Why did people always have to ask that? "Oh, nothing exciting. I'm a receptionist at a law firm." I said, trying not to sigh.

"She's a writer." Jake bragged.

I frowned, "well, not yet. I'd like to be."

"She won first prize for a short story she submitted to the San Francisco Writers' Corner."

"Third prize," I corrected, "but, that's how I'm here. I paid for the air fare with the prize money."

"I read her story. It would make a great novel or TV series. She's got talent, I tell you."

Anthony turned to Bryce, "Jeremy. It's Jeremy isn't it?"

Bryce gave him a blank stare.

"At Hachette."

"Ah, you mean Jerome."

"That's it!" Anthony turned to me, "Bryce, knows one of the editors. I'm sure he could put you in contact."

"That's very kind, but you—" Before I could finish, a waitress in a floral wrap dress and wearing a lei and several frangipani flowers in her hair approached our table. She told us the buffet would be ready soon and handed us each a complimentary Mai Tai.

Jake took a sip of his and passed it to Bryce, "You guys can have mine."

"You don't like it?" I asked it.

"Rum's a bit too strong."

"Too many rum and cokes as a kid," explained Bryce grinning.

"Yeah, the taste of either makes me sick. Even just the smell."

"Poor guy had a real problem when we were shooting *The Blood Moon Prophecies*."

"Oh, why?"

"You know, all the rum that Vincent and Sebastian drink."

"I don't follow. Surely you don't drink alcohol on set."

"No, but they'd give us flat cola instead and one mouthful would make Jake green around the gills."

"Which reminds me," Jake said, turning to me, "I haven't told you about the time Bryce dropped Jenny in it."

I shook my head suspiciously as he and Bryce roared with laughter.

Anthony rolled his eyes at me. "Here we go," he teased.

Jake continued, "There's this scene set in the 1860s when the Lady Bryant, played by Jennifer Kempen arrives at the Dubois estate. Bryce and I are waiting in attendance and Bryce is supposed to offer his hand and help her out the carriage. Right at the crucial moment, he pulls his hand back and doubles over with the hugest sneezing attack I've seen, Jenny loses her balance and falls out of the carriage face-first onto the ground. It was still muddy from the rain that morning."

"That's right, and she got mud all over the front of the dress. Wardrobe was furious." Bryce joined in.

"And then to top it off, she couldn't get up because of all the hoops in the dress so she just lay there flapping about like a fish out of water, till we pulled her to her feet."

Anthony rolled his eyes at me again, smiling, he'd obviously heard the story before. Many times.

"Oh and what about the time you messed up?" gibed Bryce.

"No!" Jake shook his head, "not that story."

"Too bad, buddy, you started it."

"Now you have to tell me," I insisted.

Bryce was laughing so much he had to take a few moments to collect himself, "Okay, okay. So we're doing a Civil War scene, right? There's a field littered with corpses and dismembered silicone limbs and we're in between takes, waiting for them to fix the smoke machine which is on the fritz again. We're on the edge of the set and Jake's getting bored and says to me, watch this, winds up and gives one hell of a kick to this arm sticking out from under a tarpaulin. We both turn to watch it fly off but instead, there's this almighty scream and we realize the arm is still attached to one very real and very much alive extra.”

“Jake, you didn’t!” I cried and burst out laughing.

Jake sat mock scowling.

“All hell breaks loose as the entire field of extras gets up to see what’s going on, the extra gets taken to hospital for a suspected fracture and the day’s shooting got set back several hours.”

“I see you still haven’t lived that down,” I said smirking at Jake for once.

“Yeah, yeah, buddy. Laugh it up.”

Our laughter was interrupted by the waitress who returned to let us know the food was ready. “Saved by the food.” Jake affectionately slapped Bryce on the shoulder as we made our way to the buffet table.

Jake, Bryce and Anthony were ahead of me in the queue, still chatting away animatedly and I listened while I piled my plate with a selection of roast vegetables and salads.

“So, there’s nothing to all the rumors about you and Kristie?” Bryce asked.

“God no!” Jake snorted.

“I just thought she might have worn you down at last.”

“Ach, Kristie can spin her stories, let the media chase their tails.”

Bryce nodded and gestured toward me, “And, what’s going on with you and Catherine?”

I pretended not to hear and reached for another scoop of potato salad.

Bryce collected a set of cutlery and stepped away from the buffet table.

“Oh, you know, it’s—” Jake did the same and the two of them moved out of earshot and returned to our table.

I froze, the serving spoon still in my hand, poised above the potato salad, a dozen permutations going through my head: it’s complicated, it’s not serious, it’s just a bit of fun... it’s nothing. Friends would scold me for being negative again, but the heaviness in his words, 'oh, you know', made it obvious that it wasn't: it's fantastic, it's the best I've ever felt... it's love.

I lost my appetite. I plunged the spoon back into the salad, collected a set of cutlery and made my way back to the table.

Bryce and Jake were thick in conversation about up-coming projects, scripts they'd read and calls from directors and agents. Anthony smiled at me when I sat down and as I pecked at my dinner

I noticed that he didn't contribute much to the conversation.

"Um, so what have you played in?" I asked.

"Goodness, no. I'm not an actor." he giggled, "I teach music at UCLA."

"Oh? Then how did you and Bryce meet, if you don't mind me asking?"

"Not at all. I met Bryce on campus. He was doing some research for his role as Joseph Breil in *His Legend*."

"So, you're not in the movie business?"

He shook his head. "Nope, well not back then. It was all quite a fluke. Bryce was meant to meet with my colleague who is the authority on Joseph Breil but she came down sick, so I met with him instead and one thing led to another. Since we've been together though, I have written a few film scores, so I'm sort of movie-business adjacent now."

"Wow," I sighed wistfully, "it was meant to be, fate."

"Perhaps. Or random luck."

"Do you think..." I whispered, "me and Jake... do I stand a chance?"

"Oh, honey..." He reached for my hand then stood up announcing, "Boys, us girls are going for a walk," and pulled me to my feet.

Jake and Bryce nodded mid-sentence and we left them to it.

We walked along the torch-lit path away from the music and dancers and found a bench beside some frangipani trees overlooking the beach below. Flickering shadows played on the lawn in front of us and the air was heady with the scent of frangipani, smoke and ocean salt.

"Jake's a really nice guy," I said after we sat down.

"Yes, he certainly is."

"I mean, he's not what I expected."

Anthony nodded.

"He stayed with me the whole time at the hospital; wouldn't leave until I'd seen the doctor. I mean, who does that for a total stranger?"

"That's Jake. He's the best. He'll do anything for his friends, for someone in need, but," he took my hand again and squeezed it, "he's a heartbreaker, and he'll break yours."

I didn't want to hear this.

"He doesn't do it intentionally," he explained. "He does it out of self-preservation, so he won't get hurt, though he'll never admit it."

"I'd never hurt him. Believe me."

"I know you think that, but it's not easy being involved with someone like him."

"I get that. But, I'm different. I don't give up on people when things get hard." I sighed heavily. "That might actually be one of my flaws. I have a misguided sense of loyalty." I went on to tell him about how David betrayed me and I had been blind to it until the moment he left me.

"Oh, sweetie," Anthony pulled me in for a hug, "I'm so sorry."

"Thanks." I sniffed.

"Jake had a long-term relationship several years ago. He was even going to propose."

"Really, who?"

"Amanda James."

"From *Carnal Retribution*?"

"That's right."

I frowned. I'd never particularly liked her as an actress. Her performances tended to be flat, two-dimensional.

Anthony continued, "They met when Jake was still starting out and had a really strong relationship for a long time. But, when Jake got the part in *The Blood Moon Prophecies*, things changed. He became a star and she was still relatively unknown. He was touring a lot, had women chasing after him all the time and though he never once cheated, she got insanely jealous and constantly accused him of sleeping around. She blamed her lack of progress on him and started drinking more and got into drugs. Jake stopped taking her to events because she'd embarrass him too much. He'd have to pick her up off the floor after she'd drunk herself stupid or watch security haul her off when she got high and yelled abuse at his colleagues. He tried everything to straighten her out and repair their relationship... rehab, counseling..." He sighed, "Bryce and I tried to get him to leave her, but he did love her, the old her, and desperately wanted to get her back, so he held on. Then one day, shooting got canceled partway through for electrical problems or something, and he went home early and found her in their bed with some guy she picked up at a bar. That was the final straw. He was broken after that."

"I had no idea. After everything I told him about my story... He never said a thing." I felt that familiar aching stab my heart. Our stories weren't all that different. "When did all this happen?"

"About five years ago now. Since then, there have been a few brief relationships, mostly flings, short romances with women overseas who were kept conveniently at a distance, and I'm sure more than a few one-night stands. He pulls the plug as soon as anyone gets close."

"Thank you for telling me." I sniffed and wiped my eyes. I had tried to blink them back, but the tears had spilled over my eyelids and were threatening to traverse my cheeks.

"Of course, honey," he hugged me again, "I don't want to see you get hurt."

I forced a brave smile.

"How about dessert? I think we need ice cream, don't you?"

I nodded and Anthony hooked his arm through mine and we made our way back to the buffet table.

When we got back to the table with our desserts, Jake and Bryce were still deep in conversation.

I ate a few spoonsful of pineapple upside-down cake and ice cream, and pushed the bowl aside. "Excuse me," I said standing up, "I'm just going to..."

Jake nodded in acknowledgement and I picked up my bag and headed for the washroom.

I freshened up and stood at the hand basin for a while, staring at myself in the mirror. *Smile, damn it!* I should be making the most of the time I had with Jake instead of thinking about how little time was left. After all my reluctance to come to Hawaii, now I didn't want to leave. I didn't want to go back to my old life. I wanted this holiday with Jake to go on forever. I wanted to believe that this was the start of something, that what we had would survive in the real world, but deep down a seed of doubt was germinating and pushing its way to the surface. I closed my eyes trying to push it back down. Maybe Anthony was wrong, maybe he didn't know Jake all that well and his warning was ungrounded. I knew what I felt in my heart was real. Jake wasn't a player. He had genuine feelings for me, I could feel it. Why else had he asked me to stay? Why else would he be making so much effort? If this didn't mean anything to him, then what did that say about me? I couldn't have gotten it all so wrong again. No, this had to be real. I wiped my eyes and touched up my makeup and headed for the door.

Jake was waiting for me outside. "You okay?" he asked.

"Just a bit of a headache," I lied, "where are Bryce and Anthony?"

"They're hitting the dance floor."

"Oh, that's nice."

"Would you? Want to dance?" His voice betrayed a hint of reluctance.

I looked towards the mass of people crammed onto the tiny dance floor and shook my head.

"Shall we leave?"

"Yes, I think so, if you don't mind."

He pulled me into a hug and kissed my forehead, "Not at all. Let's go."

He slipped his hand in mine and we cut through the mob to

find Bryce and Anthony to say our goodbyes before heading for the parking lot.

"Would you like to come up?" I asked as we pulled into the hotel courtyard. The drive had been quiet, small talk strained and limited to comments about Bryce and Anthony – what a great couple they were, what a surprise it was to see them. I sensed what Jake's answer would be, but I asked anyway.

Jake stopped the car, but kept the engine running. "I should let you get some rest." He said, keeping his hands on the steering wheel.

"Yes, of course," I mumbled and reached for the door handle. "I'll still see you tomorrow?"

"Yeah, we'll go on a short hike if you're up for it."

"Okay, yes. Well, thank you for tonight." I leaned over to kiss him, but he didn't move to meet me, only smiled weakly, a weariness in his eyes. I quickly exited the car and closed the door as fast as I dare, afraid of slamming it, and headed into the hotel without looking back. I heard him drive off towards the cabins and as I stepped into the lobby, my eyes filled up with new tears.

Chapter 21

$\mathcal{I}$ paced the bathroom floor while I brushed my teeth. Why shouldn't he want to spend the night alone? It didn't mean he was pulling away. I had to admit that I was exhausted myself and had passed out the minute my head hit the pillow. I should give him space, men hated being crowded. *Don't be so needy.*

Had Bryce and Anthony said something to him? Maybe they didn't like me. Maybe they told him I wasn't right for him. I bent over the bathroom basin and spat out a mouthful of toothpaste and angst. *Stop overthinking it!*

It didn't mean anything. That's what I wanted to believe, but this morning I couldn't shake the feeling that something had changed.

I dressed and headed downstairs to the hotel restaurant to meet Jake for breakfast. His mood was flat and we barely spoke except for the usual pleasantries. I was too afraid to ask what was on his mind, too afraid to hear what I already suspected to be true.

"Are we going for a boat trip?" I asked as we parked at a small harbor. "I thought you said we were going for a hike."

"We are. Sort of," said Jake as he pulled a backpack out of the back of the Jeep and handed me a picnic basket.

"Okay," I muttered, walking off towards the boat ramps.

"This way," he called going the other direction along the dock towards a hangar-type building.

I followed and as we rounded the corner I saw a helicopter ahead painted with distinctive brown, orange and yellow stripes.

"That's awesome!" I exclaimed, "It's the chopper from *Magnum PI*."

"Not the original, but a recreation of course."

"Of course."

"It's my buddy, Rick's."

"Rick? Really?" I said deadpan.

Jake laughed, "Yeah, though it was T.C. who had the chopper in the show."

"Ah, that's right," I said.

"Rick works with us when we need aerial shots and transport in and out of remote areas. The rest of the time he does island tours."

I stopped, "Wait, is that what we're doing today?"

"Yup. I arranged it yesterday."

"Oh," I hesitated, "I've never been in a helicopter before."

"I guessed as much, which is why I suggested the light breakfast – it's a lot different from being in a plane."

"That's really helping."

As we approached the chopper, which seemed even smaller than I imagined close up, Rick emerged from the hangar door. He was a short guy, but muscular, handsome in his own right with sandy-brown hair and a scruffy beard.

"Jake!" he exclaimed, extending his hand and pulling Jake into a one-armed handshake and pat-on-the-back man hug. "Great to see you."

"Likewise," said Jake, stooping to embrace him.

"I heard you finished shooting."

"Yeah, just last week, ahead of schedule."

"You don't say. That Andy Tanler drives a tight ship." Rick turned to me, extending his hand as Jake introduced us.

"Rick, this is Catherine. Catherine, Rick."

"Hi," I said, noticing Rick's firm grip, "nice to meet you."

"Same. So are you also in the show?" asked Rick.

I laughed, "What me? No. I'm not an actress, I'm just a..." I trailed off not voicing the word I was thinking: *nobody.*

"Really? You look like you should be." He turned and opened the chopper door for us.

Jake leaned in and whispered in my ear, "See, I told you, the right kind of guys would see the babe in you."

We loaded up and Jake helped me with the headset while Rick got in the front, "It gets pretty noisy, so you need this to talk and hear."

I nodded nervously.

"No stunts today, okay buddy," Jake told Rick, his voice crackling in the headset, "we've got a chopper virgin with us today."

"Roger that!" Rick laughed as he flicked a few switches starting the engine.

"Rick's a bit of a cowboy," Jake said to me, not reassuring me at all, as the rotors started whining and the cabin began to shake and shudder in anticipation.

"Okay, everyone comfy?" asked Rick, "We're just warming up – only takes a minute or two here in Hawaii, and then we'll be on our way."

I looked over at Jake and he gave me a double thumbs-up with a huge grin, clearly loving every moment. I smiled nervously. Though I loved flying, that was in huge jumbo jets and being in this tiny soda can with two potential daredevils worried me.

"Okay, we're good to go," Rick's voice cracked over the headset and with a slight push on the controls the chopper was airborne, as effortlessly as a leaf caught by a breeze.

My stomach lurched and I grabbed Jake's knee. He looked over at me concerned. "Are you ok? You've gone white."

"I wasn't expecting that," I said, "but, wow it's incredible, I love it!"

Jake sighed with relief, and smiling, took my hand in his as we gained altitude.

Rick took us for an hour-long flight taking in the sights of Honolulu, over Waikiki Beach, Pearl Harbor and over the volcanic cone of Diamond Head on to the O'ahu forest reserves and brought us in to land on a remote mountain plateau.

"Ah, this is where the hike comes in," I said to Jake as the chopper powered down and the rotors slowed.

He nodded, "This is part of the national reserve not open to visitors, but Rick does survey work here so got us special permission to visit.

Rick stayed in the chopper while we climbed out and took our things.

"He's not staying?" I asked as the rotors started up again once we were clear.

"Nope. We've got the place all to ourselves."

"What if something happens?"

"There's nothing to worry about," Jake said patting the backpack and lifting it onto his shoulders, "I've got my cell phone, plus a radio and my med kit. You're with a trained medic, remember."

"Okay. As long as nothing happens to you."

"It'll be fine. You're going to love it, you'll see," he said taking the picnic basket from me, "I'll carry that," and taking my hand in the other, lead me down into the forest.

I breathed deeply, filling my lungs with the damp sweet air while stepping cautiously over the thick leaf debris. The last thing I needed was to catch my foot on an exposed root and break my leg. In the distance, over the perpetual buzzing of insects, I could hear the growing sound of rushing water. After about ten minutes downhill the forest opened out into a small glade bordering a waterfall crashing down the mountainside into a large pool.

"Wow! Just, wow!" I exclaimed taking it all in, the impossibly green vegetation against polished rocks and crystal waters, the shimmering spray sending rainbows into the air.

"Told you, it would be worth it," said Jake beaming.

He seemed renewed. The hike, being surrounded by nature, removed from the outside world seemed to be the tonic he needed. Whatever had been on his mind, seemed distant now.

He went ahead and put down his pack and the basket and set about laying out a picnic blanket, while I took it all in. I kicked off my shoes and sat down on the blanket, digging my toes in the cold sand near the water's edge.

We didn't talk much. There was no need. We took our time and enjoyed the contents of the picnic basket over a glass of wine and I watched as Jake took out his camera. He wandered off taking photos of the waterfall and I lay back on the blanket. I stared up into the sky, a circle of blue edged with tropical trees and watched birds pass overhead. The rest of the world felt miles away, it even felt like the rest of O'ahu had disappeared below the ocean and we were lost on a tiny island of our own. But, I didn't want to be rescued. I wouldn't light a bonfire or set out rocks in an SOS on the beach. I wanted to stay shipwrecked here with him forever.

I heard Jake packing away his camera and I sat up and watched as he pulled off his T-shirt. I bit my lip at the thought that I had tasted that skin; run my hands over that chest. He looked over and smiled, then kicking off his shoes, he pulled off his cargo pants revealing swimming shorts underneath, and made for the water. He plunged in and I watched him swim with strong and powerful strokes, imagining what he must have looked like when he had rushed into the ocean to rescue me. He dove under the water and disappeared, surfacing near where I was sitting, in a great woosh of parting water, stood up and walked over to me, smoothing his hair back as water and sex appeal splashed down his chest and dripped from his nose and mouth, making me bite my lip.

"Come on," he said, taking my hand and tugging it, "the water's amazing," deliberately dripping water over me.

I squealed, but hesitated, "I don't know, I'm still a bit nervous."

"It's okay, I'll be right there. I won't let anything happen to you." Then he reached down and lifted my shirt, "You did put on your swimsuit, didn't you?"

"Yes," I giggled pulling my arms in as his fingers brushed my side.

"Not that you really need it," he smirked, pushing my arms out of the way and pulling my shirt off over my head. He knelt down over my legs, and leaning forward, started tickling my sides making me laugh hysterically and fall backwards onto the blanket. As I lay clutching my sides, laughing and trying to catch my breath, he unbuttoned my shorts, pulled down the zipper, and started pulling them down my legs.

"What is this?" he exclaimed, leaving my shorts round my knees and lifting up the in-built modesty skirt of my one-piece.

He pushed the frill up brushing his hand over my belly, making me quiver. I laughed and tried to push it down again, but he grabbed my hands and holding them to the ground by my sides he started kissing my thighs, "Why would you want to hide these?" he teased. Water dripped from his hair onto my skin, pinpricks of cold in the heat of his breath and the warm wetness of his lips and his tongue. My giggles caught in my throat as my breathing deepened and I surrendered, arching my back, pushing my body toward him. He leaned in, wrapping a leg over mine, holding me in place, watching my face contort with pleasure as he started to caress my legs.

"Do you want me?" he whispered as his fingers moved upwards and inwards, teasing.

"Yes," I panted, squirming, enjoying every moment of this exquisite torture.

"Say it."

"I... want... you," I gasped between moans of pleasure.

"Great!" He exclaimed, pulling his hand away and jumping up. "Then, come and get me," and rushed off back into the pool.

I sat up indignantly watching him grinning and splashing water at me. Shaking my head I stood up, taking a moment for my legs to stop wobbling, and walked over to the pool, "You're incorrigible." I hissed.

"I know," he breathed sexily and waded over to meet me.

"Oh my God, that's cold!" I exclaimed, stepping into the water.

"That's because you're so hot."

"Ha! Way more effective than a cold shower."

"It gets better." He reached out, taking my hands in his, "Watch your step, the rocks are slippery," he said helping me into the water.

"They're not the only thing," I chided, sticking my tongue in my cheek, leering at him.

Jake grinned. "How are you doing?" He asked as we waded further into deeper water, "Let me know if you feel overwhelmed."

"I'm okay," feeling safe with him near.

Once the water was waist deep he let go of my hands, but stayed close while I sank into the water, letting it wash over my shoulders and dipping the back of my head in. After I got used to the cold, being in the water was wonderful; invigorating and we spent a good hour swimming and floating staring up at the sky. Jake kept within reach of me the whole time making sure I didn't have any drowning flashbacks and helped me climb up the rocks around the waterfall so we could stand under the crashing water, feeling it pound on our backs while we held each other kissing and the sun hit the spray sending hundreds of shooting stars showering around us.

We swam back to the shallows and I climbed out to sit on a rock, dangling my legs in the water as I watched Jake swim some more. He turned back to me and dove under the water again and swam towards me, surfacing in a rush at my feet. He stood up, the water rushing from him, looking at me with his sexy smirk. I smiled, took his face in my hands and held it, studying it, this face, recognized by so many, yet how many truly knew it the way I was beginning to? I brushed my thumb over his lips and he kissed it. He took my hands in his, kissed each one, then with our fingers interlocked, we kissed again, softly, tenderly, sweetly, smiling each time our lips parted, our eyes open, gazing into each other.

Then abruptly, Jake paused and frowned, looking at me with pain in his eyes. He pulled me to him and kissed me hard, desperately, closing his eyes, shutting me out. He wrapped my legs round his waist, then moved his hands up my back. I in turn, pulled him to me, digging my fingertips into his back, clamping my legs around his waist. He pulled down the straps of my swimsuit leaving them hanging at my elbows as he hungrily kissed my shoulders as I ran my hands through his hair, pulling him to me. Before I could catch my breath he scooped me up, and carried me out of the pool and over to the picnic blanket, and as he lay me down we descended into a fevered writhing mass of flailing limbs and hot flesh. Swallowing each other whole with frenzied gulps; clinging to each other with white knuckles toward our impending doom.

Then spent, we collapsed together, lying together in a tangled heap listening to the waterfall, bird song and forest insects while softly kissing a shoulder, squeezing a hand, running a toe along a leg.

Jake's arm twitched. He had fallen asleep splayed out across me and as I stared up at the blue circle of sky, I traced my fingers over his back, hearing his soft snore in my ear, his breath warm against my cheek. I wondered what had been on his mind, what had been behind the sadness in his eyes, though I sensed I knew. Like the shadows growing longer on the ground, covering us in shade, our time was running out. I had to head back home in three days. Home to San Francisco. I struggled to picture it. Home, not San Francisco. I could see the Golden Gate Bridge, the cable cars, the Transamerica building, but home? The apartment I got with David? That wasn't home. All I could picture was Jake smiling at me. He was home. In five days he had become more home to me than anyone or anywhere else. The trees circling my view blurred as my eyes welled with tears. I sniffed them back and he stirred, rolling onto his back. I followed, rolling onto my side to face him, wrapping the picnic blanket around us, and kissed him softly on the cheek. His eyes still closed, he smiled while I playfully ran a finger down his chest.

He turned to me, opening his eyes, "Hey," he whispered, taking my hand in his and kissing it.

I snuggled in closer, looking into his eyes. "I'm falling for you," I whispered and leaned in to kiss him.

Jake pulled away, sitting up, "No. No, you can't. You can't fall for me." He sputtered, agitated.

"What do you mean?" I sat up, holding the blanket against my chest.

"You think you know me, but you don't."

"But, what I feel is real," I said.

"Maybe. But this," he gestured around him, "this isn't real."

"I don't understand."

"This is fantasy, a dream. My life isn't like this."

"Neither is mine," I said confused.

"Exactly. This is a holiday. This isn't normal."

"I know, I get it."

"This is just sex, a bit of fun."

"What? You don't believe that."

"You're just infatuated with me because I'm famous."

"That's not fair and you know it. I don't care about all that, I care about you!"

"You might think that now, but when real life sets in, you'd see, it was never me."

I looked away, sighing, "I get it. This is the it's-not-you-it's-me speech."

"Well, it is. It is me."

"You like me, but not enough to make space for me in your life. All that bullshit about finding hidden gems and you're just like all the others, too much of a coward to make a commitment of any sort."

"It's not like that."

"No, it's fine. I get it. I was a fool for thinking that someone like you could want someone like me."

"Catherine, don't be like that. I'm doing this for you."

"Sure you are. Anthony told me about Amanda."

"Then you get it."

"You're worried it'll go the same way with us."

"It will."

"You don't know that. Besides, I know what I'm getting myself into."

"No, you don't. You have no idea what it's like. You're too good, too kind. My world will eat you alive."

"I'm stronger than you think. I know you feel something for me. Why can't you let me in?"

"Don't you see?" he cried, "It's because I care about you that I have to let you go." He paused. "You've only seen the glamourous side. It's not always like this. My life is too complicated; I'm away a lot, the media follows me everywhere, there're always women and rumors. My world rips people, rips relationships, apart and tosses them aside as garbage to be scavenged on by the media. It'll destroy you. It's toxic. I'm toxic. Anyone who gets too close gets burned. You saw what happened at the pizza place. I don't want that for you. You'll meet someone else, someone who can give you what you need."

"How do you know what I need?" I hissed "I can take care of myself."

"Can you?" he snapped, "You let people walk over you, you stay in a job you hate rather than find the courage to follow your dream. How could you possibly hold your ground in my world?"

He might as well have kicked me in the stomach. I started crying, big hot tears.

He brushed the tears from my face, "I'm sorry, that was low of me."

"No. No, you're right," I said sniffing back the tears, pulling myself together, "I have only myself to blame."

"Oh God, you're so beautiful. If you were anyone else I would. But, I can't. Not to you." He placed a hand against my cheek, wiping away my tears. "You deserve so much more."

"How can I deserve more than this? Don't you understand how much you've given me already?" I said pleading, "You didn't just save my life, you saved my spirit. I was dying inside. You gave me joy again."

His expression was torn, "But when we leave here it'll never be the same. It'll never be as good as this."

"I know that. Nothing will ever be as good as this," I said choking back the tears, "that doesn't mean we have to end it."

"I know you think that, but believe me, it's best to walk away now. Before you grow to resent me."

"I could never resent you."

He stood up, grabbing his clothes, "I'm sorry, but I just can't!" he cried and stormed off.

I pulled the blanket around me in disbelief. How could he just end it like this? How was giving up on this for the best? I knew it wouldn't be easy, I wasn't naïve, but to not even try? He had risked his own life to save mine, without a second thought, without any certainty that I could be saved; yet he couldn't make that same leap of faith for love? Did I mean so little to him as a person, that I had more value as a stranger who needed saving than as someone to love?

I heard Jake approaching and wiped the tears from my face.

"We should be going, Rick will be back soon," he said.

I nodded and stood up, keeping the blanket wrapped around me and my back to him as I collected my clothes. I ducked behind some trees to dress, watching through the leaves as he packed up the picnic basket. I folded up the blanket and rejoined him, handing it to him.

"Thanks," he said and pushed it into his pack. He pulled out a water bottle and took a few gulps and offered it to me.

I shook my head though I was parched.

"Okay, let's go then," he said slipping the backpack onto his shoulders and picking up the basket, "Rick will be on his way. Sorry, it's uphill this time."

I nodded. *Whatever*. I just wanted to go. Paradise was over-rated. I should never have gone on this stupid holiday in the first place.

He reached for my hand and I snatched it away, folding my arms around me as we set off back up the winding path. The forest was quiet, darker now that the sun was getting low, and the humidity oppressive. Though it was the same route, going back seemed far longer than the way in and I was starting to feel really tired. The ground was slick with moisture and loose debris and I was battling to keep up with Jake. The path leveled off for a bit and I decided to jog ahead to try and catch up when I stepped on some leaves covering some mud and slipped. I fell forward landing heavily on my knees.

"Damn it!" I yelled.

Jake turned and rushed over to help me.

"Leave me alone!" I cried, shoving him away as I pushed myself up.

"Are you hurt?" he asked looking me over.

"What do you think?" I snapped, brushing myself off. "I'm fine," and marched off ahead of him. He followed me the rest of the way and we continued in silence up onto the plateau. I walked away from Jake and stood looking out at the view, the forest below surrounding the clearing, and off in the distance the rest of the island. I could see Waimanalo Beach, the lighthouse and Sunrise Cove. Jake put down the bags and came to stand behind me. I longed for him to put his arms around me but he didn't. I turned to glare at him and noticed his eyes were red and watering. I reached over and squeezed his hand. He smiled. Not the smirk, not that sexy mischievous grin, but a sad, resigned, heartbroken trembling curving of the lips.

"I'm sorry," he whispered.

I pulled him into a hug, "You've done nothing wrong. This was all a beautiful dream." I sighed, faltering on my words, tears dripping onto his chest as I held onto him breathing him in for the last time. He kissed my forehead softly and I lifted my head and sought out his mouth. And as our lips touched and we kissed, I knew he could taste the salt of my tears. In the distance we heard the drone of the helicopter, circling round us as it came in to land. The closer it approached the more urgent our kissing became; the tighter we held onto those last moments. Soon the downdraft hit us, flapping our clothing and sending our hair wild and we parted, but still held each other as we watched the chopper set down. We waited for the rotors to slow and for Rick to give us the thumbs-up before we crouched down and approached. Jake opened the door and helped me in and passed me the basket and his pack before climbing in and closing the door. We put on our headsets and Rick started up the rotors again.

"Pity we didn't have a camera crew with us," Rick's voice squawked over the intercom, laughing. "I could've got a great arc shot of that kiss."

I gave Jake a questioning look.

He grunted, rolling his eyes, and made a circular motion with his finger to me.

"Ah," I said, nodding. He meant where the camera circles the subject, one of those dramatic cinematic shots, usually when the hero declares his undying love and pulls the love interest into a kiss signaling their happily ever after. But, only in fiction. I turned away and looked out the window watching the mountain and the waterfall fall away.

We didn't speak at all on the drive back to the hotel and I stared out the side window the whole way.

"How about I let you freshen up and then meet you for dinner at eight?" Jake asked as we pulled into the hotel courtyard.

"Actually I think I'd just like to be alone tonight. I'm feeling rather tired." I said turning to face forward, but not looking at him, "I'll order something up to the room later."

"Okay. I understand." Jake reached over and took my hand, squeezing it, "You get some rest. Let me know if you need anything."

I nodded and reached down to pick up my bag from by my feet, blinking back the tears, "I'll see you in the morning." I lied as I climbed out of the car.

"We'll talk some more. Breakfast as usual?"

I nodded again, closing the door, knowing I would be gone by then.

"Well, good night then." He called after me.

"Goodbye," I mumbled, unable to look at him, tears clouding my eyes as I walked to the hotel, only daring to look back once I heard him drive off towards his cabin.

I held it together till I got to my room then, closing the door behind me, leaned back against it and slid down sobbing in a heap on the floor. Why did I always do that? Declare my feelings too soon and scare them off. It seemed the more I liked someone the faster I messed things up. When would I learn? I was such an idiot. *I'm falling for you?* He must hear that all the time. No wonder he got annoyed.

I just wanted to go home. I couldn't bear to stay any longer. Jake had made up his mind, and my staying wouldn't change it. Better to leave while I still had some dignity, before I might be tempted to plead with him to reconsider. I felt humiliated enough, without having to hear his protestations and denial again. And if he really believed none of this had been real, then what was the point of staying? Why invest any more time in a fantasy?

When the crying subsided and the numbness finally set in, I got up and made my way to the bathroom and ran a bath. I slipped off my T-shirt and shorts and stopped when I saw myself in the mirror, standing in my swimming suit. I looked down, and as I ran the frill through my fingers I knew I'd never be able to bring myself to wear it again. I let out a heavy sigh, took it off and stuffed it in the rubbish bin.

He thought he was so different, yet he was just like all the others, spouting the same tired lines. The melody may have been different, but the words were the same. It was all just a variation on a theme. I had heard it all before: I was flawed, a misprint, a factory second; not good enough to make commitment grade. His words simply repeated every rejection I had received from the first time a boy kissed me to David's parting note. Words that I had neatly catalogued and played on repeat: *Catherine's Broken Heart's Greatest Hits.*

I stepped into the bath and lay back, closing my eyes. I let out a heavy sigh and sank below the surface, feeling the warm water wash over me. Again the memory rushed back, the water in my nose, the taste of salt; my pounding heart and screaming lungs, but I held myself under, welcoming the sensation. It felt comforting somehow... less painful and more bearable than reliving his words. It promised escape... peace. All I had to do was let go. I opened my mouth, but the instant the soapy water flooded in, I shot up coughing and choking. Letting go wasn't that easy.

Once my hacking subsided I sank back, my head above the water and lay soaking for some time staring up at the ceiling. Slowly my churning and colliding thoughts turned to white noise and I drifted off to a place of quiet. A meadow in winter, muted, every sound swallowed up by the snow on the ground, life greyed out. Snowflakes caught on a breeze dancing a silent murmuration of ice, like birds gathering at dusk.

I started to shiver and returning to a hotel bathroom in so-called paradise, realized the water had gone cold. I got out, and wrapping a towel around me, leaned over and pulled out the plug and stood for a moment, watching my heart drain away. Numbness setting in, I dried off and slipped on the plush hotel bathrobe for the last time and went through to the main room. I made a coffee and took some fruit from the refreshed fruit bowl. Then taking the folio of hotel stationery from the credenza, I sat down in one of the armchairs and started writing.

With the coffee cup empty, the fruit uneaten, I folded the paper and slipped it into an envelope, sealed it, and wrote 'Jake' on the front. Then taking no forlorn pauses to stare off into the distance, I dressed, packed my suitcase and left the room with no parting look. I marched to the elevator welcoming the stab of pain every time my suitcase banged against my leg. It was time to do what I should have done four days ago.

"Hey Keoni," I said as I reached the reception counter.

"Ms. Marshall," he replied, then noticing my suitcase asked, "Are you leaving us so soon?"

"I'm afraid so. It's time for me to go home." I handed him the room key card, then the envelope, "Would you please see that Jake, Mr. Donovan gets this."

"Of course," he placed it in a cubby hole behind the desk, "Is there anything else I can help you with?"

"If you could call for a taxi, to take me to the airport? I'll wait outside."

"Certainly."

"Thank you for everything, you've been very kind," I smiled, feeling the urge to hug the big Hawaiian if the reception counter were not in the way.

"It's been my pleasure. I hope you'll visit us again." He beamed, picking up the phone and dialing.

Turning to take one last look at the lobby, I slung my bag over my shoulder and picked up my suitcase, cursing under my breath when it bumped my legs yet again as I lugged it outside into the forecourt.

Dumping my bags, I sat down on a bench by the fountain while I waited. The last of the light was fading and the outside lights were blinking on around the courtyard and the humid air was heady with the fragrance of frangipani. I brushed my hair behind my ear, remembering the feel of Jake's fingers tucking in the flower that first night. It was only a few days ago but already it seemed like a lifetime. In a way it was, my renewed life began the moment Jake pulled me from the ocean. He had co-signed my new lease on life. No matter how far forward I moved on with my life he would be forever tethered to me. My precious gift came with a horrible curse. How was I supposed to leave him in my past when every new breath I took reminded me of him?

I looked towards the cabins, longing for him to appear, for him to rush over and beg me not to leave. I wanted to run to his cabin, to bang on his door. I could see myself doing it in my mind, saw him embracing me and pulling me inside, but I was still sitting on the bench, gripping the seat, my heart pounding, one foot on the gas, one foot on the brake.

Jake poured a bourbon from the mini bar and stood at the large picture window staring out at the ocean watching the last rays of sunlight fade from the sky.

He was angry. Angry at himself for being so careless. It had been when they were standing there in the pool, kissing, that he saw in her eyes that she had fallen in love, and he realized he had lost control, had let her get too close. And he was angry at her. Angry that she had forced him to push her away, to say those words.

If she could have just left things alone he would have let her return to San Francisco and never contacted her again; let distance and absence break things off for him. She was right, he was a coward. He had never wanted to hurt her, yet that's how things always turned out.

He had never intended for it to go anywhere. He knew it couldn't last, right from the first day. He never meant to lead her on. If she had been from his world, she would have known that. Insiders knew the rules. They knew relationships in his world didn't last and came with no expectations, no strings attached.

People on the outside saw only the fame and fortune, the mansions and the fast cars. They mistook money for freedom. They had no idea how trapped he was. Sure, he was privileged, but it came at a price. A cost she simply couldn't comprehend. She would be putting him in an impossible situation, always needing him to protect her from the media, always needing him to reassure her that he was faithful, that the gossip she would inevitably hear was false, always needing him to encourage her when she felt overshadowed by him, always needing him to apologize for arguments she started. It was too much to ask and it wasn't his responsibility. It wasn't his fault, he wasn't the bad guy. His world was. He was just as much a victim as she was. The only answer was to walk away before they grew to hate each other. Surely she could see that.

He drained the glass, set it down on the table and left the cabin, walking then jogging along the path strung with fairy lights to the hotel. He turned away blinded by oncoming headlights and paid no attention to the yellow taxi cab as it passed him driving towards the road. When he reached the courtyard he thought he caught Catherine's perfume lingering in the air near the fountain. He stopped and turned, but the forecourt was empty. Hurrying through the lobby, he pressed the elevator button repeatedly; then headed up the stairs, two at a time. Pausing briefly to catch his breath, he walked down the hall and stopped at Catherine's door.

He made a fist and then paused, his hand poised, about to knock. Sighing, he opened his hand and pressed it softly to the door. If she opened the door there would be no talking. The second he crossed the threshold he would be lifting her up and carrying her to the bed. He had to turn back before he did something he regretted. He turned away and walked back to the elevator.

He had saved her life, but staying in it would only complicate it. It wasn't right to keep a rescued bird once it could fly again. He had to set her free.

Chapter 23

With an unremarkable thud, the wheels touched down on the runway followed by a short perfunctory roar as the air brakes engaged and the plane slowed then taxied to the terminal. All so incredibly routine and ordinary.

It's not that I wanted the plane to hurtle into the sea breaking into a thousand pieces or explode in a giant fireball on landing, but that would have been a fitting end. I imagined Jake flicking on the news and seeing the footage of the plane in flames on the tarmac and feeling sick with horror realizing I was on board. I wanted him to hurt. I wanted him to regret. I wanted him to feel my loss.

But the oxygen masks had not dropped; we hadn't had to assume brace positions or send goodbye texts in the last seconds before impact. There hadn't even been a hint of turbulence throughout the five-hour flight.

Even at the United desk, everything had gone incredibly easily. When I had told the ticket agent, I needed to change my ticket to the next flight out, I had prepared myself for a battle. I wanted to fight. I wanted to lash out, rip someone to shreds, anyone would do. But, a few taps of her keyboard and a swipe of my credit card and it was all done. Within ten minutes I was checked in and waiting at the gate.

The plane was half full, no crying children or rowdy vacationers, and quiet other than an occasional hushed murmur and distant snore. I had a window seat to myself and for most of the flight I stared out of it even though there was little to see in the darkness. I watched the lights of O'ahu fall away and let out a low cry as I realized the last blinking light to be lost below the clouds was the beam from the Makapu'u lighthouse, a last beacon to Jake. As it disappeared from view I felt I was being pulled further and further away from him in space and time. He was now behind me, beyond the horizon, but I wasn't ready for him to become part of my past. I wanted to stay in the air, forever on hold, paused, like the proverbial flipped coin suspended, neither heads nor tails; stay in Schrödinger's box, neither alive nor dead. I didn't want to go forward if I couldn't go back.

I stared out into the night, a light rain was sending rivulets of water down the outside of the window blurring the lights of the approaching terminal and ground crew arriving to offload the plane. There was no escaping the return to reality. I bit my lip feeling my eyes well up again. I'd made a mistake. I wanted to go back. I shouldn't have left. If we could have talked just one more time...

"Ma'am, are you ok? Do you need some help?"

I wiped my eyes and looked up at the cabin attendant, a young man in his early twenties. Beyond him the cabin was empty.

"Oh, sorry, I was far away." I sniffed unbuckling my seatbelt and standing up.

"Oh honey," he said, noticing my puffy eyes, "did you leave someone behind?"

I nodded as he helped me pull my shoulder bag from the overhead compartment.

"Whirlwind holiday romance?" he asked.

I nodded again, slipping my bag over my shoulder.

"I see it all the time," he said following me to the exit at the front of the plane.

"I suppose you do," I said pausing at the door, "a peril of paradise."

"You'll be okay," he said giving me a quick hug.

I smiled at him then I stepped onto the air bridge. Would I? Would I be okay? The problem with whirlwind romances is that they left a path of destruction in their wake. I had gone to Hawaii to recover from a relationship that never left the ground and left me mildly bruised, only to be caught by a tornado and dropped from the sky to return with an entirely shattered body.

My footsteps clattered on the metal floor echoing in the empty corridor as I hurried to the terminal rubbing my arms in the chill of the night air. I collected my suitcase which was waiting forlornly next to the now-still baggage claim conveyor. I heaved it onto an airport trolley and headed for the exit. The huge terminal hall was practically empty except for a few airport personnel, a security guard doing his rounds, his keys clanging against his side with each step, and in the distance the whirring of someone with a floor polisher. All the usually busy shops and kiosks were closed and silent with railings across their fronts. No announcements, no canned music. Devoid of travelers, devoid of purpose, the hall felt strangely lonely and depressing. I hurried to make my way out to get a taxi. The automatic doors swished closed behind me. I left unnoticed. Unmissed.

I leaned my head on the back of the seat, thankful for the small mercy of a taciturn taxi driver. He asked no questions, made no attempt at small talk and drove in silence. Even the radio wasn't turned on. I let out a heavy sigh and closed my eyes listening to the rain hitting the roof and the thwup thwup of the windshield wipers.

I must have drifted off as the journey seemed to take only a few minutes. I paid the fare and a generous tip for the welcome silence. The driver grunted taking the cash and popped the trunk, but stayed put. I stepped out of the taxi into the pelting rain plunging my foot straight into a puddle. By the time I made my way to the rear of the car and heaved my suitcase from the trunk, my clothes were soaked through and stuck to me as I slammed the cab's trunk shut. As I picked up my suitcase again, the taxi drove off sending a large spray of water over me. *Perfect*. Things were right in the world again.

I walked to the building entrance, stumbling in my wet sandals and slipping on the stone floor, my suitcase leaving fresh bruises on my legs as I lugged it into the elevator and along the corridor to my door. As I rummaged in my shoulder bag for my keys, drops of water dripped from my bangs into my tear-soaked eyes. I stood for a moment, holding my front door key poised over the lock. Then forcing myself, I pushed the key into the lock and turned it. The latch clicked; the door opened.

I stood on the threshold, home but not home. This was my apartment, but it had ceased being home months ago. Now, everything that had been familiar and real felt fake, and home was an empty façade, like a film set – the place I acted out the motions, pretending to be home. All that I had believed to be fake, now felt real and familiar. Reality had been inverted, the dream had become the real world, and my real world had become the dream, a nightmare. But as soon as I crossed the threshold, everything would invert again, Jake would be the dream I would wake from and I would be back in the real world.

I took a deep breath and stepped into the apartment feeling my world's poles reverse with cataclysmic shaking and eruptions sending up ash clouds that would block out the sun for months. I pulled in my suitcase, leaving it beside the stack of David's boxes, tossed my bag on top, then locked the door and made my way to my bedroom, not even turning the lights on. Not wanting to see my old reality in the light. The dim interior of the apartment smelled stale and sour, a combination of damp and the previous tenant's cat. I pulled off my wet clothes and dumped them on the floor and then climbed into bed, pulling the covers over my head.

Jake swigged back the last of his coffee and checked his watch. Nine thirty. He'd been waiting for half an hour already. Although he hadn't known Catherine that long, she hadn't kept him waiting before. He looked out the restaurant window at the ocean, watching the waves roll in. He had slept lightly and his dreams had been full of him and her together in a world where no one knew him.

They had been walking hand-in-hand down the cobbled streets of a French town; a regular couple on a regular vacation.

He sighed as the impossible image faded from his mind. In reality, there was practically nowhere in the world where he wouldn't be recognized, where he could be a regular guy. He could never be a regular guy again. Even if he quit acting and left Hollywood he would never be able to give her a normal life. He would always be that actor recognized by someone no matter where he went. Even if he wanted to leave, he had contracts to honor for the next few years before he would be free. He couldn't ask, couldn't expect her to wait for him.

There was no way around it; parting now was the right thing to do. He had to make her see that it was for the best, make her understand that he had to let her go, before the rot set in, before she became another victim of his life. He owed her that much... though over breakfast in front of a roomful of nosy hotel guests wasn't right. He quickly left the restaurant and walked to the lobby, pressed the button for the elevator. He watched the numbers count down, hoping he'd get to her room before she set out to meet him. The elevator doors opened and he was just about to step in when he heard his name called. He turned to see Keoni jogging over, holding an envelope out to him.

"Good morning, Mr. Donovan."

"Morning, Keoni."

"Ms. Marshall asked me to give you this," he said, handing Jake the envelope.

"Oh? Thanks. Did she go out?"

"You don't know?"

"Know what?"

"She left yesterday. A taxi took her to the airport around six o'clock. She said she was going back home."

The elevator doors closed leaving Jake standing in the foyer, holding the envelope. An image flashed in his mind of a yellow taxi cab passing him as he walked down to the hotel the evening before. She was already gone by the time he had got to her room.

"Mr. Donovan?"

"Sorry, yes, of course. *Mahalo*, Keoni."

Keoni nodded and went back to the reception desk. Jake followed and continued out to the front courtyard and sat down on a bench next to the fountain. He opened the envelope and pulled out a single sheet of heavy paper embossed with the hotel's logo. He unfolded it and began reading.

> *Dearest Jake,*
>
> *If this was all a fantasy, then there is no reason for me to stay.*
>
> *This may not have been real, in the way that a shooting star isn't really a star, but it has been beautiful and perfect all the same.*
>
> *Like a shooting star, rare and precious, momentary and fleeting, it's burned up now, no trace remaining, impossible to say what it really was. So the possibility remains that maybe, just maybe, it was in fact real.*
>
> *Thank you for everything. Thank you for a perfect illusion, a perfect dream. I'll never forget you.*
>
> *I hope you will remember me too.*
>
> *– Always, Catherine.*

He folded the letter and slipped it back into the envelope and sat watching the water splashing in the fountain. There was no lecturing him on his flawed thinking, no pleading for him to reconsider, no bargaining to stay in touch as friends. Had he really been so final in his words to her? He had done a lousy job of letting her down gently. As an actor, he could have acted better, given a better performance; told her some story about having a secret girlfriend to make it easier for her to hate him, easier for her to move on.

But, instead, he had chosen not to lie. And honesty was rarely gentle, rarely easy.

A cloud passed in front of the sun, sending a shadow over the courtyard. The morning breeze had turned brisk and Jake saw in the distance, the waves were building, a storm was coming. It seemed appropriate, he thought. He walked back to his cabin and packed up. There was little point staying now. Sunset had come to Sunrise Cove. It was time for him to go back to his life and let Catherine live hers.

Chapter 24

$\mathcal{I}$ passed out the moment my head hit my pillow, but my sleep was not peaceful. My dreams were filled with a mash-up of images. I'd be entangled in white sheets making love to Jake, but when I tried to see his face I'd find myself alone floating in the middle of the ocean, no land in sight, treading water. As I was overcome with exhaustion, knowing I would soon succumb, I felt a cold terror, not that I was going to die, but that I was going to die alone. Alone, invisible, unnoticed, unmissed. Then I would sink into the dark depths of the ocean and come to rest on the bottom. And lying there, head turned towards the shore, I'd watch him on the beach kissing someone else while the ocean creatures nibbled on my body pulling me apart.

A passing siren woke me and I found myself soaked in sweat. I slowly got my bearings back. Dragging myself out of bed I stumbled through to the bathroom. I picked up my clothes from the floor and as I shoved them into the laundry hamper I caught a whiff of Jake's cologne still clinging to them. I bit my lip as my eyes started to water again and climbed into the shower cubicle. It felt strangely claustrophobic and I banged against the sides while I turned on the water. I doubted anyone had ever had sex in this shower. I rested my head against the wall with the water hitting my back and closed my eyes, picturing him standing with steam rising around him, soaping his arms, turning to smile at me with that smirk. I wiped my eyes and reached for the soap, pushing him from my mind.

I stepped out of the shower and dried off, then wrapped the towel around me, tucking it in, and wiped the fog off the mirror, only to see Jake behind me nibbling on my neck, one hand cupped on a breast, the other hand cupped between my legs, fingers probing, teasing. I gripped the edge of the washbasin and bit my lip as the memory made me quiver. I groaned. I wanted him. More than I had wanted anyone before. How was I ever going to settle for less again? I didn't just want him, I craved him. Was this what addiction felt like? Was I going to go through withdrawal on top of heartbreak?

The mirror fogged over again and I left the bathroom and went back to my bedroom and dressed in a fleecy sweat-suit and socks and slippers, and wrapped myself in my gown. Dressing in my least sexy clothes to try curb my cravings and for the comfort of feeling wrapped up in a fabric hug.

I padded through to the kitchen and made myself a cup of coffee and some toast, looking out the window at the street below. It was nearly lunchtime in the real world, while here I was making my breakfast. I wasn't in any hurry to return to the real world just yet. I spread an extra thick layer of jelly on my toast then settled in the living room with my laptop.

I checked my emails, not that this had any practical use anymore other than being a depository of spam, social media notifications, job ads that I would never apply to, sales announcements and newsletters I'd never read. Over two hundred messages and nothing of importance. I selected them all and pressed delete, completing the ritual.

I closed out and opened Facebook for the first time since I'd left for Hawaii. I scrolled through the usual unnecessary notifications, mindless memes, aimless pictures of friends' meals pre-consumption, baby pictures, cat pictures, ridiculous miracle remedies and political propaganda, and gave up after three days' worth of 'news'. It was obvious I had not missed much, nor had I been missed.

I looked at the green dots alongside the faces of friends and wondered whether anyone had noticed that mine had blinked on a few days earlier than expected. I doubted they even knew I had gone away. That would have required them to actually read my posts.

I emptied my coffee, opened a new post and began typing:

> I'm back from my holiday in Hawaii. You'll never
> believe what happened! I met Jake Donovan.
> Yes, THE Jake Donovan from *Hawaii Heartbeat*!
> It was literally by accident – he rescued me
> from drowning (I had a slight misadventure
> at Waimanalo Beach) and then he took me
> sightseeing around O'ahu for the next few days.
> He is a really great guy and we

I stopped typing. There was no *we*. He *was* a really great guy. I wasn't going to see him again. There was not going to be a present or future tense in which we both appeared. From here on my relationship with him, to him, would always be in the past tense.

How ironic that the one time I had a story, a huge story to tell, a story that would be the envy of all, I couldn't share it. Who would believe me anyway? I didn't even have a single photo of him or of us both together. I couldn't bring myself to take one. I didn't want him to think I was one of *those* people. I had hoped he would offer, but he never did and now I regretted it bitterly. How could I prove to anyone else that we had been together when I couldn't even prove it to myself? I pressed the backspace key and began typing again:

> Hawaii was great. I had a lovely time sight-
> seeing and relaxing.

And even if they would believe me, even if I could prove it, why should I? Why should I share this most intimate story with people who scrolled past my posts in cyberspace without reading them, and walked past me in real life pretending not to see me? People who only followed me out of vainglorious curiosity and only sent me birthday greetings because Facebook prompted them. No, this episode of my life was too precious to share with them. There was really only one friend I would have told and she had left this world too soon. Only she would have understood my beautiful sadness.

I added a few photos from my phone, generic touristy pictures of beaches and palm trees, souvenir stores and museum entrances, pineapples and bowls of shaved ice – nothing of the hotel at Sunrise Cove, Rick's helicopter or any that included a certain Jeep; nothing that would arouse questions – and left it at that.

I entered Jake's name in Facebook's search box and clicked enter, which pulled up a long list of pages of people with the same name, imposter pages and similarly-named fan pages. I snorted as I clicked on the link at the top of the list for his official page. *Official*, one that had been formally verified by Facebook as authentic, the rest of us mere mortals were deemed too insignificant for Facebook to authenticate.

He had a photo of Waikiki Beach at sunrise as his cover photo and a moody black and white headshot of him looking to the side for his profile picture. No message button, of course. Followers: so many that it was abbreviated to 17M. Seventeen million! The entire population of several small countries and I had just 176 friends following my page. What a joke, I was just a drop in the ocean. I groaned; it was my dropping in the ocean that had got me here in the first place.

I clicked on the 'Like' button and wondered if he'd notice; if he even administered his own page. His was now the first and only celebrity page I was following. Not that he would know that.

I scrolled down and saw his most recent post. A selfie of him in the Jeep, I recognized the fraying stitching on the head rest and wondered if anyone else would notice that detail, would love him more for it. He wrote, 'Hey fans, it's a wrap on Hawaii Heartbeat, I'm now off to get some R & R on this beautiful island.' I clicked like, and added a comment, 'I hope you enjoyed your break.' I wanted to write more, declare my undying love, plead for him to be with me. It's not as if my comment would cause suspicion when every other comment was a fan declaring their love and devotion to him. My comment wouldn't be unusual at all. I wasn't unusual, no different than the seventeen million others who adored him.

I continued scrolling through his other posts. In an earlier post, he shared the picture of him with the fake bloodied shoulder and red eye and wrote, 'Bozo here got hit by a piece of the SFX. That'll teach me to pay attention during safety briefing!' It received tens of thousands of love and hugs and get-well-soon comments from fans. There were other behind-the-scenes shots of the show being filmed in Los Angeles and I smiled fondly when I saw a picture of him and Bryce, 'Good times – me and my BFF,' on an anniversary of a wrap date from the old days. Further on there was a picture of him as a young boy dressed up as a doctor for Halloween, wearing a white coat that was too big for him, 'I've been preparing for this role all my life,'. I felt a rueful pang, knowing that the photo belied a painful truth and was taken at a time when Jake's relationship with his father was still on good terms.

The more I scrolled back the more I felt like a stalker. His page was public, his messages were meant for the masses, yet I felt like I was intruding, prying. Unlike the other seventeen million, I knew things, personal and private things, about him they didn't and now sitting at my laptop thousands of miles from him, knowing I would never see him again it was as if I wasn't meant to know those things, as if my getting to know him had been an accident. A mistake.

I logged off and walked over to my suitcase still standing by the front door and opened it, rummaged about, till I found the T-shirt Jake had given me. Then leaving the rest of the suitcase contents spewing over the sides like entrails, I retreated back to the couch and curling up, held the shirt against my face. I could still smell the sea, the coconut sunscreen and the tiniest trace of his cologne. Holding the shirt like a beloved security blanket, I flicked on the TV and opened Netflix, selected episode one, season one of *The Blood Moon Prophecies* and pressed play.

The opening scene began with Jake dressed much like he was on the night we first had dinner together, in black pants and a black cotton shirt with the top button undone. He stood holding a single white rose beside a huge weeping willow tree, its graceful branches gently swaying in the breeze. He knelt down and placed the rose at the base of a praying angel tombstone. Then kissing his fingers, he pressed his hand against the stone as the camera zoomed in on the inscription above his fingers:

Elizabeth Mary Montgomery
26 June 1774 – 21 January 1793
Never possessed. Forever Loved.

The camera then drew back as Jake's voice narrated: 'on the day of my death I was granted eternal life as a vampire; on the day of her death I lost the will to live'. I clapped my hand over my mouth in anguish, my eyes welling up, blurring the scene. I reached for the box of Kleenex on the coffee table and grabbed a bundle wiping my eyes and blowing my nose. No one told me it was going to be a tear-jerker.

Jake turned his attention to the clouds out the window, for a moment, he thought he could see her in the distance, wading through the clouds, one hand held high carrying her golden sandals, one hand trailing the fluffy tops. She turned and smiled at him. He pressed his fingers to the glass of the small window and smiled, and then the clouds cleared revealing the California coast line below. Leaning his head back against the headrest he closed his eyes, to the familiar drone and shudder as the flaps extended. Soon there would be the familiar banking and descending, the whirring and thunk as the landing gear deployed. The lurching as tires made contact with the ground, re-establishing the hold on reality, a reality in which she didn't exist. He would not see her on bus stop posters or bill boards or TV shows or social media memes. He wouldn't *see* her again. He could move on without ever having to be reminded of her. He felt a pang of guilt that he was afforded a luxury she would not. She would see him everywhere.

I paid for the pizza and settled back onto the couch. Season one was just about finished. I pulled the blanket up around me and looked at Jake frozen mid-stride on the screen. My Jake, but not my Jake. I pressed play reanimating him, watching as Vincent, with his eyes red and glowing, black veins over his face, fangs extended pulled a wooden stake from his side while clutching the bad guy by the neck in the other, "you really need to work on your aim" he sneered, "pity, you won't have the time," he smirked; that gorgeous sexy smirk of his. Sinking his fangs into the man's neck he ravenously drained him of blood, then tossed him aside, "nothing like junk food when you're starving," he said turning to Bryce's character, Sebastian, "am I right, brother?" Even with fake blood coloring his teeth and dripping down his chin, staining his front, he was drop-dead gorgeous. Vincent was growing on me.

Considering I had spent so much time scoffing about the show, accusing it of being bubble-gum writing for a bubble-gum audience, I had to admit, there was a depth I hadn't expected, that probably went over the heads of the majority of viewers. Jake's character Vincent Dubois was complex, a ruthless, often brutal vampire yet he also had a vulnerable and tender side, a side he wrestled with. He was constantly at odds with wanting to give into his nature but also wanting to be a better man, to be worthy of the woman he loved. Perhaps Jake wasn't so different from Vincent. He was at odds with the person the world portrayed him as and the person he really was. The person he was with me.

Jake opened the door of his apartment, unchanged from when he left for Hawaii two months ago; the same furnishings, the same view, the same... emptiness. He sighed and took his suitcase through to the bedroom, unzipped the top and pulled out his clothes tossing them into the laundry hamper. He paused as he pulled out another shirt, the red one with tropical flowers. *Very Magnum PI,* he recalled Catherine's words as he held it to his nose, breathing in the trace of smoke from the luau and her perfume. He should throw it out, he'd never wear it again; he balled it up and aimed at the rubbish bin. Then changing his mind, he tossed it in the hamper with the rest of the laundry. He finished unpacking, stowed the suitcase and loaded the washing machine. His housekeeper usually did this for him, but there was something cathartic in doing the ordinary, the mundane right now.

With the sound of the washing machine going through the motions in the background, he sat down on his couch with his laptop and went through the motions of checking his email. He hadn't missed much since he last checked, just the usual junk and routine messages from the production team and his agent, manager and publicist touching base. Nothing that couldn't wait.

He opened Facebook and ignoring the thousands of comments by fans – it simply was not possible to read them all so he rarely read any of them – looked up Catherine's page. She had a picture of the Golden Gate Bridge as her cover photo and her profile picture was of her looking to the side, shade falling over most of her face obscuring her features. He scrolled down through the handful of equally-obscured previous profile pictures. He loved that she wasn't selfie-obsessed, but now he wished he could see more. His finger hovered over the touchpad as he stared at the friend request button. Every woman's dream, to receive a friend request from Jake Donovan, he snorted, also the M.O. of countless scammers. He could use his personal profile and contact her as Jon Donaldson, but to heed the old adage, it was probably better to let sleeping dogs lie.

He moved his finger away, closed out of Facebook and opened his photo library and connected his external hard drive. Selecting all but one of the photos from his last two months in Hawaii he moved them from his current folder to his archive, effectively moving her from present to past. The transfer complete, he opened the remaining image, the photo of the Greek goddess in the red floral blouse and white shorts wading in the ocean, one hand outstretched holding a pair of golden sandals, the other trailing the water surface. Her brown hair cascaded down, obscuring her face as she tilted her head to the side gazing out at the ocean, the sunlight reflecting off the water surrounding her with hundreds of starbursts. This image he would frame and mount on his wall.

It was Sunday afternoon, I had barely moved from the couch in nearly three days, empty pizza boxes decorated the coffee table and my rubbish bin was overflowing with sodden sad masses. I was into season three of *The Blood Moon Prophecies* and my second box of Kleenex.

It was 1793. Vincent stood with Elizabeth by the fireplace in the grand hall of his family mansion. He slipped a ring onto her left ring finger, "We need not the eyes of God to bless us, for in our own eyes we are blessed."

"In our own eyes we are blessed," repeated Elizabeth as she slipped a ring onto Vincent's finger, looking up at him with such love in her eyes.

"We are one and tonight we shall be eternal." Vincent drew her into an embrace kissing her tenderly on the lips. I closed my eyes for a moment, remembering those lips, the way they tugged at my own. He was brushing her hair from her shoulder, as she tilted her head to the side exposing her neck to him. I leaned my head to one side, mimicking her pose, able to feel Jake's breath against my own neck, as he leaned over, fixating on the pulsing in her neck. Then opening his mouth latched onto her skin, kissing her ravenously, pulling her tightly to him as she surrendered.

The door burst open as Edward Winstead broke into the room, brandishing a wooden stake, "Get your hands off her, you abomination!" he screamed.

In the blink of an eye, Vincent had ripped the stake from Edward's hand and had him pinned up against the wall by his throat. His eyes glowed red, black veins streaked his face and his fangs were extended, "You should know better than to confront a vampire in his home!" he squeezed his hand tighter around Edward's neck while he helplessly tried to pull Vincent's hands away and his legs kicked wildly a foot in the air, desperate to make contact with the ground.

"Please don't kill him, Vincent. Let him speak," pleaded Elizabeth coming to stand next to him.

"Very well." He lowered Edward to the ground and removed his hand from his throat. He pointed the stake at him, "this works, just as well on humans, I warn you."

"Elizabeth, you are not safe with this... this creature. I am here to rescue you."

Vincent raised an eyebrow in amusement.

"I do not require rescuing. I love him."

"Love him?" cursed Edward, "You are promised to me. Can you not see he has cast a spell over you? Your mind is not your own. He has stolen it."

"No Edward, he has not stolen my mind, only my heart," she said looking at Vincent showing no fear or revulsion at his terrifying vampire face, only love as if she were looking at the face of an angel.

"You know not what you are saying. He has you bewitched, glamoured."

"I have done no such a thing. Not to Elizabeth."

"No Edward, he has not."

"You cannot know that."

She pulled a thin gold and sapphire bracelet from her wrist. "You see this bracelet? It was a gift from my grandmother. I wear it always and so it made the perfect vessel." Both Edward and Vincent looked at her confused. The veins and red glow of Vincent's eyes had faded and his fangs had retracted. "When I first learned Vincent's true nature, I was afraid. I knew what my heart felt for him, and though he had done nothing and has never done anything to give me cause to fear him, my mind told me I should not trust him. I considered seeking guidance from the church, but I feared what they would do to him so instead I sought out a witch and asked her to enchant the bracelet with a spell that would protect me from any attempts by unnatural beings to possess my mind."

Vincent looked at her shocked. "You sought to protect yourself from me? You thought I would influence you?"

"Only at first. I wanted to be sure that what feelings I felt, what thoughts I thought were fully my own."

"You chose to be with him of your own free will?" exclaimed Edward in disbelief.

"I did. This is how I know Vincent has never compelled me."

"For I never sought to possess you, only to love you," said Vincent, his eyes locked on her.

She smiled at him then turned back to Edward, "The only person who sought to possess me is you."

Damn it, I started crying again as Vincent and Elizabeth embraced and kissed softly. Was I to find analogies everywhere? The camera panned round the two of them standing face to face, arms entwined when suddenly there was a loud crack and a shot rang out. Elizabeth fell limp in Vincent's arms, blood streaming from her back. The camera cut to Edward standing behind her, his arm extended holding a still-smoking musket. "If I cannot possess her, then by God, you shall not love her!" he cursed.

Vincent quickly lowered her to the ground, then launched at Edward enraged, his eyes glowing, black veins bulging, fangs extended, and plunged his hand into Edward's chest ripping out his still-beating heart and squeezed the life from it in front of Edward as he crumpled to the ground and the last glimmer left his eyes. He flung the heart to the ground, then sinking his fangs into his wrist ripped open his flesh. He fell to his knees, scooping Elizabeth up with his other arm. "Drink, drink," he pleaded as he pressed his wrist against her mouth. Her eyes stared up, unseeing, as she lay lifeless in his arms. "Please, please, don't leave me," he shook her, spilling the blood from her mouth, down her chin. It was too late. He could not save her. He could not turn her. He let out an anguished howl, "No!"

I reached for another bundle of Kleenex, blowing my nose and blubbering away, tears streaming and great gulping sobs as sad music accompanied a montage of scenes of Vincent burying Elizabeth in a plot behind the mansion, marked with a small wooden cross, snow falling. Then in the spring, placing fresh flowers on her grave and planting a willow sapling nearby. Later pulling the canvas from the angel gravestone and sitting down beside it, placing his tricorne hat on the ground next to him, loosening his cravat and the top of shirt, and holding her bracelet, moving it through his fingers like a rosary, he whispered, "Never possessed, forever loved." The montage continued with him standing at the grave as the seasons changed and the willow tree grew taller and older, and his clothing changed – Regency to Victorian to Edwardian, World War One to World War Two uniforms, then the decades, the fifties, sixties, seventies on to the present – mourning for over two hundred years at the base of the praying angel.

More tears and blubbering as the credits rolled and then the screen went black and the familiar message popped on the screen, *Are you still watching?* I knew I should hit Exit and go do something productive. I still needed to unpack my suitcase. I needed to do some laundry. I needed to get organized for work tomorrow. I needed to re-join the real world. I hit Continue. Yes, I'm still watching. The real world could wait. It's not like it missed me.

Chapter 25

*J*ake opened the new message, yet another from his manager, Carl: Heard ur back in LA. Call me! *How?!* Jake hadn't contacted anyone since he left Hawaii. Sighing he turned his phone to silent and slipped it into the saddle bag along with a water bottle and a sandwich and an apple.

"You ready, buddy?" he whispered, resting his head against the warmth of Bruno's shoulder.

The quarter horse snorted and pawed the ground, pushing against Jake.

"Ok, ok, we're going," Jake chuckled, as he mounted and settled into the saddle. They headed out the stables and out towards the ridge on the far end of the ranch. Once out in the open they set off at full gallop, a release of pent-up energy for horse, pent-up emotions for rider.

Dust filled Jake's nose as Bruno's thundering hooves kicked up the dry ground; he felt the heat from the powerful beast beneath him as he leaned into the gallop urging him on, faster and faster.

He wanted to run, put as much distance between him and Catherine as possible. Returning to Los Angeles hadn't been enough. Alone in his apartment his thoughts kept drawing him back to her. So this morning he packed up the Mercedes SL, put the top down and headed towards the ranch. Even with his foot down, flooring it, it was as if she were following behind him, keeping up, threatening to overtake.

The ridge was approaching quickly, he wanted to urge Bruno to keep going; she was still too close. He pulled on the reins, Bruno slowed to a trot as they approached the base of the ridge. There was never enough space when you needed to run from yourself.

Slowing to walk, Jake guided Bruno up a track through a bank of ancient oak trees, junipers and cottonwoods to a small clearing overlooking the ranch. He dismounted and dropped the reins letting Bruno graze while he sat on a rocky outcrop eating his sandwich watching a hawk soar in this distance, his mind quieting at last.

He reached for the apple, took a bite and chewing, looked down at the apple in his hand. *An Apple a Day.* He sighed. She was right back standing next to him. He stood up and handed the apple to Bruno who happily munched it down without second thought.

The elevator doors opened and I stepped into the foyer of Andrews and Andrews in disbelief as to how I had arrived here, like I was missing time. One minute I was sitting on the couch at home summoning up the willpower to leave and the next I had arrived. I know I left the apartment, caught the bus, walked downtown to the Wrightson building and got in the elevator, but I don't really remember actually doing it. It's like I was stationary the whole time and everything was superimposed around me as if I were standing in front of a green screen.

I'm not even sure how I managed to arrive on time. I had gone to bed far too late after finally pulling myself away from *The Blood Moon Prophecies* and overslept. I got myself ready in record time, but I was pretty sure I'd missed the bus so I sat down on the couch as I now had five minutes to kill before I needed to leave for the next one. I stared at the front door, trying to think of a credible excuse to not go. I could call in sick, say I'd got food poisoning from a bad *poké* bowl, picked up the flu from the airplane, hell I had nearly drowned, but it was just putting off the inevitable.

Then in one of those ridiculous twists of fate, my usual bus had run late too, arrived just as I got to the stop and then somehow managed to make up time en route so that I arrived at work just a couple of minutes later than usual. Lucky me.

Even late, I was the first one to arrive. I switched on the lights and walked over to the front desk. If I worked here long enough I'd wear a track in the carpet. Damn autopilot. There were times when the routine, going through the motions was a blessing, like when getting through grief. Routine, monotony, they disengaged your brain, distracted the emotions, anaesthetized the pain. But it became addictive and before you realized it, you had surrendered you free will, become dependent on it and then you ended up on time for a job you hated without realizing how you even got there.

I switched on the computer and sat down, falling momentarily when it took that split second longer than usual to make contact with the seat. Whoever had been temping was obviously a hobbit. I then proceeded to go through the predictable bobbing up and down and tilting back and forth as I struggled with the stupid levers to get the chair back to the way I liked it.

Sighing, I looked over at my work tray, piled high with files needing attention; the message light on the switchboard phone was blinking wildly, like the countdown on an impending missile launch and there were over a hundred emails in my inbox, the most recent dozen or so all marked URGENT in the subject line, just in case I might have missed the red exclamation mark pinned to each one. I felt sick.

It's not too late. My heart began to race, fight or flight instinct kicking in. *Get out! Run!* No one had seen me arrive, I could leave and they would never know. *Do it! Now!* My palms were sweaty and my legs started to shake even before I stood up. *Run and never turn back!* I switched off the computer screen, grabbed my bag and coat from behind the desk and bolted towards the elevator.

Before I could reach it, Mr. Andrews' voice hit me as the doors opened and he stepped out. "You're back, wonderful!" he boomed.

I recoiled as surely as if I had been hit by a bullet. I felt myself crumple backwards, replaying the scene when Edward shot Elizabeth, Vincent's howling *No!* echoing in my mind.

I turned and went back to my desk, "I was just–" I started, trying to explain my odd behavior, but it was obvious he either hadn't noticed or wasn't interested. I set down my bag and coat, switched on the screen, "Yes, I'm back." I said sitting down. *God help me.*

"You have a good holiday?" he asked, stopping at the front desk.

"Yes, it was lovely. I–"

"Great. Well if you could make a start with these letters first," he said patting the pile of files on my desk, "they are quite urgent. The temp was struggling with the work load, so we told her not to worry and just leave them for you, but they can't wait any longer."

"Of course, no problem," I said forcing a smile.

"Excellent. Well, now you're all rested, it's time to step up and apply yourself, yes?"

I felt my eyes starting to well up. *Jake, save me! Please!* How was I ever going to be able to go back to this infernal existence, this life sentence when I had had a taste of what my life could have been?

"I mean it, Cathy, you need to stop coasting. Show me that initiative, you said you have."

I nodded, "One hundred and ten percent."

"That's the spirit." He smiled, slapping the reception desk triumphantly before heading off to his office.

He had a point though, it was time I stopped coasting. Except I didn't need to change gear, I needed to change direction. A task that felt as monumental as trying to steer the *Titanic* away from imminent doom with a paddle.

"Cathy, you're back!" Amira cried as the elevator doors opened and the ladies spilled out, babbling away like bubbles fizzing from a soda. She rushed over to give me a hug. "How was it? Did you have a good time?"

I nodded, "Yes, it was really nice."

"You look like it did you good."

"You think so?"

"You have a kind of glow about you."

I blushed, *you have no idea*. "Well, I did catch the sun."

"Welcome back," chimed the other two as they reached my desk.

"So how was the holiday?" asked Jess.

They gathered round waiting to be debriefed.

"It was lovely. Hawaii is really beautiful and the weather was fantastic." I said.

"Come on, details!" Amira begged.

I grinned, "Oh, you know, just sun, sand, sight-seeing and..." *Sex. Lots of hot sweaty sex with JAKE DONOVAN!* "... shopping, lots of shopping."

"So nothing *exciting* then?" scoffed Alex.

"No, afraid not, it was pretty uneventful." I sucked in my lip, blushing as images of flesh on flesh, interlaced fingers pushing against white sheets, eyes locked through shared moans of ecstasy flashed in my mind.

"But, you must've heard about the big drama though?" asked Alex.

"What big drama?" I asked, my palms beginning to sweat.

"Apparently Jake Donovan saved some tourist from drowning in Waimanalo Beach."

"Really?"

"Isn't that where you were staying?" asked Jess

I nodded, feeling my stomach lurch.

"Some teenager posted a photo of Jake helping to load someone into an ambulance. Said he saw the whole thing, Jake pulling her from the ocean and doing CPR and everything."

"Can you imagine, Jake Donovan giving you mouth-to-mouth!" Jess pressed the back of her hand to her forehead in a mock swoon.

I didn't have to imagine.

"It was all over Facebook and Twitter. Surely you saw it?" said Alex.

"No, I missed it. I didn't check Facebook till I got back. So, it wasn't in the papers or anything?"

"Nah, just the tabloids, but they just rehashed the same stuff from social media," said Jess.

I let out a sigh, "Well, that's a relief," I said settling back in my chair.

"Why is that?" asked Alex confused.

I shifted awkwardly, "Oh, just that I'm sure he probably wouldn't want it splashed all over the TV news."

Alex raised an eyebrow, eyeing me, "Why not, he's a star?"

"I'm sure he'd want to protect the woman's privacy."

"I guess so," said Jess.

"I mean, no one knows her name, right?"

The ladies nodded.

"So, if she hasn't come forward with her story then I'd say she wants to keep it private." It's not that it was private, so much as *personal*. Intimate. I swallowed back the lump beginning to form in my throat.

"Pity, you couldn't have bumped into him, I'd love to know who the mystery woman is." Jess sighed.

"Mystery woman?" I choked.

"You missed that too?"

I stared at them blankly. *Shit. Shit. Shit.*

"Yeah, he and Kristie finally go public and then he's seen with some new woman," Amira added grinning, "celebs, right?"

"I'm sure it was nothing," snapped Alex, "he wouldn't do that to her."

I nodded, "Absolutely. The woman's probably his sister."

"Exactly!" Alex crowed.

Amira eyed me suspiciously.

I looked away to reach for the ringing phone. *Saved by the bell.* I breathed a sigh of relief as I answered and losing interest, the group dispersed.

Later, I looked up the news stories, to see for myself what had been said; worried that Jake would think I had betrayed his confidence. Thankfully accounts of the rescue seemed to be limited to the teen, whose photo caught only Jake's back and the rear of the ambulance, and an unnamed staff member who had confirmed that they had seen Jake with an unknown woman at the hospital. I wondered if it was the overly-chatty nurse or the orderly with exploding hair. The hospital's official statement was that they could not comment.

A search of 'Jake's mystery woman' brought up a few pictures of Jake and a woman with brown hair walking on the beach, shopping, eating together, sometimes hand-in-hand, but nothing compromising. The photos were all suitably amateur, blurry and taken at a distance, that it wasn't possible to make out the woman's features. She could've been anyone. I sighed, even on the arm of a superstar I was vanilla, easily mistaken for someone else, forgettable.

It goes without saying that I didn't get a lot of work done, despite the mountain I had to get through. I kept finding myself staring into space oblivious to the ringing phone or clients standing at the desk. I'd sit through minutes of dictation not hearing any of it, not typing a word. Instead I'd find myself staring out seeing Jake's smiling face backlit, a halo around him, seeing him present me with a frangipani flower, feeling his hand on my back, hearing his laugh, feeling his lips on my neck. Then I'd open my eyes and I'd be back staring at the blinking cursor on the computer screen.

I ended up eating my lunch at the desk while I carried on working, or at least enacted the performance of looking like I was working. I had just taken a rather large bite of my sandwich – you'd think I'd learn, especially after the relish saga – and was chewing away, my cheeks bulging, when Mr. Andrews came round the corner and dumped a package on my desk.

"Get this couriered to LA by four o'clock today."

I nearly choked and swallowed hard. "Um, I can't do that," I coughed the words out.

He turned cherry red, "Can't you interrupt your lunch for five minutes?!" he barked.

"It's not that–" I started.

"Typical! This is what I'm talking about. You're never willing to go out of your way, never willing to put yourself out. And you wonder why I didn't give you a raise. Just do your fff..." he stopped himself from saying it. Barely.

"Just do your job."

"I am," I replied tersely. "It's just that it's not possible for it to get there today."

Mr. Andrews' face grew even redder than I thought was possible. "How do you know? You haven't even called the courier yet!" he spat, barely holding back from yelling.

"I don't need to. It's half past one now, it'll take at least half an hour before the courier gets here to collect the package. Then assuming they've got no more pick-ups they've got to go all the way to the airport, although it's more likely they'd go to a central depot first. From there it's got to be sorted, loaded onto the first available flight. Then it's got a good hour and half in the air before it arrives on the other side and once it's there it's not going to go directly to the client, it's got to be offloaded, sorted..."

"Ok, ok, I get it." He grumbled, "Just make sure it gets there overnight then."

"Of course," I said with a cheery smile as I picked up the phone and dialed the courier watching him scowl and stomp off to his office.

Yes! I punched the air in triumph. *You wanted initiative. How was that?* Klaxons blazing, I was at my ship's helm at last. *Hard to starboard and arm the torpedoes!* I couldn't believe how much I was standing up for myself these days. Where was it coming from? Perhaps I really had been reborn. I smiled, feeling a lump in my throat. *Jake. Thank you.*

The ringing phone broke me from my reverie, "Andrews and Andrews, Cathy—" I paused. *Cathy's gone.* "Catherine speaking, how may I help you?" I continued, grinning.

"So, how was the holiday?" Carl leaned back in his chair.

"Good. Quiet." Jake sipped his coffee, gazing absently at the dozens of autographed celebrity headshots and movie posters on the wall behind his manager.

"Really? That's not what the media says." Carl sat forward, slapping a tabloid down on the desk, "'Is Jake cheating on Kristie?'"

Jake jumped, almost spilling his coffee, put the cup down and picked up the magazine turning to the page Carl had purposefully marked with a Post-It.

"'Who is Jake's mystery woman?'" Carl said, tossing another magazine across, "'Jake Donovan: Real Life Hero'," adding another to the pile.

"Crap," sighed Jake taking the magazines and paging through them, "I didn't think she would be the type to..." he trailed off. "When did all this break?"

"About a week ago. It was all over social media at first, then the tabloids got it. Why do you think I've been trying to reach you?"

"Yeah, sorry, I only checked my messages when I got back." Jake flicked through the magazines, skim-reading the articles.

"So, is any of this true?"

"Some of it." He sighed with relief, from the articles and photos it looked like she hadn't sold her story, but that it had been leaked to the press by the kid whose phone he borrowed and random people in the street who saw them together and shared their blurry phone snaps online.

"Okay, let's start with the hero story. Some tourist gets into trouble in the water and goes to the press with a story that Jake Donovan saved her to cover that she's a lousy swimmer and that doesn't concern you?"

"Because, I did."

"What?"

"I did rescue someone from drowning."

"Okay, tell me everything."

Jake went on to explain the events from the moment he saw the woman floating in the ocean to the moment she had been seen by the doctor."

"Why the hell didn't you tell me right away?"

"Because, you'd want to spin it for the publicity. I didn't do it for the glory. Besides I wanted to respect her privacy."

"How did she know you'd be at the beach?"

"Are you suggesting she set me up? I had no plans to be at that beach until ten minutes before I drove there, so no, there's no way she could've known. Seriously, if I hadn't seen her, if I'd arrived even a minute later it would have been, 'Jake Donovan pulls dead body from ocean'. Try putting a cheerful spin on that one."

"Okay, okay. What about the mystery woman then? Who is she?"

"The same."

"What? I thought you didn't know her."

"I didn't."

"Then how did you go from pulling her from the ocean to being seen hand-in-hand with her?"

"She was in Hawaii alone. She had no one to check on her. I just wanted to make sure she was okay, but then the more I got to know her, the more I liked her."

"Did you sleep with her?"

"What does that matter? Besides, I'm not seeing her anymore."

"So, it's over?"

Jake nodded. "It would never have worked. You know what it's like."

"Ordinarily I'd agree with you, but what the hell were you thinking?!"

"Well, clearly I wasn't, but I did the right thing. I broke it off sooner rather than later."

"Not getting involved with her in the first place, would have been the right thing." Carl sighed, "Jesus Jake, you save her life, sleep with her and then you dump her."

"I know, I know. It looks bad."

"Christ, Jake, I'm not just worried about bad optics here, you opened yourself to one hell of a potential law suit... 'Jake Donovan took advantage of me while I was vulnerable'..." he ran a hand through his thinning hair.

"It wasn't like that, Carl."

"I sure hope she knows that."

"She does. I'm sure."

"Okay. But, you know how to contact this woman if we need to bury this?

Jake nodded.

"Good. Now, what about Kristie?"

"What about her?"

"Is there any truth to that?"

"You know I can't stand the woman. That story about us getting together was completely her doing."

"Well, it certainly got the fans eager for season three to air."

"I'm pretty sure it wasn't the show's ratings she was trying to boost."

"Sure, sure, but it might be a good idea to play along till people forget about the mystery woman."

"I won't be doing that. I'm not playing her game and I wouldn't do that to Catherine."

"It would take the attention off her."

"I know, but she wasn't just a fling." Jake sighed, "It meant something. That's why I had to break it off, to save her from all the bullshit." He looked out the window at the Los Angeles skyline beyond, weariness beginning to set in. "Was there anything else?"

Carl nodded and went through upcoming events Jake was booked to attend, including an appearance on the Elaine show to promote the next season of *Hawaii Heartbeat* and also the annual *Blood Moon Prophecies* convention in November. Jake nodded and added in a few perfectly-timed yups and gotchas to maintain the appearance of actually listening.

Jake put the key in the ignition, then sat back, sinking into the leather bucket seat, rested his head back staring up at the blackened roof of the parking garage. He shouldn't have let things end the way they did. He should never have slept with her, should never have kissed her. No, he had to rewind further; he had crossed the point of no return earlier than that. He should never have taken her to dinner and gone out with her. No. Further back. He should never have brought her to the hotel in the first place. Still earlier than that. He should never have gone with her to the hospital.

The triage bay. Overcome with exhaustion and the enormity of what had just happened he had leaned over the railing of the gurney. He hadn't realized he'd sighed out loud, hadn't thought she'd noticed. Then she'd reached over and touched his arm. He'd looked over and she'd looked into his eyes – with such unselfish concern and empathy, as if she could see his soul – and told *him* everything was going to be okay. And he'd known she didn't mean physically. It had unnerved him and that was it. That was the moment when she had broken down his defenses. That was the moment he stumbled and fell.

"Damn it!" he hissed, and slammed his hand down against the steering wheel. He reached over and turned the key, starting the engine then backed out the car and headed downtown.

Chapter 26

*I*t had been two weeks and the holiday felt like it was two years ago. All trace of it had been relegated to memory. Memory? Was it a memory or was it a dream? It was like those times when you find yourself saying, *oh that's just like the time I...* and then you stop because you realize you're talking about something that never actually happened; that what you're remembering is not a memory, but in fact the memory of a dream, an ephemeral imprint of something that was never real at all.

I'd slept with Jake's T-shirt every night, but I could no longer smell him on it. I was starting to wonder if I had bought it myself, that if I reviewed the store's security footage it would show me alone in the store, talking to no one. Perhaps I had stopped breathing for longer than I realized and as a part of my brain died, the rest compensated by creating a whole narrative that I was starting to discover was fiction. I mean, it had been all too good to be true.

The more it felt like a fiction, the more my new confidence was taking a beating. I'd been trying so hard to be a new me, to be that person I was becoming while I was with Jake, but without him there didn't seem to be much point. And if he hadn't even been real, well...

Thank goodness it was Friday. Another half hour before I could go home, although the rest of the office was already in weekend mode, winding down with drinks in the boardroom. The pizzas had been ordered and from the clinking of glassware and bottles coming from the boardroom it was obvious the carousing was already well underway without me. Not that I particularly wanted to join in, I clearly wasn't being missed. It was okay for the rest of them to finish early, but if I joined in before five I'd be reprimanded for leaving the reception unattended. Yet, because I was always the last to show up, that proved my team spirit was lacking. I sighed at the double standard as I watched the minutes count down.

At least Amira had a convenient excuse for avoiding the weekly team bonding, not that her religious beliefs actually barred her from attending. Being the only one drinking orange juice was more alienating than her faith, so she played the religion card. I envied her. Without Amira, I had no one to talk with. I was never included in the conversation and banter; I'd sit in a corner on my own, sipping a half glass of wine I never finished, listening to the inane and posturing prattle with a fake smile plastered to my face.

Alex walked past me carrying three more bottles of wine from the kitchen just as the elevator chimed.

"Pizza's here!" she exclaimed putting down the bottles on my desk. Then let out an irritated sigh when a courier delivery guy stepped out carrying a package.

"I've a package for—" he started as he walked over to the desk.

Alex snatched the parcel from his hands, "Must be the Henry case files. I've been waiting all day for these!"

I smiled apologetically to him and signed his tablet for them. He tipped his baseball cap at me and hurried on his way.

"What the hell is this?" she exclaimed after tearing open the plastic wrapper to reveal several layers of bubble wrap. She squeezed the corner, "it feels like a picture frame."

I looked up mildly interested.

Alex turned the parcel over and looked at the sender's mailing address, "It's from some PO box address in Los Angeles, from…" she smoothed the creases from the label, "a J. Donaldson," she finished, screwing up her nose.

I shuddered as my heart jumped into my throat, "May I see that?" I asked choking on my words.

Alex either didn't hear or flatly ignored me, "Must've come to the wrong address," she said, turning the parcel over again to read the front address. "No," she said surprised, "it's actually addressed to you." She tossed the parcel to me, irritated, "If you're going to have stuff sent to you, you need to have it sent to your home address. This is not your personal post office." She picked up the bottles and strutted back to the boardroom.

Shaking, I pulled the bubble-wrapped package from the plastic sleeve then carefully peeled away each piece of sticky tape. I unfolded the layers of bubble wrap to expose a parcel in heavy pearl wrapping paper. Again, I carefully peeled away the sticky tape and layers of white tissue, to reveal a heavy gold embossed picture frame. A large white envelope, with 'Catherine' written on it sat on top, obscuring the picture. I picked up the envelope and looked at the picture. It was the photo Jake took of me wading in the water at Waimanalo Beach that he said reminded him of a Greek goddess. I ran my fingers over the glass, smiling. I knew it. I knew he felt something for me. He just needed time. I was going to get my happy ending after all.

A sudden roar of laughter from the boardroom startled me and I quickly wrapped up the picture and hid it under my desk. Heart pounding, I opened the envelope and pulled out a letter, hand-written on heavy paper.

Catherine,

You should have a copy of this, to remind you of
how beautiful you are.

I never meant to hurt you. I wish I had been
stronger, I should never have let things go so far.
I'm sorry for the way things ended. I wish I'd
done a better job of saying goodbye.

I'll always remember our time with fondness.
You are so special, you deserve to be happy.

*So I say goodbye properly now. Keep striving
forward and don't look back. I know you can do
it and I know you'll find someone who will love
you the way you deserve to be loved.*

*I know you wanted more and I wish I could have
been the right person for you.*

– Jake.

I read it a second time, not comprehending, like someone standing on a beach watching the ocean rush back as if draining into some unseen plughole. Then just as the connection is made, a giant wave appears and it's too late to run. A tsunami of tears reached my eyes and I broke down into uncontrollable sobs.

"Is someone going to answer that!"

Alex's yelling from the boardroom jerked me back to the ringing telephone. Choking on sobs, I wiped the tears from my cheeks and picked up the phone. I stammered the usual greeting, but the line was dead. I was too late in picking up. Too fucking bad! I slammed down the damn phone. In that moment I hated it with every fiber of my being. I fell forward burying my face in my hands.

"Catherine? What's wrong?"

I looked up to see Amira crouched beside me, her hand on my shoulder.

I sniffed and wiped away more tears. "Nothing. It's nothing."

"It doesn't look like nothing. Has something happened?"

I shook my head, nodded, shook my head, tried to smile, my lip quivering. The words I wished I could say filled my mouth, poised and ready. I swallowed them back.

"I have to go," I said hoarsely, scooping up my bag and the parcel and grabbing my coat.

"No problem, I'll take over. Go. I understand." she said, helping me with my coat.

How could she possibly understand? I smiled weakly and

hugged her, then bolted for the elevator, which mercifully opened as soon as I hit the button. The doors closed and I leaned back against the wall as fresh tears splashed down my cheeks with every shaking sob.

I couldn't find anywhere in the apartment to put the picture that didn't make me start to cry every time I looked at it, so I wrapped it and the letter in the same tissue and wrap, and placed it in my grandmother's old oak hope chest at the foot of the bed. A hope chest that contained little hope, only sadness and regret, a collection of old school journals, forgotten photo albums, travel keepsakes, unfinished stories I've written, and other unaccomplished dreams. Echoes of times that slipped away like sand sifting through fingers and moments, once full of life pressed between the pages of an old book, now faded, the color muddied, two-dimensional, see-through, fragile.

Jake was right, it would never have worked out. The magic would have worn off as routine and domesticity set in. Walking away meant we could keep it pure, undiluted. The transcendence of the encounter was in its rarity. It was as if it were an exquisite elixir, rare and potent, capable of healing in minute quantities, but increase the dose and it becomes a lethal toxin.

I began writing a letter to Jake, to thank him for the picture, but after my third draft I gave up. No matter how I tried to word it, it came across as a desperate plea for him to take me back. In the end I settled on a few vague lines thanking him for the gift and intimating that I had moved on. A lie of course, but the honest truth was too painful, too pathetic. I added my phone number and home address, leaving the door open for him in the tiny hope that he may try to contact me again. One day.

In the weeks that followed, I unfollowed Jake on social media, stopped watching *The Blood Moon Prophecies* though I still had three seasons to go, and finally washed his T-shirt. I folded it neatly, precisely, the way a flag is folded into a tight triangle at a military funeral, and as I solemnly placed it on top of the photo frame in Nan's chest, I imagined a solitary trumpet in the distance playing the last post, followed by a three-volley rifle salute. Then the sound of dirt hitting the top of the casket as I slowly lowered the heavy lid of the chest, committing yet another love that never was to my memory graveyard.

If everything happened for a reason, then perhaps I had to accept that the reason was something else, something other than finding my happily-ever-after with Jake Donovan. Perhaps, the heartbreak was the cruel price I had to pay for cheating death, a hot poker to drive me forwards. Because now, the only way left for me was forward. Everything behind me had been reduced to ash.

So, taking a deep breath of determination and staring straight ahead, I started working on turning *An Apple a Day* into a full-length novel, and I applied to the Deighton Academy in Los Angeles for their scholarship and Creative Writing for Page and Screen programs. I had nothing left to lose. And I did my best to deny that at the back of my mind, tucked away in the dark, was a tiny seed of hope that if I did get in, if I could move to LA, then maybe, just maybe I might cross paths with Jake once more.

Chapter 27

ake sat in the studio holding area, his makeup had been done and he was now being fitted with a wireless microphone pack. The sound assistant attached the tiny lapel microphone to Jake's collar and clipped the battery pack to Jake's belt behind him, under his jacket.

"Can you give us a sound check?" he asked.

Jake nodded and began counting to ten.

Hearing confirmation via his headphones from the sound engineer, he gave Jake a thumbs-up and walked off.

Jake looked over at the guest who was up after him, some self-made social media influencer. She wore a bright pink shrink-wrap pantsuit and despite the studio makeup, was checking herself in a compact, pouting her Botox lips and smoothing her hair with the palms of her hands careful not to get her bedazzled fingernails or garish rings caught in her lacquered curls. He sighed, of all the people he had to share air time with... Even Kristie would have been preferable.

She snapped the compact shut and slipped it into her matching pink box purse then leaned forward, her silicone bosom straining for freedom against her tight jacket as she reached for a glass of water.

"Mr. Donovan, you're on in five."

Jake looked up as the runner approached, busily checking things off on her clipboard, "Thanks." He said standing up.

She nodded and motioned for him to follow her. She stepped forward bumping into the pink diva's arm causing her to spill water down her front.

"Oh my God!" she screamed.

The runner looked down horrified, "Ms. Fisher, I'm so sorry," she apologized, "at least it's just water."

"Just water!" Ms. Fisher screamed, "This is Prada, you never get it wet!"

"It was an accident, I'm really sorry."

"Sorry? I'll have you fired you incompetent waste of space!"

"Some help please!" the runner called for a production assistant, "Can you take Ms. Fisher back to wardrobe," she instructed, then gesturing to Jake to follow, left the young man to suffer the rest of the woman's tirade while she walked Jake over to the wings.

"You okay?" asked Jake.

"Sure, nothing I haven't dealt with before," she sighed, "but thanks," she said handing him over to the floor director.

Jake waited in the wings, staring out at the studio audience, his mind wandering to her. He smiled as he pictured her with the breeze in her hair, the way she laughed when he caught her with her hand down her blouse. His smile faded. He missed her. Especially at times like this, surrounded by the lights and cameras and fake fawning people, he craved her unselfish authenticity more than ever. He had tried to deny it, tried to remind himself that he had made the right call, but the more time passed the more he felt a growing emptiness. He closed his eyes, bit his lip and leaned against the wall. It was too late now, what was done, was done.

"Mr. Donovan?" the floor director tapped him on the shoulder.

Jake looked up and nodded, watching him count down the seconds with his fingers and hearing the audience roar as Elaine announced his name. Then taking a deep breath, he pulled on the character of Jake Donovan, Hollywood heartthrob and superstar, smoothed out the creases and stepped out onto the stage beaming and waving while inside more of his heart atrophied.

It had been nearly two months since I wrote to Jake. I hadn't had any response. I wasn't expecting one, but I couldn't help wondering if he had even received my note. Had that even been his return address? It wasn't like I could look him up in the White Pages. Perhaps that had been the address of *Hawaii Heartbeat's* production company or his agent? Would they pass my note on to him or simply bin it or add it to a pile of fan mail he would never read?

I tried not to think about it. I had decided that if I wasn't meant to be with Jake, then our meeting was supposed to inspire me to write, to follow my dreams. It was a noble thought, but the truth was I didn't want Jake to be my inspiration. I wanted him to be my love.

But, how could it be love? We had spent only five days together, that was hardly enough time to get to know someone, let alone fall in love. I tried convincing myself that what I felt was all in my head, simply infatuation because of who he was, because someone like him had paid attention to someone like me. I tried telling myself that I wouldn't have fallen for him if he was just a regular guy. But, then I found myself remembering the way we talked for hours, the walks along the beach, the way he cooked me dinner, the way he sat with me at the hospital and I'd come back to the conclusion that even as a regular guy, I loved him.

They say time heals, but what they fail to tell you is that you first have to lose hope. As long as there is hope, the wound won't ever close. And I still had hope, a deep-seated malignant hope that was festering and invading my life. Losing Jake felt as if a part of my body had died. Gangrene had set in and was spreading. I needed an amputation otherwise the hope he'd come back threatened to destroy me. I had survived drowning only to be doomed to die of an incurable infection.

I sat watching out the window as the bus made its way along the familiar route through the city and on up the hill towards tree-lined streets of houses and apartment blocks. My new life felt a lot like my old one. Work was intolerable as ever. In fact it had gotten worse since I stood up to Mr. Andrews. Turns out he liked me better when I was subservient than when I showed initiative. I was still working on my novel, but it was progressing slowly, clumsily, making me wonder if I really had any talent at all. I felt like a fraud, I wasn't a real writer, I was just pretending. I kicked myself for applying to the Deighton Academy. I should have used the application fee on something I actually needed instead of sending away for a pricey rejection letter.

I sighed as the bus arrived at my stop and the doors sprang open. I stepped out onto the street feeling the autumn chill and I walked up to the apartment block pulling my coat tighter. I made my way inside and closing the door, switched on the lights, slowly illuminating the darkness with an insipid glow as the eco-bulbs warmed up. I paused to switch on the TV then headed to the bedroom to change out of my work clothes hearing a nasally woman's voice babbling away. *The Elaine Show.* I sighed, regretting I hadn't also hit the mute button. I detested the woman; so full of herself. I pulled on some leggings and a sweatshirt and padded back to the living room.

As I reached over the couch and picked up the remote, the studio audience went wild with cheers and screams and someone shouted, 'Jake, I love you!' I stopped, my finger poised over the remote, staring at the screen as Jake strode on to the stage. He was smiling broadly, waving to the audience. I sat down heavily. Jake, all Jake. Not Vincent Dubois or Ethan Temple, a character I could separate from the man who played them. This was him, as real as he was in Hawaii. The same clean-shaven chin, the dark hair, steel blue eyes, soft lips, the errant curl. He looked directly at the camera and it was like he was in the room standing in front of me.

The cheering and applauding died down and Jake settled in the armchair opposite Elaine.

"Welcome Jake, it's great to have you on the show."

"Thank you. It's great to be here." Jake shifted in the chair. He was smiling, but it was a smile I knew, one that told me he wasn't comfortable, at all.

"I think I can speak for all of us when I say we can't wait for season three of *Hawaii Heartbeat*, am I right?" she said raising her hands and turning to the audience, causing them to erupt in cheers once more.

Jake turned towards the audience smiling, his smile even more visibly strained and waved, then turned back to Elaine.

"Yes, that's right. It'll be dropping next month."

"The big question is, of course, are we finally going to see Ethan and Britney get together?"

"Well, that's what everyone wants to know, but you know I can't tell you. You're going to have to wait and watch the show."

"Oh come on, you can't give us a hint?"

Jake strained a smile again, shifted awkwardly, but said nothing.

"Well, it's official you and Kristie are dating?"

"Apparently so." His smile changed to his gorgeous smirk. He was playing along.

"So, that's a hint, isn't it?"

"If you say so. But, I'm sure you'll appreciate that Kristie and I would like to keep our relationship private and out of the spotlight."

I laughed. *Oh well played, Jake.* That was exactly the opposite of what she'd want.

"Of course, so the rumors that you guys were in trouble are false then?"

"I believe so."

"What about the mystery woman in Hawaii?"

"What mystery woman?"

"Oh come now, no need to keep evading. This woman," she pointed to a screen behind them displaying a series of images of Jake with a woman seen in Hawaii, long brown hair, occasionally they were holding hands. But her face, my face was never clear. I felt my stomach churn.

"A friend," Jake answered, shifting uncomfortably.

"Oh really? Do you hold hands with all your friends when you're dating someone else?"

"I'm close with many of my friends."

Elaine stared at him, waiting for him to elaborate, but he said nothing more.

Realizing he wasn't going to give her the answer she wanted, she changed tack, "Okay. So let's talk *Hawaii Heartbeat*. What *can* you tell us?"

Jake went on to talk about the show, how we would be seeing a different side of Ethan, a darker side, the part that was unravelling and facing demons from his past, which would result in him making bad decisions. He talked about how the show was becoming more character-driven around the life and moral decisions of Ethan.

"Before we move on," said Elaine cutting him off, "we can't ignore the fact that you are a hero in real life."

Jake's smile faded as she continued, turning to the audience again, motioning them to cheer and applause once again.

"You're my hero!" someone yelled in the back.

"Our Jake saved a woman from drowning while in Hawaii, isn't that right?" she said as the cheering died down.

Jake smiled stiffly.

"So, give us the details, what happened?"

"I just happened to be in the right place at the right time. I did what anyone would do."

"Such modesty," she teased to more cheers from the audience. "Tell us more."

Jake sighed, "I had stopped by the beach to drink a coffee, saw someone in trouble in the water and I took action."

"Did you have to give her mouth to mouth?"

Jake nodded uncomfortably.

"Oh, be still my beating heart!" Elaine cried, placing her hand against her chest as the audience went wild, "Every woman's – and many men's – fantasy, am I right?"

"Believe me, it was very serious. I was terrified she wasn't going to make it."

Jake's face went dark and the audience fell silent. Even Elaine's grin evaporated.

"I'm thankful I knew what to do. Though even with all the paramedic and emergency training I did to prepare for the role of Dr. Temple, I wasn't at all prepared for the real thing. I don't know how I would have coped if she hadn't made it." He paused, looking away from the camera.

I felt the familiar lump in my throat, and guilt at being responsible for his pain. What if I hadn't made it, if I had died on that beach? I would never have known he was there, but he would have been forever haunted by the unknown woman he couldn't save. I pressed my hand to my mouth, stifling a sob.

"But, she did make it, right?" Elaine's tone had changed, becoming gentler.

"Yes," Jake looked up and smiled.

"Do you know what became of her?"

Jake looked anxious, as if he expected Elaine to open a door to reveal me standing behind it. "I believe she recovered well and returned home."

"So you know her name?"

"I do, but I won't reveal it; you're hoping she'll come on the show?"

"That would be fantastic, reunite the both of you, what a story!"

"What happened to her is private and it's not for me to share it and I ask you to respect her privacy also. You're only interested in her story because of me. If someone else had rescued her, you wouldn't be interested, would you?"

"You tell her, Jake!" I exclaimed as Elaine's grin dropped at a sudden loss for words.

"I'm glad I was there to help." He continued, "That experience will be with me always. It changed me as a person, helped me gain some fresh perspectives. I'll never forget her." He looked tired, worn down.

I felt the tears welling up, he did feel something; he was talking about more than just the rescue. "I'll never forget you too," I called out at the TV. "I'm right here."

He turned looking into the camera, his expression turning

serious as if he'd heard and was talking directly to me, "I trust she's happy and moved on with her life."

No, not you too. Don't tell me to move on. I choked, tears spilling down my cheeks, and reached for the box of Kleenex on the coffee table. I didn't hear the rest as she said goodbye to Jake and I watched through tears as he got up and walked away, to more cheers of adoration. And then he was gone and replaced by dancing potato chips diving into a bowl of dip to the tune of some jingle, drowned out by my sobs.

Move on? What did that even mean? It was always said with the assumption that there was something in front of you to move on to, bandied about as if it were a benign sentiment meant to encourage, as if moving on were some kind of noble activity, a kind of spiritual transformation. The way night moves on to day, winter moves on to spring.

But in reality, moving on was brutal, agonizing. It's the kick in the guts when you're down. Like a homeless person, haggard and dirty, and pushing all they possess in a pilfered shopping cart with nowhere to go, takes refuge in a bus shelter and a burly cop kicks them where they sleep, on the cold concrete, and says 'hey you, you need to move on'.

You need to move on was just another way of saying no loitering... *Yes, I loved you, but it's over now. I have given you all I can. There's no longer any place in my life for you. You're in the way now, you can't stay here – you need to move on.*

I sniffed back the tears and wiped my face hearing Elaine's annoying voice start up again welcoming us back to her show. I looked around the couch for the remote to end her.

"Viewers in the San Francisco area can see Jake in person at *The Blood Moon Prophecies* convention at the San Francisco Park Regent on the 18th and 19th of November. My next guest is..."

I froze. Jake was going to be here? In San Francisco! How had I missed this? Why didn't he say anything in Hawaii? He must've already known back then, these things were organized months in advance.

I muted Elaine and grabbed my laptop, the 18th and 19th were just two weeks away! Shaking, I found the convention's web page. There he was, alongside Bryce and Jennifer Kempen, staring at me with that smirky smile. I ran my hand over the screen, trying to remember the feel of his skin against mine. If I could just see him again... If he could just see me again... Just once more, even if I had to pay for it. He couldn't tell me to leave, to *move on*, if I had paid to be there.

I scrolled through the ticket options. Gold passes for both days cost $750; $1300 if you wanted to be in the front row! Not that it mattered, they were already sold out. So were the silver and copper passes and all the autograph and photo opportunity passes. Of course, they were. All that was left were general admission tickets which allowed access to the merchandise vendor hall and the cast panel discussion on the Sunday afternoon, standing room only, and only gold and silver pass holders would be allowed to ask questions. Naturally. I felt my tears welling up again, how would I bear being so close, yet not be able to speak to him, to touch him? But, I couldn't *not* go either. I fetched my credit card, took a deep breath, and clicked on the purchase button.

"I just knew the stories about Jake's mystery woman were all hype," said Jess as she and Alex left the elevator.

"Of course, I mean Jake and Kristie are meant to be," crowed Alex.

I looked up, obviously they also had seen the Elaine show.

Jess let out a moan "Can you imagine being rescued by him? To die for!"

"Absolutely. I bet she wasn't really in any trouble and faked it, just to meet him."

"You're so right! I mean, who wouldn't?" Jess agreed.

"That assumes she knew he was watching and I didn't." I butted in.

Alex looked at me suspiciously, "You didn't, what?"

"Um, I just, I meant," feeling panic flush my cheeks, "I got the impression from what he said, that the woman didn't know he was there."

"You watched Elaine's interview with Jake Donovan?" asked Jess impressed.

I nodded, "It sounded like if he had arrived even a few seconds later things might have been more tragic. He seemed genuinely shaken by the whole thing, so I doubt was she faking."

"You've changed your opinion about him," said Alex, "I thought you thought he was brainless and shallow."

"I watched some of *The Blood Moon Prophecies* after I got back from Hawaii. I have to admit there's more to him than I thought."

"See!" Alex smiled triumphantly.

And for a moment there was a bond, something we had in common, some common ground. Perhaps we weren't so different. Perhaps I was the one who had to reach out on her terms; speak a language she spoke. "I hear he's going to be here in two weeks. There's a *Blood Moon Prophecies* convention." I added enthusiastically.

"I know, Jess and I are going. We can't wait!"

"You're going?" Of course, they'd be going.

"Oh yes, we booked our tickets months ago. Gold all the way, baby!" Alex high-fived Jess. "We're getting the full package, if you know what I mean," she winked, "front row seats to everything, photo ops, exclusive party with the cast, one-on-one time."

"Yeah, autographs are for the peasants." Jess laughed.

The common ground caved in as they walked off leaving me alone and left out again. I would never be one of them. Not that I really wanted to, I reminded myself. I didn't want to be like them, I just wanted to be liked by them.

I suddenly felt exhausted. I hadn't slept, my mind had kept me awake all night as it ran through dozens of scenarios of how I might conspire to see Jake. There had to be some way I could grab his attention, make him see me. Fake a fainting spell, jump up and down waving and yelling 'Jake, it's me', fake a press pass? Perhaps I could ask at the hotel's front desk to speak to Jonathan Donaldson, but I doubted that would work. If he was staying at that hotel there wouldn't be much point of checking in under his real name when he was attending a convention in his honor. Besides he probably would be staying at a different hotel, somewhere posher. The best I could come up with was to wear the T-shirt he gave me, get a place at the front of the standing crowd, and hope to catch his eye. Perhaps hold up a sign with my name on it?

It made me sick thinking how Alex and Jess would see him; that they would be close enough to touch him, and no doubt they would, while I would be consigned to the background, drowned out in the noise. All I could hold onto was that I had something they didn't. They had their gold passes, they would get their photo ops and their schmoozing, but they would never have what I had. I laughed to myself: *you get what you pay for*. The Jake they were paying to see was fake. The Jake I knew was the one that money couldn't buy, priceless and precious. No matter how much they paid, they would never know the Jake I knew.

Chapter 28

ake sat down at his designated table draped in a black sheet and stocked with stacks of prints of his headshot and a box of marker pens. The chair wobbled as he shifted his weight. *Great.* He let out a heavy sigh, the day was only half way through and he already felt drained. The morning had been spent doing five-minute interviews, a kind of journalistic speed dating event, with an endless stream of reviewers and bloggers desperate for an exclusive sound bite. They all spurted the same questions to which he regurgitated the same answers. The same old questions about Vincent's motivation as if his character's motives might have changed in the years since the series had come to an end; as if some secret had been held back to be revealed only now to a select few in a stuffy hotel convention room. The same looks of disappointment when they asked about the possibility of spinoffs, a movie, or a reboot and he gave the same answer he always gave, that currently there were no plans for further productions. And then the same glimmer of hope that 'currently' inspired: *So, there could be in the future?* Off they'd go to tell their followers to keep hoping that maybe next year the answer would be different, when he knew it wouldn't. The horse had died some time ago, but they would keep it on life support for as long as the fans kept turning up to flog it.

He looked over at Jennifer and Bryce, they had settled in at their own tables and were leaning over to chat with each other. A convention crew member stood waiting by the bolted double door at the opposite site of the room, holding back a growing commotion of excited voices. The wall clock above the door showed still five minutes to go before the onslaught. Jake blew out his cheeks and took one of the headshots from the stack, popped the lid off a marker, and started doodling over his own face, smirking as he added a cartoon handlebar mustache, beard and a pair of devil horns.

"It's time," announced the crew member as he unbolted the doors and swung them open. A sudden crescendo of cheers and screams surged towards them as the crowd flooded in and formed into queues at the respective tables. Jake let out another sigh, screwed up the print and tossed it over his shoulder behind him, and assumed his signature smile.

"Oh my God, I totally love you!" exclaimed the young woman at the head of the queue.

"Thanks. Who should I make it out to?" he asked taking a print from the stack.

"Me. I'm Candi, with an 'I'," she said while chewing gum and playing with her long blond hair.

Naturally. He nodded and started writing.

"And sign it, 'with love forever from Jakey'."

"Sure thing." He finished writing and handed the photo to her, "Next," he called out to the next person in the queue.

"Wait, that's not what I told you to write," she said glaring at him.

"Sorry, everyone gets the same thing." He looked past her and gestured to the young man behind her to step forward.

"Gees, you'd think for the price you charge for an autograph, you'd freaking write what I tell you to write!" she hissed as she marched off.

"Name?" asked Jake, his smile already waning.

"Mason. I really want to be a vampire like you. I mean, Vincent. You know, if vampires were like real."

"Yeah, that's great. Here you go."

"Thanks, man! Awesome!" the young man grinned as he took the print, holding it reverentially by the edges, careful not to smudge the signature and those immortal words: *To Mason, with best wishes, Jake Donovan.*

One after another, they continued to appear, full of excitement at their once-in-a-lifetime moment to see him in the flesh, while he struggled to keep churning out the same enthusiasm duplicated a thousand times over every day of his life. These events were in his contract, they were a necessary part of the industry machine, but the more of them he did, the more he felt like a rare tiger on display in a zoo. The star attraction that pulled in the crowds and decorated every tacky souvenir for sale in the gift shop, until the day came when he would be too old and unprofitable. And while the next star attraction replaced him in prime position, he'd be consigned to a cold dark closed-off corner, his pricey souvenirs now worthless and serving no other purpose than to memorialize a star long since faded.

Jake poured himself a glass of bourbon from the mini bar and walked out onto the balcony of his hotel room. He took a sip and let the liquid sit in his mouth for a moment, before swallowing feeling its soothing warmth release the tension in his body. The interviews and the autographs had left him feeling exhausted and though he always enjoyed catching up with Bryce and Jennifer, he had struggled to engage in the usual dinner conversation and reminiscing. It hadn't got off to a good start. Bryce had brought up the subject of Catherine by asking if he was going to see her and of course, Jennifer didn't know who they were talking about so he had had to relate the story to her before telling them both that it was over. And then he had to argue that he had made the right decision when they questioned why he ended it. After that the conversation had been strained and Jake had called it a night as soon as the dinner plates had been cleared.

The truth was, he had been thinking of Catherine all day. All throughout the autograph session he had regularly scanned the crowd hoping to see her, yet equally dreading the possibility. Would it be strained and awkward or emotional and passionate? How would they reunite in a room full of spectators ready to record the whole thing on their phones? He had considered asking the crew to keep a look out for her, but that seemed a betrayal of trust and he owed her that much. In the end, she never appeared and he found himself feeling more disappointed than he expected.

He drained the glass and leaned against the railing staring out at the city below. Somewhere amongst all those lights was one that belonged to her. Somewhere out there, possibly close enough for him to walk to... a bedside lamp as she read in bed, a kitchen light as she poured a drink, a flickering candle as she soaked in the bath. Was she standing backlit at a window right now, staring out at him?

If it hadn't been for her letter, he might have been tempted to contact her. Her words thanking him for the photograph had been brief and clear: *It is a reminder for me to leave the past behind and never look back.* He had broken her – made her suffer the consequences of his weakness. A hurt that big couldn't be fixed with a phone call or a coffee date, it would only reopen the wound.

A thousand times today he'd been told the words, 'I love you'. He was adored by millions, all in love with the idea of him, the illusion of him. Yet he was no more real to any of them than Santa Claus. None of them knew him, really knew him. He stared up at the night sky, clear but blank. The stars were there but you couldn't see them. They were lost in the light from the city, drowned out by all the noise. People stared right at him, yet they didn't see him. He was lost in all the noise. His fingers clenched round the railing and he felt tears sting his eyes. A sudden streak of white shot across the sky and was gone. Just like the shooting star the one person who had seen him had strayed too close and burned up in his atmosphere. His gravity was lethal.

"You ready?" asked the coordinator, clipboard in hand.

Jake nodded and took up his position in front of the photographic backdrop.

She turned to the photographer who was taking a final light reading and adjusting the lights. He gave her a thumbs-up.

"Okay, we'll get started then," Alice said ducking behind the curtain of the cubicle to fetch the first customer.

Jake took a deep breath and stepped into character, the Jake the fans had come to see, while the Jake who had stood on the balcony the previous night with tears in his eyes left the room.

The curtain parted and Alice stepped into the cubicle with a young woman wearing jeans and a T-shirt which had *I'm with him* printed on it.

"Lucky first of the day," said Alice ushering her in, "this is Gemma."

"Hi, Gemma. It's great to meet you." Jake gestured for her to stand next to him in front of the backdrop.

"I'm such a big fan!" she gushed as she took up her position and ventured her arm behind his back, "Is it okay if I put my arm round you?" she asked.

Jake nodded. A hug or a kiss on his cheek was a privilege given to those who paid extra for a photo opportunity; those who paid to pet the tiger.

"Oh my goodness, I think I've died and gone to heaven!" she squealed as he put his arm around her in return. "Oh, can you make sure you get my T-shirt in the photo?" she said to the photographer.

He nodded, "Yup, all good. And smile!"

The flash popped and Alice stepped forward, hurrying her along, "Thank you, Gemma. Your print will be ready for you at the desk on your way out."

"Thank you, this has been amazing, thank you. You're amazing…" she continued to babble her thanks and adorations all the way to the exit.

Jake nodded and reset his smile for the next customer. One down, near on a hundred more to go.

I sat folding and unfolding the strap of my bag over my fingers while tapping my foot as the bus neared the downtown. It was hard to believe the time was almost here. The last two weeks had dragged by and yesterday had seemed to last forever. I had stayed home all day in case he dropped by, and kept checking my phone even though I had the ringer on maximum in case he called or texted. He hadn't.

The disappointment unnerved me, whispered doubts that threatened to topple me like blocks being removed one by one in a game of Jenga. Instinct was telling me to turn back, but I felt compelled to keep heading for the cliff.

The bus pulled up to the stop and I stepped off, pulling my coat tighter around me in the sudden chill of the autumn air. Just a two-block walk to go to the Park Regent hotel... to Jake. I took a deep breath and started walking. My heart began to race and my steps quickened the closer I got, till I was practically running and then I was taking the stairs to the hotel entrance two at a time.

A blast of hot air and noise hit me as I entered the hotel's foyer. I followed a group of teens dressed as Vincent, Elizabeth and Sebastian to the atrium and presented my ticket to the door attendant. She handed back the stub and I stepped through to see huge banners of the cast hanging from the balconies and I felt my cheeks flush when I found myself looking ahead at a two-story tall image of Jake as Vincent, blood dripping from his fangs, staring back at me. I turned away from the central area which was lined with vendor stalls selling *Blood Moon Prophecies* merchandise and following the signs made a left and headed straight for the stairs to the convention rooms.

There was still a good hour to go before the panel discussion, but as I only had a peasant ticket I decided to arrive early in the hopes of getting a good position in view of the panel so that Jake might see me. I had exhumed the T-shirt he bought me in Hawaii and was wearing it with the same taupe skirt I wore that day. I even had a fabric frangipani flower that I found in a dollar store ready in my bag and waiting for me to slip it behind my ear. I had replayed the scenario a hundred times already. He'd be on the stage talking about the show and then he'd see me across the room. Our eyes would meet and he'd walk over to me in front of everyone, in front of Alex and Jess, pull me into his arms and kiss me.

I turned the corner toward an arrow pointing to the Washington room to find the corridor already full of people queuing up that I couldn't even see the door. I fell back against the wall and slid down it to sit on the floor, hanging my head in my hands. I would need a miracle for him to see me and considering it was a miracle that we met in the first place, I doubted I would be that lucky again. I felt sick knowing that Alex and Jess would be in the front row. I sniffed back the bitterness and took off my coat and bunching it up, placed it behind my head against the wall and stared up at the ceiling to drown out the chatter and noise, and lost myself in the memory of when I had looked up into the sky and saw the unshaven face of an angel.

Jake took a drink from his water bottle as the curtain parted and Alice stepped in with two women with bleached blond hair and spray-tans and wearing nearly matching tight-fitting short dresses. They didn't wait to be announced.

"Oh-em-gee, oh-em-gee!" the taller of the two shrieked, "I can't believe I'm finally getting to get to meet you!" as they rushed over, teetering on their heels, and hugged him.

Jake carefully extricated himself from their grip, "Hi, it's great to meet you too. I didn't get your names?"

"I'm Alex," said the taller, dressed in pink and motioned to her friend, "and this is Jess."

She wore a similar turquoise dress that barely covered the essentials. "We absolutely love you!" she cooed, "We're your biggest fans."

Of course you are, just like everyone else here. He suppressed a sigh, ushering them to the backdrop and they took up their positions, draping themselves on each side of him, giggling away like giddy school girls, posing with their lips puckered against his cheeks.

The flash popped and Jake peeled himself away from them once again, "Well, thank you ladies, it was nice meeting you."

"We've got a double ticket for the both of us, doesn't that mean we get another photo?" Alex chided.

Jake closed his eyes for a moment, seeking out that place of calm – for an instant, a subliminal frame – he saw her smile and then she was gone. "You're right. Of course."

The took up their positions again and Alex leaned in, placing her hand on his chest and hitching up her leg against his side so that her bare thigh rested against his crotch and then at the last second licked his ear.

The flash popped again and Jake stood motionless as they removed themselves from him, focusing on that calm place and stepping outside of himself, he took her by the hand and they walked towards the ocean.

"Thank you," said Jess, yanking him back to reality. At least she had some courtesy. "Though, we'll see you again soon at the panel session. We're in the front row."

"And, again tonight at the gold pass party." Alex winked, licking her lips seductively, "We're here for the *full* package."

Jake's stage smile dropped. God help him, he was going to have to endure these two airheads again.

"Ladies," Alice motioned to the exit, "you can collect your prints at the desk on the way out."

"Oh, I nearly forgot, said Alex pulling out an expensive bottle of rum from her bag. "This is for you. I know how much you love rum."

"It's from both of us," Jess added, glaring at Alex.

Jake strained a smile, "Wow, thank you. That's awesome." He took the bottle and noticed a business card attached to a ribbon and pulled it free. "Andrews and Andrews," he read it out loud, recognizing the name. He turned to Alex, remembering. *Just like Reese Witherspoon's character in Legally Blond.* "You're Alex!" he blurted.

"Um, yeah," she shot Jess a puzzled look, "That's what it says on the card. That's me. You know, in case you need—"

"She didn't tell you about Hawaii?"

"What about Hawaii?" Alex looked enquiringly at Jess who shrugged her shoulders.

"How is she? Is she here with you?"

"Who? It's just the two of us."

"I mean, Ca—" he paused, taking in their confusion. "No, never mind, sorry. I was thinking of someone else."

Alice stepped in again, "If you don't mind, ladies. Your time is up; we really need to move on."

"Fine! We're going." Alex snapped. She slipped her arm through Jess's and the two of them turned and blew kisses to Jake as they walked back to the curtain.

"What was all that about?" Jess asked Alex.

"I have no idea. Maybe he was thinking about Kristie. I do look like her, don't you think?" she sniggered as they disappeared behind the curtain.

He ran his thumb over the embossed lettering, shaking his head in disbelief. They were clueless.

She'd kept her word. She hadn't spoken about him. He couldn't ask about her without betraying her secret. *Their* secret. He had trivialized her feelings for him, and given her every reason to exploit their encounter, yet she had never come forward with her story, apparently not even shared it within her own circles. He had come to expect what he gave of himself to be sold off to the highest bidder that he had stopped letting people in a long time ago. Yet she was out there going about her day, carrying a part of him with her that no one else knew about, keeping it hidden. Keeping it safe.

"Jake? Are you okay?"

Jake turned to see Alice with the next customer. He nodded and dropped the card in the rubbish bin, "Yeah, sure. Just miles away." He returned to his position in front of the backdrop, his smile heavy as he gazed into the distance at the woman wading in the water with a pair of golden sandals hanging from her outstretched hand being showered in a thousand shooting stars.

Chapter 29

The crowd surging forward broke me from my thoughts and I grabbed my coat and scrabbled to my feet. I pulled out the frangipani flower from my bag and clutched it tightly while I followed the queue through the doors into the Washington room.

There was a small stage set with several chairs and a podium at the front of the room followed by rows of seating for the gold and silver pass holders. The lucky elite were already seated, having entered through a different doorway, and I couldn't see beyond the back row.

The last of the peasant rows were filled and I joined a group of people standing at the back. My legs were shaking so much that I pressed up against the wall for support. I slipped the frangipani flower above my ear and straightened my T-shirt even though I was lost behind all the people in front of me.

A hush fell over the room as the panel host came onto the stage and walked over to the podium. He introduced himself, ran through a few rules regarding the discussion, thanked various sponsors, and then welcomed the panel onto the stage. The room erupted in applause and cheering as Jake, Bryce and Jennifer walked onto the stage and took their seats. I couldn't help it, I yelled out Jake's name, calling him to see me, but my words were lost in the fray. The cheering died down and I stood frozen in place, staring at Jake, willing him to look in my direction, to see me.

The panel started with them talking about life since *The Blood*

Moon Prophecies, projects they were working on now, and though there were no current plans to do so, their hopes for the series to be rebooted in the future.

"Of course, the reason we're all here is to hear about the good times," the host said, "so can you share some of the fun times with us?"

"I'll start," said Jennifer taking the microphone and glaring at Bryce and Jake which set them off in fits of laughter. I smiled. They knew what was coming and so did I. She went on to tell the story of the carriage scene where the two of them let her fall in the mud.

"And there I was, facedown in the mud, hoop skirt making it impossible for me to get up and these two are laughing their heads off," she continued with a big affectionate grin.

The audience was clapping and laughing, and I watched Bryce and Jake giggling and mock punching each other like young boys.

Bryce leaned over and kissed Jennifer on the cheek, taking the microphone from her. He grinned at Jake who shook his head in mock protest. "Don't you dare!" he cried laughing.

"Sorry, buddy, the truth must out," Bryce grinned and started relating the story about the civil war scene when Jake kicked an extra.

Jake was leaned back in his chair, laughing and playing along. I suspected they brought out the same stories at every convention and though the banter wasn't scripted, they must have replayed this scene many times before. Even when he was being real he was playing a role and I felt a sudden wave of sadness for him, as if the real him was lost under layers of paint and lacquer, like a set of Russian dolls. He sat forward and for a moment stared into the crowd, straight at me.

I raised my hand above my head, wanting to wave, wanting to call out his name, but I couldn't. I just stood there looking at him, my mouth hanging open, my eyes locked on his, willing him to see me.

A staff member person in black jeans and a 'crew' T-shirt with and ID badge swinging on a neck lanyard came onto the stage and quietly approached Jake. She crouched beside him and whispered to him. Jake's smile faded and he stood up quickly and bolted off the stage. A murmur spread through the audience and Bryce and Jennifer turned to each other confused. The crew member went over and whispered to the host who then walked back to the podium and tapped the microphone.

"Unfortunately due to unforeseen circumstances, Jake has had to leave and will not be with us for the rest of the panel discussion. I know you're disappointed, but we ask that you remain till the..."

I stopped hearing the host's words and the grunts and sighs from the audience as the reality hit me. I lost my chance. I wasn't going to see him. And even if I had, it wouldn't have changed anything. I shouldn't have come. I had let myself hope on a daydream. A stupid, pathetic daydream. I pulled the frangipani flower from my hair and stuffed it in my coat pocket as my eyes welled up and I felt my stomach lurch.

I inched towards the door. A burly man dressed in the signature black and neck lanyard stood guarding it.

"I need to leave," I whispered.

"You have to wait until the panel's finished." He grunted.

"I understand, but I think I'm going to be sick," I pleaded, cupping my hand over my mouth.

"Okay, but I can't let you back in," he said stepping aside and opening the door for me.

I nodded and ran the moment I cleared the door.

I made a wrong turn and ended up going down a different stairway which deposited me at the opposite end of the atrium. There was no escaping it this time and I was swept forward by the people coming down the stairs behind me. Unable to turn back, I found myself walking through a hall lined with stalls selling *Blood Moon Prophecies* merchandise, like a nightmarish carnival hall of mirrors. Everywhere I looked I saw Jake staring back at me. His face printed on posters, T-shirts, books, mugs, key chains; every piece of useless plastic imaginable. Scenes from the show played on TV screens and the theme music played on repeat before every advertisement and announcement from overhead loud speakers in between belting out superstore music. All around me, people were browsing shelves of premium Jake, scratching through bins of reduced-to-clear Jake, handing over wads of cash, swiping cards to take home their tacky souvenir, their relic, the graven image of their idol.

The room started spinning and I started to run towards the foyer, only to trip over someone's foot and stumble into a stall selling Barbie-sized dolls of the *Blood Moon Prophecies* characters. As I regained my balance I came face-to-face with several dozen plastic Jakes staring at me from inside boxes with cellophane windows, and I was overcome by a wave of nausea. I cupped a hand over my mouth and headed for the washrooms, nearly knocking over a life-size cardboard cut-out of Jake in the corridor.

I narrowly made it into a stall in time, slamming the door behind me before retching up the remnants of my lunch. I grabbed some toilet paper and cleaned up, flipped down the lid, and sat down holding my face in my hands as my tears spilled down onto my lap.

I had let my own pride fool me into thinking I was immune to the spell, that I couldn't fall for an illusion, that I alone had seen the truth, the real man behind the idol. But, I was just as delusional as everyone else here. Worse. I hadn't just drunk the Kool-Aid, I'd put it in a syringe and shot up on it.

Who had I even been with in Hawaii? I wanted to believe the Jake I had come to know was the real one, that this Jake being worshipped here was the fake, but the truth was, the Jake I had fallen for was the illusion. I was so high that I had built him up in my mind to be someone he wasn't and now I was sober I was seeing the truth for the first time. He was right. I had fallen for a fantasy... that I was special. I was such an idiot for ever thinking I was different, that he could be different for me.

I took a deep breath, straightened my clothes, wiped my eyes a last time, and left the washroom for the corridor. It was empty and as I passed the cardboard cut-out of Jake I pushed it over to land facedown on the carpet. I focused on the exit as I headed back through the atrium, trying to block out the noise and echoes of Jake all around me. I passed yet another stall selling T-shirts as I left the atrium into the foyer. I bit my lip, sniffing back my tears and snorted thinking they needed to add one to their range with the words: 'I slept with Jake Donovan and all I got was this lousy T-shirt'.

The world outside had turned grey and as I paused to put my coat back on, the fabric frangipani flower fell out of the pocket. I picked it up and turned, looking for a rubbish bin. I spotted one next to a desk near the entrance to the atrium and walked over. I stood, my hand poised over the rim, ready to drop it in when I looked over at the desk and noticed the sign above it which read: 'Gifts for the cast'. A crew member sat slouched in a chair absorbed in his phone, not paying much attention as people dropped things into the three large boxes that sat on the desk with Bryce's, Jennifer's and Jake's names printed on them.

I pulled my hand back, dug in my bag for a pen and went over to the desk. I wrote a few words on the flower and then dropped it into the box for Jake watching it disappear into the cracks amongst the many cards, soft toys, pieces of underwear and other gifts. Then pulling my coat tight around me I left the hotel. And as I walked to the bus stop, my heart breaking, I imagined the frangipani flower floating on the surface of the ocean, the water lapping over it dissolving the ink, washing away my words. Then slowly the flower sinking below the surface, swaying back and forth as it sank lower and lower until it finally came to rest on the ocean floor next to shells of bottom-feeders and an old corroded soda can.

I slipped the key in the lock and as I turned the door handle to my apartment I looked down and noticed an envelope sticking out from under the door. My heart started racing again as I bent down and pulled it free. I tore it open, my hands shaking. And then, with a single motion of unfolding the letter, my heart plummeted. Again.

I slammed the door behind me, screaming as I screwed up the

landlord's letter and threw it across the room. I dumped my bag and pulled off my coat dropping it to the floor as I headed to the kitchen. I opened the cabinet and pulled out the bottle of Vodka David had left behind and poured a glass. How the hell was I going to cover a rent increase when I was barely keeping up since David moved out? I took a swig of the vile liquid and choked it down. The alcohol burned my throat causing me to cough forcefully. I turned and tipped the contents of the glass into the sink and emptied the bottle, watching it splash down the drain. I'd have to get a new place now, at the worst possible time for the year. What kind of jerk ups the rent just before December?

I had wasted so much time fixating on Jake, stupidly thinking he was my destiny. But, my time with him was not fate or destiny; it was a glitch, a giant cosmic error. I had been given a glimpse of an alternative universe version of me. A version of me that could not exist in this universe, because some laws of nature are immutable – snow does not fall in the jungle, lead cannot be turned into gold, men like Jake do not choose women like me.

It had all been a cruel joke, at my expense. It's like I had been set up, been given the part meant for someone like Alex and now the universe was self-correcting, laughing at me, ridiculing me; punishing me for ever believing it had been real.

I ripped off Jake's Hawaii T-shirt, bunched it up and walked to the kitchen bin, stepped down on the pedal flipping up the lid, and shoved it down into the pasta sauce I had burned, molding banana skins, eggshells, and other garbage where it belonged.

Chapter 30

The elevator doors opened releasing the expected wave of excitement and I braced myself as Alex and Jess washed towards me.

"Good morning," I said from behind the security of the reception desk, "I see you guys had a good time at the convention."

"The best!" squealed Jess

"Well, it would have been better if we had got our money's worth," Alex sighed, glaring at Jess.

"Oh? What happened?" I asked, feigning ignorance.

"Jake left the panel discussion, like ten minutes after it started."

"And he never turned up for the cast party!" Alex hissed, "And they wouldn't even refund our tickets. I mean the whole point of us going was to see him."

"Oh, that's awful," I said biting my lip and suppressing the urge to grin. Their disappointment was making me feel so much better. "Still, I'm sure he must have had a good reason for not being there."

"What could be so urgent that it couldn't wait until after the convention?"

"He's just an actor, it's not like he had to rush off to perform heart surgery or something," Jess added.

"But, you did at least get your photo op?" I asked.

"Thank God, yes. It was fantastic. He's so amazing..." Jess started the debrief.

I sank into my seat, regretting I had asked as the two of them gushed away about how wonderful it was to spend time with him.

"And oh-em-gee, I don't know what cologne he wears, but he smelled divine!" Alex closed her eyes, running her tongue over her lips. "Mm-hmm."

I slumped against the desk feeling the color drain from my cheeks as a wave of dizziness overcame me.

"I was ready to jump him there and then!" She cackled.

"Me too." Jess laughed, not to be outdone.

I felt sick as the picture of them with him forced its way into my mind, desecrating the remaining sanctity of my memory of him.

"And he loved the bottle of rum we gave him. You know how he loves the stuff." Jess said, thankfully interrupting the sickening mental image.

"Vincent," I said flatly, staring off into the distance.

Alex looked at me annoyed, "What?"

"Vincent. Jake's character. He developed the taste for it during his human life when he spent time in the West Indies." They stared at me blankly and I elaborated, "Jake doesn't drink the stuff. It makes him ill."

Alex eyed me suspiciously, "How do you know?"

My cheeks flushed and my heart started pounding, "I... err... read it somewhere." I stammered, praying they'd buy it.

"How could we make such a rookie mistake?" Alex exclaimed, shoving Jess, "Why did I let you talk me into getting the rum? I feel like such an idiot!"

I sighed with relief under my breath. I'd come too close to revealing my precious truth, thankfully the Barbie Twins were too focused on themselves to notice.

"Well, it serves you right for saying it was from you and not the both of us." Jess argued, "I paid half of it! I was sure he said he liked it in an interview I saw."

Amira walked into the office carrying a box file under arm. She smiled guessing the topic of the chatter, "So, do you have the photos with you?" she asked.

"Of course!" Alex cried and they both took out their phones.

"They give you prints at the convention and then also email you JPEG versions," Jess added while they showed us the pictures. They both had the same photos of the two of them wearing near-matching impossibly short tight dresses and draped on either side of him. Jess was more modest; she stood beside him, her arms wrapped around his left arm and resting her head against his shoulder. Alex had her hand against his chest and a leg up, her naked thigh pressed against his crotch. It sickened me, her lack of modesty, her lack of respect for the very idol she worshipped.

"They're great," I said, letting out a heavy sigh, "I wish I could've gotten a slot."

"Maybe next year, sweetie. If you save up hard." Alex sniggered, transfixed with the picture on her phone.

I looked away, feeling my eyes well up.

"Though, next year he better fucking turn up to everything I pay for, especially the damn party!" She snapped, putting her phone away.

"Sorry to interrupt, these are the notes you wanted from Kensington Legal," Amira said, handing the box file to Alex and turning to me with concern.

"Oh right, thanks. I need to get on that." She nodded to Jess and the two of them strutted off down the corridor.

"Are you okay?" Amira asked.

"Yes, fine. Just allergies," I sniffed, "sounds like they had a great time with Jake," wiping my eyes.

"They sure did, though I'm not sure it was the same for him. Poor guy."

I smiled, "No, probably not."

"I bet he ran and caught the first flight out of here the minute he finished their photo op just to avoid seeing the two of them again."

I burst out laughing. Amira always knew just what to say to make me feel better even when she had no idea.

"Thanks. That means a lot." I said after I caught my breath.

"You're welcome." She furrowed her eyebrows at me, "I didn't realize you'd become such a big fan."

"No. I'm not really..." I looked away, fearful she'd guess the truth. "It's just Alex, getting under my skin again."

She nodded, patting me on the shoulder and turned for the corridor. I fought back the tears as I watched her leave the office. I wished I could tell her, share with her the secret I carried. The longer I carried it, the heavier it got. I had tried to drop it and leave it behind, but it remained attached to me, dragging behind me wherever I went. My beautiful sad heavy secret.

A new email popped up from Mr. Andrews, subject: staff meeting in 10 minutes. *Great.* At best, it would be fifteen minutes of boredom, at worst an announcement of some new office policy that invariably meant more pointless work for me.

We all assembled in the boardroom taking a seat at the oval table with Mr. Andrews at the head of the table as always. Alex was sitting to his right and beaming. Obviously the meeting had something to do with her. Jess took the seat opposite her and Amira and I sat down at the opposite end of the table, the furthest away from two of them that we could get.

"Any idea what this is about?" Amira whispered.

"None, but I think it must have something to do with Alex, don't you think?" I whispered, nodding towards the grinning face.

"Hmm, whatever gave you that idea?" She sighed, rolling her eyes.

I snorted and Alex frowned at me, and I quickly feigned coughing into my fist and looked away.

Mr. Andrews tapped on the table and stood up.

I groaned under my breath and whispered to Amira, "Here we go..."

"Right, I'll keep this short," he started.

"Well, that's a relief," Amira whispered to me.

"I expect most of you can guess what this is about." Mr. Andrews continued, "As you know, Alex has performed spectacularly over the last few years. Her dedication to the firm, her diligence, unwavering work ethic, always putting in one-hundred-and-ten percent, always going the extra mile—"

I sat on my hands to restrain myself from turning to Amira and making a gesture of putting my finger down my throat. Amira rolled her eyes at me and I looked away stifling a laugh and stared down at the table, zoning out to the rest of his sickening speech. It amazed me how he could be so oblivious to how much Alex actually got away with. She had him so wrapped around her finger that one could almost wonder if there was something going on between the two of them. But the idea of it was too nauseating to take seriously. I glanced over at her, sitting there in a singlet blouse to show off her bronzed skin and bleached hair that was getting the same frizz as a Barbie doll that's had its hair brushed too much. She caught me looking at her and turned up her nose and turned back to Mr. Andrews, smiling and fawning. She felt the same contempt for me as I felt for her. Still, I think I would rather be a plain, boring loser than be like her. Plastic and fake. Empty.

"So…" Mr. Andrews paused for effect, "it gives me great pleasure to announce that I have promoted her to partner, as of today."

Oh god, no. As if her ego needed any more boosting. I fell limp in my seat and clapped my hands for show, while the rest of the office gave her a big hand of congratulations.

Jess jumped up, rushed over and hugged Alex excitedly, "And we've having a cocktail party in your honor next Wednesday!" she squealed.

"On my birthday!" cried Alex.

Oh, for crying out loud. As if being promoted wasn't enough.

"Yes, that's right." Mr. Andrews confirmed, glaring at Jess who had apparently beaten him to it. "It's going to be at the Park Regent.

Seriously!? The Park Regent!?

"I organized the whole event and you didn't suspect a thing!" Jess babbled on.

I zoned out again as Alex lapped up the praise and made a speech of her own, thanking everyone (except me and Amira of course) and pledging to make us all proud.

"Cathy, could I have a word please," Mr. Andrews asked as we filed out of the boardroom.

I hung back feeling another wave of dread hit me.

"Yes, Mr. Andrews?" I asked through gritted teeth.

"Now that Alex is a partner she's going to have more responsibilities which means she's going to need more help, so I would like you to take on the role of her personal assistant."

"You're moving me off reception?" I asked, beginning to hope.

"No, there's no need for that. You'll just assist her as necessary in addition to your current duties."

I nodded. *Ah. So, not a personal assistant then.*

"Will I be getting a raise?"

"No." He looked at me as if I was stupid for even asking. "Alex got the promotion, not you."

Of course not. Just more of the same shitty work for the same pay and the same bullshit. Nothing was ever going to change for me. Not here.

"Of course. I look forward to getting started." I strained a smile then trudged back to my desk dragging my sad secrets, disappointments and broken dreams behind me.

I couldn't get home fast enough, on this, the worst Monday in the history of Mondays. I collapsed on the couch and dug into my Chinese takeout. I got halfway through the vegetarian noodles and put it aside, hungry yet too sick to eat. I picked up the fortune cookie, broke it open and read the strip of paper inside. *Good things come to those who wait.* I grunted and crumpled it up, along with the cookie.

"No!" I exclaimed as the memory of that night with Jake started to surface. The face he had made when I had read the note from my fortune cookie, the way we had laughed. I grabbed the carton and marched through to the kitchen and dumped it into the bin. It landed on top of Jake's Hawaii T-shirt and I stood staring into the stinking dark abyss, my foot pressed on the lid pedal. This was it. The destination of my loser life. I may as well surrender to it now. Climb in and let the lid fall down, trapping me in my inevitable destiny.

Or... I could run. I removed my foot and the lid slammed shut. As much as I hated the idea of retreating with my tail between my legs, it was time to go home. David was a mistake. Moving with him to San Francisco, an even greater one. And Hawaii... that was a mistake of epic proportions. It was time to wipe the slate clean and start again. I went back to the living room and fetched my laptop, settling again on the couch. I opened a new Word document and began typing. Just one freeing paragraph. I saved it to a USB drive and popped it in my bag to print out at work. Then I opened *An Apple a Day* and with a sense of peace that I hadn't felt in years, I continued working on my novel.

I knocked on Mr. Andrews' door and opened it partially, popping my head round, "Do you have five minutes?"

He looked up from his desk, "You'll have to make it quick. I'm due in court soon."

Perfect! I had no desire on hanging around after I had pulled the pin on my paper grenade.

I sat down, holding the letter on my lap, tapping my foot. "There's something I need to tell you."

"Yes?"

"I'm going home."

"Has something happened?" he asked, sighing.

"I mean, I'm leaving. This is my four weeks' notice." I shook as I passed him the letter.

"You're quitting?" he barked, "Now, at this time of the year," shaking his head, his skin flushing, "do you realize how much of an inconvenience this will be!"

Not my problem! I bit my lip to stop myself from smirking.

"Can't you wait until the new year?"

"No, I'm afraid not. I've promised my mum I'd be home for Christmas." I lied. "I could always leave earlier if that would make it easier for you to find a replacement."

A vein bulged on the side of his head. I probably shouldn't have said that.

"Fine, go! I haven't got time for this." He stood up and almost tipped me out the chair as he rushed round and ushered me out the office, a hand pressed firmly against my back. He slammed the door loudly after me. I let out an excited whoop under my breath and skipped down the hall like a giddy schoolgirl.

My legs gave out when I got to my seat and I sat down heavily, shaking all over with adrenaline. I did it! I had cut the lifeline. I had jumped without a safety net and now I was starting to feel ill. What the hell was I doing? I didn't have a plan. Or maybe I did. It was just that in the past I had always been following everyone else's plans and for the first time in my life, I was starting to make plans of my own. I might be going back home, but I was going back on *my* terms.

When I was with Jake, it was like I had been the person I had always wished I could be. I thought it was him, that I needed him in my life for me to be that person. But, now I was starting to see that perhaps I could be that person on my own. Maybe that was Jake's purpose, to help me see and believe in my own potential. He had given me a trial run of the new me.

Chapter 31

Jake sat at the grand piano playing the opening notes of the Moonlight Sonata over and over. For so many of his teenage years he'd hated this piano. It was just another reminder of his failure to live up to his father's expectations. Though he loved music and performing, Jake never progressed beyond the basics. He ditched lessons to go play ball with his friends and found any excuse not to practice. If he was going to play, then he wanted to learn play music from his generation, like Billy Joel or Bruce Hornsby, not Beethoven and Mozart.

Yet now, hearing the hammer strike each note sending out a pure crystal tone and the damper moving down, the mechanics vibrating the piano cabinet with a woody undertone, all he wanted more than anything was to go back to the time when he was too small to reach the pedals and sit next to his father while he played Beethoven's famous sonata.

He glanced over at the notebook resting on the lid, open to a blank page. He had yet to write a single line. Every time he tried to commit pen to paper, he'd catch sight of her in the corner of his eye, watching him, smiling, the breeze in her hair. But when he turned to get up and leave the book in the sand, she'd be gone and he'd be back in this forlorn living room.

He'd let her go, for what? To keep doing the same bullshit interviews, smiling for the cameras and being paraded around at conventions? He'd ripped out her heart as a sacrifice for that? For stuff he didn't even want anymore, for an idol he had ceased to believe in.

Four months ago he thought he knew what he wanted, what he *should* want, but now he wasn't so sure any of that mattered. It's like the mirror broke and now when he looked at his reflection, Jake saw a stranger, a broken version of his self. He'd created Jake Donovan to separate himself from his past, but now that his past was no longer pursing him, he didn't know who he was. Or who he should be.

She knew. She had seen him, the real man... understood him better than he knew himself. She had been like the guardian of his soul. And he had rejected her. He might as well have thrown her back into the sea.

Sarah Donaldson finished her tea and placed the delicate cup carefully on the saucer on the coffee table and walked over to the piano. She sat down next to Jake, running her narrow fingers over the keys tenderly.

"The nights haven't been the same." She sighed.

"I wish I could play for you like he did, Mum." Jake said, his eyes watering, "I never put any effort into learning; I knew I'd never be as good as him."

"Yes, your father certainly was talented."

Jake nodded looking down at the keys, "He was. In everything he did. He left big shoes to fill. Too big for me." He closed the notebook and pushed it aside, "I don't know if I can do this."

"You've given speeches before."

"Speeches. Not a eulogy. Danielle should do it. She was always his favorite."

"People will be expecting you to."

"Because I'm famous? That's the last thing he would want."

"Because, you're the eldest. The son. You know what this family is like."

"I'm not even a Donaldson anymore. He never forgave me for that. You know that."

"Precisely why you need to. To let go of the past."

"How can I honor him when I was such a big disappointment to him?"

"He was never disappointed in you."

She stood up carefully, "Come with me," she said taking his hand, "there's something you should see."

She led him out the living room and down the hallway full of framed family memories to his father's study. Jake looked around at the imposing space. He and his sister were rarely allowed in it as children and he hadn't been set foot in it since he left for Los Angeles years ago. The room smelled of furniture polish, old books and vintage antiseptic. A large mahogany desk and leather chair sat in front of a giant picture window bordered by heavy curtains drawn aside with tasseled tie-backs. One wall was lined with tall bookshelves full of medical books and journals, some authored by his father. Apothecary bottles, antique medical instruments and anatomy models decorated the shelves. Sarah directed his gaze to the wall behind them. Like the hallway, it was full of framed photographs and certificates.

Jake sighed, "Ah yes, Dad's wall of fame." He turned away, familiar with the contents: photos of his father at various crowning moments in his career and of Danielle as she followed in his footsteps.

"Take a closer look," Sarah urged.

He turned back and glanced over the pictures. He recognized the many pictures of his father graduating medical school, receiving numerous awards and performing surgeries, as well as similar photos of Danielle receiving prizes at school, her graduation from medical school, her first day on the job wearing the typical white coat with stethoscope slung round the neck.

Jake stepped closer, a new series of pictures had been added: photos of him on the red carpet at premieres, signed headshots, him holding his Emmy award, both times he won and a framed copy of the *People* article titled *Jake Donovan: Real Life Hero*.

"I don't understand. He framed the pictures I sent you?"

Sarah nodded.

"And the article...?"

"I saw the magazine in the shops. You should have told us."

"Not after all the flack Dad gave me for putting in so much work to train to be a 'pretend doctor' when I couldn't do it for the real thing."

"You weren't pretending that day."

"Being a doctor, real or fake, had little to do with it. It was sheer luck that I was able to help."

"I'm sure that's not true."

"Maybe, but I didn't want to hear him tell me again how I was wasting my potential. He always disapproved of my career."

"Only at first. He thought you were throwing away your education and opportunities on a silly whim."

"I remember, 'dreamer', 'head in the clouds'..." Jake grunted.

She sighed with regret and moved the thin wire-framed glasses up her nose, "He didn't understand. Not in the beginning."

"He never realized that the impossibly high standard he set guaranteed I'd never live up to it."

"It was never intentional. For him medicine was easy. It was familiar; it's what his father did. When he went on to be a doctor like your grandfather, he was simply following the established path in front of him. He expected it would be the same for you."

"Like it was for Danielle."

"Yes, she has the same technical brain as your father. But, you were always different."

"Different." Jake snorted, "Not something this family approves of."

Sarah smiled, "No, but when he saw how hard it was for you to get started in Hollywood he began to see he'd underestimated you."

Jake furrowed his eyebrows. "I'm not sure I believe that."

"The longer you kept at it, the more rejections you got and you didn't give up, the prouder of you he became."

"Proud?" Jake choked, "of my acting?"

"Of your strength, your determination. Your courage."

Jake said nothing, processing his mother's words.

"Did you know that your father dreamed of being a concert pianist?"

"Really?"

Sarah nodded, smiling. "He often confessed longing to give up his work to play with an orchestra in a huge auditorium full of people."

"He certainly was good enough."

"He was. But, he was afraid. It was too much of a gamble for him. But, you... You risked everything for the dream." She turned to the pictures of Jake at the Emmys. "And then you achieved it."

Jake smiled in disbelief, "Dad envied me?"

"He did. And he couldn't have been prouder than when you rescued that young lady from drowning." She pointed to the framed article, "He said to me, 'Danielle and I save lives every day, but we never have to risk our own lives the way Jake risked his'."

"I never thought about it that way," Jake said staring at the article.

"When she was being swept out to sea, she didn't need a department head with several doctorates and dozens of medical papers to their name, she needed someone with courage. And that someone was you." She paused, "Your father was so proud of your courage. You had the courage to go after your dreams, and the courage to risk everything for the life of a stranger."

Jake exhaled heavily, taking it all in. "Why didn't he ever say anything to me?"

"You know your father, he was a proud man. It was hard for him to admit he was wrong. You were always better at self-expression."

She reached up, pressing her hands against his cheeks, pulling his head towards her and kissed his forehead. "He was never disappointed in you. He loved you very much."

Jake reached round and hugged his mother, "Thanks, Mum." He whispered, closing his eyes as tears filled them.

She parted from him and gently wiped the tears from his cheeks, her own eyes red and watering, "Okay, kiddo," she said, her lips trembling, "I'm going upstairs to rest for a while."

Jake nodded and kissed her on the forehead. "Sleep well." He called after her as she left the room.

He remained in the study, staring at the pictures. So much time had been lost through assumptions, prejudice and pride. What an irony – that his father could be proud of him, yet too proud to tell him. And, what of his own pride? Too proud to tell his father that he looked up to him. Too proud to extend the proverbial olive branch, always putting it off for the 'right time', always thinking there would be more time.

"So, this is where you are."

Jake turned from his thoughts to see his sister walk in the room carrying a large cardboard box.

"Oh hey, sis."

"This arrived for you." Danielle set the box down on the desk.

"Oh, who's it from?"

She leaned over and read the label, "The official Jake Donovan fan club. Lucky you."

"It'll be from the convention. Don't know why they sent it to me here though." Jake sighed, turning back to the article.

Danielle walked over and joined him. She rested her head against his shoulder, "You're quite the hero."

"No, I'm not. I messed up." Jake sighed.

Danielle turned to look at him, puzzled, "What do you mean?"

Jake walked away and went to sit down in his father's desk chair, leaning back heavily. "You didn't see the other stories then?"

Danielle frowned, shaking her head. "No. You know I don't pay any attention to the gossip pages. I'm always hoping my brother will actually tell me what's going on in his life." She walked over to the desk and perched on the edge.

He looked away out the window, "I hooked up with her afterwards."

"What do you mean 'hooked up'?" she eyed him suspiciously.

Jake stared out the window lost in thought.

"You got involved with the woman you rescued?"

He nodded slowly.

"I know you're not actually a doctor, but that still seems a bit... unethical."

"I never intended for it to happen. It just did."

"How? How does it *just* happen?"

Jake recounted the story of how that fateful decision to go with her to the hospital had led to a five-day holiday romance.

"She was in Hawaii alone. I just wanted to make sure she was okay and before I knew it, things had gone too far. I should never have got involved. I let her think it meant something when it didn't." he finished.

She stared at him, "You don't sound convinced."

Jake sighed, "How could it? It was all a fantasy. It would never have worked in the real world. I had to end it before my world chewed her up."

"I'm sorry. I wish it was easier for you." She said and reached over and squeezed Jake's shoulder.

He turned to her with a wistful smile. "Thanks." He let out a long sigh.

Danielle brushed her hands through her long dark hair and turned her attention to the box, "So are you going to open it or what?"

"Nah, you go ahead. It'll be gifts from fans. I get inundated with the stuff."

She opened the box, sifting through an assortment of photos, letters, cards, soft toys, and pieces of underwear. She lifted a G-string out on the tip of her finger and read aloud the note written in black felt-tip marker across the tiny triangle of red satin, "'I love you! Marry me! Katy'. And there's a telephone number on the back."

Jake grimaced.

"I'm obviously in the wrong profession," she teased, dropping the thong back into the box.

"What? You've never had a patient propose to you?"

"Only those jacked up on morphine."

Jake laughed. "Any candy in there? I could do with a sugar hit."

"Hmm, will a bag of gummy vampire fangs do? 'Love from Emma, to the best vampire ever'," she said reading the note.

"That'll do."

She tore open the bag and pulled out a fistful and passed the bag to Jake, returning her attention to the contents of the box.

"Well, this is different," she said pulling out a fabric frangipani flower and turning it over. "No name, just 'You were real to me. C.'. How odd."

Jake looked up. "Let me see that." He took it and carefully turned it over to read the message.

"Catherine."

Danielle raised an eyebrow.

"She came." He fell back against the chair.

"The woman from Hawaii?"

Jake nodded, smiling, "I gave her a frangipani flower the first night I took her to dinner. I tucked it behind her ear." He touched the flower to his nose, remembering the fragrance. "She wore a floral cotton dress with spaghetti straps and sandals. So real, so genuine, so unpretentious."

"So, it did mean something."

He sighed heavily, "Everyone has an assumption about who I am and that is who they see. But with her, it was like she could see the real me. I didn't have to play a role with her. I could just be myself.

Danielle cocked her head to one side, surprised, "You're in love with her."

"I couldn't see it then. I didn't think it was possible." Jake let out a groan. "But, I haven't stopped thinking about her since I left Hawaii."

"Have you told her?"

"I can't. Not after the way I treated her."

"She's obviously still thinking about you."

"I don't know. The odds are it won't work and I don't want to hurt her again.

"Maybe, but from where I sit, it seems the odds were actually in your favor."

"What do you mean?"

"You're Jake Donovan, Hollywood superstar. The circles you move in are pretty small, pretty tight, right?"

He nodded.

"So what are the odds that you would have met her within your world?"

"Practically zero."

"Exactly. So maybe you weren't in the right place at the right time to save *her*. Perhaps she happened to collapse in the right ocean, at just the right moment to be seen by *you*, because at any other moment, at any other place your paths would never have crossed."

Jake looked at her thoughtfully.

"Looks to me like God didn't put you in her path; He put Catherine in *your* path. Anyone could have been at that beach that day, but He chose *you*. That has to mean something."

"That may be so, but I blew it. I let her go. She's better off without me."

"What makes you think she will be? How do you know that she won't hold a torch for you, that you haven't doomed her to be heart-broken for the rest of her life because no one else will ever measure up to you? What if you were her Prince Charming and you sent her back to her tower, to a life of kissing frogs?"

"Come on sis, you're being overly dramatic."

"You are one of Hollywood's most eligible bachelors. It's going to be hard for her to top that."

Jake laughed, "She's not that shallow."

"It's not because you're a celebrity. It's because on top of that you're also kind, honest, loyal, generous..." she paused, "what?"

"I just remembered something she said to me on the first day we spent together."

"What?"

"She said she liked me not because I was Jake Donovan, but in spite of it."

"See?" She smiled.

"But, I'm scared," Jake whispered, blowing out his cheeks, "I'm afraid my world will change her, the way it changed Amanda. I don't want that to happen to her."

"Of course she'll change," Danielle reached over and squeezed his hand, "but maybe it's time for you to change too. You can change with her. Spend more time on your ranch, plant that vineyard, start your production company." She turned back to the box and pulled out the G-string again, "You don't have to be this Jake Donovan forever."

Jake sat back in the chair staring at his sister in awe, "Where did you learn to be so wise, little sis?"

Danielle hopped off the desk and went over and wrapped her arms around Jake, "Probably from my big brother," she grinned and kissed him on the forehead.

She snatched the bag of gummy fangs from the desk, popped one in her mouth winking at him and left the room leaving him to his thoughts. His gaze returned to the framed *People* article. What had happened to his courage? He had had the courage to follow his dreams to LA and live on pizza and couch surfing till he got his first break. He'd had the courage to rush into the ocean to rescue someone he didn't know. Yet, the moment she told him she loved him he panicked and ran, too afraid to tell her he felt the same. Where was his courage then?

The rest of the week dragged by. Things had only got worse since I dropped my bombshell. Mr. Andrews' temper was shorter than ever, Alex's rudeness had taken on a whole new level and everyone else in the office followed suit. All except for Amira, of course. I didn't know how I was going to get through another three weeks of it, not that I had a plan yet for what I was going to do after I left. I hadn't even told my parents yet. I was leaving that phone call for the weekend.

I looked up at the clock, half an hour to go before knock-off. I sank into my chair, blowing out my cheeks to an empty front office while hearing the sound of laughter and the clinking of wine glasses filter down the corridor. The usual Friday wind-down was already in full swing.

Sod it! I sighed and switched off the computer. Then jumped up, grabbed my bag and coat and marched over to the elevator. I hit the button and stood tapping my foot. The office phone started ringing and I hit the elevator button again repeatedly. *Hurry up!*

"Can someone answer the fucking phone!" Alex yelled as she came round the corner into the front office carrying a wine glass.

"Where are you going?" she barked at me just as the ringing finally stopped and the elevator doors opened.

"Home." I said, holding the door, "Since you lot have finished for the day, so have I."

I let go of the door and stepped in, letting the doors close behind me. I fell back against the wall of the elevator and burst out laughing when I heard the phone ringing again and Alex screaming for Amira, whom she hadn't noticed had been away on leave for the past two days.

One thing had changed since I gave in my notice. I no longer cared and it was intoxicating. Now when Mr. Andrews huffed and puffed at me, I rolled my eyes and when Alex was rude, I was rude back. The confidence that came from having nothing left to lose combined with all the bitterness and hurt I had suffered was turning me dark. It was like I had been turned into a vampire and embracing my new life, losing the last vestiges of my humanity just as Vincent turned cruel and ruthless after Elizabeth was taken from him. By the time I did leave this shithole job, I'd be full bitch. So be it. I was sick of being nice. Nice had got me nowhere.

The rain and bus journey home helped numb my mind and as I climbed the stairs to my apartment I felt everything melt away with the simple joy of getting to start my evening earlier than usual. I got to my door to find a pile of empty boxes and newspapers stacked in front. I smiled. My next door neighbor had dropped them off already. It was only yesterday when I had told him that I was moving and he offered to find some boxes for me. In the two years I had lived here I had only spoken to him a couple of times that I hadn't expected him to pay attention, let alone follow through so fast.

I brought the boxes inside, leaving them in the living room behind the couch, next to David's boxes, which he still hadn't collected. I kicked off my shoes and changed out of my work clothes. I went through to the kitchen and poured a can of soup into a pan, putting it on the stove to heat up while getting some dinner rolls from the bread box to warm in the stove. I opened the cupboard and took out a bowl and plate for my dinner. Pausing, I reached in and pulled out the whole stack of bowls and plates and put them on the counter. I fetched a box and several newspapers from the living room, setting the box on the floor and the papers on top of the sink cabinet, then started wrapping the bowls from the counter.

There was still plenty of time before I needed to start packing, but there was something cathartic about the process. The sooner I could pack away the pieces of my life in San Francisco, the sooner I'd be able to put the whole sorry chapter behind me.

The oven timer beeped and I turned off the burner and took out the rolls. I went over to the sink to wash the news print off my hands and while I dried them I idly glanced at the papers on the cabinet. A headline caught my attention: 'Johns Hopkins top surgeon farewelled by famous son'. I leaned in for a closer look at the photograph below. It was of a man with dark hair standing behind a podium. He was turned away and shaking hands with another man wearing a doctor's white coat to his left. To his right, stood a tall woman with long dark hair dressed in a smart business skirt suit, white coat and ID badge clipped to the pocket. She looked familiar somehow. I looked at the top of the paper looking for the date when I heard a knock at my door.

"Coming," I called and tossed the towel on top of the papers. No one really did anything anymore without expecting for something in return. I looked down at my faded sweat suit, noticing the soup had splashed up over my top. *Typical.* Still, maybe my appearance would lower his expectations of the kind of reward fetching boxes and newspaper might promise.

"I'm on my way!" I yelled to the sound of more knocking.

I took the door chain and slid it through the groove, securing it and then unlocked the latch and opened the door till it hit against the chain. There was no one there and I looked down the hall to see a man dressed in jeans, hoodie pulled over his head, carrying a large duffel bag, walking away, his head down looking at the floor. I let out a sigh of relief and started pushing the door closed when an unmistakable scent wafted to my nose.

"Jake?" I unlatched the chain and wrenched the door open, adrenalin flooding my system. My heart sped up and every muscle tensed, ready to launch me out the door after him.

He turned and looked at me with dark bloodshot eyes. Stubble growth shadowed his chin and his skin was pale and drawn. For a moment I thought I was mistaken. It couldn't be him.

"Catherine." He gasped, straining a smile and walked towards me, hunched over, the duffel bag weighing heavy from his shoulder.

It was all wrong. This wasn't the dramatic reunion I had pictured. He was supposed to run to me with outstretched arms, sweep me off my feet and kiss me passionately. But there was no powerful cinematic soundtrack; no moody lighting and soft focus camera angles.

This was the scene I had starred in many times before. The one where I got played for a fool, suckered into doing a favor with promises of being paid back one day; the one where I got friend-zoned and used.

"What are you doing here?" I croaked when he got to the doorway.

He paused, turning away. "I'm sorry," he whispered, "I shouldn't have come," his voice faltering with a rawness that unnerved me.

I reached out and pulled him into a hug. The moment he made contact with me, it's as if the forces that held him together were shattered and he collapsed into my arms, burying his head into the crook of my neck and wrapping his arms around me.

I helped him into the apartment, kicking the door shut and guided him over to the couch. I sat down beside him, taking his hands in mine, "What's going on?" I asked.

He struggled to look me in the eyes. "My father... he's gone." He said, staring past me.

"Oh Jake, I'm so sorry." I pulled him into another hug.

I held him against me, stroking his back, feeling the tension in his body ease, the heaviness fall away as each breath grew deeper and slower. I closed my eyes breathing in his scent and for a moment it was like no time had passed. We were back in Hawaii and I felt home again. How could it be that something not meant for me could feel so right? I bit my lip to fight back my own tears.

Jake pulled away and sat up taking a deep breath.

"Do you want to talk about it?"

He nodded, but didn't speak.

"Was it expected?"

He shook his head, pain contorting his face. "It was sudden. A stroke. I was at the convention, I was on the panel listening to Bryce tell that god-awful story once again and someone taps me on my shoulder telling me my sister's trying to contact me urgently."

My stomach lurched and a sudden cold shiver shook me as I remembered the moment he left the stage.

"I phoned her back and she tells me she and Mum are rushing Dad to the hospital with a suspected stroke and before I can even get to the airport she's calling me back to tell me he's gone."

He sat kneading his hands and for the next hour he told me everything that had happened since the convention. I let him talk without interruption until at last the outpouring slowed and the burden was eased.

"And now? Why did you come here?" I asked.

"To be honest, I'm not really sure." He put his hand in his hoodie pocket and pulled out his hand, holding something in his fist. "When Danielle told me I had to come home all I could think about was how much I wanted to see you." He opened his hand to reveal the fabric frangipani flower I had left him, "And then I found this and... instead of returning to LA, I came here."

I looked at the flower in his hand. "You got it." I said stunned, "I didn't think you would."

"I nearly didn't." he smiled weakly. "You came to the convention. I hoped to see you there."

"If you'd invited me, you would have. By the time I realized it was happening everything was sold out. I only made it into the panel discussion, which, well you know..."

He shifted uncomfortably, "Yeah, I'm sorry. You made it clear you had moved on. I didn't want to intrude."

I snorted. "I only said what I thought you wanted to hear."

Jake's eyes lit up, "I was hoping that if I saw you at the convention... maybe..."

I leaned over on the armrest, leaving a gap between us. "I was hoping too. I wore the T-shirt you gave me—"

"You still have it?"

I turned away, staring at the floor and continued, "I put the frangipani flower in my hair. I was right at the back and watched you the whole time, like I was willing you to see me. You even looked in my direction – I tried to wave – I was sure you had seen me. But you didn't and then you left. I felt like such an idiot."

"But, you left the frangipani flower."

"I was going to throw it in the trash on my way out, but I found myself at the gifts drop-off and I... I don't really know why I left it. I hadn't intended to." I paused. "A last attempt at a lost cause, I suppose."

"I'm sorry." Jake reached for my hand and I pulled it away.

"Oh, and Monday was unbearable. Listening to Alex and Jess boast about their photo op with you while never knowing that you and I were... had been... that I... knew you personally." I spoke slowly, deliberately, to fight off the tears that were threatening to break through.

"I know. It was so hard not to ask them about you."

"You recognized them?"

"They were exactly as you described them," Jake smiled, "But, it was clear they didn't know anything about you and me."

"I never said anything. Not to anyone."

"It means a lot to me that you didn't."

"I didn't do it for you. When I got back it all felt like a dream and talking about it seemed... Well, no one would have believed me anyway, so I didn't."

"I'm sorry. I hate that I put you in that situation."

"It killed me that they and thousands of others got to have a photo with you, yet I didn't have a single picture of us together. I couldn't bring myself to ask you to pose for one... I didn't want to think I was like everyone else."

"I never thought that."

"I think your exact words were 'you're just infatuated with me because I'm famous'."

Jake grimaced, "I shouldn't have said that."

I sighed, "Well, you were probably right. I got carried away with the fairy tale."

"And I got scared."

I looked at him in the eyes, frowning. "You got scared?"

"I was so used to people only ever seeing the mask, that it unnerved me when you got so close to the person I am underneath." Jake reached out for my hand again and taking it, squeezed it gently. "I messed up. I'm sorry."

I said nothing, unsure of how to answer and he moved closer to me. He brushed the hair from my face and traced his fingers over my lips. "You're so beautiful," he whispered as he leaned in and kissed me.

I felt my heart race and heat flood my body as every part of my being ached for him and his tongue sought out mine. He pulled me tighter to him and his hands slipped under my sweatshirt sending waves of electricity through me as skin met skin. At last, the craving would be satiated. All those weeks of hunger would be ended. But, then I remembered the dismemberment, the uncontrollable bleeding, the nerve endings on fire as a piece of me was ripped away.

"I can't do this." I croaked, pushing him off me. "I want to. God, I want to." I said biting my lip and stroking his face, "But, you're only here because you're hurting. You wouldn't have come otherwise."

Jake sat back and sighed. "You're right. About the timing, but not about how I feel. I had time to think while I was back home; to see things from a new perspective."

"I've had time to think too, and you were right. Our lives are too different. The distance. Your commitments. Your high profile. It would never work." I folded my arms, "The truth is, if we had met in real life, you would never have given me a second glance. We weren't meant to meet. It was an anomaly, a cosmic error. You and I aren't meant to be." I said, tears starting to roll.

He dropped to the floor, kneeling in front of me and gripped my knees, looking at me intensely. "I thought so too, but then Danielle helped me see that it wasn't a mistake, it was a miracle."

"Yes, I know. You saved my life and I'm grateful for that."

"No, I don't mean it like that. It's like... that was the only way the universe could get my attention, to make sure I would meet you. It's like the flower. Usually the fan gifts go straight to my assistants in LA. They sort through them and donate them to various charities and I never see them. But this time they were sent to me at my parents' house and Danielle opened the box while I was in the room. She saw the frangipani flower and asked if I knew what the message meant. I knew it was you immediately. If it hadn't been for Dani... It's like the universe was making sure I'd find it."

"You're saying the kind of things I usually say, about the universe and fate..." I sighed. "I'm not sure I believe that stuff anymore."

"And, I never used to. But, now I think I should. I was so lucky to find you. I just didn't see it at the time." He reached up and wiped the tears from my cheeks. "I was a colossal ass. Can you give forgive me?"

"I don't know. I need time." I stood up quickly and walked to the kitchen. I paused in the doorway, "Have you eaten?" I asked. "I've got soup and I can make you a sandwich, if that's okay?"

"That would be great." He got up and followed me to the kitchen, noticing the boxes behind the couch and the half-packed box of crockery on the counter. "You're moving?" he asked.

"Most of those are David's, he still hasn't fetched them, but yes," I said as I reheated the soup and started making sandwiches with the dinner rolls, "I'm going back home."

"Is that a good idea?"

"Probably not. But I can't afford to stay here any longer and I quit my job on Tuesday. I'm done with Andrews and Andrews."

"What will you do?"

"Move back in with my parents. Probably get a job waiting tables or something. And keep writing my novel."

"You're writing it?" Jake cheered, grabbing me by the shoulders and squeezing them.

"I'm up to chapter four and it's going really well." I grinned.

"Tell me more." He took up the butter knife and finished making the sandwiches while I took the soup off the heat and poured it into soup mugs.

"You actually sparked some great ideas. I created a new character, the detective who suspects Martha but the more he investigates her, the more he realizes how much of a monster her husband was and in the end, he intentionally overlooks a key piece of evidence and lets her get away with it."

"Because he feels she's suffered enough." Jake continued, "through him the reader develops sympathy for the murderer rather than the victim. Brilliant. I love it."

"Thanks. I wouldn't have done it without your encouragement." I sighed, then told him the rest, "I also applied to the Deighton Academy for their scholarship and Creative Writing for Page and Screen program, but I didn't get in."

"That's too bad. But, there are other schools. I know you can do it. It's just a matter of time." He whispered, looking at me with those smoldering eyes as he moved in to kiss me.

I turned aside deliberately and his lips made contact with my cheek, but I didn't move away. Nor did he and instead we both leaned in toward each other, his forehead resting against my temple. We stood, motionless and paused. Feeling each other's warmth. Feeling each other's breathing. Feeling the severed nerve endings starting to regrow, sending out thousands of tiny bursts of energy, rippling outward, like microscopic fungal mycelia searching each other out in the darkness.

"We should eat before it gets cold," I stepped away before the spell could take hold and turned to put the soup pot in the sink. I glanced over at the paper open on the cabinet while I rinsed it. "Oh God," I gasped, holding the paper up to Jake, "I didn't read it, but this article's about you, your father."

I pointed to the photo, "That's you and... your sister?"

He nodded, "Yes, that's Danielle."

"You look very much alike," I said studying his profile, the nose, the eyebrows, those eyes.

He took the paper from me and scanned it. "Good. I asked the press not to mention me by name, though I'm sure someone will leak it eventually. I set up a scholarship at John Hopkins in my dad's name."

I squeezed his arm, "I'm sure he would appreciate that."

"Thanks. I just wish we could have talked... you know, made our peace before..." His voice wavered.

I took the paper from him, folded it up and tucked it out of sight in the box of packed crockery. "He knows," I whispered and pulled him into a hug. A platonic hug. I moved away before it could be mistaken for anything more, before I might be tempted to let it be more. "Come, let's eat." I handed him a mug of soup and I took mine and the plate of sandwiches through to the living room.

"Sorry, I haven't anything posher to offer you," I said placing the plate on the coffee table as we settled on the couch, the food's not very fancy,"

"No, this is great," he said, reaching for a sandwich. "I'm starving."

I smiled as I sipped my soup, my fingers wrapped round the warm mug, my feet tucked under me while I watched him wolf down two more sandwiches and the color returned to his face.

He noticed me watching him. "What?" he mumbled with his mouth full and looking down his front to see if he'd dropped something.

"Nothing. It's just, you're looking more like your old self."

He raised an eyebrow and smiled – that signature smirk – sending a flood of warmth through my body. I looked away and gulped down the last of my soup.

"I saw your segment on the Elaine show," I said, leaning over to put my empty soup mug on the coffee table.

"Ugh." He sighed.

"I liked the way you avoided giving her the answers she wanted. She's such a stirrer."

He raised an eyebrow, "You're not a fan?"

"Not at all. I never watch her show; I only watched that episode because you were in it and that was by accident."

"Yeah, those interviews are a necessary pain in the butt."

"I bet." I frowned. "I'm sorry you had to deal with all that extra attention because of me."

"Oh, she wasn't nearly as brutal as Carl."

"Carl?"

"My manager. He was afraid you had set me up."

I laughed, "That's what Alex and Jess thought."

"I thought you didn't tell them."

"I didn't. They saw the Elaine interview too and they were convinced that she, *me*, must have known you were there and deliberately feigned drowning to meet you." I giggled, "I mean you are sexy and famous and all, but I wouldn't be *that* desperate to meet you."

Jake laughed, "More like something they would do."

"Absolutely!" I snorted.

"They thought themselves pretty clever when they handed me a bottle of rum during their photo op."

"You should have seen their faces when they told me about it on Monday, all triumphant and showing off, and I said you don't touch the stuff."

"How did you explain that one away?"

"I said I had read it somewhere." I grinned.

"Clever. I gave the bottle to Bryce."

"How is Bryce?"

"He's good. He asked about you at the convention."

"Oh?"

"Yeah, he gave me an earful for letting you go."

"You should listen to him." I sighed, "He knows you well."

"Yeah, he's a good friend."

We fell silent, lost in our own thoughts for a while.

"This is nice," Jake murmured and leaned against me.

"It is," I whispered.

He let out a weary yawn, pulling his feet onto the couch, and curled up beside me with his head on my lap. "Can I stay here forever?" he whispered.

I rested my arm on his shoulder and stroked his hair while he continued to mumble, "Don't make me go back..." he yawned again. "No more world... Just here... with you..."

His body went limp and a soft snore blew from his lips.

"Jake?" I gently shook his shoulder and when he didn't rouse I carefully shifted over, easing him onto the couch as I stood up. I fetched some bedding from the hall closet and covered him in a blanket and slipped a pillow under his head. Then paused, and kissed him on the forehead before switching off the light and heading to bed.

Chapter 33

I lay staring at the clock radio watching the red glow mark off the hours. I hadn't slept. I kept replaying the previous night in my mind. And when I wasn't overthinking every word that had been spoken, every glance and every touch, I was indulging my imagination. Fantasizing of sneaking through to the living room wearing nothing but a silk gown, gently kissing him awake and then, letting the gown slip to the floor to reveal my nakedness in the moonlight. Or of him throwing open my bedroom door, pulling the bedclothes aside and pinning me down as he ravaged my body making me cry out in ecstasy. I pushed those thoughts from my mind. That was not going to happen. Not if things were going to end the same way as before.

Every time I heard a noise or random creak, I strained to hear more, worried he was leaving. And now, as the sunlight started to filter into the room and I still had not heard any sign of life from the other room, I feared he had left after all, stolen away into the night.

The red glow blinked again, ten past eight. There wasn't any point in lying in bed and delaying it much longer. I'd have to face the empty apartment eventually. I pushed myself up, sighing heavily and stopped suddenly at the sounds of shuffling footsteps, a low thud followed by muffled cursing at a stubbed toe and then light appeared under my door after the living room light switch was discovered. I smiled and crept back under the covers, not wanting him to think he had woken me.

A soft knock on my door woke me just as I had drifted off.

"Come in," I called, sitting up and pulling the covers around me.

Jake came in carrying a mug. "I brought you a coffee," he said handing it to me, being careful to turn it so that I took it by the handle, "milk, one sugar."

"You remembered," I said in awe.

"Thanks for the couch."

"You're welcome. I hope you didn't have anywhere you had to be. You were sleeping so soundly, I didn't want to wake you."

He shook his head.

I eyed Jake curiously. His hair was messy, the stubble shadow darker and he changed into a T-shirt and long plaid flannel draw-string pants.

"What?" he asked.

"I never imagined you to be the pajamas type." I grinned, sipping the coffee.

"Well, I did just come back from my parents' house."

I laughed, "I guess so," and cocked my head to the side, "it suits you though."

He smiled and turned, "enjoy the coffee, I'm making pancakes." He said as he closed the door behind him.

I looked at the coffee mug in amazement. In all the years I had been with David, he had never once got my coffee right, let alone made me breakfast. I put the mug down and climbed out of bed. I put on my fleecy gown over my own modest pajamas and slipped on my house slippers, then picked up the mug, wrapping my fingers around it and padded through to the kitchen. As I passed through the living room I noticed he had folded up the sheets and blankets and laid them neatly in a pile at one end of the couch.

I stood in the doorway leaning against the door frame sipping the coffee as I watched him heat some oil in a pan.

"I was going to bring them to you in bed," he said seeing me.

"I wanted to watch. It's not everyday someone makes me breakfast."

He grinned and poured some batter into the pan and started moving it about.

I finished my coffee and set out plates, cutlery and a selection of fruit and syrup while he finished up. We sat down at the kitchen bench with fresh coffee and chatted about ordinary normal things like the weather and plans for the day.

"When do you go back to LA?" I asked.

"I don't have to be back for a few days." He answered, hopeful. "I was hoping we could spend some time together?"

"That would be nice, but I still have to work and I have packing to do."

"I can help you with that. I'm skilled at packing boxes."

"Where are you staying?"

Jake frowned, "I don't know. I guess I should find a hotel."

"That would probably be for the best." I nodded, "I mean… unless you don't mind the couch."

"Your couch's perfect. I'm sick of hotels."

"Okay. But, I don't know what we'll do all weekend."

"I'm sure we can think of something." He winked, but when I didn't take the bait he continued, "I haven't seen much of San Francisco even though I've been here many times."

I inhaled thoughtfully, "It would mean slumming it on foot or by BART and taxi."

"No problem, that's the best way to see any city."

"It is, right?" I smiled as I collected up the plates.

"I can do that." Jake offered, taking them from me and stacking the dishwasher.

"All right then. Sightseeing it is."

"Excellent."

"I'm going to take a shower. Thanks for breakfast." I kissed him on the cheek and headed to the bathroom.

Jake packed away the breakfast items, set the dishwasher and was busy wiping down the counter tops when he heard the apartment door open slam. He tossed the cloth in the sink and went through to the living room to check. A man dressed in chinos and a pink shirt with the typical preppy navy sweater slung round his neck dropped some letters on the bookshelf next to the door then bent down to take a closer look at Jake's duffel bag.

"Is there something in particular you're looking for?" Jake asked casually.

The man bolted upright. "What the devil... who the hell are you?!" he exclaimed.

"I feel like I'm the one who should be asking the questions."

"This is my damn apartment."

"Oh... *you're* David." Jake grinned.

"Have we met? I feel I know you from somewhere." David glared at him.

"No. But, I know all about you."

"Where's Cath? I need to talk to her."

"Catherine's taking a shower," Jake smirked, "we just got up."

"I can wait."

"Can I get you anything? Coffee? There's still a fresh pot—"

"I don't fucking want coffee! I want you to leave my apartment so I can talk to Cath."

"She prefers to be called Catherine and I'm not going any-where."

"Is everything okay?" I called as I shut off the shower. I pulled on my bathrobe and rushed through to the living room, "I heard shouting."

"Everything's okay. You have a visitor." Jake said turning to me.

"David." I sighed, pulling my robe tighter around me and brushing back my wet hair. "What do you want?"

"I need to talk to you. Can you tell this buffoon to please leave?"

Jake turned to me with a look of amusement, "Buffoon?" he mouthed the word.

"The 'buffoon'," I gestured in air quotes as I walked over to stand beside Jake, "is my boyfriend, and anything you want to say, you can say in front of Jake."

"Jake? Wait... as in Jake Donovan?" David blurted.

"Yes, that's right."

"But, how?"

"We met in Hawaii." I said, "During the holiday you wanted me to give you and your plaything."

"But... *you*... him... *together*?" He stammered.

"I get it." Jake agreed, looking at me with adoring eyes "You're thinking, how can someone as gorgeous as her, want to be with an ordinary guy like me, right?"

I gasped and David's jaw dropped. Jake slipped his arm around me and I turned and kissed him on the lips in front of David, slow and lingering, for maximum effect.

"I need you to take your stuff," I said, my eyes still locked on Jake's, "otherwise I'm throwing it out. And I need your key back. I'm moving soon. To be with Jake."

Jake raised an eyebrow and furrowed his brow, questioningly. "You are?" he whispered.

I stared at him, pleading silently.

"That's right. She's moving in with me," he declared.

I mouthed back, "thank you," and then turned to David, "Your key! Now, David!"

David fumbled in his pocket and pulled out his keys, "Okay, but can we talk? Please."

"There's nothing left to talk about," I said as Jake snatched David's keys from him.

"Which one is it?" he asked, holding the keys out to me, and I pointed it out.

Jake pulled out the key and slipped it in the pocket of my bathrobe then tossed David's keychain back at him. He missed catching it and it clattered to the floor.

"Please Cath, just give me five minutes. It's important," David pleaded, picking the keys off the floor.

"What is it, then?" I sighed.

Taking the cue, Jake moved away and started moving David's boxes out into the hall.

"I made a mistake."

"You what?" I snorted

"Tiffany and I broke up."

"What, I thought you were *meant to be*?"

"She left me for a twenty-something drummer."

"She left you for someone younger?" I burst out laughing, "Karma is a bitch!"

"Yes, yes, I know. I learned my lesson."

"Oh? And what? Now you want me back?"

"I don't expect you to... not right away... If you'd just listen..." He reached for my hand, "I was such a fool."

"Yes, you were. And so was I." I drew back, crossing my arms firmly.

A look of hope flashed across David's face. "Yes, you see it too, don't you?"

Jake finished moving the boxes into the hall and stood discreetly out of view in the doorway, listening.

I shook my head in disbelief.

"What we had was real. I just didn't see it at the time." David continued.

"No, David. What you and I had was never real. It was a show put on to satisfy everyone's expectations. It was just an act. It was Jake who helped me see that."

"What? But, you can't possibly think whatever you have with, with..." he grappled to say his name so just pointed to the doorway, "...with *him* is going to last! It's obvious he's just using you."

From the corner of my eye, I noticed Jake's expression sadden and he hung his head looking down at the floor.

"No!" I cried, "*you're* the one who used me! You made me move here, made me give up my friends, give up writing, made me get this place... all to support you. And then you dropped me the minute you no longer needed me. Maybe things won't work out for us, but if there is one thing I am certain of, it's that Jake is *not* using me!"

Jake looked up, locked his eyes on mine and strode straight over to me pulling me into a tight embrace and kissed me hard. My knees went weak and I held onto his arm to steady myself when we parted. He turned to David and said, "It's time for you to leave."

"You need to go." I nodded and walked over to the door and ushered him out not listening to his muttering.

I shut the door and leaned against it, smiling at Jake as he walked over, staring at me with his smirky grin. I reached forward and grabbed the drawstrings of his pajama pants and pulled him to me. Our mouths connected and we drew each other in, desperate to lose ourselves in the other. The deeper we ventured, the more urgent our hunger became and the harder we clung on as we moved in unison banging against the door. It shook in its frame and rattled the lock and chain, creating a fevered crescendo of banging, jangling, panting and moaning.

I could hear David on the other side of door dealing with his boxes. The thought that he surely could hear us made me want Jake more and I dug my fingernails into his back urging him on. He lunged forward, sending me off balance and I reached out for the bookshelf to steady myself, knocking several envelopes off it. From the corner of my eye, I caught sight of an unmistakable logo fluttering to the ground and stopped dead.

"Sorry, I got carried away—" Jake stammered.

"No, it wasn't that." I bent down and gathered up the envelopes, setting aside the usual bills and marketing material and held up the envelope with the Pegasus logo to Jake. "It's from the Deighton Academy."

"I thought you said you didn't get in."

"I never heard back from them, so I assumed... But, look," I pointed to my address, a line had been drawn through '*Buxley*', and a hand-written note added: '*try Huxley Street*', "it was misdirected. And anyway who sends letters anymore?"

"Well, come on, open it then."

I shoved it at him, "You do it."

He took the envelope and carefully pried it open. "And the Oscar goes to..." he announced as he slipped out the paper and unfolded it slowly. He read the letter and said nothing.

I grimaced, "I knew it."

"Dear Ms. Marshall," Jake read out loud, "it is our pleasure to welcome you to—"

"I got in?" I shrieked.

Jake nodded grinning, "You got in."

"Let me see that," I took the letter from him. "I don't believe it. I got in. *And* I got a scholarship."

Jake smiled proudly, watching me read the letter a second time to be sure. "I knew you would."

"I'm going to LA." I said dumbfounded, "I've got to pack. I've got to get a place—"

"You have a place." Jake smiled, "I have a couch."

I laughed, "I'm sure it's better than mine."

"Seriously, you can stay with me. No..." he paused, "Don't just stay with me. Move in with me. For real," he winked.

I sighed. "I don't know if that's..."

He got down on his knees and took my hands in his, "I can't be the person the world wants me to be anymore." He started, "I'm done. I'm going to quit that crappy show and the media circus. I want to make movies that move people. I want to plant a vineyard and raise horses. I want to be the Jake I was when I was with you in Hawaii. I want to watch the sun set every night with you by my side and make love to you, till it rises again, under a thousand shooting stars. I want to be your Jake, if you'll have me."

I sucked in my lips, nodding as tears blurred my vision.

Jake stood up and I jumped into his arms and he spun me round, the letter crumpling in my hand as I wrapped my arms around him. "Yes." I whispered, "Yes, yes, yes."

He scooped me up and carried me through to the bedroom. He laid me on the bed and whipping off his T-shirt climbed on top and straddling me, pulled open my bathrobe. He paused for a moment considering where to strike, then leaned down and began devouring me.

I closed my eyes and arched my back, offering myself to him, feeling myself lose my way in him, enveloped in pleasure, unapologetic and greedy. My mind went back to how we had just made out against the door in earshot of David, passionate and fevered. I pictured us doing it at work, against the boardroom wall, silhouetted through the frosted glass while they all listened, while Alex...

I sat bolt upright, nearly smacking my elbow against Jake's head.

"Did I hurt you?" he gasped, pulling back to a safe distance.

"No, no." I laughed, "The opposite." I let out a satisfied groan and fell back against my pillows.

"Then what's going on?" He lay down next to me and pulled the covers over us.

I eyed him with a raised eyebrow, "I'll move in with you on one condition."

His smile turned serious and he answered cautiously, "Okay... what condition?"

"Be my date to Alex's promotion party on Wednesday."

"Sure. No problem."

"Really? You'll come? Just like that."

"Of course. That's what boyfriends do."

"Oh, so you're my boyfriend, are you?"

"Well, I believe that's what you told David."

I blushed, "I guess I did."

"Now, where was I?" He mumbled no longer listening, leaning over me again.

"I believe you were ravishing me." I giggled.

"Ah, yes, the ravishing. Shall I take it from the top?"

"I think that would be wise. You wouldn't want to miss anything."

"Definitely not. We wouldn't want that." He breathed as he leaned over and started nibbling my neck, "I pride myself on being thorough."

I awoke to find myself with my head resting against Jake's chest while he lay, staring up at the ceiling, with one arm behind his head and caressed my back with the other.

"Hey you," he whispered.

"Hey yourself," I murmured looking up at him and then over at the nightstand for the time.

"It's down there somewhere." He gestured to the floor with his head, "We must have knocked it over at some point."

"Ah. Oh well, too bad. I'm not moving."

"Good choice."

Jake inhaled thoughtfully, "So... this party, will there be press?"

I looked up at him, seeing the worry in his eyes. "No, it's not that newsworthy. It'll mostly be everyone from work, their partners and around thirty selected clients."

Jake sighed with relief, "Okay. And dress code?"

"Formal. Black tie. Which makes me realize..." I said hopping out of bed and walking over to my wardrobe, "I've got nothing to wear."

"Pity, you have to wear anything at all," Jake smirked, leering at me as I stood naked, going through my wardrobe, looking at various options.

"Ha!" I turned round and stuck my tongue out at him. "All I've got, that's remotely cocktail party-appropriate, is this," I said pulling out the infamous short blue dress, and holding it against myself.

"You've actually worn that?" Jake raised an eyebrow.

"Only once and only to the hospital. It's the dress from David's Christmas party disaster when I cut my hand."

"Ah, that explains it."

"I hate it. It's kinda—"

"Slutty?"

"Oh my god, yes!" I laughed, "See? You get it."

Jake smiled, "Bin it. We'll go shopping. I'll need to pick up a suit myself."

I tossed the dress on the floor, "I think Macy's got a sale—" I mumbled, losing track of what I was saying, distracted by the Adonis lying naked on my bed with the sheet draped strategically across his groin like a nude in a renaissance painting.

Jake raised an eyebrow, "Baby, where we're going is only open by appointment." He reached out and pulled me back towards the bed.

I drew my hand back, "Oh, you devil. No more! I need a shower, followed by something to eat."

"I'll join you." He said jumping up and following me out the door, his hands on my waist.

"I'm not sure that's a good idea."

"Aww, I promise I'll behave." He teased, nibbling on my neck as we made our way to the bathroom.

"That's not the problem," I laughed as we crossed the threshold and I opened the shower door.

Jake looked up from over my shoulder into the tiny cubicle, "Right. Nope. That's not happening. Looks like a sci-fi coffin. You go ahead, I'll wait."

I stepped in and closed the door behind me and turned on the water. I stood with my back to the door, soaking in the heat of the water and steam while I soaped up and lost myself in the afterglow of the last few hours. I ran my hands through my hair, rinsing out the shampoo, bringing myself to the present and turned around to feel the water pound against my back. I opened my eyes and jolted upright with surprise. I thought Jake had left the room, but he was standing in front of the shower door with his hands and face pressed up against the glass. I burst out laughing and wiped the steam off the door while he kissed and licked the glass like a teenager practicing French kissing on a mirror. I turned off the water and stepped out reaching for a towel.

"You!" I laughed, stepping aside for him, "All yours." I gestured, and as he walked in I slapped him on the backside.

"Cheeky!" he yelped, grabbing his butt, grinning.

"I'm going to order some pizza, okay," I said as he closed the door. He turned and gave me a thumbs-up.

"Don't forget the pineapple!" He called after me, turning on the shower.

I smiled. How could I forget?

We settled on the couch, both dressed slouchy for an evening of pizza, Netflix and relaxing. Jake opened the pizza boxes and poured the wine while I opened Netflix and started scrolling through titles.

"I started watching *The Blood Moon Prophecies* after I got back."

"Oh?" Jake asked, handing me a glass of wine, "and what do you think?"

"I was pleasantly surprised. There's a lot more depth to it than I expected."

"See, I wouldn't have all those millions of fans if it was bad." he grinned, munching on a mouthful of pizza.

"I don't think the storyline is really the reason for that." I smiled, taking a sip of wine.

"To be honest, I haven't watched much of it myself."

"What? After all the gibing me in Hawaii that I hadn't seen it and you've never watched the show that made you a star?"

"I've seen parts, but I never got round to seeing the whole thing."

"Well, we can fix that right now," I selected *The Blood Moon Prophecies* and hit play, picking up on where I had left off.

It was surreal watching him on screen while he was curled up with me on my couch. It was like some kind of out-of-body experience, but instead of stepping outside of your body to exist as pure energy, the fictional character on the screen, existing of pixels and energy, had stepped out of the screen and materialized into real flesh and blood in front of me. I almost believed that as soon as the episode ended, he would disappear and I would find myself alone again.

I looked back at the screen. Vincent stood with his mouth clenched over some thug's neck, savagely biting him, blood gushing into his mouth and down the man's front. With a satisfied grunt Vincent tossed the drained body aside. "Sucks for you," he leered with a wicked smile, his mouth red and blood dripping from his teeth and down his chin.

"Oh man, those fangs!" Jake laughed, "They gave me a lisp.

It took me forever to learn to talk with them." He turned to me baring his teeth and inching towards my neck all serious and broody-looking, "I'm Vinthent, thuper thexthy vampire, here to thuck your blood till you thkweam with ecthtathy."

I burst out laughing as he nibbled my neck, "You're such a—"

"Buffoon?" he asked, grinning.

"Yes. You're my beautiful buffoon." I smiled and kissed him. He leaned over, curling up on the couch and rested his head on my lap while we continued to watch.

$\mathcal{I}$ sat on the couch and typed out a new text message on my phone to Amira telling her I had a stomach bug and would not be in to work for probably two days. It was a lie of course, and I felt bad, not for blowing off work, but that she would have to fill in for me on top of doing her own job. Somehow, I'd make it up to her.

Jake was singing to himself in the kitchen and I smiled while I listened and scrolled through the photos I had taken the day before when we had spent the whole Sunday exploring the city. It had been a long time since I had done the tourist route and doing it with Jake felt like I was seeing the city for the first time. We did a whirlwind tour of as many famous landmarks as we could and at every one Jake made a point of posing for me and of us taking selfies together. I now had several dozen photos of us from riding the cable cars, walking Lombard Street, and visiting museums to watching the sun set the Gold Gate Bridge on fire in the evening.

My phone beeped with a message from Amira saying she would take care of everything and hoped I felt better soon.

"Everything okay?" Jake asked as he handed me a mug of coffee and sat down on the couch next to me.

"Yup, all good. I am officially off work with a stomach bug."

Jake grinned wickedly, "You're so bad."

"I don't know what's gotten into me." I teased.

We made a list of everything that needed to be done in the next few days from canceling utilities, booking movers, and packing up my belongings.

"Divide and conquer," said Jake handing me my half of the list. "Last one to finish cooks dinner."

"You're on." I laughed.

Jake opened the browser on my laptop while I dialed the number of the utilities company on my phone. After selecting the various options I was put on hold as expected and while I half listened to awful canned music I looked over to see what Jake was looking up. He was at a website with a stylish corporate design and the words *Exclusive Connections* across the banner.

"Exclusive Connections?" I mocked, "Sounds like a dating site," I said giving him the evil eye.

Jake laughed, "It does, doesn't it?" He scrolled down and a number of small luxury aircraft appeared on the screen, "I'm booking our flights back to LA."

"You're hiring a private jet?"

"Actually, they're turbo-props, but yeah, this way we won't have to waste time waiting around or deal with gawping fans. And you can bring some extra luggage along."

"So, purely for practical reasons?" I grinned.

"Naturally." He nodded straight-faced.

I raised an eyebrow.

"Okay. It's also really cool," he said laughing.

"Ah, I—" A voice interrupted the hold music, bringing me back to the mundane task of canceling my utilities and I left Jake to finish booking the flights.

By mid-morning everything had been arranged, and there was one final call to make.

"Hi, Mum," I said when she answered, "There's something I have to tell you and Dad."

After lunch we set off downtown to get our outfits for Alex's promotion party. Since I was supposed to be ill at home in bed and Jake, was well, Jake, neither of us wanted to be recognized so we both covered up to be incognito. We wore sunglasses even though the day was overcast and drizzling. Jake had the hood of his hoodie pulled down low over his face and I wore a pashmina shawl over my head and my long trench coat with the collar upturned. We set off, probably looking more conspicuous than not, but hopeful that we projected a don't-approach-us vibe.

We were headed towards Chinatown past the big brand stores, places I never dared enter for fear of being asked to leave because I didn't fit the profile of their clientele, places that were the natural habitat of people like Alex and Jess.

"I love this store." I mused stopping in front of the huge glass window of Farinelli's to admire the glittering collection of opulent furniture, antiques, giant porcelain vases, fine art and crystal chandeliers. "I've always wanted to go inside."

"Well, why don't you?" Jake asked.

"Me, in a place like that? I'm too afraid I'll knock something over."

Jake laughed and pulling me by the hand headed for the door.

Within seconds of removing his sunglasses and pushing his hoodie back, he was recognized and a store assistant glided over to us, "Mr. Donovan, what a pleasure to have you in the store today!" she gushed, "Is there something in particular I can help you find?"

She didn't realize I was with Jake and stared at me with a look that threatened to call the police if I stepped any closer.

Jake slipped his arm around me, "We're just browsing for now, thank you."

"Certainly, I'll leave you to—" she sputtered while we walked away and I glared at her triumphantly.

We lost ourselves browsing in the Aladdin's cave of priceless one-of-kind objects, sumptuous Victorian chairs with velvet cushions and polished wood work, gold rimmed china sets, marble statues, jeweled ornaments, precious paintings with ornate frames and luxury Christmas decorations.

"Wow, just wow," I whispered, absolutely gobsmacked by it all.

"It's fantastic, isn't it?"

"It's like being in a fairy-tale royal palace." I stood staring at a glass case of sparkling Swarovski crystal ornaments. "It's mesmerizing, the way they sparkle like that."

Jake looked over my shoulder at the collection of faceted glass animals, flowers and figurines. "They really are something…" he paused, momentarily distracted, "I just need to make a call."

I nodded, not taking my eyes from the glittering pieces. He walked off and I was left alone. After a while I looked up to find Jake, but couldn't see him anywhere. The more I looked around, the more aware I became of security cameras and several store assistants watching me. I looked down putting my hands in my pockets and walked towards the entrance doing my best to look casual and innocent. Beads of sweat started to form in all the wrong places and I pulled my hands out of my pockets again as I passed the checkout desk fearing they might think I was concealing something. I darted out onto the sidewalk drawing my coat around me in the sudden chill and looked back at the store half expecting a security guard to grab me and pull me back in. Sighing with relief, I leaned back against a lamppost to wait for Jake while I caught my breath watching it escape from me in clouds.

A few minutes later Jake found me. "Why didn't you wait for me inside?" he asked, pulling up his hoodie again, "It's cold out here."

"I was beginning to feel watched, like they expected me to try and slip something in my pocket."

Jake laughed, "Well, the trench coat does have a cagey look to it."

It wasn't the coat. It was me. They were right to suspect me. I was guilty. Not of potential shoplifting but of being an imposter. I didn't belong in places like this… *Yet*. It hit me that that was all going to change.

We continued walking for another block until we reached a doorway tucked in amongst street-facing shops. There was an intercom and Jake pressed the buzzer.

"Hello?" a shrill voice answered.

"Hi, it's Jake."

"Darling! Come on up."

The door buzzed and clicked open and we stepped through to a small lobby with a flight of stairs. We went up and entered into a large space sumptuously decorated with chaise lounges and heavy velvet curtains and various racks of suits and dresses in expensive fabrics and decorated with beads, sequins, feathers and diamantes. We stood taking it in, as a middle-aged gentleman in pin-stripe dark purple suit with lilac cravat entered the room.

"Darling!" He pulled Jake into an embrace, kissing him on each cheek European style, "It's been too long."

"Julian, it's really good to see you," said Jake, pulling back and gesturing towards me, "this is Catherine."

Julian reached out an elegant manicured hand, "*Enchante.*"

"Hello, it's a pleasure to meet you," I said taking his hand, "Jake has said great things about you."

"*Moi*?" He winked at Jake and pulled me into an embrace and kissed my cheeks, "But, of course."

We moved over to the chaises and Julian motioned for us to sit while he went over to a table with wine bucket and glasses, "Champagne?"

We nodded and he poured us each a glass before sitting down with us.

Jake turned to me and held up his glass, "To your new life."

"To *our* new life," I said, clinking my glass against his and taking a sip.

"We're moving in together." Jake explained to Julian, "And she got accepted to the Deighton Academy."

"This is good news, yes!" he squealed and jumped up to pour himself a glass of champagne, "*Félicitations!*" he clinked his glass against ours and downed the contents in one go.

Jake and I smiled at each other with amusement.

"Right, to business," Julian declared, smacking the glass down on the table, "this party you are attending, it is a premiere?"

Jake shook his head and motioned to me to explain.

"It's a work thing, cocktail party after hours, black tie."

Jake nodded, "I'll need a tuxedo for the night, preferably a peak or notch lapel – you know the style I like, bow tie, cuff links. You still have my measurements?"

Julian nodded. "And, for madam?"

I looked at them both completely lost, "I have no idea."

Jake continued, "Well, the night is all about her, so the full works, pull out all the stops."

"Lovely!" Julian clapped his hands with glee. "Please, stand for me," he motioned to me.

I stood up awkwardly.

"Turn, turn. Let me see," he said, twirling his hand.

"I'd prefer not to wear anything too short or revealing. I'm a bit old-fashioned."

"Ha! Old-fashioned! No, no, you are a classic. And classic is never old or out of fashion," he cheered as I looked over at Jake and he gave me a thumbs-up, "as they say, in a world of Kardashians, you are an Audrey Hepburn." He pointed to a decorated screen, "you can undress behind there."

"I'm sorry?" I blurted.

"Just down to your underwear. I must take measurements."

I hesitated and he took my hand pulling me to my feet, "Come, come. Quickly." he pushed me towards the screen, "Besides, darling, I'd much rather see Jake in his briefs."

Like a musical montage in romantic comedy, Julian had me try on many different outfits from a modest and simple little black dress to an over-the-top modern fuchsia pantsuit with giant flounce on one shoulder. Finally we settled on a dress we both liked.

"This is the one," I said, looking at myself in the mirror. I wore a crimson velvet dress, floor length with a slit on one side right up to just below the hip. It was sleeveless and strapless with layers of fabric draped around the shoulders like a shrug. Dramatic yet classic, sexy but not slutty.

"Perfectamente!" pronounced Julian, clasping his hands in success. He pulled the screen aside and gestured for me to go ahead.

"What do you think?" I asked Jake as I stepped forward.

His jaw dropped and he stood up staring at me in wonder, "Stunning! Takes my breath away."

I ran my hands down the slender form, feeling the richness of the velvet, "I love it!"

Julian tugged at the dress from behind, "I just need to bring it in a bit, but otherwise its perfect, and I think the hair works best up," he lifted my hair and set it on top.

"Definitely up," Jake nodded, "makes me want to sink my teeth into that neck." He turned to me and winked, licking his lips.

"You behave!" I pulled my hair down round my shoulders and darted behind the screen to change back into my normal clothes.

We finished with Julian, arranging a time for Jake to collect the garments and then headed back downtown to find somewhere to eat.

The waitress took our order and we both let out contented sigh. "Jinx," grinned Jake.

We sat in a cozy booth beside a roaring fire at the back of one of the city's best Italian restaurants. Its rustic country décor belied its exclusivity. Exclusivity meant privacy and no one to disturb us.

Jake shifted, digging in his pocket and pulled out a small box. He placed it on the table and pushed it over to me.

"What's this?" I asked.

"Open it."

My hands shaking, heart pounding, I slowly raised the lid. Inside nestled in a velvet-lined hollow sat a crystal Pegasus rearing up with its wings spread out as if about to take flight.

"Oh Jake, it's gorgeous!" I ran my finger over the cut glass, "this is what you were doing when you disappeared in Farinelli's?"

He nodded, "I saw it and it made me think of the Deighton Academy."

"It's their logo, of course."

"I just know you're going to fly that Pegasus all the way to the top."

"It's perfect. Thank you." I reached over and kissed him. He scooted over to sit next to me on my side of the booth and we leaned against each other, holding hands until our meal arrived.

Chapter 35

"Catherine? What is it?" Amira asked when I stepped out the elevator and rushed up to the front desk where she sat minding the phone.

"Where is everyone?" I scanned the office and sneaked a look down the hall.

"Mr. Andrews is in a meeting with Alex and Jess. Kim's not in yet. What's going on?"

I hung up my coat and dropped my bag, and leaned against the reception counter, tapping my fingers on the top. "I don't know how to tell you this."

"You're okay, aren't you? Don't tell me it's serious?"

"What? No. I wasn't actually sick."

Amira tucked her hijab back, "Okay, I'm lost. Explain." She narrowed her eyes at me.

I broke into a huge grin, "I don't think you're going to believe me." I pulled up a chair next to her.

"Believe what? Tell me!"

"Okay," I took a deep breath, "Remember back in July when we joked that it would funny if I went to Hawaii and met Jake Donovan?"

She nodded her head.

"Well, um... I... did."

"Did what?"

"I met Jake Donovan."

"Ooo..kayyy... So, you met him, what like in getting his autograph or something?"

I sucked in my lip, "More than that. He um—"

"Wait, you're not the woman he rescued from drowning, are you?" she shrieked.

"Ssshhh!" I hissed, nodding.

"But, why didn't you say anything? You nearly died, you poor thing!" She grabbed my hands and squeezed them.

"Because it's complicated, because there's more to it than that." I went on to explain everything from the moment I waded too far into the ocean to the moment Jake had kissed me on the cheek this morning in my very own doorway before I left for work.

Amira stared at me in a state of shock.

"I know. I can hardly believe it myself. It's like a dream."

I opened the gallery on my phone and scrolled through pictures I had taken of the two of us traveling around the city: Jake goofing around, Jake posing next to San Francisco landmarks, selfies of the two of us together.

"I can't believe that's Jake Donovan. He looks like just a normal guy."

"I know. He's nothing like I expected." I said "Oh and don't you love this," I showed her a picture of the crystal Pegasus, "He gave it to me for getting into the Deighton Academy, it's their logo."

"Aw, it's beautiful, and congratulations," she reached over and gave me a hug, "I just know you're going to make it."

"Thanks."

She leaned back and paused, frowning thoughtfully. "You don't think it's all a bit fast? Moving in with him so soon?"

"I know. But, playing it safe has worked out *so well* for me in the past," I muttered sarcastically, "so, I'm making a blind leap of faith. Besides, what's the worst that could happen? I've already nearly died once."

"Okay," Amira smiled satisfied, "then go for it. Grab it with both hands!" she declared excitedly, "you're getting out of here! Tomorrow!"

"Mr. Andrews is going to explode, I grinned. "Though, we contacted the temp agency, someone will be here in the morning and he can use my pay, so it's all taken care of. I just have to *tell* him."

"And what about the others, I take it none of them know about you and Jake?"

I shook my head and grinned, "All will be revealed tonight."

Amira's eyes twinkled with delight, "he's coming?"

"Yup, he's my date."

"I can't wait to—" she was interrupted by the sound of Mr. Andrews' door opening and the Barbie Twins voices coming down the hall. "I better go. Let me know when you need me to cover you while you do the dirty," she winked.

I knocked on Mr. Andrews' door and opening it partially, popped my head round, "Do you have five minutes?"

He looked up from his desk, "You'll have to make it quick; I'm due in court soon."

"No problem." I had no desire to hang around. This time I wasn't just throwing him a grenade, I was dropping a nuclear bomb.

"This had better be an explanation of your absence yesterday. It's obvious you weren't sick."

"Well, sort of. There's something I need to tell you."

"Yes?" he drew out the s, barely holding back a 'what now' burst of fury.

"I'm leaving sooner than expected."

"How much sooner?"

Shaking, I pulled the bomb release lever, "Today is my last day. I'm moving to Los Angeles tomorrow."

"Tomorrow?!" he exploded "You can't do that!"

I said nothing, waiting for the shock waves to pass, feeling the searing heat tear through me and imagined myself as a glowing skeleton as a giant mushroom cloud rose from his shoulders. It obscured the world map behind him, laying waste to every continent, reducing every country to radioactive ash.

"And since when have you been planning to move to LA? I

thought you were going back home."

"Yes, there's been a change of plans. I've been accepted to a writing school there and my boyfriend asked me to move in with him."

"Okay, but why the bloody rush?"

"I understand it's very sudden. It's been all very unexpected..." I sighed. What was the point of trying to explain? "Look, I'm really sorry for the inconvenience. We have arranged for a temp to be here first thing tomorrow and I've spoken with Amira, she knows what to do."

"Fine, though I'll be docking your pay!"

"Of course, please do." I tried to stop myself, but I couldn't help it, I broke into a smirk, "As you made clear in my review, I'm easily replaced so I'm sure you won't have any trouble finding my replacement."

Seething, Mr. Andrews grabbed the folder on his desk, "I have to be in court. I haven't got time for this!"

I jumped out the way and he flew out the office. I stood for a moment to catch my breath, then punched the air and marched triumphant back to the front office.

Alex and Jess had heard the commotion and were gathered around the front desk with Amira waiting to be debriefed.

"What the hell was that all about?" asked Alex, gloating at my apparent dressing down, "You must have seriously pissed him off."

"Yes, he's not too happy with me," I said taking my chair back from Amira. I winked at her, sucking in my lip as I sat down and she broke into a grin.

"So, what did you do?" Jess prodded.

"It's not so much what I did, as what I am about to do. I've had a slight change of plans... I'm leaving sooner than expected."

"Oh? When?" chimed the Barbie Twins.

I took a deep breath, "Today's my last day."

"What?! Why so soon?" Alex shrieked.

"I've been accepted into the Deighton Academy writing school, so I'm moving to LA instead of going back home."

"Oh wow, congratulations!" Jess exclaimed and rushed over and hugged me for the first time in our acquaintance.

"Thanks," I said, genuinely surprised by her uncharacteristic show of support.

"But, why the rush? Surely your course doesn't start till the New Year?" Alex continued, while giving Jess the evil eye.

"No, that's right, it doesn't. But, my boyfriend and I want to spend some time together, just the two of us, before the holidays."

"Boyfriend!" Alex spat, "Since when have you had a boyfriend?"

"Since my holiday – we met in Hawaii." I bit my lip trying not to grin too much. "He lives in LA and now that I'm moving to LA, we're moving in together."

"Oh my God, that's so exciting!" gushed Jess, "what's his name?"

"Jonathan Donaldson." I struggled to keep a straight face, this was too good.

Amira looked at me, grinning. She was enjoying this as much as me. "And what does he do?" she asked, playing along, trying not to laugh.

"He works in TV and film."

Alex rolled her eyes, "Oh God, what a cliché. *Everyone* in LA is in TV and film," she groaned.

"He's in town at the moment, so you'll be able to meet him tonight."

"You're bringing him tonight? You're still coming?"

"I wouldn't miss it."

"Oh yay, looking forward to it." Alex sighed and turned to Jess, "Come on. It's time for lunch." They left the desk briefly to fetch their handbags while Amira and I stared at each other, trying not to laugh, with huge smiles plastered on our faces.

"Enjoy your lunch," we called in unison as the Barbie Twins passed us and headed to the elevator.

"So, what do you suppose he does?" Jess asked Alex, making no attempt to whisper.

"He's probably the dork that holds the sound pole thing," Alex laughed, fully intending for me to hear, "and, what kind of name is Jonathan Donaldson?"

"The kind of name that gets a kid beat up during recess," mocked Jess as she pressed the elevator button.

We waited for the elevator door to close on their cackling, before bursting into laughter. Amira grabbed me and hugged me tightly, "I can't wait for tonight."

"Me too," I murmured, "it's going to be—"

My phone beeped with a message.

"It's from Jake," I said reading it, "he's downstairs now."

"Here?" Amira gasped.

I nodded, "He's brought my dress for tonight." I tapped a quick reply. "I'll be back in a moment."

Amira nodded, staring at me in awe.

"Come with me." I blurted, looking around the empty office.

"I don't know, we can't just leave the office unattended."

"I'll switch the phone to the answer service and lock the front door. We'll only be gone a few minutes. It'll be fine."

"Umm, I—"

"Oh, come on, be a rebel." I grinned, "It's great fun!"

"Oh, all right. You've twisted my arm. Let's go."

The elevator doors opened and we stepped into the lobby. A giant Christmas tree decorated with huge baubles and over-sized tinsel dominated the area.

"I don't see him," Amira said, scanning the space.

"That's him," I pointed to a guy in jeans and hoodie pulled over a baseball cap and wearing sunglasses and a woolly scarf lurking in a corner beside a potted yucca. He stood in the blind spot of the security cameras and was carrying a bag of takeaways and held two suit protectors over his shoulder with one finger.

"Wait, that creepy guy's Jake Donovan?"

"Yup, that's him. Incognito."

"Are you sure?" she whispered as she followed me over to him.

"Yes, that's my scarf."

Amira laughed, "The Barbie Twins probably walked right past him without noticing."

"You're right!" I snorted, "They'd never look twice at someone dressed like that." I tapped him on the shoulder, "Hi handsome."

"Hey there, beautiful." He turned and handed me the bag and kissed me on the cheek, "I bought you some lunch."

I took a peek inside, "Oooh, sushi, yum!" then gestured to Amira, "Jake, this Amira. Amira, Jake."

He took off his sunglasses and slipped them through his collar. "Oh hey," he extended his hand warmly, "I've heard great things about you."

"Likewise." Amira shook his hand, gobsmacked. Then collecting herself, she placed her other hand on top of his, "I'm sorry to hear about your father."

He nodded, "Thank you, that's kind of you."

He started to pull his hand away and she squeezed it tighter, "And, thank you for saving Catherine's life."

For the first time, I saw Jake's cheeks flush and he stammered bashfully, "You're welcome. I mean, I did what anyone would do."

"*Mashallah*. That's what we like to believe, but I don't think it's necessarily true," she pulled him into a hug and whispered, "she's been such a good friend to me." She let him go and turning to me said under her breath, "He's awesome."

I grinned from ear to ear.

"I should probably head back upstairs and let you two talk." She held out her hand and I gave her the keys. "It's been lovely to meet you." She said turning to Jake, then took her leave and headed to the elevator.

"How's it going upstairs?" Jake asked.

"Not too bad. And you?"

"Packing's done and the movers will be by first thing."

"Brilliant. Thank you for doing all that."

He handed me one of the suit protectors, "And here's your dress."

"Thank you, Sir." I kissed him on the cheek. "I better go. I'm already persona non grata upstairs, so I—"

"Oh, one more thing, I booked us a suite at the Palace Hotel for tonight."

"Really?"

"Yeah, I thought you might like to spend your last night here in comfort rather than sleeping amongst boxes."

"You're amazing, you know that?"

He flashed his smirky smile.

"Right. I've really got to go. I'll see you tonight." I grinned and turned for the elevator.

He grabbed my hand and pulled me back again, and pressing me against the lobby wall kissed me hard on the lips and then pulled away, winked at me and darted for the exit.

"This is it!" Amira declared, as we settled into the backseat of the premium Uber we hired to take us to the hotel.

I exhaled slowly, trying to calm my nerves, "I still can't believe it."

"Well, you deserve it and can I say, you look stunning."

I ran my hand over the rich velvet of my dress. "Thanks. And thanks for helping me get dressed. It was a great idea to change at the office."

"And for the luxury Uber, I feel like royalty."

I grinned, "It's worth it, isn't it?"

"For sure!" she nodded.

"I love your dress," I said admiring her long-sleeve, floor-length royal blue silk caftan-type dress. It was decorated with layers of chiffon, and embroidered with silver beads and sequins, and she wore a matching hijab.

"Thanks, it's an abaya. I got it in Dubai, for my cousin's wedding. I've only worn it once before, but being that I am the token brown person in the office, I thought I'd dust it off and go full traditional."

I laughed, "Brilliant! You do you!"

She reached over and squeezed my hand, "There's no stopping us now, right?"

"You better believe it."

We arrived at the hotel in good time and headed upstairs to the Lincoln Room, turning a few heads on our way from business-men attending dinner meetings and hotel guests checking in. We were the last from the office to arrive and we found a quiet corner across from the door to watch and wait. More guests continued to arrive and we scanned the room in the meantime. We spotted Mr. Andrews with his wife and their son. We remarked that Max must have been roped into putting in an appearance as the silent partner in Andrews and Andrews. They were talking with Kim and her doctor husband and several influential clients. I quickly lost inter-est in people watching and returned my attention to the entrance, keeping my eyes glued on the doorway. Jake had texted me while we were in the cab to say he was about twenty minutes away. My heart began to race, it wouldn't be long now.

I let out a low groan, "Don't look now," I whispered to Amira, "the Barbie Twins are coming this way. She looked over and snorted at the sight of them. Predictably, they were dressed in almost matching outfits, tight body-contouring dresses that accentuated all the curves and left nothing to the imagination, like the plastic seal around the neck of a bottle; both teetering on impossibly high heels.

"Oh, you poor thing!" Jess exclaimed, looking at Amira.

"What?" Amira asked confused.

"You're forced to wear that!"

Amira groaned, "Actually, I *chose* to wear this."

Alex eyed my dress, puzzled, "Your dress is amazing."

"Thank you." I stammered, surprised at the rare compliment.

"For a knock-off it's pretty convincing."

"Sorry?"

She sighed impatiently, "It looks like a Julian Renoir. Where did you get it?"

"Um... from Julian Renoir."

"No, I mean, where—" she started, wanting to argue further, but was interrupted by the arrival of a medium-height bulky man whose suit strained to conceal his muscle bulges, and his collar and tie threatened to cut off his circulation.

Alex hooked her arm through his, "This is my date, Tony."

Amira leaned over and whispered to me, "Must be the latest flavor of the month."

He nodded and grunted in monosyllables acknowledging us, obviously possessing little to no vocabulary. "He's a personal trainer." Alex crowed.

"Of course, he is," I whispered back to Amira and we suppressed a mutual giggle.

Alex motioned towards the buffet table and sent him away to fetch her a drink. "So, where is this man of yours?" she sneered, "not coming after all?"

"He'll be here," I assured her, although inside I was beginning to panic. What if he had changed his mind and was heading back to LA?

Alex rolled her eyes and let out another condescending sigh and the panic knotting in my stomach was about to go up a notch when a sudden hush fell over the room. Everyone turned with muffled whispers to stare at the doorway. A tall man with dark hair, wearing an obviously expensive tuxedo, crisp white linen shirt with black buttons and black bowtie stood on the threshold.

He adjusted a cufflink, scanning the crowd; then dropping his arms, shrugged his shoulders and strode into the room. The crowd parted in front of him and he walked towards us, his calm blue eyes locked on mine. An errant curl brushed his forehead and he raised an eyebrow smiling at me with that signature smile.

"Oh-em-gee, you guys!" screeched Alex, "how on earth did you arrange this?" She rushed towards Jake extending her hand, teetering on her heels.

He walked straight past her, not even noticing her or anyone else for that matter, ignoring the gasps of surprise and confused chatter. He kept his eyes on mine till he was in front of me then slipping his arm around my waist drew me to him and kissed me on the mouth, long and unrushed, tugging on my lip, eyes on mine the whole time, taking my breath away and making my knees wobble. I felt like the room was spinning, as if there was a camera circling us doing a 360° shot, freezing us in slow motion while the rest of the room dissolved away.

"Sorry, I'm late," he said pulling back and slipping his hand into mine.

"Perfect timing, actually," I said breathlessly. The Barbie Twins stared at me wide-eyed and open-mouthed, while Amira was grinning from ear to ear. "Ladies, let me introduce you to my boyfriend, Jonathan Donaldson."

"What the hell?!" stammered Alex, "Is this some kind of joke? That's Jake Donovan!"

Jake smiled, "Yeah, that's generally what people call me."

"Jonathan's his real name," I explained, "before he changed it."

"Jake Donovan has a better ring to it, don't you think?" said Jake.

Alex looked back and forth between Jake and me, "But, you... and him... how?"

I smiled, "Remember the story about the idiot tourist that Jake saved from drowning? Yes well, that was me."

Jake nodded, "I went with her to the hospital and one thing lead to another."

"Jake takes his life-saving very seriously," I laughed, "and decided it was safer to chaperone me for the rest of my visit."

Alex was horrified. "That's how you met, by some random accident?"

"More like cosmic destiny," said Jake looking at me with adoration, "it was fated in the stars." He pulled me tighter to him and kissed me on my cheek.

"Let me introduce you," I announced, breaking the spell, and gestured to each in turn, "this is Alex and Jess..."

"Ah yes, the rum girls," Jake remarked, extending his hand.

Jess shook it eagerly, "You remember? We—"

"Yes, sorry about that." Alex cut her off, "We heard you don't drink rum." She turned and glared at me.

I grinned sheepishly, "Yeah. I didn't read it somewhere."

"Hey, no problem. I gave it to Bryce. He and his husband acquired the taste for it."

"Maybe that's who I was thinking of," Jess mumbled.

Jake continued, shaking Alex's hand, "And congratulations on the promotion and birthday."

"Thank you," she brightened.

"And of course, you know Amira," I said, turning to her.

"Wait, you know Amira too?!" cried Alex.

"He dropped by when you two were at lunch," Amira said with delight, extending her hand.

"Amira..." Jake took her hand in both of his and squeezed it fondly, "your abaya is stunning. Dubai, right?"

"Where else?" she beamed, "Have you been?"

"A short stopover a few years ago. I got several great tailored suits while I was there."

I stood by, happy to see Jake and Amira swap notes about their visits to UAE. It meant a lot to me that he was making the effort to get to know my friend. I could sense the jealousy emanating from Alex and Jess expanding like a foul-smelling cloud, and I was glad when Tony re-joined the group. Alex greeted him with an annoyed groan as if she had forgotten she had invited him along. He introduced himself to Jake, shaking his hand with a vice-like grip and the two men chatted briefly about weight training and work-out routines. I spotted Mr. Andrews near the buffet table and hooked my arm through Jake's. "Time to meet the boss," I whispered as I nudged him in that direction. We excused ourselves from the group and made our way over.

"Mr. Andrews, I'd like you to meet my boyfriend, Jake."

He turned but showed no flicker of recognition, "I thought you said his name was Jonathan."

"It is." Jake said, extending his hand, "Jake's a... a nickname."

Mr. Andrews eyed him suspiciously, straightening his stance and puffed out his chest, before shaking Jake's hand, "Trevor Andrews, attorney, senior partner."

Not missing a beat, Jake straightened up and puffed his own chest, "Jake Donovan, actor, double Emmy award winner. Pleased to meet you."

"Actor? The one Alex is always going on about?" Mr. Andrews drew back his hand and raised a questioning eyebrow at me.

"The same," I nodded.

Jake took the lead, "I understand you have some issues with Catherine leaving you short-staffed, so I'd like to offer to pay for a temporary replacement until you find a permanent staff member. It seems only fair. We have arranged for someone to be available from tomorrow until you find a permanent replacement."

I agreed, "And Amira knows what needs to be done, she's filled in for me before, so there really won't be any problems. You won't even miss me."

Mr. Andrews exhaled heavily, "Very well, it seems I have little choice in the matter."

"Thank you." I touched his arm lightly, "And I really am sorry for the inconvenience."

Mr. Andrews grunted and turned to Jake, "If I could have a word with you alone."

"Certainly," Jake nodded and turned to me frowning and shrugging his shoulders.

"I guess," I whispered, frowning in return, then made my exit and re-joined Amira and the Barbie Twins. Alex's Ken doll had disappeared again in search of food.

Alex narrowed her eyes and glared at me, "Wait a minute... Are you the reason Jake bailed on the convention and cast party?" She had obviously been going over the events of the last few weeks in her mind.

"Yeah?" Jess chimed in, only now making the connection. "Did he blow off the fans to be with you?"

"No. That had nothing to do with me." I shot a look over to confirm Jake was still talking to Mr. Andrews and explained, "Jake's father passed away suddenly and he had to go back to Baltimore for the funeral."

"Oh, that's awful." Jess gasped.

"Well, at least it was—" Alex started.

"Alex!"

We turned towards a familiar and unwelcome voice.

"I just wanted to congratulate you personally," Alistair Steele, extended his hand, exuding his usual sleazy self-importance and arrogance.

"Alistair, thank you. Your support means so much. Has the merger been—"

"And who is this tasty morsel?" he jeered, looking me up and down.

"That's Cathy," said Alex flatly

"And why haven't I met you before?"

"You have," I replied.

"Oh, believe me, I'd remember a hottie like you."

"Try picturing me behind a reception desk."

"Hmm... I don't know about behind, but definitely on top," he reached out to pat me on the hip and I darted out the way just as Jake appeared carrying two glasses of champagne.

"Is there a problem here?" he asked.

I took a glass from him and splashed its contents in Alistair Steele's face, "Not at all." I declared triumphantly.

"You bitch!" he yelled, "I'll have your job!"

"Good luck with that," I sneered, grabbing Jake's hand and pulling him to follow me.

Jake turned on his heel and paused for a moment to look back at the shocked crowd while pointing at me with his free hand and exclaiming boastfully, "I'm with *her*!"

"Well played," Jake remarked, handing me the other glass of champagne as we walked away.

"Thanks." I grinned and took a long sip, "I've been wanting to do that for a long time." I passed the glass back to him. "What did Trevor want?" I dispensed with the 'Mr. Andrews'. After all, he was no longer my boss.

Jake emptied the glass, "Just to go over the finer details of our arrangement."

"Ah," I nodded.

"And he..."

"What?" I stopped and eyed him curiously.

"You won't believe me."

"Come on, what did he say?"

"He told me not to mess up."

"Huh?"

"He said you deserve to be happy, so I better treat you right."

I stared at Jake dumbfounded, "Well, I never—"

"Here, give me your glass." Jake took my empty glass and left it on a side table along with his before taking me by the hand to an open space on the floor away from the other guests.

"What is it?"

"The song," he murmured, pulling me to face him, and slipping his free hand around my waist, "you're my lady in red."

I smiled as I recognized the iconic song by Chris de Burgh, "I love this song."

Jake curled my hand inwards, holding it against his chest, and I rested my arm on his shoulder while we swayed in time to the music, our cheeks pressed together.

And as the last notes faded away, his lips against my ear, he whispered, "I love you."

I pulled away a bit to look him in the eye, not sure if he had simply repeated the last words of the song. He looked back at me, eye-to-eye, no question in his mind, nor mine, and he said it again, "I love you."

"I love you too." I beamed. Our lips met and we kissed, slow and tender, swept away in our own movie montage, oblivious to the heads turned to watch us, lost in our moments past, present and future that seemed to play out around us scratched and flickering like precious family videos.

The music changed and we continued to dance. It was ages since I danced with a partner, but it came naturally with Jake and those watching him lead me through turns and dips must've thought we had been dancing together for years.

Then with a screech of feedback and a tap on a microphone Trevor called for everyone's attention.

We hung back at the rear of the crowd, Jake standing behind me with his arms around my waist; my arms on his and my head against his shoulder, while we listened to Trevor formally welcome everybody. He continued to give a speech about Alex, outlining her progress through the firm and praising her outstanding dedication and work ethic. I caught Amira turning to roll her eyes at me and I smiled though I wasn't paying much attention. It wasn't my life anymore. I no longer had to play that role.

As Trevor wrapped up his speech, Jess interrupted him to remind everyone that it was also Alex's birthday and insisted we sing her happy birthday. Trevor was not impressed by the frivolity of it all, but Alex loved every moment and I actually felt happy for her. This was her world and she deserved to be in the center of it.

Afterwards, we mingled for a while, chatting with guests and others from the office. Jake always stayed near me, his arm in mine or with his hand resting on my hip or the small of my back – not in a possessive way, but in a reassuring, protective way, and for the first time in my life I enjoyed being at a work do with my partner.

I always hated that term... 'partner'. It sounded so transactional, conditional – like business partner, lab partner, partner in crime. But perhaps, partner was the right word... in the sense of 'fellow participant', like co-pilot. A co-pilot shares the workload and doesn't leave you to fly through the rough weather alone. A co-pilot has your back and slips his fingers through yours while listening to tedious speeches at your boring work function.

Though it looked like the party might continue till late, Jake and I decided to leave early.

We made our way around the group saying our goodbyes and came at last to Amira. Her eyes were glistening and her lips trembling.

"Don't you start," I sniffed, pulling her into a tight hug. "You'll set me off."

"I'm going to miss you." She sobbed, tears falling as she wrapped her arms around me.

"I'll miss you too." I croaked, "But, we'll keep in touch okay."

She nodded, wiping her eyes.

"And you're welcome to visit us. Anytime," added Jake.

"Thank you." She reached over and hugged him, "You look after her, okay?"

"I will." He drew back and taking my hand, turned to me with an enquiring look.

I nodded and wiping my eyes we paused and waved a final goodbye to everyone before heading for the door.

"You ready?" asked Jake as we left the room and headed down the hall.

I slipped my arm through his and rested my head against his shoulder, "Like you wouldn't believe."

Epilogue

The limo turned the corner and I stared down at the double diamond engagement and wedding band set on my ring finger and took a deep breath.

"You've got this," Jake murmured in my ear and squeezed my knee.

In nearly two years I still hadn't got used to these events and tonight's was especially significant. My nerves were in overdrive. The car slowed to a stop in front of a canopied entrance and our driver got out and opened the door on Jake's side to an instant cacophony of cheering fans and strobing camera flashes. Jake stepped out and waved to the crowd while I scooted over to the door. He turned back and offered me his hand.

Maneuvering in my dress and heels was proving to be something of a challenge. I was wearing another of Julian Renoir's originals – a shoulder-to-ankle coral silhouette with layers of sequined chiffon cascading from the shoulders and waist at the back, creating a train of fabric that trailed behind me and was presently bunched up on the seat next to me. It didn't help that I was carrying some extra weight and felt like a beached whale. I grabbed hold of both Jake's arms to pull myself up, to hell if it didn't look particularly photogenic, but it would be better than falling flat on my face.

Once firmly vertical and all the layers of fabric were suitably arranged the reason for the sheath form of the dress became obvious. It was purposefully figure-hugging to show off my developing baby bump. More cheers rang out from the crowd as they saw the visual proof that the rumors were true.

We took a moment to wave to the press and fans who had gathered to support us. Though, I wasn't waving as Jake's wife, the envy of women everywhere, I was waving as a celebrity in my own right, a best-selling author.

My novel was a huge success and while there were the critics and haters who said my success was only because of Jake, and in a way they were right, it wasn't in the way they implied. I had worked for my successes, but if he hadn't rescued me that day in Hawaii, none of it would have been possible. It wasn't so much that he saved my life physically. It was that he saved my spirit. He had seen it trapped inside a cage and set it free.

Things were difficult in the beginning – it was a huge culture shock getting used to his world. We decided early on to beat the media at their own game and to minimize rumors and scandal, we announced our relationship in the most public of arenas – by doing a follow-up interview together on the Elaine show where we revealed our relationship and what had really happened in Hawaii. It caused quite a media storm for a few weeks but by pre-empting the gossip feeding frenzy people soon lost interest and we became old news.

Season three of *Hawaii Heartbeat*, which Jake had finished shooting when we met, was a hit, so his decision to leave the show was heavily criticized and people said he was committing career suicide and feared for the show's ratings. In the end, Jake's character was killed off early in season four in a dramatic car accident that I couldn't bring myself to watch. A new leading man, a native Hawaiian, was introduced and had the unexpected effect of actually boosting ratings.

Once Jake was freed from his contract we spent more and more time at the ranch. He formed a community outreach program providing work to disadvantaged youths to help with planting the first grape vines and building new stables. I would watch from the loft window while I sat at an antique writing desk we picked up at an estate sale and worked on my novel.

We had only been living together for six months when Jake proposed. We sat on a picnic blanket at the top of the ridge that overlooks the ranch eating sandwiches and drinking homemade lemonade while our horses grazed, tied to a nearby tree. Jake knelt in front of me and pulled a ring from his pocket. I said yes before he even finished the question.

We married four months later in a small ceremony on the beach at Sunrise Cove. Amira was my maid of honor and Bryce was Jake's best man. After the reception, Rick flew in and landed the chopper in that tiny parking area and whisked us away to our honeymoon on Big Island where we spent two weeks losing ourselves in the pristine rainforests, waterfalls, untouched beaches and the slopes of primordial volcanoes.

Amira and I kept in touch regularly and she kept me updated with all the gossip from Andrews and Andrews. She told me Alex and Jess went from barely noticing my existence to bragging after I left that they were 'friends with Jake Donovan's girlfriend'. *Typical.* Amira quit a month after I left and went on to a junior lawyer position at a human rights law firm.

Jake slipped his arm through mine, breaking me from my thoughts and we made our way up the red carpet towards the auditorium. Once inside we spoke to various reporters and bloggers providing them with the required sound bites and posed for the official press photos, Jake beaming with pride as he stood side-on to me with his hand resting lovingly on my belly.

We continued inside and found Bryce and Anthony already seated. After helping me into my seat, Jake sat down and was soon chatting excitedly with Bryce about the big reveal. I sat back, staring out at the audience full of Hollywood stars and filmmakers in disbelief. *I* made it. *We* made it.

A hush fell over the crowd as the film's director stood up and said a few words introducing the movie and then the lights began to dim.

Jake took my hand and leaned over, kissing me on the cheek, and whispered, "This is for you, babe. I'm so proud of you."

I turned and pressing my hand to his face kissed him softly, "I love you so much." I murmured, my eyes beginning to water.

Bryce and Anthony both bent forward in their seats, grinning widely and gave me a thumbs-up, making me break into an affectionate smile.

The theatre went dark and we sat back and watched as an animated star streaked across the screen, followed by the words Shooting Star Productions. The name of Jake and Bryce's company dissolved and was replaced by more opening credits. Then the opening scene of an apple orchard bathed in golden light from the setting sun filled the screen overlaid with the words: *An Apple a Day*, based on the novel by Catherine Marshall.

ACKNOWLEDGMENTS

This feels like my Oscar moment, so I'd like to say thank you to all those who helped and supported me along this incredible journey.

For practical help and advice, I'd like to say a special thank you to the following...

To director and filmmaker, Derrick Sims for checking the behind-the-scenes filmmaking parts and for his invaluable feedback and being so generous with his insider knowledge.

To Dr. Arielle Kasindi for checking the medical scenes.

To pilot, Joseph Kasindi for providing the correct aviation jargon.

To Velma Christie and Caroline Donovan for final proofreading and helping me catch those pesky errors hiding in plain sight.

And, though I ended up not using it, thank you to Sergeant Patrick O'Donnell for his advice on US police procedure for an earlier draft of Jake's TV scene.

Lastly, to the multi-millionaire businessman who shall remain nameless and broke my heart after a whirlwind romance twenty years ago, but gave me so much to draw on. I moved on, but I never forgot you.

I have to admit to stealing the part about Jake's mishap with an extra. I can't recall who it was, but I remember a guest on the *Graham Norton Show* recounting the story and I thought it was pure gold. I hope you will forgive me for borrowing it. Though of course, I did change the details and context to fit my narrative.

There were many times when I doubted I'd make it to the end and felt tempted to give up, and I'd like to say thank you to all my friends and family who encouraged and inspired me to keep going.

In particular, a heartfelt thank you to my friend Randy Tan, of Ajatan Studios in North Vancouver, for inspiring me all those years ago to aim high and dream big.

Of course, no Oscar moment is complete without acknowledging one's teachers, so I'd like to say a big thank you to Mrs. Polchet, Mrs. Hooper, Mr. Gilmore and especially Mr. Gurney for praising my work and instilling in me a love of English and encouraging me to keep writing.

And I can't mention school without also acknowledging all those Writers' Circle meetings that saved my spirit, kept me strong and got me through high school. Dee, this is for you. I kept my promise. I'll see you soon.

About the Author

Skye Bothma is terminally single and lives a quiet life in rural New Zealand with a family of furry, fishy and feathered friends – some she adopted and some who adopted her. Born in South Africa, she considers herself a global citizen by effort. As a person with several chronic conditions, she is an advocate for raising awareness and acceptance of neurodiversity, chronic illness and invisible disability issues. She enjoys travel, learning about the world, arts and crafts, gardening and attempting the occasional DIY disaster.

This is her first and long-overdue novel.

Visit her website at www.skyebothma.com

Made in United States
Troutdale, OR
03/18/2024

18568689R00206